Watermelon Row

Watermelon ROW

A NOVEL

Michael Holmes

ARSENAL PULP PRESS
Vancouver

WATERMELON ROW
Copyright © 2000 by Michael Holmes

ARSENAL PULP PRESS
103, 1014 Homer Street
Vancouver, BC
Canada V6B 2W9
www.arsenalpulp.com

The publisher gratefully acknowledges the support of the Canada Council
of the Arts and the BC Arts Council for its publishing program,
and the Department of Canadian Heritage through the Book Publishing
Industry Development Program for its publishing activities.

Canadä

The Canada Council | Le Conseil des Arts
for the Arts | du Canada

This is a work of fiction.
Any resemblance of characters to persons,
living or dead, is purely coincidental.

Typeset by Solo
Printed and bound in Canada

CANADIAN CATALOGUING IN PUBLICATION DATA:
Holmes, Michael, 1966-
Watermelon row

ISBN 1-55152-080-X

I. Title.
PS8565.O6366W37 2000   C8313'.54   C00-910223-X
PR9199.3.H5815W37 2000

For Herta Adamson, Brigitte Holmes, and Lynn Crosbie
– your strength, wisdom, and astonishing love

ACKNOWLEDGEMENTS

For their invaluable support, advice, and encouragement in this, and many other endeavours, I am indebted, as always, to Tony Burgess, Lynn Crosbie, Stephen Heighton, David McGimpsey, Michael Turner, and R.M. Vaughan.

I would also like to thank Doug Crosbie, Patrick Crean, Jack David, Bruce McDonald, and Martha Sharpe. Each have, in their own way, been instrumental to this project.

Without Blaine Kyllo and Brian Lam of Arsenal Pulp Press this book would not exist: I am honoured by both their belief and commitment.

Finally, I would like to acknowledge The Toronto Arts Council and the Ontario Arts Council for their support, as well as *This Magazine*, for first publishing what would become the opening chapters.

But God forbid you ever had to wake up to hear the news . . .
'Cause then you really might know what it's like . . .
to have to lose.

EVERLAST

O you who turn the wheel and look to windward,
Consider Phlebas, who was once handsome and tall as you.

T.S. ELIOT
The Waste Land

Here comes a regular. . . .
Am I the only one
who feels ashamed?

THE REPLACEMENTS

ONE

SATURDAY, OCTOBER 4th

He beat the hell out of her.

Some guys manage to control it. A short, measured elbow to the gut. Sharp, quick twists of the wrist. Half-nelson games of uncle. At worst an open palm, just a little quick smack.

And then it's over and they feel like shit. You know, right? How it goes? What it's like?

Jesus, baby, I'm sorry. Begging and pleading don't leave me, finding their wits. Promise, promise, promise. Manipulate the situation, pull back and out to level all the possible emotional threats.

Baby, I'm under so much stress. I'm gonna get straight, I swear. You know me. You know that's not who I am. I'm not like this. God, I'm gonna fucking kill myself.

Cry softly, so gently, gentle man.

You fucking know better. Don't provoke me. Don't. Don't fucking push.

I'm such a bastard, you'd be better off without me. Jesus, I'm no good.

Cry harder. Become a pathetic, purple-faced baby.

Yes. Exactly. Make all 118 pounds of her want, need, to save you.

Wrap it up with a bow like a big fat joke.

But this guy? This time? Something different entirely. This time the guy followed through his backhand. His nails stung and his arm snapped back. Automatic. Then bang: a lazy, reckless appendage balls up into a fist. A thumb folds over four tightly curled, taut fingers. Knuckles angle to a kind of knife-edge, haywire lever cartwheeling around the maniac an elbow becomes, biceps pumping, vibrating to attention. Everything falls apart this quick: a sliver of pain pushes a body to a place no one in their right mind ever dreams exists.

Like really flashing a jab at a girl's cheek. Dancing into a stance that takes in her rocking body. Another coming out of nowhere to glance off her ear. Actually feeling the sharp back of the stud piercing into that soft place where a neck becomes skull. A delicate old earring. A horrible new hole.

Everything in the guy's head gave up on him in that instant. Important synapses shut down in unison, the wrong ones firing a chemical chorus of "lost cause," the tango called "let's get the fuck out." Where there used to be a picture of a woman he says he loves there's now a heavy bag or a Springer guest or a frozen side of beef.

And so he throws a right.

Coaxed, the bone and cartilage of a nose will venture into places it's reluctant to occupy, into the flesh and muscle economy of a face. Sometimes the exploration is even bolder. At best, a fist leaving you like that, gloved or not, looks blacker than black. If you're used to it, understand the phenomenon and know what to look for, maybe there's some burgundy and plum. But mostly there's just, well, black. And yes, there are stars. Cruel ones. Pricks of light that make fun of your smashed-in face and hurt more than almost anything else, even the betrayal. You're almost glad you've been blinded, especially when things get this messy.

She *doesn't* see, thank God, her flesh swell purple over her eyes so bad she *can't* see. And she doesn't actually feel her lip split so far open that a flap comes off like an old cola can tab. So, when she falls to her knees and his fist connects with her temple it sounds better than it really is, almost like a choir, angels or beautiful boys. Shock makes that kind of fracture and concussion seem easy, pain so bad it's like you can't feel or know anything for sure. Not even the pain, or who's responsible for the shape you're in. If a life flashes before your eyes it's out of sync. No, the toe of his boot breaking two ribs was nothing. Same with all that mad weight coming down through one knee to break her wrist. The eighty-year-old cuckoo clock she'd inherited from her grandmother, ripped from the wall and disintegrating against her shoulder? Timeless now, the displaced minute hand nests in the new copper highlights of her blood-streaked hair.

She thinks of Buddy – he hasn't been fed and his cage needs to be cleaned – because she believes she hears a tiny happy budgie peep from above, at the upper corner of the bay window where the black of a night sky is probably blueing into the dawn she can't find. Christ, he's not going to remember.

There's talk of frost tomorrow. Tonight. Today. Yesterday? The radio didn't think so but the TV said maybe. Anyway, that's pretty cold. Summer's really over. The breeze coming in off the water makes it feel even worse. Where'd I put my long coat? My gloves? It's so cold. Too damn cold.

How long have I been here?
A few minutes? Hours? A day maybe?
It feels like forever.

HAIR OF
THE DOG

FRIDAY, OCTOBER 3rd

12:01 AM

Ed Harrison is entertaining. He smiles and tilts the long neck of his Bud towards the much younger woman, then to his lips. After he drains the last of his beer he places it back on a small, square, thickly varnished table as solid and storied as the fifty years between them. It fits back into the ring of condensation, perfectly. His tongue pushes his new teeth forward, habitually, though before he continues he sucks them back in. Briefly, through the rank and din, his voice is strong and clear and riveting. But there is too much of everything here, and focus cannot be maintained. What's perfectly clear inevitably fades: "So I'm sitting there, beat all to hell, mind, I'm sitting there, in the Emerge, and the doc says to me, he says—"

· • • ·

A single, perfect black bead flames orange and then disappears.

It reappears black and round and floating, darts a little to the left, back a little to the right.

There are many obstacles to acknowledge. First? The business end of an unfiltered Camel, the heater flaring a rain of phosphorous sparks. Blink and it's gone, nothing to be afraid of. But open your eye. . . .

He doesn't belong here and he's scared, his heart racing, bursting, faster than his frantic thoughts: Find a way out; there's no way out. The room is stuffy and claustrophobic and packed and dim, filled with smoke and mirrors that trick black lights and a rainbow glow of neons and yellow spots into a speedy kaleidoscope. It seems bottomless, this mazy place, like the wet and stinking, threadbare low-pile red-black carpet is no ground at all; the illusion of a foundation, nothing more. The cacophony is terrifying, too: the pulse of deep, too-loud bass, machine gun snare drums, chainsaw guitars. Glasses tinkling and banging, through it all. An entire ocean of incomprehensible conversation. Always a hush, lascivious, beneath the roar. People dancing and hooting and laughing. And the place smells. It smells of so many smells that it smells of one new smell, also incomprehensible. From where he sits, twitching and panting and hiding, he tries, in vain, to catalogue them: a thousand thousand alcohols mixed with a thousand thousand sweats and body odours; baby oil and hash oil; mustard and candle wax and rubber and processed nacho cheese food. Rosewater and glycerin and vomit and Vaseline. Thirty, forty perfumes. Paco Rabanne and Dune and Old Spice.

Together these things are the atmosphere and sound and smell of desperation, deception, killing time. He wants to retch but cowers in a corner behind a table where two men watch women dancing. The women's heels are high and their legs are taut and tanning-booth tanned.

The room is limited and confining and huge and mocking; he feels dwarfed by everything, a thousand thousand times smaller than he's ever thought possible. Looking down the length of the long mahogany bar, over glasses filled and half-filled and empty and toppled, over the arms of men and women who loop and weave cigarettes in the air around them as they talk and drink, he sees his own eye flash in orange light. Yet another tiny perfect version of his terror, another cruelly deceptive, inviting, distorting mirror. Yes, blink and it's gone.

No, it's not. He is small and his chest is pounding and he is afraid and alien and lost. This is not an anxiety attack. This is real. Okay, right, life or death.

A woman in sheer, radiant fabric and leather and silver chains approaches the men whose backs shelter him, and even though she hasn't seen him he's flitting again, moving away, darting. Causing a commotion now, conspicuous, he senses terror, annoyance, derision, dismay. It hurtles at him from everywhere, fuzzy in speed trails. Eyes momentarily blinded by shards of yellow and pink thrown from the disco ball, he ducks and dives wildly, brushes against the arm of a lonely, black-haired young man with vacant, red-rimmed eyes. This man, still a boy really, as sensitive as stone and full-lipped and pock-marked and drunk and staring into his lonely shooter glass, notices nothing: not even the tequila worm.

Sorry, buddy.

The apology is not acknowledged, but in the moment of contact, as terrified as he is, he understands everything and too much. Self-pity and destruction more horrible, more real than he had thought possible.

Sorry, buddy. Really. I'm so, so sorry.

Looking over his shoulder and still moving much too fast, his body burning off days and days of what a body needs, he manages to pivot around a woman's shaking head, the snare of her long blonde tresses, but can't avoid crashing into another guy. He stops and falls; stunned, immobile for a moment, he looks up from the improbable bottom of this abyss at the back of a well-kempt, close-cropped head.

The head spins and looks but misses him, barking: "What the fuck?" A hand runs through important hair; the other men at his table laugh and point to the floor.

"There he is!" they say.

The guy can't find him. "Where? Where?"

Sorry buddy, he says. You alright?

When the guy's Swatch flashes in the black light there's another distortion of his perspective. He twitches once more and rises but it happens again; the window opens: he sees a heart tainted, tarnished, black with deception.

Oh my. Buddy's fucked.

Even more confused, hellbent on escape, he circles quickly around the bar and back, still searching for an exit. Mirrors everywhere try to tempt him with at least twice as much room. Every eye in the place is on him now, even though the music's changed and the dancers half-heartedly dance new versions of the same dances. A beautiful voice is singing about a brand new key.

Listen, people, I'd take any old fucking key, just let me out of here.

An elderly gentleman's left hand flies out then, cigaretteless at least, in the middle of making a point, probably about him, with the woman he's talking to. The cool gold of the guy's wedding band snaps off his leg.

Sorry, sir, he says, wincing.

It's not pain he feels, just weight. The unbelievable weight of this man's secret sadness.

And then, through the cigarette smoke and dry ice and haze of human sweat he finds it: a meridian of natural light. The moon, peering in through a breach.

That's it. That's where everything went wrong. Where I came in. How I'll get out.

· · • · ·

In the crowsnest booth the club's DJ is counting twenties into the hands of a weedy young thing who, after a long day, is wearing black Adidas tearaways and a fuzzy white long-sleeved sweatshirt. She's cool and impatient and bored all at once, desperate to head out. He's not really paying attention and moving very slowly.

Through the club's only window, a ridiculous little fissure, a soft breeze ushers in just the hint of a moonbeam.

"Jesus," he says. "Jesus. Look at that, would ya? Look at that."

The DJ's staring out through the mirrored glass onto the floor below. Dancers ducking, drinkers weaving – not like usual, you know, in odd ways.

"Jesus. What's going on, you figure?"

"Whatever," she says. "Look, I'm kinda in a hurry here."

"Yeah, yeah. Sorry, Jules. Um, look, sorry. Here you are."

Jules counts the twenties again, then stuffs the bills into the money belt she's got tucked under her sweatshirt.

As she turns to leave the DJ says: "You splitting now?"

"Nah. Waiting."

"Yeah?"

"Yeah."

"Going out later?"

She shoots him a don't-be-so-goddamned-stupid look, then cracks a sly smile. "No, baby, I'm waitin' for my, ah, friend."

"Oh, yeah? Cool."

"Whatever."

"Sure you don't want a hit of this?" He points to the folded origami envelope that rests on the jewel case for the *Boogie Nights* soundtrack.

"Naw, that shit'll fuck you up."

"Funny."

She shrugs her shoulders and as she does all the commotion that was contained outside enters. A tiny budgie, frantic and confused, bounces off her bruised arm and tumbles, end over end, into the DJ's lap.

He scoops it up gently: it's twitching and hyperventilating.

"Ohmyfuckinggod," the DJ says. "Jules, can you believe this? I mean, look. A bird."

The bored girl, still standing in the doorway, half-turned to leave, shrugs her shoulders again.

"Yeah. Fuck."

The budgie peeps, frantic, rotating a wild black eye toward the girl.

Listen, lady, be careful. You gotta listen to me. Something bad's gonna happen. I don't know how I know, you know. But be careful.

"Noisy little fucker," Jules says.

The DJ rises from his seat, still holding the tiny little guy. "He's scared, that's all. Somebody's pet. Poor fella. Wow, cool. You can feel his heart beating a mile a minute. So cool. Touch him. It's going a mile a minute."

She shakes her head when he pushes the bird towards her.

"Look," he says, "we gotta get him out of here."

"No way. Not me. Buddy, forget it. I got plans. Besides, he likes you." She's laughing and pointing at the dollop of budgie crap the bird's just dropped. It's missed the DJ but landed squarely between his feet.

"At least hang out here then, and change the next couple of CDs. They're all lined up. And we're in the middle of a set. All you have to do is push the buttons."

"Buddy, I can't. . . ."

"C'mon. I'll be ten minutes, tops."

"You got exactly ten. Then I split. What buttons do I push?"

Still cradling the chirping bird, the DJ pockets his coke and shows the woman what to do. As he's leaving he says thanks and then laughs: "You know, there's books, a couple of 'em anyway, books that say, like, you know, a bird coming inside, like this, a bird in the house is, like, a bad thing."

"Right. Whatever. Buddy, look, you got nine minutes now."

· · ● · ·

Walking downstairs and through the club, the DJ, a young, pear-shaped man, held the bird close to his face and whispered sweet, calming ministrations.

"It's okay, little buddy, I'll get you out. You're gonna be okay. Okay? Yeah. I live, like, three minutes up the street and I'll take you home and you'll be safe. Okay? Yes, it is. You're a good little guy, aren't ya, buddy? You and me, we'll be good together, right? Yes, we will."

Being carried back through the asylum he'd just escaped, the bird, feeling trapped and terrified and even more disoriented, saw them all again — those he'd touched, self-annihilating and barely maintaining and inscrutable men — dappled amongst the laughing and pointing and sneering and bored and unknowable people who danced and drank and talked and yelled.

He pecked the DJ's nicotined thumb. Buddy, I'm scared. I don't feel so good. What's happening to me? Why can't I get this shit out of my head? See those guys, buddy? See them? They're really freaking me out.

· · ● · ·

". . . Poor little fella, Jesus, I mean, who'd let their goddamned budgie get away like that? At least that fat-assed little freak's getting him outta here. Right, anyway, like I was saying, this guy, he says to me, there in the Emerge, in front of that fat bitch nurse and the young one and everybody, 'Eddie,' he says, 'Ed, you've got a serious problem and it'll kill ya.

If you don't stop, and stop right now, mind, you're done.' And so I say to him, look him straight in the eye and say, 'Doc, this is how God made me.' And then I say, 'I'm too damned old and stubborn to change, besides.' And he just smiles all prissy like through his little college boy spectacles, and shakes his head. I'm thinking, of course I'm thinking, well, Fuck you, Mr. Fancypants. But I say, I say, 'Doc,' I say, 'Doc, I'm a man who drinks. My father is a man who drinks. His father, too. God bless 'em now. My brothers? The same. We're drinkers, not drunks. Sure, there's gonna be trouble sometimes, but I, none of us, I, we, we don't go looking for it. We're there if it happens, though. Oh yes we are. And yes, sometimes the booze acts up and something bad happens to somebody, but there you go. Boys'll be boys,' I say. 'And besides,' I tell him, calm as anything, 'besides, what needs to get done gets taken care of. My gran, my mom, my wife, Alice, my wife. . . .' Alice, God, she was lovely then; just half as beautiful as now though. Half. I said, 'None of 'em ever had, have, to worry about making the rent or feeding the kids.' Sure, they'd bitch sometimes, specially when they got a call saying they'd have to come down and make bail, but they knew their place. They sure as hell know where they stand, those women. Strong though, fucking strong. And then I said, 'Doc, we've never been outta work more than a day. Any of us. Not during the depression. Or after a night in a cell. Never. We fought wars, see, built the goddamned country you call home. And so we drink. How you gonna change that? It's what we are.' And so he says, after pushing my nose back where it should be, and pulling a thread through the corner of my eye, he says, 'All that may be true, Mr. Harrison. . . .' And I know where he's heading and I hate the damned way he says my name, like I'm a drunken ignorant sonofabitch he assumes, the asshole he is, ain't read a college boy book in his life. And I'm thinking of firing off a line from Virgil, something 'bout warriors in their cups, but I settle for my own translation, and I say, 'Damn straight.' But he won't shut up, this one, lecturing me of all fucking people, knit one and purl two-ing through my fucking eyelid, he goes, like a broken record he goes, 'All that may be true, Mr. Harrison, but your liver is not a drinker, and it will kill you, soon, very soon, if you do not stop. Your problem with alcohol, Mr. Harrison,' he says, 'your problem with alcohol cannot continue unchecked, not without dire consequences.' Dire fucking consequences the pretentious little prick says, like he's gonna impress his pitiful little antiseptic audience, dire fucking consequences. And I'm thinking, I'll show you the dire fucking consequences of my problem Doctor fucking Fancypants, and I'm considering punching him in the teeth, but the man's got a fucking needle in my eye. So instead, instead I give him

24

a little gem I learned from Mr. F. Scott Fitzgerald himself, not the words exactly, of course not these exact words, but again, a reasonable contemporary translation, so I say, really, I just say, 'Fuck you, Doc. Fuck you and the horse you rode in on.' And that was forty-two years ago. He just huffed and snorted, like I'd offended him or something. 'Well,' he said. 'Well, you've been told.' I was a red-blooded man, then, you know, in my prime. Twenty-six or seven and full of piss. And he's talking to me like a child, some puny fucking college boy still wet behind the ears. The tee-totalling little four-eyed geek's been dead himself since '79. Cancer, I heard. Just fucking riddled with it, the poor sonofabitch. Too young, now that's just too damned young. Sad, yeah, but the point is, he's still dead, and I'm still here."

The waitress, who'd been standing beside the table-for-two for all of this, smiled back as he flashed his new teeth, popping them forward slightly, and nodding, up and down, up and down: damn straight. "Would you like another, Mr. Harrison?"

"Yes please, darling. And Miss, you know you can call me Ed. Mr. Harrison was my dad, and he's been gone a long time now. God rest."

"Okay, Mr. Harrison, sir. Ed, I mean. Ed. Sir."

"Not *sir*, darling. Just plain old Ed. And you Miss Johnston. How are you doing with that? How 'bout another?" He touched the hand of the relaxed younger woman seated with him.

The gesture was assertive, she thought. Gallant, not proprietary. Not an intrusion. Not at all flirtatious. She liked the way he said her name. Liked, too, the way he called her Miss. "Yes, Mr. Harrison. Yes, I believe I would."

"Please, Miss Johnston, the same goes for you. I'm Ed. Miss Johnston would like another cocktail, Miss Addams. And I could do with a shot of bourbon as well, please and thank you."

The waitress smiled again, turned and headed toward the bar. Her spill-rag hung over the side of her black tray and a filthy dribble of gin and beer and ash and salt cascaded down onto her skin, just below the cuff of her white, short-sleeved, button-up waitressing dress shirt. She stopped for a second, sighed, and used her right hand to wipe off the sticky wetness. Readjusting the rag, she snuck a glance back at the table where Mr. Harrison and the woman he called Miss Johnston sat. He was talking up a storm again. Like he does whenever he's in here.

Polite and gracious and formidable and funny, he was one of her favourite customers. Maybe her only favourite. She looked around the club. Everybody drinking, spending way too much money. Guys chatting up women. Women hitting on guys. People hiding in the dimmest corners, looking through one another, or licking their lips and zeroing in. The old guy was different. He's not here like *that,* she thought, so *why?* What's his gaff?

. . . . .

"You know, Mr. Harrison, she's been working here three months, ever since they changed owners, and I didn't know her name was Addams. She was always just Ronnie. Or, the new girl. I think there's something wrong with me." The younger woman looked into the blue eyes of the grey-haired man who was buying her a drink and shook her head. "Really, you know, I don't know what's wrong."

"No, Miss Johnston. Nope. There's not a single little thing wrong with you. And I'll tell you why. You just do what they call maintenance, Miss Johnston, you maintain, preserve. Keep a bit of yourself back. I've noticed this, Catharine. No offence, dear. No, Miss Catharine Johnston, I want to make a point. And I'm gonna impose and use your Christian name now, Catharine, because I'm an old married dog who's got a thing or two figured and a few drinks in him. You're a good person. There's a fair bit of my girls in the way you are, my poor, lost Belle and my grand-daughter Krystal. And I know, Catharine. I know you. I know there's respect bred in your bones. Self-preservation. See, there's nothing wrong with you. It's just this place. A place, a situation, can do things to people, make them need to forget. Not want to know. A war, a jail, a hospital – it's no different. You didn't know Veronica's name was Addams because you didn't want to let that piece of familiarity become a part of who you are in a joint like this. And I respect that, Miss Catharine Johnston, I do. You maintain. Take that sonofabitch, for example. The one Miss Kupaceck's speaking to, with all those other fancy fellows in suits. Why do you think he comes here? You've seen him before, I know you have. What is this handsome, married young man in spiffy clothes and shiny shoes doing here at all hours of the day? You've asked yourself Miss Johnston, again, I know you have. And you might tell yourself a little story that explains this away, but you wouldn't ask him about it, and if you did he wouldn't tell you the truth. Because in here he's barely maintaining, too. But I know the truth, Miss. I do. Jesus H., I do."

Catharine Johnston, of course, recognized the man Ed was talking about. The first night she was ever here, in fact, he made a point of introducing himself, more than once, buying her drink after overpriced drink. Hell, everybody knew what they needed to know about him: his name was Scott, he drank too much, threw money around, was always impeccably dressed. He told her he was a lawyer or something. Middle-aged, he was kinda handsome in a sorta movie star way. It was hard to place, though, exactly which movie star. Lately he was in here more and more. Every day. Usually pretty early. Like he wasn't working. Funny thing was, he seemed to be even more flush now. Like he'd won the lottery or something.

"And him, Christ, would you look at that, by the stage."

Catharine followed Ed's nod across the room. Another regular. A source of tension, one of the club's many problem children.

"The scarfaced boy, him. That's what I call him, the scarfaced boy. Yeah, him too. He's here day in and day out, drinking slow and steady. Slower than Miss Addams' boss would like, I suspect, but steady enough to stay out of trouble. The boy who's forever vying for Miss Jefferson's attention. Waving at her, trying for a word. And she has to ignore him, doesn't she? Or put up with it all. We've all seen it, him following her around the place, out even. We've watched as other gentlemen have told him, time and time again, to leave her be. Yet he's always coming back, isn't he? The scarfaced boy. And what is it about him? Why is he so comfortable in this place? So comfortable with its rhythms? Why's he come here, even when he's not wanted? That boy can't have anything in common with those suits, can he? Him in his dirty jeans and motorcycle jacket and t-shirts and long black hair? That young man should be out working. 'What happened to his uniform?' you may well ask. The uncomfortable brown uniform he used to wear? What happened, indeed. . . ."

Ed was talking about Jenna's stalker. Catherine knew more about his story than most of the others' because Jenna'd told her a bit about him. A guy from her past. Pete something. Alcoholic. Unemployed. Lives at home. A fucked up, mama's boy. Rumour was he'd beat the hell out of Jenna once.

Stay away.

"Jesus, a big man like that, a brick of a man with a strong young back, should be working. Instead, when he's on his best behaviour he's in here bobbing to your music, so slightly, ever so slightly, that he figures no one will ever notice. I've watched him and so have you. And deep down you probably know what I'm gonna tell you even though you don't really want to know. Not here, at any rate. But I know his truth, too, and I'll tell you now, this once, Miss Johnston, because I'm just a crazy old man who knows this about that. His truth is the same, exactly the same, as the truth of Mr. Executive over there. They're fucked up, Miss Johnston. They're fucked up and mad and shit-fucking scared."

The mousy waitress had placed Ed Harrison's Bud and Jack Daniels on the small square table and was handing Catharine Johnston her gin and tonic just as he finished. The striking young woman's eyes were locked into the older man's. She was oblivious, to the drink, the noise, the place. To everything but Ed Harrison's eyes and voice. She clutched the sweating highball glass to herself automatically. He slid his right hand into his shirt pocket and pulled out a twenty.

"Is this enough, Miss Addams?"

"Sure, I'll get you change."

"No, you'll keep that, Miss Addams, you'll keep that."

"Thank you, sir."

"Ed, please, just Ed."

"Thank you, Ed," she said again, uneasy with the faraway look the other woman still wore.

"You okay, Cara?"

"Fine, Ronnie, just fine." Cara blinked then. Pulling her eyes from Ed, she shifted in her seat, and spoke directly, warmly, to the waitress. "I mean, yes, Veronica. I'm just fine. I'm maintaining, Veronica. I'm good. And, Veronica Addams, it's really nice to meet you. I'm Catharine Johnston. So you can call me Catharine, okay?"

"Uh, sure."

As Veronica Addams waved an unconvincing, frustrated *I see you across the room so wait one goddamned minute* at another table, Ed Harrison toasted Catharine Johnston with his Bud, drank, and then gently touched her arm with his free hand. The gold of his wedding band, only slightly tarnished by the gaudy light, was warm against the young woman's skin.

In the neon of this bar no one noticed that the condensation from Catharine's drink had wet an open bedroom window through the thin fabric of her white baby doll. Through it you could see everything – a flash of stainless steel, an opal bead, a ring of pinkish brown gooseflesh, a beating heart.

A half-hour later, by the time she took off the lingerie, three quarters of the way through the first song of her last set, the window was gone.

· · • · ·

The tuxedoed bouncer pushed and held open the door and a cool, crisp blast of early, early morning October air hit the DJ and the budgie at precisely the same time. They both shivered and breathed a deep, calming draught.

"I'll be back in five, dude," the DJ said to Jason, and then held the bird up for him to see. The bouncer grunted.

For a moment, DJ and bird, bathed in the marquee glow, stood motionless together. In front of The Rail, their four eyes adjusted to new lights: the moon, many other fizzing neons, the halogens of oncoming traffic. There was a different kind of pulse outside, too. Both more relaxed and more dangerous: less contained. The heavy door to the strip club swung shut behind them and a gust sent the DJ on his way. He began walking quickly, south, towards the water.

"It's not far," he said to his new friend. "See, just up there and across the street. Above the coffee shop. That's where you're gonna live."

They made it to the lights, waited for a green, and then crossed. The bird stared back at the club and then up, longingly, to the sky. He saw a huge billboard – *Roadwolf* written in giant blood-red letters – and a nest of some sort on its upper ledge. It fascinated him.

Four teenagers idling at the intersection watched the two of them walk. The DJ had the bird cradled close to his face again, was still telling him not to worry.

Of course the driver, egged on by his friends, rode his horn, and everybody in the car yelled at once.

"Freako!"

"Hey, bird boy!"

"Lardass!"

"Fag!"

Startled and embarrassed and a little frightened, the DJ lost his grip.

Startled and incensed and terrified, the budgie struggled to break free. And he did.

In the air, foolishly looking back as he flew, the bird was hit with another confusing jolt of recognition.

Thanks, buddy, but Jesus, get a grip. I mean, think about it. There's something inside you that ain't quite right.

"Hey," the DJ screamed after his lost little friend, watching him fly headlong into downtown traffic, "watch out!"

When the squeal of brakes died, the kids in the car laughed and honked again. The light had changed.

The DJ was composed enough to get out of their way.

Then, muttering a little prayer that involved asking God to kill them all in a drunken, high-speed police chase, he was struck with the most curious feeling. Like something passed through him. Something about the bird. Something better, maybe, than the carnage he craved.

And then the feeling dissipated.

He shivered and noticed he had the light again, envisioned bodies burned beyond recognition. Dental identifications. An unholy mess. By the time he reached The Rail he'd lost heart and the malice was empty, fruitless. Opening the heavy door, he took a last look up the street and twitched and shrugged. His little friend was gone.

Somehow, though, in the disintegrating, human core of him maybe, a tiny little bit of the budgie stuck to the DJ, hung on for dear life. It clawed and clung and nested deep inside.

And then it walked on into the bar.

4:06 AM

THE PEELERS ARE LEAVING.

When he realizes this, Scott Venn's saying "I love you, man" and clutching his buddy Kirk in a blood-brother handshake-bearhug: the kind where the four fingers of your right hand curl over the thumb of his into a mutual fist while your left arms reach over opposing shoulders to make two separate chests clash in hollow fraternity. Andy and Alex are already in the back seat of the black and orange '91 Chevy Cavalier. The front passenger door hangs open over the sidewalk and the engine coughs; naked neon is mirrored off the club's facade onto the taxi's windshield in red and blue breasts, great jugs of light.

It's pretty, the way Kirk slips from Scott and into the front seat. Alex passed out immediately behind the driver. On this side, Andy is waving and saying, "Night, dude."

"Çiao, boys." Scott smiles and runs clean, delicate, manicured fingers through his beer and Sambuca-drunk hair. It springs back to a slightly thinning perfection that his wife says makes him look like a Brad Pitt-Billy Zane mongrel as he slams the cab door shut. *Seven* eyes, *Titanic* highlights – Scott Venn fucked.

Too bad Tony couldn't make it, he thinks, then smiles, perversely. Dude. Man oh man, dude, what a blast.

Scott's tie, Armani's deep green and red silk, flops rumpled and limp in the warm updraft hissing from the vent below his Oxfords. There's the wretch of an indecisive transmission deciding to go, a bucking Scott hears as the kind of death-rattle that's only made-in-America – a car trying to be too smart for its own good, a tiny digital sensor that's more Hollywood than Silicon Valley or import production values, confusing the simple need to move. His friends are gone, receding down the strip into diminishing streaks of yellowish summation. Good night. And he's jaywalking, amazed, between tired spurts of traffic, trying to flag down something heading south. Amanda's at home. Probably sleeping. Tossing and fretful, but maybe dreaming.

Things between them have been bad, crumbling, and he's wondering if they've gotten any worse. Anything could have happened. A whole world that he's absented himself from could have fucked with his life while he and Kirk were presiding over Alex's stag. Anyone could have called. And Amanda had been there alone in the house they'd bought together a couple of years earlier, when everything was easy with promise, watching TV on the couch or reading in the big chair by the living room window, being lulled into a false sense of security by the faint sounds of small waves rolling onto the beach just a hundred yards away. Someone could have phoned, innocently, to commiserate, and he'd be sunk. That's exactly how it slips. It could be a scrap of information that might make her suspicious, something simple that would get her prying, maybe even going through his things, or a full-blown disclosure. Worst-case scenario: she's up and waiting in ambush and he's got nowhere to stand, a dirty rotten liar with no way out. He'd have to tell her. They'd fight of course, and it would be hell. Vicious. That's if things go well.

But then, at least, it'd be over. Besides, it's his fucking life. His business. Deal with it.

Waiting for the ride that isn't in a hurry to come, watching women move in either direction away from the tits-and-ass marquee and heavy brass doors of The Rail, his mind toys with it again: the peelers are leaving.

He's been here a million times. Not this place, exactly. But then he enjoys convincing himself that they're all this place. The movement of his life, he figures, from the time he'd bothered to remember it, say high school to now, twenty years more or less, could be mapped onto a couple of continents of these clubs. Countries and states and provinces and cities and towns shaped like stages and runways lit with pots and spots or those cute little Christmas lights that are just like the ones that're supposed to come on in the event of an emergency landing.

In his head there was a course in history to go with this geography: lecture after lecture on brass poles, G-strings, ragged comforters, and mirrored-in DJ booths. How travelling carnival girly shows and burlesque houses became choreographed lasers, mermaid-sized fish tanks, and couch dances. Catwalks and table-dance stools are the site of remarkable battles. Urinals and VIP rooms? Object-lessons: the wisdom – perspective, at least – you get from bitter defeat.

Right now Shannon and Holly are laughing at some joke the bouncer Jason cracks, holding open the door with his ass and the gesture of a gallant arm. The girls' clothes are startlingly plain. Jeans, Nikes, Vans. Shannon's Budweiser sweatshirt and old blue K-Way wind-breaker. Holly's leather jacket and oversized black T. Mercedes's already at the next set of lights, head down, smoking, listening to a yellow sports Walkman. Each of them has a nondescript nylon gym-bag slung over a shoulder. They all look incredibly normal.

The black '95 BMW that stops in front of The Rail, idling, momentarily obscures everything but the three laughing heads. Then Shannon and Holly are off, heading in the same direction as Scott. For a second he almost believes yelling to see if they want to share a cab might be a good idea. He and his friends had invested at least $420 in the two of them that night, lapdances for Alex, the last rites for his singularity. When Shannon screams "Wait up" and Madison, the slightly heavy-set blonde, spins and stops outside the sub shop down the street, his courageous flight of fancy's crushed.

Who the hell am I kidding? I can't get *that* drunk anymore. Not often.

White boy hip-hop, House of Pain Celtic style – kinda old school, but something new – seeps from the BMW and the car pulls focus. Jason's turned into the club and it looks like he's relaying a message. Absolutely huge in his tuxedo, he's all smiles when he looks back through the now open passenger door and flashes his right index finger, mouthing one minute at the driver.

The music's really loud. One helluva stereo, but too loud.

Scott thinks he can place the song, tries, but then gives up. Some millionaire kid, straight outta college – the Pac 10, probably – not Compton, will make it his mission to educate him.

It's not like it's real music, you know, live musicians, words that mean something. Not great music – art – like old Genesis or King Crimson or U2 or the Furs or Tom Waits.

Tom Waits, now there's a fucking genius, a goddamned poet.

With this new stuff it's like you need to know a whole other language. How can you get it? And who listens to tunes that loud?

Arrogant dicks.

Scott tries to see the person behind the wheel, but the reflection from the red and yellow and white Coffee Time lights behind him make it nearly impossible. Probably a guy. His mind races, figuring it's some creep come to get his girl. Images of pimps and small-time gangsters. A wiry, coked-up badass, maybe. Or a Neanderthal whose life is intimidation, muscle. He tries to match a girl with the car. On the inside, there's a number of likely candidates. Like Janna: all silicone and attitude and extra-special lapdances. Or her twin, Jenna. (I can't see the difference. Can you see the difference?) Freaky duo shows like that make it all fair game: *Smells Like Teen Spirit*. Maybe Cara, a human box-cutter with tattoos and piercings and fuck-me eyes, the one who's always grinding out bored sets to Dr. Dre and Snoop Doggy Dogg. Or this week's feature, Mistress Krys. Last time she was here she was known as Krystal Kupps, the time before that – Special K. A bargain basement version of Tori Spelling's botched, venous tit job packed behind nipples that'd cut glass, she's a shaved, bleached blonde metal queen whose tight leather minis and ample chain-mail bustiers squeak and rattle when she prowls the bar, a perma-tanned amazon bitch goddess, in high PVC boots with six-inch iron spikes. Hell, it could even be Jules – so heroin thin when she writhes to Sammy Hagar's Van Halen, on bad nights moonlighting blowjobs in the private booths – who always looks content and a little too bruised. Right Now.

He goes through a mental Filofax of twenty or thirty other girls named Candy and Amber and Tiffany and Devon. He's on the verge of nominating Cara when he realizes a hack has passed, going his way. Shit. He waves frantic for a second hoping to catch the cabbie's eye in the rear-view mirror, but the car continues south, actually speeds up, either oblivious or mocking. Scott feels stupid, sick, and cold. Pathetic, just standing there; actually vulnerable. Impatient, he's about to walk a block to a busier intersection with some west-east traffic when the music and engine stop. The black driver's side door opens and somebody emerges. Christ, he couldn't have been more wrong.

Of course it's a dude that gets out of the BMW, but there's no way you could mistake him for a tough guy. In fact, he looks like a college kid, almost an awkward teenager, a pussy. Little rounded silver glasses, no shoulders. No way he's a pimp or wanna-be Gotti. Maybe a computer programmer or chartered accountant for one of the big international firms a few blocks away in those glass high-rises where all the money is. The only "tech" in this little guy's life is on-line support. Dude closes his door delicately. Shoves his hands into pants pockets. Slouches and walks around to Jason and the front of The Rail like a shy puppy. The guy is tall though, but it's the kind of size that's embarrassed, desperately trying not to be noticed. And now that he's standing with the bouncer, Scott sees a comic book before-and-after ad come to life, Charles Atlas, sand in the face, the whole bit.

When Janna – no Jenna, no, yeah, Janna, has to be, her sister left early – bounds through the door, actually giddy and warm, and hugs beamer boy, Scott figures the whole world's as insane as he feels. This can't be right, she can't be with him. Nobody's really that rich, are they? Ha ha. At least not legitimately. And then he thinks, maybe he is. Life's had a way, lately, of pointing out just how unfair it means to be. So maybe this guy's her pencil-necked sugar daddy. Her very own Billy Gates, taking, and being taken, for a walk on the wild side. Is that what she's so fucking happy about? Usually it's like Janna's won a lottery if her boredom doesn't rear up and threaten to kill. Tonight all this means the stick man's probably got a ten-inch dick to go with the car and the stripper girlfriend.

And then another cab catches his eye. In time, thank God, for Scott to flag it down. Whatever, he knows Amanda's going to be a bitch. It's really late; too late, maybe, for even the stag excuse to fly. There have been too many nights like this, nights where there isn't an adequate, acceptable explanation. Besides, lately it seems she's always pissed. There's always a reason. Sometimes even a good one.

Getting into the taxi, he's bathed in a couple of years worth of smoke and puke and pine and BO. The driver, a bull-necked, scruffy white guy with an Eastern European accent, is talking to somebody on a cell phone and doesn't seem in too much of a hurry to ask him where he wants to go. Seems content, in fact, just to idle where they are. Leaning into the front seat to interrupt, Scott says, "The Beach." But still they're not moving.

Scott slumps back against the Plymouth Colt's tattered vinyl. His stage sigh fades into a really annoyed, "Jesus."

"And this from another fucking Serb," are the thick words he makes out as the cabbie rests the phone between his ear and shoulder and puts the car into gear. They lurch maybe three feet, and then stop, the meter running. The light, which never seems to go red at this time of night, has actually changed; the guy returns his full attention to his conversation.

Closing his eyes to rub them with the back of his right hand, Scott feels like he's trying to clear the pus – of what awaits him at home – from his already challenged vision. The stasis seems interminable, like they'll never move. His hand trailing away from his face, he turns his head and blinks onto the scene outside the bar again. Jason and Janna and the beamer boy are still there. Only now, the little waitress, the nervous one with big brown eyes behind sturdy glasses and mousy hair and the nice smile, is standing with them; talking, it seems, to the sidewalk. Even outside the club she looks out of place. In The Rail she's definitely not like the other girls, the peelers or the other waitresses. Her skirt's a little long to be good-tip short, her white dress shirt is always starched, her shoes really flat, and her nylons a shade too opaque. She's unremarkable except for these delicate pearl earrings and the simple gold charm bracelet that sometimes tinkles against sweating beer bottles. He's not even sure he remembers her name, though he's positive she told him one afternoon: Beth or Emily or Vanessa or something. Really, when she wears her hair

34

back in a tight ponytail you think Olympic fucking women's rowing. Or donut chain ads. Maybe the health food stores or snotty kitsch antique shops across town.

"Whores and drug addicts," the cabbie says, nodding to the strip joint as the light changes back to green. At some point in the last few seconds he must have finished with his call. His observation floats around his car, not necessarily directed at his passenger. They're moving south now and Scott's attention is drawn to the back of the driver's salt-and-pepper head, then to the photograph of the guy pasted onto his taxi-registration. It hangs, tattered, inside a yellowing rectangle of plastic behind the passenger-side headrest. He's looking into the ugly square face of Goran Vlastic.

"The Beach," he says. "Right on the water. The development by the old track."

As Scott pivots his head to look over his left shoulder out the rear windshield, he realizes that Cara and Janna and Jules, each of them in track pants, have joined everybody in front of the club. They're all rapidly diminishing, lost in so many lights, when he thinks he sees three of the girls get into the black BMW. One of them appears to be the waitress. The guy and Janna and Cara, probably, giving her a lift.

He laughs out loud and closes his eyes again; thinking, the peelers are leaving, like it's profound.

That's what never gets talked about. No matter what, everybody's got to go home, sometime.

7:18 AM

HONEY! GET UP. BREAKFAST IS GETTING COLD!"

For the last eighteen minutes Peter James has been blinking and wheezing, at times groaning softly. Only his mouth is dry. What little spit does pool under his swollen tongue or between his chapped and cracked lower lip and yellowish teeth is gummy and bitter. Inside his head a metronome switches between pain and dread. He's overwhelmed by his own foul night sweat. It clouds the small room, a stew of liver and kidney and rot. He wonders if he's pissed the bed. Considers checking to see. From under the closet door a game defence of mothballs attempts to cut through the thick wetness. From the hallway crisp bacon tries to insinuate itself. Alternately, it seems, these smells make small advances. But the reek of less than three hours of sleep, of last night and his life, decimates them.

35

His elbow at a right angle to his chin, Peter rubs at an itch playing hide-and-seek in his blue-black bedhead. The queen-size mattress and box spring below him are ancient and he fits neatly into one of two well-worn grooves. The thinning paper blind behind the sheer curtains does little to block the light pouring in through the second-floor bay window. If he could see past the pain and the brightness, through the translucent filters covering the yellowed glass, a whole city would be bearing down on him from three directions: royally pissed and loaded for bear.

"Peter, darling, rise and shine! You don't want to be late."

His mother's voice is ghost radio, haunted FM broadcasting endless fall high school mornings: a sing-song wake-up cart stuck on infinite repeat, the day that came two or three weeks into the newness of each year, the day when next summer fixed itself an eternity away in impossibility and longing.

"Shut up," he says, his voice a barely audible whisper. The first two words he spills into the blessing of the kind of clear, crisp day his mother will, in less than another twenty-two minutes, say is, "Proof, Petey, of God's bounty," are little more than a simple confirmation of the miracle of respiration.

Still, it takes more effort than his body can countenance, and, with an automatic, exasperated jerk, Peter pulls the pillow out from under his head before his neck can brace itself against the force of the useless object it supports being unceremoniously dropped. He hides his face under the damp pillowcase, a clumsy hand mashing himself back into septic darkness. Years of abuse have disintegrated the foam encased in the yellowed cotton into tiny packing beads. A thousand hypoallergenic synthetic roaches ungulate and pick at his cheeks and eyelids and nose. Almost awake, Peter believes there's a peerless, active malevolence in the belly of his pillow, that it might be capable of doing the one thing he can't stomach; that it would gladly end this misery to spare itself the terror, the horrible oil and fear and mustiness he breeds into it nightly.

Unsure of so much, this man believes he will never again remember his dreams. If there was someone he was still close to, though, someone for him to confide in, he'd argue that the atmospheric effect his sleeping body had on a room was quantifiable proof that he, in fact, was still actively dreaming. And he'd be right, of course. His body might be dead drunk, put down for the night, but his mind, like all willful, vertiginous things, still resurrects itself in happy little poltergeists that, in this room, go about the business of having a life.

Last night, for example, megalomania and intrigue and the true heart's core of romance pulsed within these browning, eggshell walls.

It began on the black swivel chair by the oak table his father had given him as his first desk almost fifteen years ago, furniture – presented to symbolize hard work; most definitely not the pursuit of knowledge – Peter believed was the worst, most hateful, oppressive birthday present a ten-year-old had ever received. An empty cardboard video case for the Tom Cruise vehicle *Cocktail* became digitally animated. Actually, it did a *T2* thing and morphed into the shape of an up-and-coming filmmaker who looked and spoke remarkably like Nick Cage in *Vampire's Kiss*. Still flush with the unprecedented critical and popular box-office success of his full-length feature debut, the man clicked "send" on an e-mail that pulled him out of a multi-million dollar Hollywood project on a whim. Part Orson Welles, part Francis Ford Coppola, part Gus Van Sant, the renegade cinematographic genius bristled at a perceived national media slight, and an agent's and studio's and producer's indifference regarding his latest idiosyncratic, though quite brilliant, casting decisions.

"Fuck you all," this Peter had signed off and cc'd into the electronic ether that led to the succession of terrified and speechless production assistants and TriStar and William Morris underlings who would have to carry a hard copy of the news, with their heads, to their respective employers on silver platters embossed with all manner of horrors, from Mickey Mouse and Pluto to Elliot and E.T. and baby Drew Barrymore.

Five minutes later the black Vista phone rang with a conference call of apologies, promises, and new contract riders; the kind of ass-kissing a very important person like this Peter has the luxury of taking for granted.

Meanwhile, under the bed, pressed flat on washboard abs and powerful thighs that ripple through cotton khaki on the short-pile beige carpet, his breathing shallow and almost silent, the twenty-year-old G.I. Joe, an uncle's more thoughtful birthday gift, had grown five feet to a flesh and blood man's full stature. His mind raced, anticipating the completion of his most dangerous mission. He was a soldier, for sure, not a spy or an assassin, the garroting wire uncoiling in the dry nimble fingers of his muscular right hand. No convention governed, the rules of war could not be appealed to or interpreted. The man on the phone was his enemy, the single impediment to securing the stronghold he had so cunningly infiltrated for such a just cause. Hundreds, thousands, of lives were at stake. The fate of the free world depended on his stealth. Ruddy stubble on the back of his head flagged proudly at the familiarity of the thought. And so on, and so on. The same old drill.

This Peter shed a tear, not for the Hollywood Peter whose life burbled away as his body flopped in the chair in front of the oak desk, but with the relief that comes from knowing that personal psychological sacrifice and success means the suffering of others, dependents, will terminate.

At the same time, in perfect, oblivious harmony, a nine-year-old mash note from a quite thoroughly forgotten, gawky young girl who was a grade behind Peter at high school, hidden in a shoebox in the darkest recesses of the closet – behind the mouldy and reeking hockey bag, the damp goalie pads, and assorted excessively taped sticks, red blades, and regulation white butts, under the shattered pieces of an unmarked video-cassette and the first draft of a filmscript for something called "Wolf on the Road" – broke through its chrysalis. A butterfly named only with two shy initials – V.A. – dried her wings in long violin bow pulls and flourishes, then levitated up from under the crack created by a roughly fitting door like a newly-pretty schoolgirl's breath. Free, she arced in lazy circles about the carnage, processed all the sordid details of the sleeping Peter's existence, and did what it took to become the unlikely focal point of his life.

Twelve minutes later, ignoring the phone off the hook, the smell of hard plastic and parachute silk, and the lifeless body, slumped now, over the lip of the desk, the winged words of crushing love had aged the way of all Lepidoptera. It was a matter of mere seconds before V. was a forty-five-year-old woman with two kids: Ryan, a teenage boy who secretly marks the calendar he's hidden in his underwear drawer with X's that count down the days until he gets his learner's permit; and Sophie, a twelve-year-old figure skater/department store Young Miss catalogue model, whose two best friends are both named Krystal. A mature, successful, powerful woman, V. knew that a single initial wouldn't cut it, considering the life she led, so she chose a new, fitting, moniker: Jennifer.

Absolutely Jennifer now, a former Miss Coppertone – her handlers had saddled her with the unlikely, ironic stage name, Miss Pismo-Ventura-Monterey – she was currently a contented and highly productive ad company executive who sat with her forty-six-year-old heart surgeon husband, her first and only true love – yes, the man of *her* dreams – on the edge of the bed by the sleeping Peter's left foot. The kids were asleep down the hall and the loving couple had just finished watching *Cocktail* for an impossible, sadomasochistic, seventeenth time. This Peter had just recited Young Flanagan's bartending poem: *Give me a kiss, you sexy beast.* It was the 103rd such occasion (he knew she secretly kept count, overheard her telling her twin sister last summer at the cottage while he did the dishes) and he never tired of his wife's response – delight, real joy, inexplicable passion – to the sexy, effortless way he reeled off the list of shooters: *The Sex-On-The-Beach, the Schnapps made from peach – the Velvet*

Hammer, the Alabama Slamma. . . . Silent now, not looking at each other but not away either, this Peter and the woman of *his* dreams simply held hands.

And then. And then the alarm on the dead-drunk Peter's clock radio proved worthy of the faith millions place in such subtle but terrifying technologies like bedtime prayer: the Hammer of the Gods. Black coffee. Sleep apnea. A flatline. Another unwrapped gift from a negligent dad.

It sounded and destroyed the next dream, as it always did. The dream this Peter never dreamt. Never fully, never to completion. Jennifer again, transformed. Younger, different, familiar, real. Not a dream at all, in fact, but an awful, dreamlike memory. Peter as himself, this Peter, drunk, flailing. The back of a hand making contact with a soft, tear-caressed cheek. This Jennifer, so real, falling, backwards; her left shoulder just about to make dislocating contact with the corner of an almost fifteen-year-old oak table. . . .

The words "I'm sorry, babe, I'm so sorry." Those words evanescing.

But of course, thankfully, the clock radio pulsed its annoying squawking pulse exactly as it had every Monday through Friday for ten months and nine days: "Merry Christmas, son," it droned, the raw electronic translation a perfect digital capture of a father who would die, suddenly, as suddenly as years and years of alcohol can ever assist a suicide, six days after speaking this exact recording with automatic, bell-toned indifference.

Oh yeah, you ugly sonofabitch. Happy fucking New Year, too.

And then. And then his mother's voice. As always.

And now there's wet cotton darkness and the crazy school of silverfish in his head. An ache from his bladder. A rasp from his right lung, the shifting tide of the viscous brown ocean in there. Knuckles lightly on his door.

"Peter, you'll be late for work. You don't want to keep Uncle Joe waiting again. You know how he gets. Peter. Peter? It's time to get up, son."

"Yeah." Muffled.

"Are you up."

"Um-hmm."

"Peter?"

Nothing.

Maybe Peter hears the brass knob turning and sixty-two-year-old feet padding five steps across the carpet. Maybe, but probably not.

"Oh honey, I thought you were up."

He definitely hears this. And he feels the quick dart of his mother to the window. A sharp tug on the blind sends a light breeze across his elbows, tickles the fingers he's splayed over the pillow. His window being slid open sends a knife of lightning and one of thunder through the parts of him that want to retch. A blast of clean, cold air calls him stupid.

"You really need to freshen up this room. And throw it together. At least for the open house this weekend. Really, you have to let the agent do her job. Like she says, the market's so bad we have to put on our best face. She's bringing a couple by later today, and I just don't know how she manages to avoid your room. Wake up now, Peter. It's time to get up."

"I'm up. Christ, I'm up." His whine becomes menacing, that quick. "Christ." The pillow jettisoned violently, replaced by a cupped, palpitating hand. His thumb and forefinger brushing through eyebrows to rub thick black hairs and dander into swollen eyelids.

"Do you want coffee, honey?"

"What do you think?"

Peter had begun every day for the last nine years with a vacant stare and two cups of Nescafé – a muddy taupe, half-and-half, no sugar, the *Black Hole* mug, the red one if the *Black Hole* was still in the dishwasher.

"Orange juice, maybe? Honey?"

"Coffee. Just a coffee." Then, under his fetid, rasping breath, "Fuck."

"You're coming down for breakfast?"

"I'm up, I said."

7:19 AM

SHE WATCHED OVER HIM WHILE HE SLEPT. In the stillness of the room his almost toothless mouth-breathing was a hypnotic Atlantic pulse, as good and rapacious as perfect silence. Terrible gulls hung and glided and raged and thrashed in the purple and gold and Halloween fires over the water and beach. The world bowed to contain their curses and screams, the automatic little demons in their vicious evil heads, and the swell buffeted its scratchy flotsam off the thick, leaded bedroom window. Stung by the gentleness, the sick new warmth of daybreak, their anger pitched and roiled and peaked into a psychosis so feral and pure that no horror, no future indignity or sin remained unimagined. The worst flew maniacally ahead into the intruding corona of the sun, burning and dumb with hate, insulted by the beautiful and mocking reflection that wedged into the fish and sulphur-stinking water below. It chased a smaller devil, one vector swearing to rip another to shreds. My hate is better and I will kill you.

And then the light tricked, or the breeze tacked, or an impulse came unbidden and the suicidal mission was aborted. Seagull, not Icarus.

It was over, the cannibal hunt broken as momentarily and irrationally as it began. Daybreak wasn't so bad. Not such an offence now. No longer too beautiful. No longer unbearable. The part of the world that's death and pestilence and outrage filled it up. The shine was off. The worst gull dove into the blue below to skim and spear some fat morsel of sewage or a choice bit of carrion. It touched down on the beach huge and demented. Terrible and ravenous and paranoid and frenzied.

The first sunbeam inched further up her legs and still he slept. It carried the worst gull's hunger within its light; absorbing some of everything it touched, it was already a relentless stream of inscrutable energies by the time it wedged again and bent through the crack in the cotton drapes she'd handsewn decades earlier. This room confirmed everything, could teach the light nothing new. But now the sunbeam warmed and played with the white skin of her calves, only slightly more diffuse in its teasing of her than the pulse that bristled and electrified the grey of his beard, his floating teeth. And now, even through the scrim of everything gull and garbage and glass and him sleeping, it was not gull or garbage or glass or him; it was as beautiful as Alice.

In the dark, sitting on the edge of their double bed in his yellowing undershirt and shorts and worn brown socks before sleep, he had remembered and tried to tell her this. This precisely.

"But then I couldn't tell you and I'm the fool for it. And it wasn't just the once. Like me, isn't it? Talk and talk and talk and never say a damned thing. Jesus. But it was the one time, the one time I should've just opened my mouth and told you so then you'd know. I guess it started when Teddy came. He couldn't have been more than a few weeks old anyway. And we were still so young and I'd be lying here dead asleep and then just be, you know, aware. And awake. My eyes were closed and I was still sleeping, I guess, but somehow I was also wide awake. Between the two, I guess. And I'd be aware of the whole place. Of our baby finally asleep and you being up and down with him all night. The light might be coming in and warming and the air might be cold and the blankets wrapped tight and safe around me. And it might've seemed like I was asleep. But I knew you were there and awake and watching over me. Even though I didn't say nothing, Alice, I knew. I felt you looking and it felt good and I wouldn't, couldn't disturb it for the world. No matter what I'd done or said, or how we fought the day before, I knew you were there. Watching. And Christ that felt right. So I never said.

"Well, it happened again and again over the years. Sometimes I'd go awhile between realizing, of course. I guess sometimes I was too damned pigheaded or dumb or hungover to realize. But I always knew and it always felt good. And I never told.

"Then one morning, we'd been married at least forty years by then, I can tell you exactly, darling, I remember the very day because it was the day Ted's Krystal was born, it happened and I finally truly understood. And I was lying there half asleep and half not, my eyes closed and feeling you watching, and I knew and I just started. The tears came, Alice, and I was embarrassed and sure you'd know. Even though I was facing the window and seeming to sleep, I could feel it trickle down my face, drops rolling onto the pillow and the screams building in my gut and through my throat. Great sobs of it ready to bust out and make me look like a fucking idiot baby – I couldn't stop it.

"And then you woke me, Alice. Remember, sweetheart? You said, you ran your hand through my hair and held me and rocked me and said, 'Ed, darling, you're dreaming, you're having a bad dream.' And then it was all over for me, and it just came, and I let it out. You holding me, Alice, and I let it out and stared out the window through the tears of rage and joy and pain and cried. 'What is it, darling? What were you dreaming?' you said. And I sobbed and said, remember how I said I was dreaming of our Belle and how I wanted her to come home? And you said she was safe, remember? You told me it was best, that she'd find her way. Said we'd call her that day, that the college wasn't far. And maybe we'd visit come Thanksgiving, or she'd come home. You held me, Alice, and I let you, and you comforted me, and I let you. Because I said it was all a bad dream.

"But I was lying, Alice. I lied to you then. And I'm sorry, sweetness. I just couldn't say what it was, I felt like such a damned fool, so I lied instead. It was easier and I'm sorry. I lied when I said I was dreaming, Alice, it was no dream. You see that morning was the morning when after forty years I finally realized. After all that time I finally understood the feeling. Finally understood why I'd be half-awake and just know you were watching me. Christ, I could barely feel your breath on the back of my neck. You were so still, I couldn't hear a damned thing. And after all that time of knowing and not saying anything and it feeling good, that day, finally, that day I realized. Jesus. I knew. I knew you were afraid. You were afraid and you were watching to make sure I was still alive. You were afraid of being alone. And I never knew until that day, and then I knew and never told you. Christ, hon, now I know. I never told you before but I know now what it was. Jesus, you loved me. And you sat there watching over me like a prayer, afraid you'd be alone. It broke my heart, Alice. I was bawling because my heart was broken by how much you loved me. And I loved you back so hard then, you were so god-damned beautiful and precious. And you really loved an old sonofabitch like me, and I couldn't tell you then what I'm telling you now.

"And darling, I swear, you'll never be alone."

· · • · ·

The light has crept further up Alice Harrison's legs, and still she watches. Her husband's sleep is fitful, the sunbeam's gotten in.

Ed's breathing is erratic, begins to gallop. Gulls pick at his peace, torment him with a twelve-year-old malice, rub sharp beaksful of ocean salt into the wound.

This hate is bitter, but this hate is better. A daughter's not a daughter when she's a junkie. When she does that with her body.

Belle's a junkie, Ed. A slut and an addict.

She never came home. She never will.

Forget her, Ed.

Hate her.

7:21 AM

Home. Close by, actually, and painfully sober. Scott Venn can see most of the large second-floor bedroom window through the turning leaves of the big ash and young red maple from where he sits, an empty beer bottle and three stale cigarettes in a soggy pack beside him, cross-legged and compulsively stroking his thighs, in the dewy, cool sand.

When the cab pulled up in front of his place he was still just about drunk; the graveyard DJ was blowing into his coffee, sighing a hushing throw over the whispers and first groove of the next tune. Funky nightmusic. "4:31 in the AM and time for a little of Mr. Marvin Gaye's 'Sexual Healing.' Get up, get up. . . . Wake up, wake up. . . ."

· · · · ·

Goran the hack had talked, raged actually, along every downtown one-way street, across the short stretch of highway he caught to save time, and up the industrial backroads that gave way to the whitebread canopied laneways which cosseted the houses where people like Scott lived. The whole long, nauseating ride south-east was scored with his scattershot analysis of everything wrong with the continent, the country, the city, the neighbourhoods, and the unsuspecting citizens asleep all around them. Frenetic but familiar, to Scott his voice was as jagged and compelling as speed. Go, don't stop. Don't ever stop, go.

An indecisive signal and sudden right-hand turn started him on lazy fucking pig-ignorant immigrants who couldn't and shouldn't drive, his voice creepy and deep and thick with uneasy syllables. A rainbow of skin tones not white. He then cruised past neighbourhoods in the west end you'd be insane to drive through at this time of night, snaked down his

43

dread of those types of calls. Crackheads, thieves, and murderers. He'll drive five more hours before passing the car back over to his little brother who's studying to be a pharmacist at the university. Hasn't even paid for the shift yet. Exits onto how young Stephan Vlastic isn't as smart about these things and never sleeps. Goes anywhere, picks up everyone. Yeah, you speed up and pass them, those people, they're all criminals. A violent fuck you, knife or short lead pipe. There's pepper spray in his red and gold Niners jacket, and plumbing supplies of his own under the seat. It happened to some guy just yesterday. His head bashed in for forty bucks, could've had his throat cut. And he was Black. Ethiopian or some goddamn thing. But what're you going to do? You need the stinking money, right? To survive. This banked into his own engineering degree, useless here. And his brother again, Stephan, getting out but not soon enough. Stupid kid. Having an affair with a married woman, older too. Where's he find the time? Never sleeps. He's twenty-three and should know better. Arrogant little shit. Idiot fucking husband. Anybody too fucking stupid to know a bitch is doing that to him deserves it. A sudden detour next, onto the world economy, and the violence of it, and then a dogleg to local politics. The fucking mayor. All the money he makes off the hundreds of cab licences he hoards and hides under the names of relatives close and distant and non-existent; how it's impossible to make ends meet as a cabbie in this city when rich bastards like that grab up all the licences. Fucking used-car salesman, hair-plugged sonofabitch.

Something about the way his voice raced, veering off into the suburban waterfront enclave, made Scott know he was angling for a bigger tip, setting up snares of guilt, handing out a pop quiz.

Pass or fail. Mensch or asshole. Either or.

No choice at all, really. There was still a buzz to go with the lurch in his gut, the dull throb toying at his temples, so Scott Venn did what you do when it's four in the morning and you're kind of sort of drunk and you're in the back of some psycho's taxi and it's still far too far from your place to even imagine the walk: he mumbled encouragements, uh huhs, little agreements – then decided to just like the guy. Simply give in.

Because that's what's easiest.

Idling at a slow light at the end of the strip, in front of where the classy hotels and convention centres spread out before the harbour, he and Goran Vlastic got it over with, did that thing that means you and your driver have bonded.

The moment, the compact, was as miniature and geometric and limited as it's supposed to be: they made silent eye contact in the rear-view mirror.

And it happened like it always happens. Goran's eyes shifted unnaturally, bulged, up and way too far right. They became the entire shiny rectangle, the whole rear-view. At that exact time Scott stared directly into the blue-grey, focussed on the big black speedy pupils, the eerie band of pink flesh and dark brows that made a cave around them. The glow of the red light they waited at made everything else dissolve.

Next, of course, Goran's head bobbed again, up a little more, down slightly. His burgundy lips surfaced for a moment, curled over white teeth in a tentative half-smile. Then, quick, there's a dart back down to nothing but contorted eyes and Scott bobbing his own head, leaning forward in the right rear seat. His right elbow was on his knee, his right thumb under his chin and index finger arced over his nose. Scott dropped the fingers that covered his own mouth and smiled, too: Okay, I'm in.

Discharging this obligation and entering into the polite society of the driver-fare relationship almost from the start meant they both could get on with the business of getting to where you're going to end up anyway.

The light turns green.

Go, don't stop. Don't ever stop. Go.

Goran had his licence to vent, Scott to become congenially distant, lulled by the ebb and flow of his driver's problems into the snakepit of his own. Of course his problems were of the necessarily subvocal variety, the ones that come with the kind of warning that's only ever found in the fine print of this kind of contract, being taken for this kind of ride: objects in the mirror *are* closer than they appear.

Always.

Like Amanda. And the lie. The big fuck-up. His job and his marriage. Amanda and work. His wife and the job he no longer actually has. Hasn't had for three weeks and six days.

When Goran made the left at the light and started into his jag about criminals of colour, Scott found the comfortable rhythm of mumbled ascent and quickly lost himself in the psychic fingercuffs, the blues and purples and crimsons, the '70s power and prog rock colours of his own abysmal, illicit fall. He couldn't remember precisely when he entered the impossible funhouse maze, or who or what dropped the chainsaw-wielding madman into the centre to turn it into an out and out blood curdling house of horrors, but the harder he pulled at the burnt and fraying ends of his problems, the more he struggled with the idea of responsibility and ramifications, the more desperate he became. No fun at all.

And the more he lied and the deeper he got, the worse he was fucked.

So far the way it played out wasn't too bad. Nothing had really happened. No real action had been taken. It was all polite, civilized.

Deferred. But that was the problem: nothing had really happened. Not yet.

Outwardly, he believed, his life appeared unchanged, maintained. Mechanically upper-middle-class, almost mundane. Cocktails and dinner parties and TV and peeler bars after "work." But inside? Inside, the wait was destroying him. Unable to move or act he bounced between a few, well-defined moods: mostly there was disgusting, often drunken self-pity. Terrifying, always drunken, micro-psychosis came a close second. Occasionally, though, there were moments of mere bored, semi-sober annoyance, moments when Scott was indistinguishable from his old, technically law-abiding self. There'd been more of those blissful moments lately, but in the back of Goran's cab it was the maudlin stuff that got him thinking: Hey, at least the cuffs aren't stainless steel, biting at my wrists. Plenty of folks get by with a couple of stuck digits, a neurotic, obsessively chatty conscience. Plugged, you adapt.

Amanda, or her father, hadn't had to bail him out, eyes averted, unable to meet his gaze. Not yet.

Of course, he'd been fired. They'd caught him cheating on the math test, and they'd said the words: *March straight home, young man, and wait for your father to. . . .* So that's what he did: his face went red and he hung his head and he stamped his feet and he waited to be punished. A lifelong acquaintance with the cruel sting of tough leather, the loving snap of the belt, however, meant he wasn't about to buy into any "this is going to hurt me worse than it hurts you" crap. And he definitely wasn't going to do anything to hasten the blows, to piss Mom off to the point where *she* opens the kitchen drawer and pulls out the wooden spoon. So, for almost a month, he'd been lying to his wife. Getting up and pretending to go about business as usual, finding pretty damned fine excuses – if he did say so himself, to himself – to become more and more absent; telling her things around the four silver and black decorated floors of the slick financial district office were crazy, that he'd been told to cut down on personal time at work, that he'd take all her calls on his cell – it seemed like he was always in negotiations anyway, bottom-lining GMs or sweet-talking young clients, budding stars, and their parents.

But then, in the strictest terms, he wasn't really fired. Not really. Not on paper. The high-powered partners at Shooting Stars Players' Representatives, Inc. suggested that leaving, that willingly transferring his boys to others within the organization, might be prudent, and he'd quickly agreed. Without a pink slip or press conference, he'd retired. He wasn't even, he figured, technically, lying – he just hadn't mentioned anything to Amanda.

There'd been no arrest, thank God. Not even a formal police investigation. Nothing. Not yet.

The company's lawyers, two middle-aged suits more straightlaced and fit and humourless than his former co-workers, had met with him, not at the office, but in a board room high and deep inside the Harbour Hilton. He'd mumbled answers to their questions, his responses alternating somewhere between cocky and sheepish, and spent most of those mornings staring out at small yachts and zippy sailboats and tubby fireboats lazily circling the islands while they shuffled papers and compared ledgers and accountants' reports and the files they'd removed, with his consent, from his cabinets. The way the hermetically sealed glass of the climate-controlled room framed the nautical play was subtle and perfect: out there, below, almost unreal and definitely beyond his reach, the difference between the things he always wants and the thing he most certainly needs.

On each of those three occasions they were also joined by the partners' jittery damage control team. Nervous, ridiculous men. Lawyers too, but not scary, hardly real councillors at all. Privileged jock wannabes, junior league or high school or college ball mediocrities at best. Older guys who'd bought him countless shooters at The Rail to celebrate a hot new superstar signing for the firm. Their multimillion dollar deals meant table dances.

These men were his mentors, advisors who were free and easy with the avuncular pep talk, though loath to let him land a big money client of his own. Not friends. Not Jerry fucking Maguire. Like Scott, they had struggled through law degrees, somewhere in the bottom third of their class, and then lucked into this fantasy camp of a career – they were precisely what Amanda said she was afraid he'd become. Deep down, he knew her fears were justifiable. Sometimes ashen-faced, sometimes glowing like shameful little beets, they were three of the most senior guys, puffy-eyed and heavy-set veterans, soft and overfed dinosaurs weeks away from the next company coronary, another Hallmark sympathy or get-well-soon card passed around the office.

And then there was the fucking harpy, Margaret Chisholm. Behind her arrow-straight back the guys, who had a nickname for everyone, called her "The Chisel." Her with her LPGA hopefuls and closeted figure skaters and those prepubescent tennis chicks that hockey players were always desperate to fuck when they weren't sweet-talking their way into the high-cut panties folded neatly inside sitcom dressing-room bureaus labelled "Candace" – breaking new ground for the firm, taking them to places most of the guys had thought of as strictly bush league. The bitch of it being she was good, made Shooting Stars buckets of cash, hand over fist. Amanda liked the thought of her – too much. Rode him hard, very hard, about her miraculously quick rise to full partner – six years and change younger than he was, not even thirty. About thinking about following her lead. She'd even clipped articles on amateur skating and female skiers and snowboarders and tucked them into his briefcase. Cute. But there was no way he was watching that shit on a Sunday afternoon in November, even if it was the national championships or some legendary downhill. Too much football and hockey and basketball happening. All the big baseball deals about ready to go down. Under his breath he'd mutter about how he'd rather get involved in North American pro soccer, then smile, pleased at his own joke.

Soccer. In America. Again.

Yeah, right.

Scott despised Margaret Chisholm: she was fucking with a perfectly sweet thing. No fucking way figure skating and ladies' golf and tennis was sports.

Not in my air force.

The doughy, lesser stooges weren't a problem. They chuffed and nodded once in a while, cleared their collective constricting throats often, wheezed constantly, but added nothing more than the odd, inaudible whisper amongst themselves. Margaret, however, was being such a razorbacked bitch that even Shemp and the two Joes would flash him the occasional look of sympathy.

Jesus. Sorry, son.

Her holier-than-thou outrage on behalf of SSPR was actually embarrassing. The way her lean but barbed, late-twenty-something body tensed, the muscles of her throat pulling dangerously taut before each explosion of by-the-book indignation ripped out of her unnaturally large and sharply pointed face, made her look all the more like a satiated praying mantis. Yeah, she fucked him worse with each outburst, and the violence of her ethical posturing verged on cannibalism. Not surprising, really. They were, after all, pro sports agents. And agents always screw and eat their own.

After the first piss-break on that first morning of informal examinations – a voluntary exchange of information they called it, nothing like a real legal proceeding, more of a good faith thing, fact finding – not even an hour into the damned mess, the Stooges actually shifted over one seat, distanced themselves from Margaret around the long, oval table. As close to Scott, now, their disgraced former co-worker, as their respected colleague, he thought he heard one of the pudgy Joes say something.

Maybe. Words bubbled out from a shiny head buried in one of the yellow legal scratch pads they all doodled on and stared at, during her fifth or sixth high decibel rant: "Castrating bitch. Out of control. Not good for anyone. Gawd-damn. Damage, damage-control."

By the third week of the inquisition Scott's apprehension and annoyance had swelled into active, violent hatred. While he stewed over worst-case scenarios, wallowed in the misery that stalked him, he also fantasized, continuously, about making Margaret Chisholm pay. At every moment he believed SSPR would end the charade and call for the cops. The real lawyers, he was sure, had it all figured.

They know *what* I did. Embezzlement, graft, whatever you want to call it, I swung deals that fucked my boys – just a little, not enough to hurt – directed money away from the company, and built a tidy little fucking offshore nest-egg. They've got names and dates – reams and reams of goddamned paper. Just get out the adding machines and put it all together. Game over.

So what were they waiting for? What else were they after?

Stick in the fork, guys, I'm done.

But no, they kept at him, asking oddly open-ended, vague, almost stupidly tentative questions. It was like they were waiting for him to drop another bombshell, they were giving him that much room. What was the point? It's not like he was going to itemize it for them. Not like he could, in fact, confess to anything they didn't already know.

Yeah, I get it: I'm fucked.

The only thing that kept him from going completely squirrely was a single, pure, happily mischievous thought: Hell, why not add one more little crime to my rap sheet?

Chisholm.

Scott's obsession with Margaret's vendetta twisted into fantasies so ugly, so brutal – pulling the maddening shock of her blunted, wiry hair, slapping those vicious mandibles, twisting her needle nose and administering vicious pokes to her eyes, jagging her with a bat, the broomstick she rode in on, searing irons upside her head, good old-fashioned Larry-Curly-Moe love, baby – he caught himself almost beginning to chuckle and had to fake a sneezing fit.

One truly funny thing? The month without an income hadn't become a problem. He could go on for years, maybe ten or fifteen, living in the manner to which he and his wife had become accustomed. Better even, with a few sound investments. No hardship there. Not yet.

Every payday, days like today – as dark as it was outside the cab, it already felt like a new Friday morning – he'd get up early, spread out the sports pages from all the big papers, dial in on his laptop from the kitchen, sip the foam off his cappuccino, and direct the bank in Zurich to transfer the appropriate funds to the branch downtown where he and his wife had set up their joint account seven years earlier. They'd opened it together, after years of getting by on Amanda's money, the unreasonably low five figures she made at the pharmaceutical manufacturing company her father owned, and that she'd one day inherit from the miserly sonofabitch. It was also the day when his parents had paid back the thousands he'd owed on student loans, the day he'd been called to the bar, and the very day he'd received the letter from SSPR offering him the same junior position he had recently lost. Hell, it was the first time his shitfuck surgeon father had ever ponied up for anything, so Scott was flying high. The ten grand he'd thrown in – just to get you started, *but* pay me back when you can – was what they used to start the account.

For the past three Friday mornings he'd play a little game to amuse himself: match the lies he'd been telling Amanda to what his commission should be for the week. He'd do the math on the Windows 98 calculator, trying to remember what the figures were from the deals he'd said he'd locked, then add his cut to his base salary plus a reasonable sum of the expenses which were always staggered one month behind the current pay period. When he found the magic number he pressed the magic button, converted enough Swiss francs to real money, and, presto, he paid himself.

Lately, in fact, things had been going so well at work he was thinking about giving himself a raise. Maybe even a promotion to Associate Partner. Nobody, especially Amanda, was any wiser, though it had been hard keeping the details of his new employment straight.

Did I get that Czech defenceman his new contract last week, or is the ink still drying? I better start writing this stuff down.

When you've got 1.5 million in found money to play with, it's surprisingly easy to become complacent.

Goran pulled onto his street, two blocks away from his place. "Fucking used car salesman. How did you make him mayor?"

"Uh, um, I don't know. Not me. Them. You're right. Regional support."

"Fucking hair-plugged sonofabitch."

"Yeah."

"Like this man is fooling anyone."

Like I am, Scott thought. Just like me: by maintaining the status quo and keeping your mouth shut. And nobody's doing a damn thing about it. Not yet.

This morning though, a few hours from now, it's all over. Margaret Chisholm screws me and I'm fucked royally. Chewed up and spat out. The last meeting they called it.

More like my last fucking meal. Crow, for sure. Shit, any way you cut it. My head on a platter. Sirens, maybe. Real cuffs. Hard ones.

· · • · ·

"Get up, get up. . . . Wake up, wake up. . . ."

Scott's fishing a twenty and a five from his wallet, dazed by the burn of the interior light the cabbie's sparked for his convenience. The meter says $18.25.

"Keep the change. And a receipt? You know, taxes."

"Yes. They take you wherever they want you. Yes. Fucking taxes. Thanks. You take care of you. This is your business now, my friend. You fill this out?"

"Sure."

Goran hands him the company business card that doubles as a receipt, then says, "Be very careful, my friend. These people. Criminals. All criminals. They will fuck you whenever they can. Rip your fucking head off and shit down your throat. They do this as soon as look at you, my friend. Don't vote for him again. He's a bad man. Too many bad men, here. This is a good place, a good place with too many bad men."

"Yup. Well, goodnight. Uh, I guess, no. Good morning."

Slamming the door behind him, Scott appraises the distance to his front porch and begins the blind zombie march toward home. The backfire from Goran Vlastic's ride makes him shudder and rear up, notice the darkness of the place, pitch black.

In exactly ten slow, precise steps he will trip the motion detector. Look every bit the jailbreak star, floodlit, centre stage.

· · • · ·

Keys cradled gently in his hand, balanced light and soundless, immobile not to jangle, the heavy front door eased shut, its lock slowly reset, Scott listens, still, in total darkness, between the mirrored closet he knows melts into the white oak arch which gapes onto the plush front sitting room, and the large vase and bench and exposed brick to his right. No sound. He places his briefcase down with his other hand, gently.

No sound.

No sound.

One sound. Ruffling in the living room, dream spasms. The bird settles.

51

No sound. Amanda upstairs, asleep. Nothing awry, nothing amiss.

No sound.

Except what?

Scott falls into the rhythm of his own breathing, annoyed by its heaviness, the tidebreak each time he exhales. What the hell am I going to do? Everything mesmerizes. I don't even know how to go home.

One sound.

The alarm. Christ, the alarm.

An almost inaudible blip has peeped just behind his right shoulder; in the black ice of the closet mirrors he sees a tiny green pulse becoming fever pitched, about to explode into sirens of red.

His first thought? She armed the fucking thing. She set the fucking alarm to fuck me.

His second: What does she know?

As Scott's head empties of unnecessary, useless notions, he begins a dervish spin to the right, his left arm, flailing, up. An angry flock of house keys dart from their nest. Leaving his right palm they bite at the brick in a metallic splat, then die, slap down into a chipping ceramic splash.

Lots of sound now.

Too many sounds. Loud ones.

During the wild unwinding, his left leg becomes a spaz for a second, jumping stupidly, too far behind the rest of him. It smashes into its counterpart at the front of the bench, its ankle meeting a solid wooden one in the dark. The chance encounter is not civil and the idiot limb discovers a will and a voice of its own. In no uncertain terms it pipes up, telling Scott, "That really fucking hurt, asshole." Aware, now, of the usually mute limb's outrage, Scott responds in the only way appropriate. *He* screams.

"Aw fuck fuck fuck!"

As he's screaming, with a foot stuck hard, much too hard, against the leg of a bench, his upper body torquing toward an alarm about to raise the dead and bring the cops, he does the only thing a man in his position can do: he accepts the fact that the intersection of pain and momentum, for a failed college athlete, a wide receiver and a left winger turned jock lawyer, must lead to chaos. And so his extended right hand sweeps by the alarm, just missing it, of course, and he topples, fast. Scott's right elbow cracks off the door first, then his shoulder's thrown into the thing for good measure. Faced with such a roadblock, his whirling momentum shifts. Down. He lands with a thud, square on his ass.

"Fuck fuck shit fuck!"

From the floor he can see the green light's blinking so fast it's almost solid. Rising to it again, a desperate, confused lightning bolt, he knows he has three maybe five seconds to punch in the four numbers his pain has conveniently convinced him to forget.

His left hand hovers over the key pad and takes control. "Get a grip, you lazy sonofabitch. I got it."

The index finger points and presses, sighing, shaking its little nailed head. 99. 69. Just like him; his whole character, numerologically, automatic: Gretzky and sex.

The epileptic green fit stopped, the point of light solid again, his mind readmits its recent evacuees. Of course, Scott's next real thought comes like the cruel little thing it is: Thank God, it's over. The fourth car on this bullet train of mental activity is simply practical: Christ, I'm in a lot of pain here. Finally, something more evolved, a complicated, foreboding little caboose, sneaks into his head and immediately displaces and derails the first four thoughts for the annoying, irrelevant certainties they are. In essence it's the familiar, sobering, low-grade panic he's lived with for a month. Events of the last thirty seconds, however, have added new twists. Probably warrant upgrading his creeping dread to full scale terror. But he'll have plenty of time to work out the nuances of living that life, to imagine the garish suit and tie of paranoia he'll learn to wear. For now the expression is embarrassingly blunt: Amanda – what's going on?

"Amanda?"

The maelstrom he unleashed in the hallway must have roused her. At the best of times her sleep was fitful, light. Always has been. He can't figure out why she isn't inching down the stairs, calling his name. Or screaming from the bedroom, barricaded, threatening to call the cops.

"Hon?"

Nothing. In the dark his eyes scale the brick wall to where the stairs begin their ascent. He expects a glow from above, her bedside lamp seething with the rage she'll level him with at any moment.

"Hey, Amanda, you up? I'm sorry. Baby, I'm sorry I woke you."

The fragile silence and relentless darkness piss him off.

"Look, Man, this ain't fucking funny. I said I'm sorry."

Scott breathes in the stillness of his own house, shudders, and snaps. His ankle throbs encouragements, pushes for violence.

"Fuck. Man! What the fuck's going on? You gonna say something, or what? I said I'm fucking sorry."

His knuckles skin the brick as he punches up the hall light. He takes the stairs in twos. "A-man-da! Don't make me come up there!"

At the top of the stairs he ignores his office, the blinking message-waiting signal of the Vista phone. He turns to his left and punches on another light just outside the bathroom. Here, surprise, surprise, Scott fails to notice the toilet seat.

It's up.

Now this is just another insignificant little domestic detail. More of a cultural running gag, really. And you can hardly blame a man with Scott Venn's worries and rage for missing it. But, in fairness, it's definitely another thing for his wife to be pissed about. Ask her: she's fallen in. A cold wet shot in the dark. And that's never any fun. So why shouldn't she want his balls on a platter? Because if Amanda had told him once, she'd told him a million times: "Put the fucking lid down when you're done you fucking pig."

But here it is, again. Up. There's even the patterned splatter of a wild and vigorous backspray.

Not that Scott sees it, though.

Nope.

Another small difference on another different night: another tiny clue overlooked.

He's forgotten, too, that he'd stopped forgetting to put the damn thing back down years ago. A very sympathetic husband, now, he's sensitive to his wife's plight. A little afraid, even. The demented, incomprehensible screams that boomed off the bathroom tiles when it happened in the past were a wake-up call for guy's guys everywhere. Yes, Scott Venn's been toilet trained.

Burdened with his guilty rage, though, overconfident in his manipulations, an incredulous, trusting sucker, hoodwinked and dulled by both the legacy of his masculinity and the subtle reprogramming of sensitivity training, he walks on down the hall. And then he stops and flexes, runs the pad of his index finger down the face of a brick until it dips into mortar. He jabs the tip in, scratches until he feels something bad.

The bedroom door is ajar. His left hand flies out to slap it open. He pulls it back, quick, in an arc across his body, then flicks a snap at the head of a dimmer switch. A row of track lights blush. Too hot, not dim at all.

His tiny, furious pupils swell to mock him, taking the room in high definition slow-motion: dupe.

Scott recognizes, first, the familiar king-sized bed, positioned to look out onto the water. Its warm, deep blue duvet cover is patterned to undulate like waves. Six pudgy, soft pillows in light blue cases crest at the head; slipping under, leaden, deeper, he always feels like he's floating before he falls asleep.

The second thing he sees in the merciless light is that the bed is empty.

The duvet is pulled taut, perfectly draped to spread an eerie calm over the massive blue ocean.

"Fuck, Amanda. Where the fuck are you?"

Exhausted now, with nothing to do with his rage, Scott dives onto the duvet. He buries his face in blue and mutters, "Jesus."

Smelling her, Ivory and Joy, mixed faintly behind dust and fractal skin flakes and very old sex and very new nightmares, he almost sobs. Gulps, for sure. Sighs. He's sorry and he misses her and he knows he's got a serious situation here.

"Aw, Christ. This is bad. This is very, very bad."

The words come out wet and muffled and his lips, pressed tight into cloth, are covered in cold Sambuca and Heineken and bile-flavoured spit.

"And buddy? Hey, buddy! Fuck, bud. Why the hell are you talking to yourself?"

His face buried in the cunning and cruel wet spot that's spreading around his jabbering lips, he laughs up more drool and coughs. Rolls back onto his side. His left ear's in the puddle now, displeased with sobriety, displeased and wet and uncomfortable. He stares out the window, into the moon hovering high and huge and full, a shiny new paper plate, over the water. It's a crazy moon, perfect and improbable and as out of control as Scott knows, in the twisting, burning, jump ropes of his guts, his life's become tonight.

Amanda's not here. This has never happened before.

She's always here. She knows. I'm toast. She's left me.

Amanda's not here. Maybe I should be worried about her.

Amanda's not here. I miss her. I'm screwed. I'm scared.

What if something's wrong? What if something's happened to her?

Amanda's not here. She knows. She's left me.

In an aching explosion of movement, Scott's left ear sucks back from the duvet in a pop as he props himself up on his elbow and swings his legs over the edge of the bed. "Amanda," he says, "where are you?" Everything about him that can still be frantic takes over. He's no longer imposing and enraged; in fact, he's flitting and jittery, ranging through the upstairs, looking for his wife but noticing nothing.

He sticks his head into the guest bedroom across the hall. She's not there. Moving back past the bathroom to the office, he stops at the doorway then scoots back to the can. He turns on the light and actually pulls back the shower curtain to look in the tub. He decides he needs to piss, then forgets. Scott's oblivious to Amanda's makeup drawers, hanging open in the way that always pissed him off. Every overhead light upstairs is on now, except for the one in his office. He takes care of that. Looks around the room, hoping, maybe, just maybe, to find a note. There isn't one: Amanda never goes into his office. She's not like him. Not suspicious really, not an inveterate spy, a snoop.

Nope, buddy, she's a trusting soul.

He spins again and rushes downstairs, hangs a right and turns on the lights in the front sitting room. No sign of her. Another quick spin and he's moving through the dining room toward the kitchen. More track lights are punched on. Under the dining room table a powdery little grey-blue pill, a power-packed bundle of pharmacological joy, snug, secure in the knowledge that it's the preferred party favour of both good Cajun boys and successfully banal ex-pat Canadian thespians, has nestled itself against a hitching post. It rests comfortably under the mahogany shadow of the chair leg, softly on the plush rug, and Scott does nothing to disturb its happy presence. In the kitchen, there's an empty Chardonnay bottle in the recycling box. He misses that, too. And, of course, the dishwasher's still warm. Inside a couple of plates and wine-glasses dry spottily in their sauna. But who checks the dishwasher at this time of the morning?

Scott scans the kitchen counter for the notepad Amanda keeps for to-do lists and grocery reminders. Bingo. There it is, beside the block of Brie you really should wrap and put back into the fridge when you're done.

A note.

He snatches it up, prepares to be levelled, then reads: *Get more Kleenex. Scott – Driveway? Safe-T-Salt – Wal-Mart?*

Another spin and he's moving through the leaded glass of the French doors that lead to the living room, the very back of the house – the ornate, narrow, and heavily curtained archway from the dining room is the only other way. One last switch and the place is lit up like Christmas. Except there's no presents. No tree or decorations. No wonderful choco-late and turkey and eggnog surprises.

Just a couch, a loveseat, a leather recliner. A home entertainment cen-tre. A fireplace mantle with pictures of Amanda's family. A bookshelf with more videos than books. An antique wooden clock. A sliding patio door behind thick blue curtains drawn together and tied in the middle.

No trace of his wife. No note, no nothing.

The bird ruffles its feathers high in its corner and Scott jumps.

"Shit! Damn – hey, bird. Where the fuck's Man?"

The bird cocks its head, one eye piercing through Scott, judging him. Saying nothing.

"Thanks, Buddy. Thanks a hell of a fucking lot."

Hurt, the budgie blinks once, swivels its head away and then stares at a barely smoked cigarette that's rolled under the couch. The thing looks aborted, butted out as soon as it was lit. Strange: Amanda doesn't smoke, and the guy who never feeds me quit a year ago. What's that gonna taste like, you figure?

Aimless now, defeated and followed by many track-lights, Scott ambles back to the kitchen. Poking around the fridge he tests the Tupperware: cold meats and pasta, some kind of stew. A medium pizza box. He pulls out a slice and takes two bites, drops the crust-half back, grabs a Grolsch from the door, closes the cardboard lid, and clumsily slams the thing shut.

Leaning against the counter, the edge of the stainless steel sink cool against his elbow, he pops the fancy spring loaded stopper of his beer, raises the green bottle and takes a deep draught. He's dying for a butt and doesn't know why.

Finally, maybe it's the beer, lubricating his edges a bit, Scott gets a clue: duh. There's another blinking phone. A phone, just three-and-a-half feet away. The Venn household is full of phones. Many, many phones. This one, blinking. And a blinking phone means a message.

Bobbling the receiver, clunking the side of his head with it, Scott pushes *98, waits for Amanda's horrifying giggle which means he's into the system, then automatically punches in his universal PIN number: 9969.

He gets the fucking cyborg and there's no way to override her metallic ghosting, the electronic caps, hollow-points, she's hellbent on putting into Scott's head: "The following message will be deleted from your mailbox. Message from: an outside caller."

"Well, who the fuck else would it be!" he spits.

"Sent: Thursday, September 26th. At: 8:32 PM."

"Enough already."

"Hello, Scott Venn, this is Al from the garage. Your brakes are shot, buddy. Listen. . . ."

Scott punches the 3 twice. Then the /.

Cyborg-girl responds: "Message erased."

There's a beat before anything happens. Scott's actually mumbling, "C'mon, c'mon."

"The following message will be deleted. . . ."

"Oh, for chrissake."

He waits for the first word. "Amanda?" Her mother. Then it's 337.

"The following message. . . ."

"Doesn't anyone ever fucking write this shit down? Christ!"

Another hopeful beginning. Another 337.

"The following. . . ."

"Why do you hate me? That's it. I'm switching fucking phone companies. Fuck you, Bell, fuck you!"

He's about to hurl the thing against the wall, but stops himself. First, get these messages.

337.

And then, finally, "You have one new message. One skipped message. Press one one to listen. . . ."

A skipped message? Oh shit. A skipped fucking message. Oh fucking Christ. Amanda never skips messages. She always saves them. I'm the lazy one. I skip them. Man never does, always listens to every fucking word. Always. Oh fuck, Amanda. Oh fuck, fuck, fuck. She likes to tell me about them later, likes leaving those fucking notes to remind me to deal with them. And I do, the important ones at least. So, fuck, why's she skipping now?

The cyborg: "First new message." A pause. "Scott, just in case you call and I'm not here. . . ." It's Amanda, unusual, vacant, distracted. "I've, um." There's something undistinguishable, a gulp maybe. "Listen, Scott, I'm going out to ah. . . ." A what? Or was that something else? A sigh? No, couldn't be. She's pissed. Fighting to pick the words that'll reveal the least. Saving that for later. "Flick. With my . . . with my mom. Look, Scott, there's some things we have to discuss. Ahh, um. Yes. Discuss. About, about, well, you know. Things. Around here. I'll be back around midnight. I know you'll be . . . um. Yeah. Late. And, at least, be careful, Scott. Try to stay sober. We do have to talk. Ahh, and don't let Kirk make you do anything too crazy. And watch out for Alex, for godsake, he's getting married this weekend. Jesus. Um, okay. Look, we'll talk later, okay? Right? Yeah, talk. Bye."

Click. Scott pushes 7. Amanda's erased, and he regrets it immediately. Something about the words, the pauses, still bugs him. He wishes he could replay the damn thing. Analyse it further. Stupid fucking electronic voicemail.

And all this stuff about talk? What are we going to talk about, Man? Talk? Oh Jesus, that's not good.

"First skipped message." Cyborg-girl doesn't give a rat's ass for him or his need to clear his head.

"Hey, buddy, I'm back. Just got in. Hello, Amanda." It was Tones, Tony Lewis, Scott's best friend since law school. Fatally ambitious, he had worked his way up to full partner with a branch of the firm run by an ex-NHL superstar defenceman. From a cellar-dweller like Scott to the top of the heap in five years. For the past six weeks he'd been globe-trotting, spending most of his time in Kazakhstan and the Ukraine. Side trips to Sweden and Finland, Yugoslavia and Greece, and one to Hong Kong even, meant that he'd nabbed the rights to negotiate for five of the hottest seventeen-year-old European hockey prospects in years. The Swedish twins, of course, were his real coup. And hell, the seven-footers he'd signed from the Euro pro leagues and China were the kinds of long-shots that just might make the NBA. Who knows? One of them could be the next Divak. "Listen, I love you guys. And I've missed you. So I called as soon as I heard. Jesus. This sucks, buddy. . . ."

Oh fuck, oh fuck, oh fuck.

"If there's anything you need. Anything. Just call. Look, the 411's pretty sketchy around here, Scott. Nobody's talking, not even on your side, and definitely not on mine. So, I'm digging. But it looks like they've really gotta come down hard. Are the cops involved yet? How much money was it? Why, buddy? You could've come to me if you were in trouble. Christ, I'm sorry, I'm rambling. You two must be going through hell. Listen, buddy, I'm here for you. I'm gonna help straighten this out. Don't worry. At least the media isn't all over it yet. We've still got time to get together the damage control here. We don't want an Eagleson thing blowing up in your face. And, well, if worst comes to worst, I think I might just have an ace or two up my sleeve. Stay loose and call me, okay? Hang in there, guys. And Amanda, don't you worry about it. It's gonna be alright."

Click.

Dazed, Scott pushes 7. Bye, Tones. Hits the star twice. Automatically replaces the receiver.

Oh, God. That's it. It's over. She knows.

Fuck.

He drains the rest of his beer, walks mechanically to the fridge for another. Springs its mechanism and takes another long draught. Says: "Christ, I need a smoke."

And then: "I'm sorry. Oh Jesus, baby baby, I'm sorry. Man, I'm sorry."

Wandering, amazed at how quickly a life disintegrates, Scott negotiates the labyrinth of the downstairs, out through the kitchen, avoiding the centre island. Cradling his cold Grolsch, taking the long way around the dining room table, his baby toe, snug in a leather Oxford, brushes the table leg that protects the fluffy pastille dreams nestled against it. Outside the dining room he finds some of his wits returning. What he remembers of the two phone calls, he believes, will help reconstruct the events of the last night of his life as he's known it.

Ascending, he starts, mustering up all the logic in the world, drinking himself stone cold sober in the process. Okay. Tony called. Amanda was out. She was going to call to leave a message about going to a flick. Decided to check for a message from me first. Discovered Tony's message. Freaked. Yup, she lost her fucking mind, but was too embarrassed to lose it totally in front of her mother. She masks well, Amanda does. Such a fucking private Daddy's girl. She'd never let her mom in on it. Not until she had it out with me. Not until the moving van was packed. No, Daddy'll hear about it first. Tomorrow. After she crucifies me. As bad as Tony's message sounded, she'd assume things were worse but would be more pissed at me for hiding it.

Scott's at the top of the stairs again. Resting against the bricks there he takes another swig.

She knows and I'm fucked. That's why her message was so weird. So disjointed. Why we have to talk. Talk. Fuck, more like World War Three. Oh, fuck.

Again he ignores his office, unaware that a phone function he's already taken for granted might offer him a new perspective on the course of the evening's events.

Back in his bedroom Scott Venn stares out the window. He desperately wants to cry but the tears won't come. There's too many voices, mocking, angry voices, fighting for his full attention. They bite, tear at one another. And at his thoughts.

· · • · ·

On the desk in the mess of Scott's office the Vista phone no longer blinks red. But even without the warning lights the call display still casts its green effulgence: 2 New Callers. If Scott was in this room, scrolling down his callers menu, he'd see, first: 24 AllPro, and below it, Tony's switchboard number. Then: 25 Private name Private number. If he was just a bit more attentive he'd also have noticed that the first call read: Oct 2 8:08 PM. The second, Amanda's odd, private message, was also registered at that time.

But this is simply more of what Scott Venn never notices; because, staring out a window now, utterly absorbed in the water and his failure, his life's ruination, he will never find an unfamiliar Chardonnay in the recycling box or a trickly little Vicodin on the dining room area rug; he will never check the dishwasher or the wonderful bit of technological advancement from his good friends at Bell.

No one useful ever will.

Yes, Amanda was obviously the second caller. And yes, she left her message after Tony spilled the beans.

60

Or, more precisely, while Tony was doing so.

What only Amanda Venn knows is this: she had been calling her own phone number on a borrowed cell phone, while she was actually right there, at home. Yes, her ass was up on the moveable centre island in her stylish kitchen, and her hair was an unruly, seductive mess. The phone in the kitchen, a few feet away, rang four times – just as it was supposed to. She could hear it ringing. In both ears. She expected to hear the click and then their outgoing message; in unison: It's Scott and Man, leave a message. Instead, the line just disconnected. Strange. Amanda then pressed the redial button of the borrowed Fido. The line rang once in her ear but not in the kitchen. This time her call went directly into the voicemail service. Ah, okay. She understood.

Somebody else had called at exactly the same time. Funny, eh? They were both leaving messages right now.

Only she wasn't laughing, certainly not outwardly, not as she began her message.

Instead, as she started speaking to her absent husband, a young man's hands worked their way up her thighs and under her dress. Trying to talk, she had to push his face away, twice, from the spontaneously unbuttoned crevice that opened upon the flesh so perfectly buoyed by her Miracle Bra. Bothered? God, was she bothered. Not necessarily in a bad way, but she was still having a hell of a time getting out her words – especially when a muscular thumb brushed ever so electrically light over the thin fabric of her black lace thong. After mumbling her way through a lie she could barely remember, it was all Amanda could do to get off the phone. To end the call undetected.

A man more attuned to his wife's subtleties might have replayed her voice over and over again. Might have savoured this horrible opportunity. This man might have heard things. Gulps, maybe. Or sighs. Definitely misplaced sighs. He might have even heard the unmistakeable rasp of fabric being hiked. Or even the odd atmospheric shift of a button being popped.

Scott Venn was not this man. Scott Venn, remember, erased his wife's message.

After hanging up, but before her husband erased her, Amanda briefly indulged the man, the boy really, on her island. She'd given him the spare set of keys two weeks ago, to let himself in, as long as he called first – their little code call, one ring, hang up, two rings, hang up, call – and he'd used them often. The attention – like now, his tongue circling slowly against her neck, the flesh just below her right ear, his large hands cupping her breasts, fingers toying gently with her nipples – was, frankly, and this is the word that burned through her endorphin-charged mind, *unfuckinbelievable*.

She was a bit uneasy about her situation, though, knowing that she and Scott really should talk about so many things, like her plans for her father's sixty-fifth birthday party and forgetting about that riverside cottage they'd been thinking of buying since last summer. About all the things, little and big, that Scott had been putting off for more than a month. Her, too. She wondered, as well, whether he'd finally cop to everything, confirm what she'd known for weeks. The sonofabitch. Give her the satisfaction of fessing up to her own extra-curricular activities. And then, still, screwing him royally.

So, despite the purpled lips pulling at her right lobe, the hot breath circling deep into her ear like the promise of an immaculately wicked tongue, Amanda knew something wasn't right. Plus, she was unnerved by the coincidence of the other call, so she playfully cast her guy adrift.

The younger man smiled and ran his right hand through his thick black hair. Churlish, he grinned and popped the lid of a vial. Then fished out three, no, sneaky, four blue-grey pills. He popped one in his mouth, then washed it away with some Chardonnay. Amanda smiled and laughed, then finished off her wine as he reached out with her little present. The transfer was awkward, and one fell to the floor, then skedaddled. Neither of them noticed. Amanda took the two Vicodin under her tongue and savoured the bitter dissolve.

Bad girl.

"Listen," she said to her gentleman caller, "can you get things together down here? I want to get out right away. Maybe catch a movie? Or, we could just go to your place. Whatever. As long as we're not here. Something doesn't feel right. Not tonight. Okay?"

"Yeah, sure. Ah, what about the wine?"

"Oh, just finish off the bottle and get rid of it. Put the glasses in the dishwasher and turn it on. And make sure you get rid of your butts, okay? I'll just grab a couple things from upstairs, and we're out of here."

Passing the lonely little blue-grey boy that'd come to rest in her dining room, Amanda went upstairs. She pissed, pulled sharply at the toilet paper: out, down. Done, she flushed, shut the lid, then rifled through her makeup. She touched up her lips, her eyes, and tousled at her wild hair. The mirror's kind. She's flying, really, happy as she's been in months. But turning off the light she shuddered, involuntarily. It's not guilt. Amanda's so over guilt. It's something else: more like curiosity. Something more thrilling. Like the possibility of being caught. Of confrontation. Of finality.

Who else was calling here? What if it was Scott, to say he'd be home early? What if the myopic sonofabitch actually stumbled into this?

Momentarily freaked, she bolted to her husband's office and punched in for the message: come on, come on. What if he was calling from the corner, to say he wasn't going to the stag. And, was there anything they needed from the store?

Amanda's taking her turn in the game called self-absorption here, so she doesn't notice that the new man in her life has followed her up the stairs. She doesn't realize that he, too, is taking a moment to relieve himself. And she certainly doesn't notice, even though the door's wide upon, the sounds of a very manly, healthy stream of urine, flying long and strong. Hell, she even ignores the fact that she doesn't hear the toilet flush, or that the seat stands at attention, also very manly, very up.

Come on, come on. She's past the cyborg, listening: Two new callers. First unheard message: "Hey, buddy, I'm back. Hello, Amanda. . . ."

It's just Tony. Shithead's back in town.

Relieved, she quickly pushed the pound key, then disconnected. Scott's buddy had always weirded her out. Swear to God, he meant it, really did make a pass. On our fucking wedding day. But oh no, Scott wouldn't believe it. Dupe.

For another brief moment she thought about re-recording her own halting message. Considering her options she poked around the mess of Scott's papers. There was nothing of interest out in the open, and she was content, knowing she'd already found the incriminating stuff behind some boxes weeks earlier: another of Scott's pathetic attempts to keep his life a mystery. Finally, she decided her performance wasn't up to par, and again picked up the receiver. She'd dialled *98 and was about to key in the stupid password, but the feeling of her island man's hands on her ass plucked the notion right out of her head. Fuck him.

She replaced the receiver.

And then she thought: Fuck him? In Scott's office? The idea thrilled her. Take him in, from behind, right here, right now, on the desk.

But no. Really now, that's a bit much. I'm not that high. This is fine. Fun. It's all good. But nobody should get that high. That's just dumb, porno movie shit.

Not completely convinced, she again removed his large, strong, soft hands.

"Lover, let's get out of here. Okay?"

"Was that your husband?"

"Nope, just one of his idiot drinking buddies."

"A problem, though. You seem tense. If you want me to leave. . . ."

"No, no problem. I just want to go someplace where we can relax. Completely relax. Some place not home."

"Sure, precious. Sure. You know, I think I could fall in love with you. I think, maybe, I am."

Taking his hands, Amanda pulled him close and kissed him hard, biting his lips. The boy growled. Pulling back and spinning, still holding his hand, she led him down the stairs. Arm in arm with her lover at the front door then, she armed the alarm.

It's the kind of thing you do, automatic, when you go out. It's also her little joke on a husband who always expects her to be there waiting. Just in case, though it's not bloody likely, he'll be home first.

With the little green light blinking, Amanda and her new guy passed through the door. As she fiddled with the key to lock the deadbolt, he lit a Rothman's. The words he spoke accumulated, inscribed in the cold night air. "I meant to tell you, I've got to get the car to my brother. He needs it tonight. It's only a block from my place. Do you mind the walk?"

She kissed him quick on the doorstep, smushing a "No" into his mouth before he could take a second drag.

· · ● · ·

Staring out his bedroom window, the only blissful thing left in Scott's life is his bored ignorance, his utter inability to see things any other way. The thoughts picking and tearing at his mind are so familiar they've become comfortable blinders. To the usual refrain of "I'm fucked" and its variants, a new phrase marches along with the others: Amanda knows.

I'm fucked. I'm going to jail. My life's over. Amanda knows. I'm fucked.

It's really late now. Really early. Pre-dawn. Scott opens the window to hear his thoughts carried on the waves. To see them break, rhythmically, upon the same black waters on which he's being broken.

In and out: I'm fucked. I'm going to jail. My life's over. Amanda knows. I'm fucked.

He cries out then, one twisted, squawking word: "Amanda!"

And from somewhere above, the worst gull, malicious and circling, more vulture or monster than seagull, answers, satiated almost, nearly satisfied: Ah.

Scott's oblivious to this, of course, but downstairs, in the living room, a little bird shivers. His head swivels, dives under a wing. Nests there, thinking: It's not nice to laugh at pain. It's not right.

Popping its head out again, this tiny budgie casts a compassionate eye out through the double patio doors. He sees the big house plant, the frightening one that sits below his cage when the weather turns.

The bird feels cold and lonely and hopes the plant will come inside soon. It really should. It must be cold and lonely, too.

A few minutes later, when Scott passes through the living room and out onto the patio carrying another beer and the stale, half-empty, year-and-a-half old package of cigarettes he'd dug out from an accordion-folder squirrelled away under his desk, the bird considers saying something cheering or instructive. Something like: Hey, dufus! You quit. Don't pack it all in now.

He settles for the practical: Bring in the plant, for chrissake. At least bring in the plant. It's too cold out there.

Never having expected much from Scott, the bird's not surprised he's ignored. Not surprised at all that the man who rarely feeds him jostles the large house plant as he passes and heads down to the water, as oblivious as always, to wait. Eventually, when the sun starts to rise, he can see Scott bathed in pink and purple light, ass and elbows planted in the sand. When he feels the first rays warm the glass, he's relieved. Okay, another day should be fine. The big fella should be all right. Maybe Amanda will remember. She remembers those things. I can't do everything. Jesus, it's too cold out there. Am I right? Okay. Amanda usually remembers.

7:40 AM

He LIT A MATCH, circled it before himself three times to free its sulphuric magic, then dropped it into the bowl. Another for his cigarette. The muscles across his chest heaved in throbs, still frantically urging him to vomit, unwilling to admit even that painful failure. A ritual morning death spasm, a loping string of yellow bile. That's all. Pulling hard to replace the sour metallic taste, Mr. Clean with a hint of lemon Pledge, equal parts sleep and mescal and Jack Daniels and beer, the smoke bit through his body – a parasitic mastiff, violent and final. This felt good, a shudder of normalcy. He pulled mucus through his sinuses into his throat, swallowed, shuddered again, retched another dry heave, and spat more bile into the sink. Better, feeling better.

Couldn't feel much worse.

His cigarette perched in an ashtray he's nestled into the steel soapdish plumbers recessed into the maze of mildewy blue and white tile above the bathroom sink thirty years earlier, the water running cold, Peter James raises the alms bowl he's made of his hands to his face. The clinging wrap of shrunken dirt and oil and sweat becomes unstable. Reluctantly, it dissolves, then washes away. His face appears, stubbled, hard. All puffiness recedes. In these miraculous, precious moments before it all begins again his eyes see older eyes, eyes that are deep, alert, and blue. Not grey; for once, not grey and blood-red at all.

And then they see The Rail's shooter girl, her tray and bottle and salt shaker and lime wedges. Her money belt and sly smile. Her big tattooed tits. She's talking to the new one, a shy, sort-of-pretty girl. The four-eyed mouse points and shrugs.

Do I know her from somewhere? Is she buying me a drink?

The shooter girl, walking his way, gum-cracking and cleavage. The dregs of the bottle, cloudy. The worm in his shot glass, as desiccated as he is. Trying to be cool, to flirt.

"Wow," he'd said, "I guess I'm early."

"What?"

"You know, the early bird?"

"What?"

"Uh, gets the worm...."

"Listen, buddy, whatever, it's five bucks."

"Uh, yeah."

He smiles now, rabid, almost laughs. Then the bottom falls out of his mouth, and his jaw juts forward and he bares his yellowing teeth. His right fist flies toward the mirror. Stops just before making contact and hangs there.

His hand relaxes and his fingers spread to obscure himself, a poor man's Eric Roberts, blotting himself out.

Yeah, I'm early, baby. Fuck. Bad, bad fucking birddog, bad.

The face Peter's most familiar with returns when he's shaving, passing the rechargeable Braun he never unplugs across the extra padding that rises from his throat. Circles of strange yellow and blue-black under his familiar eyes, livid splotches of tricky crimson dancing here and there on his cheeks, pock marks and scars. Whiteheads burst through the razor's foil, the two or three that always appear in the morning to mock years of Acutane. They're glued to tiny points of hair and dust by jigging blades.

Rubbing alcohol becomes aftershave, spread to burn with the generic quilted cotton pads Maria brings home from work. Water and splayed fingers clean and style his straight, shoulder-length blue-black hair. His chest is still damp from the water rubbed around there, and a thin stand of hair springs back to hook through the cotton t-shirt that clings to his belly and nipples. Peter shoves the Speed Stick through the left armhole: two quick, perfunctory passes. An ambidextrous switch, then the same happens to the right.

Negotiating the stairs, down, tentatively, Peter carries his beer- and coffee- and sweat-stained jeans under his left arm. They're filthy, yellow and black and brown more than faded blue, two pinprick burn holes just left of the crotch: hot embers before ash, an exploding seed. His pants are a heavy and lopsided ball. There's exactly five dollars and eighty-three cents worth of change, a thin bumpy cone of tinfoil, and nine keys on a plastic Black Flag ring in the front right pocket; a watch, a miniature red Bic lighter, an oblong blue condom in foil and plastic, and a long dead pager, now a charm, in the front left. His wallet, empty except for his revoked driver's licence and ATM card, a half-empty pack of Zig-Zag rolling papers, two bus tickets, rides light, high in the back left. Hidden and forgotten under the fold of the wallet's lining, there's also half of a nine-year-old photo booth strip. A black and white teenaged boy and girl, laughing, kissing, ripped asunder: the words "Jen & Pete 19-" in the blue ink of a girl's high school hand fading into a jagged strip on the back.

Peter half-stumbles down the last two steps but doesn't fall, doesn't hurt himself. Miraculously he doesn't drop anything. Wedged against his side with his right arm, still, are his beaten black Nikes, a frayed hole gaping out of the left instep. In the fingers of that hand he's still got a firm grip on his cheap Aiwa walkman, his good Sony headphones bouncing behind him as if everything's par for the course.

Wearing white sports socks, a wrinkled plain classic black t-shirt, and rumpled Jockey boxers, another cigarette dangling from his lips and his eyes squinting against the smoke and heat that's stinging them redder and greyer by the second, Peter turns the corner into the kitchen. He releases everything but the pseudo-walkman and the smoke and they thud into two reckless mountains just inside the doorframe. Maria doesn't turn from the kitchen sink where she's eating a half-slice of margarine-soaked toast. Crumbs fall onto the Javex-scratched stainless steel with imperceptible pings. The light through the kitchen window makes the Wonder Bread bag, the fallen dominoes of bread, more beautiful because there's no one there to notice. Nobody, in fact, could notice this because the light, the morning, the day itself, is far too beautiful, far too manipulative. And it hoards all the praise, the wonder. It holds all the cards.

Peter puts out his smoke in the brown clay ashtray his mother and father brought back from the Bahamas when he was sixteen. It's damp in the valleys between the ridges that spell the tropical name. Black lagoons in the B and A's. He thinks: Christ, how many times have I asked, how many times have I told you?

Peter James hates wet ashtrays for what they do to a smoke, how they

67

kill it and destroy a perfectly good cigarette. Always the best you've had in a long time. Relighting the butt is pointless, the taste of nothing but ash and ruin. And no matter what you do, no matter how soon you light another, it's just not the first. Not the same. Nowhere near, inevitably nowhere near as good. The fact that he'd finished with the butt is beside the point, he could have just lit the thing. And then it would've been ruined. He's going to say something to his mother, explain all of this once and for all, but he decides against it, can't find the words.

Really, Peter thinks, don't open that breach. *Don't, not yet.*

Reaching for his coffee, he knocks over the plastic rooster pepper dispenser and an arc of black spreads across the white Formica breakfast nook tabletop. The salt hen beside it wobbles but doesn't topple. A bit of fortune, anyway, to start the day. He can't help thinking this, amazed at the extremes of his own banality: a man with no dreams, even less luck, and no "day," actually, to speak of. But he forgets about it, lets these thoughts die out immediately, raises the Black Hole mug to his lips, swallows and sighs. Better, feeling just a bit better.

Couldn't feel much worse.

"Better," he mumbles, a spurt of taupe coffee escaping his mouth and arcing onto his shirt, his hairy white thigh.

"It's in the fridge, son. But I've already put the marj on your toast. Should I make you some more, have you got time?" Maria had pivoted away from the sink before the first syllable left her son's lips, grateful for an opening, the possibility, any possibility, of having a conversation with her only child. She still clung to the hope that something good might come from her husband's death, that it might have a profound, liberating effect on her son: it hadn't. No tears. No epiphany. No resurrection. In fact, the only change she'd noted was the bloating resignation, the way time can take everything bad and make it just a little bit worse. Now, still chewing, expectant, a shower of toastflakes, no two identical, dusts her pink rose-patterned robe and the linoleum of the kitchen floor. "It won't take a minute," she continues. "If you've got time. Darling, is there time?"

"What?"

"The butter, Peter. You just asked for butter. But I've already put the Parkay on your toast. You never have butter any more, so I just assumed. But I'll put more bread in the toaster if—"

"What're you talking about?" Confused, Peter thinks of the undisturbed slabs of butter, perfect silver-foiled monoliths, he occasionally finds when taking out the garbage. Maria dutifully tosses them out when they reach their "best before" date. Twenty-four hours later, they're replaced by an identical slab of precisely the same brand of unsalted butter.

Neither Peter nor his mother has used the confection for years. It's for the guests they never entertain, a dead tyrant's favourite brand.

"Didn't you ask for butter?"

Peter shakes his head.

"Oh, I'm sorry, dear. So, what were you saying?"

Fishing into the waistband of his Jockeys, Peter frees his cigarettes. He pulls another out, reaches across the pepper arc to the wooden fruit bowl filled with packs of matches, and mechanically lights his smoke.

"Honey?"

He inhales and shakes, no, slightly.

"I'm sure you said something, darling. I'm sure you did." His mother's not about to give up on this opportunity. "You should eat, dear, your uncle will be here in fifteen minutes. Don't you want your eggs? I can fix you some Shreddies."

Looking down at the sunnyside eyes and bacon mouth, Peter imagines his cigarette flaring red into the yellow cornea, his fist coming down to bust a fat pig lip. He takes another drag, considers actually following his inclination and ruining his mother's happy gesture, then blinks the thought away: *Not now, not yet.*

"Come on, Peter, you have to eat. Dear, do you think maybe you're smoking too much? Why don't you put that thing out and try to get something good inside you?"

Maybe? Maybe now? Wait.

Peter James takes the penultimate drag from his smoke, hooks a crisp, cold slice of bacon into the right yolk, bites off an inch, chews twice, and swallows. Another drag and wash of coffee. His head lolls back on his shoulders as he stubs out the cigarette, obliterating the first wet A.

"Ma, I'm not hungry," he says, staring at the smoke-yellowed stucco of the kitchen ceiling.

"That's okay, dear, you'll feel more yourself later. I've packed a banana and some cookies with your lunch. Maybe you'll try those, okay?"

"Yup."

"You're not planning on wearing these are you? They're filthy." Maria James points to the faded blue jean ball on the floor in her kitchen doorway.

"They're fine."

"Oh honey, I've washed your black ones. They're in the laundry room on the ironing board. I'll get them for you."

As his mother darts away, Peter closes his eyes. He's absorbed in the contours of the stucco peaks and valleys the ceiling imprints there, disappearing into this landscape. Exploring the terrain, he wonders if he'll ever manage to convince his mother that you don't iron creases into jeans.

"Here you go, son."

Startled back to the kitchen, the smell of eggs and toast and fresh Wonder Bread, Peter lowers his head to see his mother standing before him, holding out his black Levis, delicately, by the V the open zipper makes.

Automatically, he mumbles, "Thanks, Ma."

A sunbeam breaks off from the flood of light, overwhelming the kitchen counter and throwing a glorious spot over Maria. Still sitting at the breakfast nook bench, Peter slides his white-socked feet into the stiff, rectangular legs of his pants.

"It's a lovely day, son. Beautiful. Everything will work out, turn around today. Look out that window dear. My lord, it's gorgeous. Proof, Petey, of God's . . ."

"What the fuck?"

Now.

". . . bounty."

"How the fuck'd this shit get in here?"

"Peter?"

"My keys! My fucking wallet! My stuff!"

"Calm down, honey. Peter, I was only trying to help."

"You what? Fuck!"

"I was going down anyway, Peter, and I just figured I'd save you a trip. You know I do the laundry anyway. I was just trying to be helpful." Maria thinks her good-natured, rapid-fire explanation might diffuse her son's rage. "I wasn't snooping. Really, I just wanted to make sure you looked nice, that you weren't late. So I picked up your dirty pants on the way down and moved your stuff. Everything's exactly where you had it, Peter. Honestly, I'm your mother. You've got to learn to relax about these things." Her sunbeam trembles, expecting the worst of the furious, red-faced twenty-four-year-old who menaces it.

"Just. Don't. Ever." Peter spits out his words, zipping up his fly, only half of his black t-shirt tucked in at the waist. "I've told you not to go through my crap!"

"I'm sorry, Peter. Really, if I knew you'd be upset, I'd never have."

A short, burping blast from the horn of Joe James's mint Oldsmobile Eighty-Eight Royale interrupts Maria's apology.

"There's Uncle Joe. I'm sorry, Peter, really. But you have to get a move on now."

Maria James's only child stomps to the doorframe and fumbles with his shoes. Unlaced, stiff with rage, he lumbers toward the front door. Reaching for the handle, he stops and turns and begins stomping back.

In the kitchen he blows past his mother and the sunbeam, scoops up his cigarettes and walkman, without saying a word.

Still irate, Peter plugs his ears with tiny pieces of fitted black plastic before he reaches the front door again. He grabs the beaten leather and heavily zippered motorcycle jacket that lays strewn on a chair, pressing play just as his mother says, "I love you, son. Have a nice day."

Stopped short by the brilliant, unoccluded blue sky, the intensity of the early morning light, the door he's slamming behind himself hits Peter in the ass, sends a burner through his funnybone and up his left arm, punctuating his mother's farewell.

· · • · ·

Inconsiderate and rude. Mean, even. Yes, okay, maybe. But it could also be as simple as this: Peter might not have acknowledged his mother because of the throbbing hangover pain in his head. Or he may not have heard anything at all. Rage, perhaps, played a part. Or it might have been the action of swinging open the sticky oak door which drowned out Maria's sad voice. The fact that Uncle Joe leaned on the horn, more annoyed and emphatic this time, at precisely the same moment, couldn't have helped either. Mostly though it was Motörhead that drowned her out, Lemmy Killmister screaming: "You win some, you lose some, it's all the same to me! The Ace of Spades! The Ace of Spades!"

Hurt for Maria James, widow and mother of an adult child too big for his britches or to be babied, her compassionate sunbeam urged the day to play its next card. Obliging, just for Peter and those very much like him, it drew from the bottom of the deck. Pulsing like a Fender Precision bass through a dozen 100-watt heads, it covered Lemmy's wicked heavy metal afterthought: "And don't forget the Joker."

Buddy, it said, don't you dare forget.

8:29 AM

IN FRAYING, COMFY BLUE SLIPPERS, soft brown slacks picky with coffee-coloured balls of fluff and undone at the fly, wearing yet another yellowing undershirt, elbows on the kitchen table, Ed Harrison forks a mouthful of goo-covered egg and heavily peppered tomato up to his lips. The people who run those financial planning ads on TV might not want you to know it – their vision of how folks should spend their golden years always features some nattily-dressed couple in their late sixties breezing by on yachts or climbing mountains – but as the fork ascends he's the

71

very picture of a hardworking man thoroughly enjoying his retirement. No plans, no pressure, no worries: just a damned fine meal to start the day. Engrossed as he is in the pre-season roundup on page S3 of his paper, however, Ed's strong, white-furred and tattooed arm misdirects this bit of one of the three different breakfasts Alice Harrison had prepared for more than fifty years. A chunk of sticky brown egg scrambles, taking a few seeds and some of the wet, black-flecked meat of the tomato with it.

Now, if he'd been eating two slices of dry toast and a bowl of hot oatmeal, as he had yesterday, or even the simple, sugar-doused, milk-logged bowl of corn flakes of a couple days back, he'd have been handling a tricky spoon and probably would've been paying a little more attention. Ed hated making a mess, hated knowing that Alice would fuss and make him change.

But it was a Friday, and the day before ten of the NHL season openers, and that meant well-done scrambled eggs, six tomato slices dusted with freshly ground pepper, five strips of crispy bacon, and A1 sauce. Definitely a fork day.

The only spoon on the table lay beside one of the two cups of coffee he'd have every morning. Double-double – though when Alice wasn't looking he'd sometimes sneak an extra sugar. And because the idiot the tabloid called a hockey expert was pontificating about how management had screwed things up royally for twenty-some years, and how last season's playoff appearance was a freak occurrence that only a fool would believe they'd duplicate, Ed was somewhere in the middle of either flying off the handle or picking up a phone and laying down some real money through an old Army buddy in Atlantic City. Worse, S4 and the headline beside the picture of the goddamneduglyreactionarybroad they for some godforsaken reason let write stupid hockey editorials – Christ, how can they let her bitch about hockey; isn't that shit she writes about the cops in her regular column bad enough? – had also caught his eye: it badmouthed his team's coach, his reputation as a hard-ass who pushes players beyond reasonable limits. Well, boofuckinghoo.

So, as his powerful, steady arm guided the shiny stainless steel Friday breakfast fork, a tremor so tiny it belied the violence of his response made the food dive faster than a Russian feeling the ghost of a furious Canadian backchecker: goddamnit, these were his Bruins. The legacy of Milt Schmidt. His Espo and Bucyk and Orr. Wencyk and O'Reilly. Middleton and Neely and Borque. Sinden's and Cherry's and Burns' boys. These were fighting words. And what the hell did an enemy rag know about his team anyway? Jealous, too; because the hometown bums look to be the league's laughingstock again this year – even with expansion into the heart of goddamned Nashville and Atlanta, again, on the horizon.

"Aw, hell! Jesus H, now look what you've gone and done."

Ed drops the fork in disgust, then jabs a fat, menacing finger into the crease between S3 and S4. With his fork-free hand he picks up the lime-green linen breakfast napkin Alice always insisted they use. A different colour for every meal. And not just for company. They weren't about to start using paper towels: this is the way her mother did it, and it would always be that way in their house. After wiping off the smear of A1 and the bit of egg that did manage to find its way to the corner of his mouth, he licked at a clean corner of the napkin, then lowered it to furiously rub at the brown and yellow and red mess on his white undershirt.

"Christ. Alice, I'm sorry, hon. I don't know where my head was at. My damned paper's got me all riled again. They just can't leave Boston alone. Yeah, I know, I know, it's only the paper, but it's just that it makes me furious, you know? Of course you do. They're young and strong this year, and this fella Burns knows a thing or two about lighting a fire under an ass that needs one lit. Mark my words. Why'd they think this guy's coach of the year with every team he takes on? Lays down the law, he does. A good kid. There's going to be more than a few of these fellows with egg on their face come spring."

From across the room, hovering by the stove, Alice looks down on her husband, smiling. In the sunlight pouring in between the small azure square of the window frame, her silver hair reflects a glorious halo. Ed still daubs at the mess he's made of himself. He squints up at her.

"Now, hon, don't you go making a fuss. Look, I'll take it off and put it in the hamper. You really are right there, eh, Alice? Maybe the old man needs a bib."

Ed's untangling himself from his stained undershirt, his beautifully incongruous round belly jiggling around the rest of his lean, seventy-two-year-old frame, grey tummy hairs dancing in their freedom, when the tiny bird in the ancient cuckoo clock close to Alice pokes out its head and says hello. Balling up his shirt and dropping it at his feet, he checks the time then fishes into his pants pocket and pulls out his watch.

"Alice, the thing's still slow. You know, Ted's taken that clock in three times now, and it still ain't right." He looks to his wife for her opinion, then lowers his eyes to his plate.

"I know, I know. All these years and I keep forgetting to wind her up. I'm getting worse, too. There's probably nothing wrong with her – just needs a little more attention. I'm getting a bit forgetful in my old age. Maybe a touch of the Alzheimer's, eh, darling?"

They've shared this joke a hundred times in the last few years, and every time they both laugh. Neither one of them had ever been sharper. Ed's retirement, all the extra time they found they had together, even while maintaining many of their daily routines – some old habits die hard; some habits, in fact, never die at all – meant they talked more, listened more, became more attuned to the world around them. And to each other.

Even when Ed lost himself in the paper, as he had just done once again, shirtless, and munching on a strip of bacon, he was aware of his wife, her subtle presence, the things that mattered to her.

Like now, for example: as deep as he was in the sports pages, checking the final standings and expanded stats from last season, he heard her station playing on the small Emerson radio she'd set up by the toaster behind the ridiculous rabbit salt and pepper shakers little Krystal had given them for Christmas when she was just six. Ed cringed at the poncy fake British accent of that godawful zealot they'd given a goddamned morning talk show. Just because he understood it didn't mean he thought it was right: Martin Creighton always managed to rouse the worst of the rabble, so no matter who he offended, no matter how much hate he mongered, the usually middle-of-the-road AM station kept him on the air.

Both Harrisons despised Creighton's petty viciousness, his holier-than-thou duplicity and downright stupidity. Alice called him the worst kind of right-wing reactionary, a heartless, gutless faker, and she despised him for the cosseted and weak ivory-tower bully he was. But what pissed Ed off the most was that the guy's rants had, on occasion, actually driven his wife to tears. He swore that if he'd ever met the sissy – oh yes, he'd seen the bald-headed little pencil-necked weasel shilling for an auto-repair company on a local cable station, and there's was no way in hell the guy could even change his own damned oil – he'd kick his stinking teeth in. When Ed said this out loud one morning, Alice actually looked at him, afraid. Not for Ed, but for the talk-show fool. She knew her husband's temper, that he really meant it. She didn't doubt for a second that he could back up his threat, that he would, in fact, if the encounter ever occurred. It scared her enough, though the chance of the two of them ever meeting was more than unlikely, that she made him swear he wouldn't start anything. Ed put her off for a while, scowling. Mumbling about how *Mahr-tin* had it coming. Finally he tried to humour her – she knew it, and kept at him.

"Now, Ed, I don't care if you were kidding," she had said. "Promise me. Promise that you'd never hurt this man. No matter what."

Ed, of course, bristled, but then softened, thinking about his wife's concern, her gentle kindness. "Aw, Alice. All right, I promise."

This morning, for the millionth time, the idiot had found his way into nastily berating some poor young girl about the evils, the unholiness of abortion. Even with an annoying sliver of hard meat jabbing between his dentures, and contemplating Jason Allison's unbelievable +/- figure and team-leading shooting percentage – he's just got to take more shots, that's all, and he'd lead the league in goddamned goals, he would – Ed jumped from his seat to switch stations. Flicking to the FM dial, he found the nice man and woman who'd taken over one of the national network's morning shows.

The truth was, the abortion nonsense, the vitriol, hurt him, too; he felt Creighton's cruelty like a kidney blow.

He remembered being forty-two and thrilled at the thought of another child, another pair of soft, tiny feet padding around the place. And he also remembered Alice, ashen-faced as the door opened and she walked out, unable to meet his gaze, almost in slow motion, from the doctor's office.

All she would say, all she ever said, during the long streetcar ride home, was "Ed, I'm so sorry."

Later that day, Ed returned to the office, brushed off the secretary's warnings, and burst in on the quack. The doctor explained it to him: "Complications."

Ed grabbed the man by his white coat and screamed: "Don't talk to me like I'm a fucking retard! Tell me what the fuck's going on, right now!"

"Mr. Harrison, please, try and calm down."

"I am fucking calm, buddy. You don't want to see me when I ain't calm. Now, what the fuck did you say to my wife?"

"She didn't tell you?"

"Tell me what!"

"Oh my God, I'm sorry, Mr. Harrison. I am truly sorry."

"Stop calling me Mister, Doc, and start telling me what the fuck's going on with my wife! She was just fine when she came in here. What the hell did you do to her?"

The doctor explained everything. About toxaemia, about his wife's age, about the way the baby would grow inside her. That she would be in terrible danger if the pregnancy went its full duration. He believed, of course, that the fetus would spontaneously abort. But if she did carry to term. . . . Well, they would have to see what could be done. There might be some deformity. Or a stillbirth. Or even, in the worst possible scenario, both Alice and the child might be lost.

Ed went home and held his wife, tight. "Darling, I know. I know everything now. It's okay. Everything will be alright."

Alice cried. Her husband ran his fingers down her face, brushing the tears from her eyes, and then stiffened and left the room.

Ed picked up the phone, dialled the specialist's secretary at the General, and arranged for the abortion.

Alice wanted to discuss their options, wanted to wait to be sure.

"I'm sorry, darling," he said. "I won't have you go through this. It's for the best. We're going next Friday. I'm sorry. But that's it."

Alice tried, for the next week, to get her husband to talk. He couldn't and the day came and they got on the bus and it was done and Ed took her home in a cab. The drugs were already starting to wear off.

Alice began crying when they got home and found Ted, with his baby sister Belle propped up beside him, playing tabletop hockey with Ed's brother, Frank. She sobbed in bed, doubled up, for most of the weekend. He told the young boy his mother was sick. That she'd be alright, though, in a few days. Ed stalked the place, kept their son away from his mother, left the bedroom and returned dozens of times. He wanted to comfort her, to take her in his arms and explain why he'd done what he'd done. Why it was right.

But Ed didn't. And they never spoke of it again.

· · • · ·

Picking up the salt and pepper bunnies, Ed turned to look at his wife.

"Remember the card Krystal drew to go with these things, Alice? Gramma and Grampa bunnies. Where's that gotten to, you figure? I want to pull some of that stuff out for her to see, if they ever get her here, eh? Ha. She'll get a kick out of some of her dad's junk, too. Especially that. Now, where . . . yeah, wait, that's right. You put all the kids' cards and drawings and things in one of those big old hatboxes in the back room, didn't you? That's good, darling. I like knowing where everything is, don't you?"

Alice Harrison's alabaster arms reached through her daffodil and emerald sundress and held fast to her love for her husband as he walked past her and down the hall toward the closet. She didn't mind that he'd left his dirty undershirt on the floor. That'd get picked up later.

9:14 AM

IN PURPLE AND BLACK VELVETEEN, the monkeysuited fellow, a doorman or car jockey or valet or something, is obviously frustrated, annoyed at having to repeat himself. He's just a kid really, with a couple of small, menacing zits around the right corner of his lower lip. There's another, an angry red casualty, smack dab in the middle of his forehead, but he's still a handsomely boyish teen with a cruel, lascivious mouth. Whatever, the minimum-wage hotel lackey in the ridiculous getup and crisp new hat and shiny black shoes has asked him, twice, a bit warily, but politely enough, actually, exceedingly politely, if he needs a taxi.

Patting himself down, Scott Venn ignores the question.

Again: "Sir? Can I call you a cab?"

Scott gives in and acknowledges him this time: "Uh, yeah. I mean, no. I'm fine. Hey, I guess I'm early."

"Yes, sir," the kid says, thinking: *Whatever*. He's trying not to look, for a third time, at Scott's pants, the very noticeable white crusty stain that's set down his inseam. The young man tries, as well, not to assume the worst.

But that's hard, isn't it?

In fact, the kid's pretty much positive – justifiably so – that the guy's planning a quick, brisk, open-air wank.

Just look at the way he's touching himself. Here and there and up and down, obsessively.

Like, okay, besides the stain, dude here seems to have his shit together, right? Except for the stain, he's looking pretty fine. Decent, anyway.

But then, how can you miss that stuff, the long white crusty smear running down his leg? And, of course, as well, his face is, just, you know, kind of crazy. Also, there's the fact that this guy's so sketched. You know, like, look: he's just, like, working up and down all over himself. And it's like this: he starts on his own nipples – outside his coat, then inside, then over his shirt. Worse, he keeps going down. Left front pants, right. Left, right, left. Then he's all, like, patting his ass: here and there and then, like, starting the whole damned crazy pattern again and again.

The kid's seen it all before, though. Right here, a couple times. He's only been on the job forever, like, at least three months. So he knows.

And it's not just the bums and guys in raincoats who cruise the white-sand-filled ashtrays looking for tasty half-spent butts. It's all kinds of freaky mothers. Rich ones, even.

Guys who pull a Jag or Lexus or Merc out of the underground lot and roll up slow and idle and wave him over with a fat, flashy-ringed finger. Yeah, businessmen, lawyers, and doctors and stuff. Every one of them in town for some big deal conference. All kinds of guys with dreamy lost eyes, the kind who spy a boy – or is it just him? – and power down their window and point below the wheel: guys with a pudgy white slab of pasty cock flopped out of their fancy Matinique zippers and a hungry wet smile on their puffing lips.

Guys who, cool as anything, grin and whisper: "I'm back at nine. You must be ... bored ... out here all day. Why not come up, 1402, and visit. Oh, and it'll be worth your while."

Yeah, they say it like it was part of your job, then wink and flip on dark Alain Mikli shades and gun the engine before they speed off. So dope, these guys. Yeah, right. The bomb.

And unbelievably rich. Dying to throw away their scratch for just a little taste.

So damned down with it you never have time to say a single word. Nothing. Not even fuck off.

Or even: well, um, you *know.* . . .

Anyway, the kid's learned, naturally enough, not to lead, so to speak, this kind of dance. But that doesn't mean he won't have a little fun with all the freaky-deaky dudes. Sometimes, yeah, when there's no one around, he decides he wants to play, jerk their chain.

Sometimes. Like now.

Hey, he's earned it. Right?

"And, sir, I assume you won't need me to *help* with your ... bag?"

"Hmm?" Scott's still not really paying attention: he's too busy look-ing for something to put into his panicky mouth.

"I was just wondering, sir. Whether you wanted *me* to assist. With your ... bag, sir. You're checking in, perhaps?"

Fine, okay, maybe there's a bit more paranoia influencing him than usual, but Scott feels like boil-boy's words are smug or disgusted, maybe even a bit flirtatious. Chock full of some kind of attitude at any rate. And even though he's still nervously – okay, obsessively – checking his pock-ets, he feels the need to put the pimply little dick in his place: "Look, I got a big meeting up there and I don't fuckin' need–"

"Yes, sir."

Shit, all of a sudden the kid looks, well, just like a kid.

"I'm sorry, sir. I just. . . ."

Hell, he's just a teenaged boy. Working for minimum wage and tourist tips, the little puke's doing a shitty job the way he's been told he better – fawn and ass-kiss. Or else.

"Aw, look, forget about it," Scott says, now once again furiously tug-ging around the inside of his right pants pocket.

The kid raises an eyebrow, begins to smirk: Oh my God, he's not. Is he? Please, God, don't let him pull it out here. It's way too early.

"Christ, where'd I put it? I just got it."

"I'm sure I wouldn't know, sir. But maybe in your briefcase?"

"What? Look, kid, was I talking to you?

"I'm so sorry, sir. I thought you were. And you obviously seem to have misplaced something, uh, important. I just thought...."

Ignoring him, but pissed, Scott says, "I'll be a second here. Just forget about me, okay? Jesus, where's my fucking smokes!"

Trying not to laugh out loud, the kid manages, smiling, "Your brief- case, maybe. Have you checked there?"

"All right kid. Nothing personal, but fuck off. All right? Fuck right off."

Turning on his heel, the teen rolls his eyes and whispers: "Filthy psy- cho asshole." Then, reaching inside his uniform to his own breast pocket, he feels the duct-taped butt of the .32 he planned on giving his little brother at lunch – just to equalize things, to make sure that small indis- cretion with some cocktease girlfriend of the high school's star point guard didn't escalate into a family embarrassment, something his little bro wasn't prepared for.

The kid, this good scout of a brother, purses his lips and thinks, with a hell of a lot more terrifying swagger to his almost seventeen-year-old sense of himself than the physical world acknowledges, and even more menace to the cruel voice he hears inside his head, a voice so unlike the squeaky, geeky one Scott hears: Oh fuck, dudes. You're both so fucking lucky I don't fucking whack you, dudes. Mess with my fucking bro. Mess with me. I'm gonna fuck you up, motherfuckers.

Yes, he's definitely an amused little Quentin Tarantino action figure when he spins to face the dude and whips something out of his pocket, firmly, between his thumb and trigger finger.

"Take this."

Scott jumps, startled. Composing himself he barks: "Look, I thought I told you...."

Realizing what the kid's got in his hand, he speaks more slowly, "Hey, Jesus. What? What're you doing? What's that for?"

"It's for you."

Taking the cigarette and flipping it to his lips, Scott plunges his left hand back into his pocket. He's searching for a light. "Thanks kid. You don't look old enough to smoke. Above and beyond, this. Do they even let you grab a butt out here?"

"Not here, sir. And not until our break."

Beginning the whole where-the-hell-did-I-put-it comedy again, Scott says, "Hey, I'll get you next time. Alright?"

"Sure," the kid says, flicking open, from out of nowhere, a gunmetal

Zippo embossed with a black widow spider. It explodes in a dangerous flash, right in Scott's face. "Sure."

By the time Scott's taken his first deep drag, exhaled and relaxed a touch, the friendly juvenile sociopath's moved twenty feet away. He's ushering up a taxi for a middle-aged couple in white GAP baseball caps, thick, matching lavender and purple Benneton sweaters, and baggy, unzipped, red Roots jackets. A pre-teen blonde girl sulks a couple of feet behind them in baggy cargo jeans and running shoes that look like Apollo mission moonboots. Each of the adults carries a camera, one Sony video, and one Kodak DC240-Zoom digital still. The girl's wearing headphones, and her taupe-painted nails fiddle with a Sony CDman. The tourist's pointing down at a hotel gift map and asking about "the big spaceship-looking place," in a distinctively east-coast accent that Scott's too lazy and skittish to place accurately, while his wife and daughter slide into the back of the cab.

Fading in and out, a shaky receiver, Scott overhears the kid giving the driver clear, specific directions, and telling the tourist, with a snide, snorting laugh, something about not worrying, about not being able to miss it. Then the guy with the video camera and map, still outside of the cab with the kid, is fishing around his pockets for a tip and asking something else, something about tomorrow, his daughter, and a cemetery. He hollers into the back of the cab, asking for the name of the place. Saint something's. The kid says he doesn't know it, asks the driver, who's also unsure.

"If you can wait just one minute, sir, I'll ask Francis. My co-worker. He'll know."

Scott sees the kid wave over another guy in an identical monkey suit. Francis, who looks seventy-five if he's a day, has been watching everything from his post. He winks and grins at Scott as he passes.

"Morning, Captain. Beautiful, eh? Gorgeous day."

"Uh, yeah, morning," Scott says, taking another deep drag and wondering why in the hell everyone's looking at him funny.

And what's up with the Captain shit, buddy?

When he reaches the taxi Francis gets into a slow but animated discussion with the kid, the tourist, and the cabbie. The four of them are trying to figure out exactly which graveyard, there are so many.

Saint Joseph's? Saint Thomas'? Saint Paul's?

Probably Saint Stephen's, Scott thinks, the reception pretty good as he's filling his lungs with more smoke.

From the back of the cab the girl, who's unhooked her headphones, scowls and says: "Rick, let's go. Now!"

"Krystal! Jeesh. Hang on a second. We're talking here."

The woman in the GAP cap joins in, just to put the girl in her place: "Krystal, you calm down. And don't you dare talk to your father like that. Do I make myself clear? Let us figure this out. Got it? Alright?"

Turning her attention to her husband she adds, "Richard, c'mon. Now. We *don't* have all day. And I still want to get to that mall."

The guy in the purple with the Handicam says, "One second, hon, Christ," and then gets into it again with the cabbie and the two hotel employees.

Scott's still riveted as a five-way discussion about the city's major Catholic churches and cemeteries erupts, each and every participant talking at once and at cross purposes. The adults completely ignore the little girl. Posh little Krystal's mouthing a hiss as she replaces her headphones and cranks the volume, thinking: Ricky's not my father, bitch. Just fucking forget about it. Dad gave me the fucking address before I left, you fucking idiots.

It's almost funny, and he feels for the girl, he really does, but inevitably Scott loses interest. There's too much information to process, far too much cross-chatter. Completely tuned out, he goes back to the only thing that can really occupy his attention: Amanda.

Amanda, what's going on?

· · • · ·

Its rage came explosive and clawed and unforgiving, as terrifying and sudden and violent as its malevolence and hate and will would always be. A thick, sulphuric, white hot rage from the bowels of a place that might as well be hell.

Scott Venn sat in the sand, knees up, leaning back with one elbow behind his head supporting his weight. Watching the sky fire-up he polished off the warm backwash of his Grolsch and smoked his second-last stale damp smoke. He was cold, but didn't want his ass to get wet and covered in dewy sand, so he was reclining on his overcoat. The sky, red and pink and orange, and the rhubarb and strawberry jam-covered English muffin of a sun, half a large burning dappled ball hovering over the blue-grey water, was the most beautiful thing he'd ever seen.

How long had he lived there?

And he'd never gone out through his own backyard, crossed the goddamned boardwalk and watched a fucking sunrise?

Jesus.

The worst gull targeted Scott from a quarter of a mile away. Flying east in its fury, following the shoreline, it screamed its foul-mouthed

hatred in teen-slasher-film Dolby THX orchestration: a hunting, predatory, repetition of analog delay. One hundred yards from its target the
worst gull shot up, tacked, circled, and began its descent.

It gauged its approach, eased off the throttle and began to glide. It
descended, current surfing with an aerodynamic grace, down – down to
forty-five feet from 400. Its velocity assessed, confirmed, rechecked, the
bird knew conditions – air temperature, drafts, currents, sheers – were
ideal.

And the gull logged it all, a wicked aviator. Counted it off for poster-
ity, the history of evil.

Distance closing. Ninety yards. Eighty: target engaged. Seventy: system armed. Sixty: abort? Negative. Fifty: target locked. Twenty-five:
clearance? Check. Ten: missile launched.

Bombs away.

Scott didn't hear the gull coming, didn't register its approach anyway,
its stealth, and he certainly didn't notice it tip its wings as it sped by and
climbed and banked back out over the water. In fact, he didn't see the
gull at all.

He felt the explosion, though. The warm blast. From above. All over,
like his head had been blown off.

"Shit!"

Running the fingers of his left hand through his hair, Scott touched it,
thick, oozing slowly down the back of his pinkish ear.

"Shit! Shit! Shit!"

He sprang to his feet, sending more of the gullshit down the arm of
his sportscoat.

"Christ, you little fucking bastard! You fucking shit on me!" he
screamed after the phantom bomber.

And then he looked at the hand he'd automatically shot through his
perfect hair. His manicured nails, and soft, tanned fingers, now micro-
scopically yellowing from his freshly re-engaged and utterly hotwired
habit, were spattered with white goo. The flecks of black in the bird's shit
made his belly lurch. He wanted to retch and scream and kill and cry.

Instead he almost laughed, bared his capped teeth as he sighed, then
coughed.

"Perfect. Great. Venn! Yo, shithead!"

Bending down to wipe his hands in the wet sand, Scott stumbled, still
slightly drunk. His pinky, a fine brush, added tantalizing, perfect highlights to his pant leg on the way down.

Another subtle stroke for Scott never to notice.

He did notice, however, that birdshit-covered hands, plunged into sand, did not emerge miraculously cleansed, purified, shitfree.

No, they were simply glazed: sandy, birdshit-covered hands.

Horrified by the mess of himself, knowing he was covered in excrement, that it was on his face, probably, for godsake, he realized the water was good for something.

Not just a pretty fucking picture anymore.

Alone on a very long stretch of one of the city's most popular beaches, three minutes after sunrise, a man in a rumpled but expensive sportscoat, fine, slightly creased, slacks and expensive, sandy shoes, Scott Venn looked like a lunatic Jesus as he approached the water: hands spread wide, palms up.

. . • . .

Entering his living room a few minutes later, struggling with the screen riding offtrack between two sliding glass doors, Scott's gullshit-smeared leg brushes the huge, monstrous leaf of the insane tropical plant that waits there, outside. It leaves a fine white check mark: a living thing, present and accounted for.

He slides the doors shut behind him one by one, too hard; they rattle from the power in his sweeping dismissal and a tiny, nearly imperceptible crack in the bottom of the inner-most pane grows a new branch. Scott clamps the lock down, just as forcefully. The little bird shakes his downy head.

Jeesh, buddy. What happened to you? You look, well, you look like shit.

Scott tosses his sand-covered overcoat at the couch; a long right arm flops to the floor, its cuff drapes over the still-moist filter of a hastily stubbed Rothman's. He rips off his sportscoat and drops it in a ball at his feet, the old pack that contains his last smoke falls too, and lands squarely over a large dollop of birdshit. He paces then, ranges the length of the living room, telling his worry-beads: I'm fucked. Amanda. I'm going to jail. Margaret fucking Chisholm. This morning. A few hours. I haven't slept. I'm half drunk but not drunk enough and I'm going to go to jail. In a few hours. I'm fucked. Amanda.

He punches on the TV to distract himself. The chipper local morning anchor – pretty and blonde in a lean, angular way, Scott remembers she's also a former jock, a skier or track star or something – is throwing to the chunky morning sports guy. Definitely never an athlete, not a real one. Not looking like that.

"Coming up next: major league scandal."

Not a good omen.

Scott punches off the set before the station's environment dissolves to commercial, picks up another remote and clicks on the stereo. The all-talk sports station is previewing the start of the new hockey season. A sad-sack former GM is running down a list of teams from the Eastern Conference's Northeast Division, talking about Boston's bubble being set to burst.

A hyperactive interjection from the overgrown schoolyard bully who's the station's professional sports freak/circus geek, a prime adult Ritalin candidate if there ever was one, is enough to distract him, make Scott realize he's got to pull himself together. Out of the jumble his best thought is: Coffee.

Pinning down the unopened, foil-sealed, freeze-dried Nabob he's pulled from the fridge's crisper with his right hand, his left shakes uncontrollably as he stabs at the thing with dulled kitchen scissors. Cool, compacted flakes of coffee explode out of the foil in a puff, settling, finally, all over the counter and floor.

"Fuck!"

Giving up on his brightest and best idea, he decides to switch to instant. Scott plugs the kettle into the stove while wiping at the brown-flaked counter with a damp sponge. Nescafé was the smart decision, for someone as unfocussed, absorbed, and ungrounded as Scott. Only problem? The stove – hell, for its age it's in pretty good shape, even if it came with the house, better than the fridge anyway, which smelled like spoiled milk and rotten vegetables no matter what Amanda scrubbed the damned thing with – wasn't quite grounded either.

An arc of electricity bridges across one arm, through Scott's neck, and down the other. It shoots down, too, through his groin and into his legs, his toes. Becoming human jelly, after a night of no sleep, before your first cup of coffee, is also bad. Very, very bad.

Numb all over, picking himself up off the kitchen floor, a few coffee grounds stuck to his ass, Scott doesn't realize, thankfully, that he's lost, literally, another ten seconds of his life.

"Jesus fuckin' Christ!" he says, every molecule in his lips and tongue jiggling.

From the living room the bird calls: You okay in there, buddy?

"Okay, Christ, okay. Okay? Just a cup of coffee. Jesus, all I want's a cup. Just some motherfucking coffee. Alright? Christ." The jolt's got Scott talking to himself again, still ignoring the budgie singing from the other room. He's about to reach down to the dishwasher, to pull out his favourite red mug, when he sees it: there behind glass on the shelf above the sink, beside the birdseed.

"There you are, Red. Coffee?"

He manages the oversized Nescafé's red lid, even digs around successfully with a teaspoon, and pours boiling water without incident. The half-and-half's no problem, and the delicate act of raising a mug to his lips goes exceedingly well.

So why the spit take?

Why's vile coffee spurting all over the counter, the sink, and Scott's Armani tie and Arrow shirt?

The strong, ugly tang of generic, green, bacteria-fighting detergent that bites at his tongue and lips and throat explains everything. His favourite red mug had been handwashed, badly.

"Arghh, fuh-uck," is all he can manage as he smashes the mug, polluted coffee and all, down into its stainless-steel final resting place. More of the taupe liquid splashes back up, of course, making his shirt even worse and causing a nasty little burn on the left arm he raised to shield his face from exploding pottery shards.

"Damn, damn, damn. Shit. Damn!" And then: "Sorry, Red, sorry. Fuck. Sorry. Ha ha. Amanda, use the fucking dishwasher, okay? Christ! At least rinse the fucking dishes for once, okay? Fine!"

He's violently unnoosing his tie with one hand while forcing the buttons of his shirt with another when the bird asks, really concerned now: What's going on?

The budgie knows enough not to expect a reply. But he can't help caring, can he?

Oh my, he adds, watching the popcorn buttons – tiny, wide-eyed, happy faces with painfully shocked, blank expressions – fly off Scott's shirt and bounce into the living room. Sorry, buddy. Hell of a day, huh?

Naked from the waist up now, Scott realizes that his arm's burnt, just above his Swatch. The watch is covered in coffee, too, and the strap bites at his reddening wrist. He pulls it off and lets it fall on the piled shirt and tie at his feet – one bad bounce, off this spongy makeshift trampoline and the thing backflips, crystal first, onto tile.

Exhausted and cold, he still needs a cup of coffee, badly. His mind tells him this, but his pummelled ego, his body even, tries to talk him out of the embarrassment of another attempt.

Listen, juice maybe. How about some juice? There's a couple nice, safe drinking boxes in the fridge. . . .

Shut up! Everybody relax!

I can do this, he thinks.

"I can do this. Just a cup of coffee, right? I can do this."

Scott ignores the bird's *Attaboy!* as he leaves the kitchen and heads upstairs for the bathroom, sipping a damned fine and creamy cup of instant, from a lime-coloured mug he's just named Greener.

· · • · ·

Pissing, his dick in one hand and a cup of coffee in the other, Scott's already dying for another smoke.

Downstairs, the pack's downstairs. I have to go down there again. And I'm gonna need more smokes. And a lighter. I'm gonna need a lighter. I have to clear my fucking head and get to that meeting in one piece. I have to talk to Amanda.

And then, shaking and tucking himself back into his pants, he catches sight of himself in the mirror.

"Oh, shit."

Scott desperately needs a shave, some Visine for sure. His lips are dry and cracked; his gums and teeth, well, they feel disgusting. He probably smells.

And, of course, his hair's gelled with gullshit.

Sighing, he flushes and dutifully lowers the toilet seat that gaped hello when he got there. "Scott, son, you're really not doing too well today, are you?"

The Scott in the mirror shakes his head: No.

Both Scotts raise their left arms and check the matching Swatches that should be there but aren't. In unison they mumble: "Oh yeah. Shower. No, bath. Shave. Dress. Deal with Man. Drive to the hotel. Got no idea. Wonder how much time I have?"

Scott leaves himself in the mirror for a second. Pops into the spare bedroom to look at the digital alarm clock.

His words echo round the tub and tiles: "No, Jesus, no! I'm gonna be late. What fucking next?" Once he's raced back to the bathroom his reflection's shrugging its shoulders, too.

The first thing Scott does is dunk his head under the faucet in the bathroom sink, without really bothering to gauge the water's temperature. It's cold, terribly cold, but while he struggles to adjust the hot tap, his eyes shut firmly to prevent acidic birdshit from washing in, the blast of cold makes him sharper than he's been in hours. Forgetting to get shampoo from the tub forces him to improvise, so he pumps the Ivory handsoap dispenser right onto his scalp. It lathers rather nicely, in fact. Yes, it'll do.

Rubbing his head with a fluffy black towel, checking himself as closely as time allows, he's convinced he's cleaned himself up, that he's presentable. Added bonus: a little Fudge sculpting cream, a tug here and there with a deft, practiced, vain hand, and his hair's responding better than it does with his fancy salon shampoo.

Brushing his teeth, bristling up and down his tongue even, he convinces himself he looks rugged, commanding, in an Alec Baldwin kind of way, with a nine-in-the-morning shadow.

Racing around the bedroom, he rifles bureaus and drawers for a clean shirt. It's dark blue and a little more casual than usual, but it'll make him seem relaxed, carefree, won't it? Next, he grabs another Armani tie, a very pale yellow this time, and another smart sportscoat – blue-black Belgian chocolate. Wondering about his ass, he turns to peer over his shoulder in the bureau mirror. After brushing off a little sand, he figures the pants will do for another day. He gathers his bundle and races back to the bathroom, sniffs at his underarms and crinkles his nose. Frantically, he smears on Body Shop antiperspirant. Finally, he questions the wisdom of going with last night's undergarments.

Take 'em off?

Nah, no time. He takes Greener from the counter and carefully drains the last of his coffee.

Scott's got his shirt on, hanging open at his waist just over his belt, and his coat and tie draped over one arm when he lands downstairs. While he's buttoning and tucking and fidgeting with his tie, he kicks off his mucked-up shoes, not bothering with the laces. After quickly glancing at his sweaty, stinky feet, and shrugging, he begins forcing them into a brand new pair of deck shoes. He's decided against the freshly polished pair of black Oxfords, identical to the one's he'd worn last night. They, too, were still laced tight, the left one was knotted in fact, and he couldn't be bothered.

Yeah, I'm casual today. No problems, no worries. Forget about it: not a work shoe day. He's always ruining the backs of the damned things, Man says, because he never undoes the laces. Looking at himself in the hallway mirror, he almost believes he's pulled it off. I'll make it. Just. And then he remembers.

"Oh shit. Man," he says as he's buttoning up his cuffs. "What the hell am I gonna do about Amanda? She's gotta be at her folks, and the three of them are just ready to fucking crucify me. Shit."

Another thought, finally, worms its way in.

Wait. What if something else's happened? What if she went to the movies like she said? What if she'd come home after to confront him? And then something – something bad – happened. What if she's in a hospital: a horrific accident in a cab or something? What if I'm a heartless idiot who should be calling the fucking morgue? The cops might be driving up here any second. Two uniforms, not coming for me, but a man and a woman with their hats under their arms and grim expressions: Mr. Venn, may we come in? This isn't easy, maybe you should have a seat. Mr. Venn, there's been a tragic—

Nah. No way.

She's waiting to fuck me. Waiting for me to come crawling, whining. Please, darling, I can explain. I'm so sorry. Please, just listen. Don't leave me. . . .

Even if I call, he rationalizes, there's no guarantee she'll talk. She's pissed all right, probably too pissed to say word one. She'll probably wait, make me sweat a day or two. Have me call over and over so her mom or dad can brush me off, those frigid fuckers.

Scott. She does not *wish* to speak with *you*.

Or worse: Scott, you've disappointed us. How could you?

Oh fuck. Amanda. I'm fucked. Chisholm will fuck me in an hour, and then a couple of cops, for real, both cruel, heartless guys this time, will slap on the cuffs and duck my head into the back seat of a cruiser, pushing me a little harder then they have to, and then I'm going to jail and then my wife will fuck me and her family will fuck me and my parents will disown, then fuck me, and Man'll divorce me and. . . .

I'm fucking fucked.

I can't do it. Not now. I can't call her now. No time. It'll take too long.

First fuck first, right? Eh, Margaret? You get your little piece of Scotty first, you chisel-faced bitch. Man, sorry. You're gonna have to wait. For you, darling, it's sloppy fucking seconds.

Resigned to it all now, Scott decides to play what remains of his life as a free man as cool and indifferent as he possibly can. Instead of phoning his wife at his in-laws he decides to put her off, to call the reverse that'll pitch the ball out wide and defer the inevitable. Seeing his briefcase, he unclasps the unlocked gold tabs. Raising its lid, his fingers warm to the beaded leather. He reaches in and pulls out his cellphone, then dials his own number. From the kitchen he hears it ringing. The voicemail kicks in, their voices, saying: It's Scott and Man, leave a message.

And Scott does: "Listen, Man," sigh, "I know you'll pick this up eventually. You're right, we need to talk." Sneeze. "Shit. Sorry. Christ, I'm getting sick now. Sorry. Okay. Listen," another deep breath, another slow exhale, "I know you're at your folks, right? Okay. I'm worried sick. I haven't slept all night. I didn't want to wake anyone there. You're mad. Yeah, I know. But it's early hon. And, um, I wanted to give you space. And, well, I've got a meeting soon. So call me, okay? Call me on the cell, later. And we'll talk. Call me this afternoon. And we'll talk about every-thing then."

Putting on his sportscoat, Scott drops the cell phone back into his briefcase and then snaps the thing shut. He checks his hair again and picks up his briefcase, then he opens the front door with his left hand, automatically turning the knob lock as he steps outside.

Standing on his front porch, Scott Venn experiences a number of rapid-fire revelations.

First, the newspaper hasn't arrived yet. Either the neighbour's stolen it again, or the kid who delivers it is slower than usual. Christ, it always used to arrive by eight. And what, it's gotta be a quarter past nine now, right?

Second, looking at his wrist to check the time, he discovers that he's left his watch inside. To hell with it, probably covered in birdshit anyway.

Third, as he reaches into his pants pocket to fish out his keys to lock the deadbolt, he remembers he's forgot to reset the alarm.

Fourth, as he digs madly through one pocket, and then another, and then checks every pocket on his person, he realizes that he doesn't have his keys at all. What happened last night? Oh shit, the alarm. The last time he remembered seeing them was as they arced out of his hand while he tried to get the alarm. No house keys then.

Fifth, no house keys, no car keys. How the hell was he going to make the meeting now?

And finally: it's cold. He's wearing a light sportscoat. His good over-coat was covered in sand. His other coat was just behind the locked door in front of him. Like his keys. Like the one cigarette he has left – the one that, at this moment, he needs desperately.

Scott actually bangs his forehead against the door, twice, three times, in frustration. His shoulders fall and say it for him: Why me?

Then he's off, remembering something, actually racing around the back of the house, to the sliding doors. When he gets there he can see his cigarette, lying in the open pack on yesterday's sportscoat. The bird. His overcoat draped over the couch. He can see it all because he's left on every light in the place.

Amanda, did you? Please, God, say she did.

Out of breath, Scott moves the big, heavy tropical plant in the huge clay pot, its leaves inching as he shifts it, following the slow path of the sun. It's the first attention he's paid to the thing since he'd moved it out there in the spring.

The bird was watching him, hopeful: Yes. Finally. That's it, buddy.

But Scott isn't really interested in the plant. Instead, he's looking for the spare keys Amanda had hidden there for just such an emergency.

The bird realizes what's happened before Scott can even begin to wonder, and tries to tell him: Forget it, buddy. She gave 'em to the other guy.

Like the little match girl, Scott places both hands on the glass doors he'd furiously locked such a very short while ago. Seeing his smokes, the mess he's made of the place and his life, something low, almost a groan, escapes his throat. It's suspended for a second when he notices the clock on the VCR.

8:05. Not the right time, really, but close.

Oh yeah. Ha. Shit. The clock radio in the spare bedroom was an hour off. He wasn't late at all. In fact, he was terribly, stupidly, early. And terribly, stupidly chilly. Underdressed.

He bangs his head against glass this time. Once, for good measure. The small crack shoots out yet another branch, just as his throat releases the whine.

"Amanda."

Slumping on the patio stones beside the plant, already in the throes of nicotine withdrawal, and almost, clearly, losing his mind, Scott opens his briefcase and does the only thing he can do. He flips open his cell phone and calls a cab.

In ten minutes the ugly square face of Goran Vlastic, at the very end of a long, angry shift, will pull up in front of the Venn house. Again. In a different light, in any light, after miles of automatic passage and revenant danger, this place looks unfamiliar. The beautiful morning sun will tickle Goran's red and swollen-rimmed, bloodshot grey eyes while he waits for his fare and rides his horn. His compact with Scott was broken hours ago, forgotten.

For each and every second of those ten minutes a tiny bird, inside a well-lit living room, will sing an emotional aria, one that scales everything from disgust to pure pity. Anger and empathy. Its song begins like this: Hey dufus, the lights. You've left on every light in the place. The stereo, too. You never hear of conservation, buddy? And for godsake, remember to do something about the plant. Look at it, please, ya putz, it's cold. Too cold. . . .

The end is softer somehow: Hey buddy, it'll be okay. Pull yourself together. Tough day. It could happen to anybody. And, before you go – I can hear your ride pulling up now – look. Look at your pants for godsake. I hate to be the one to tell you this, but you've still got birdshit all over you. Hey buddy, I'm sorry, don't shoot the messenger. But I should know, right? Am I right? Huh, buddy? Buddy?

For ten minutes Scott Venn withdraws, shivering, sitting on patio stones, his back to the glass door, trying not to think about the cigarette trapped inside. He ignores the plant beside him, doesn't see a large check-marked leaf reaching to absolve him, to touch his sad face, as the sunlight crosses and caresses his slightly warming cheek.

Picking himself up, swinging his briefcase so it bounces off his sore knee to remind him, again, of the travesty of a man he's become, he hears a hateful, mocking screech carried on the gentle breeze that comes from the west. Scott's let a bird in, finally. The wrong one.

The worst gull, still bellowing its ritual morning warcry, strafes the boardwalk with compact cruise missiles as it follows the wooden wends and doglegs of the shoreline. The heart of the city approaching, it breaks from its flight path and arcs up, higher and higher, out over the water. Its mean black eye scans the beach as it gives way to concrete and then it recognizes the abandoned and converted warehouses by the harbour. It recognizes carrion and suffering and disease and death and it celebrates each of them with a clarion call: This I do for me, it says, for this glorious morning's fiends. I acknowledge the world that made me and give thanks and pray.

And, hearing it all with terrifying clarity, so does Scott: I'm fucked. Margaret. Man. Man oh man, am I fucked, or what?

· · • · ·

Naked and salty and sticky, Amanda Venn is curled, almost fetal, her heavily lidded, mascara-stuck eyes speedy with dreams, on a strange futon in a cheap, low-slung, wooden frame. The weight of her upper body, her shoulder and back, pin the right arm of her younger lover. One of her arms rests on his flat, hard, naked stomach. The cauled head of a big sleepy uncircumcised penis pokes out from the thin black cotton sheet that's risen and fallen and bucked and shifted many times during the course of an improbable night. Bundled like that, the intrepid member is safe from the sunbeam that tries to tickle it plump and awake. Amanda's other arm raises her own small, firm breasts across her body, and the sunbeam sports there, too.

Her new guy's eyes spring to life, comically, big and wide and rudely awakened. Probably the unholy racket of the gulls outside the old warehouse window cracked open with a crushed beer can; that, or, the heavy rapping at the wide, pulley operated door of his loft.

He looks frantically to the alarm clock he'd forgot to set.

9:14 AM. Really.

"Ohmigaw," he mumbles, his mouth cottony. "Amanda. Get up. We fell asleep. Christ, get up."

As he pulls himself up from under her, his right arm a dead, useless thing, Amanda moans, rolls over toward the window, trying to hang on to a dream, still mostly asleep. He's almost panicky, and definitely knows that everything's gone wrong. He has to get the car again. Work four hours. Go to class for three more. Work for five more. Maybe dinner then, maybe get laid. All of this was supposed to begin fourteen minutes ago.

The young man's muscular back glistens, sheened with nightsweat and sex. He finds his full voice as he's walking to a hook on the wall, grabbing a robe. "One second. Just a goddamned second!"

Amanda starts: "What. . . ."

Hauling the door by the heavy linked chain that always feels oily, the new man in Amanda Venn's life stares into the face of his older brother. His only living relative.

"I'm late with work. There. I brought the coffee we share," the greying guy says, holding a cardboard tray and two plastic-lidded cups of the finest donut store blend. The red and white and yellow bag in his other hand means chocolate chip muffins that taste like cake. "Christ," he says, "what has happened in your home? My brother, this is not fucking good, no. Not good. And you. Look at you. You are not ready?"

"Look," Amanda's guy says, rubbing his eyes, "the alarm didn't go off. Alright?"

"Shit. This is no excuse. No. This is not a reason. I have told you. But do you listen to your brother? No. Not you. You think only of yourself, and this, this is not good. You can't do this with your life. This is too much."

"I'm sorry."

"Do not be sorry with me. I want no apology. Not from you, not from my brother. Let me in. We have coffee now. The car is outside. Then you will go. Put clothes on and go."

"I can't let you in."

"What does this mean?"

"Uh. . . ."

"Ah, I see. The girl. You have the girl. Well. You are a fucking idiot. Yes. Yes you are. You are my brother, but you are a fucking idiot. This woman is here? In your home? How can you do this? This is not good; no, not right."

"I know."

"You say this. You say this, but do you? Do you know?"

"Listen, fuck, I said I know," the younger brother says, his temper gone in a familiar, familial, irrational flash. Even with all the years that separate them, they are identically, dangerously, twinned.

"No fuck. You don't fuck me! Do not make that mistake, my brother. Not with me. Don't start this foolish thing with me. Something you will not, never, ever, my brother, be able to finish."

The younger man glares. From inside his cavernous loft, Amanda's voice, awake finally, breaks things up.

"Oh my God! Oh Christ! Oh Jesus! How? It's almost nine fucking thirty! Oh Christ! Hey lover, where are you? What's going on?"

In the doorway, the older of the two brothers sets his hard jaw. With unblinking grey eyes he says: "Get the bitch out of here. Send her back. Now. You get to work."

And then he turns to leave.

Before the square, greying man is more than ten feet away he pivots and shakes his disapproving head. The younger man stands, still, in the wide open door, a greasy, blackened metal chain balled up in his fist. When a ring with two keys to a beat up '93 Plymouth Colt is tossed at him, he makes no move to catch it. It bounces off his broad chest and falls to the concrete, an enraged metallic snap, dead at his feet.

9:29 AM

COFFEE TIME.

Okay, anytime's coffee time here. It's always open: twenty hours a day, seven days a week, 365 days a year. There's muffins and an array of pastries and soups and sandwiches, a rainbow of slick, bland pasta salads even – the commercials for the chain always make a big deal about these things – but mostly it's about donuts and coffee. Especially the coffee. That's why the place exists, the exact same brew of the exact same brand of coffee, day or night, in every location. Of course, you can get juices and pops and a couple different kinds of pure spring water in ribbed or collapsible plastic bottles – but no one ever does. Do they? And there's always the same two girls, women, working behind the counter. Polyester visor cap, hair pulled back into a tight ponytail, no makeup. They're seventeen or sixty-three but it doesn't make a difference. Right now, in more than 1,000 different locations, more than twenty-two hundred female employees are wearing and doing the same thing. Pouring cups of coffee, pressing the automatic creamer button, occasionally bagging or boxing some donuts or a cake-like muffin, wiping counters, making change. Every twenty minutes, guaranteed, they're getting a fresh batch brewing. Just exchange the pot, scoop out the old filter pack, insert the new one, pour in the precise amount of

water, and press the button. No cappuccinos, frappuccinos, or mochac-
cinos – just pure, unadulterated, Grade A American standard blend.

Yeah, this is Coffee Time. And everything here is always slightly off in
the same, reassuring way. The clock's fast, the service slow. Sometimes,
well, sometimes, hey, the opposite's true. Even the lights are mischievous,
wicked hallucinogens, pinkish neons, and occasionally, a little smoke-fil-
tered sunlight – predatory emanations, beams, and rays. Mostly, though,
it's the colours that get you. Every possible combination of red and yellow and cream.

Coffee Time's the mental health hypochondriac's worst nightmare; a
micropsychotic trigger for everyone from the full-blown psychopath to
the slightly, giddily neurotic. It has something to do with the subtle
machinations of all corporate takeovers, the wary residue of unfriendly
mergers: same paint by numbers outlines, different paints. In Coffee
Time nothing really matches, nothing quite works. Damn it all, though,
it's very close, isn't it? And you can't get much simpler than three different colours, right? But nobody ever figures on all the possible permuta-
tions, all the things that can go so gleefully wrong. Like, what are the
odds that both the design staff's chief decorator and its head of purchasing could be colour blind – in radically different ways?

Well, that's Coffee Time.

Actually, it really is coffee time for Peter James. Or, if things had
worked out differently, it would have been. Close enough, at any rate.

It would be time, right now, for Peter's first break. And that would
mean a run for a fresh cup of coffee. His second large take-out of an
eight-to-four work day. Yes, now would be Peter's very own coffee time
– if he still had his job. Or even the one before that. He'd be at the counter picking up his large paintbox red and primrose and hoary cup, then
he'd hurry outside for a quick smoke before heading back to the grind.

Instead, he's been sitting at the banana and cherry and high-glossed
creamed-coffee-coloured wood table in a canary yellow and cardinal and
buff and taupe plastic and cloth chair for an hour and a half. It's the same
seat he's sat in, his leathers beneath his ass, back to the window, in the
far corner of the place, every weekday morning for about a month. He's
already rolled up the white rim of three large fucking red and yellow and
white paper cups today and won sweet bugger all. No surprise.

In all this time he's cashed in on exactly one large coffee. Oh, there's
bigger prizes promised, a low five-figure cheque, eight all-expenses-paid
vacations, four cars, even a yacht. The contest rules, etched in the tiniest
black print down a long strip above the cup's seam, claim that one in
every twelve cups wins.

Do the math: say you average five cups a day, five days a week, for four weeks. That's one in a hundred, give or take.

Surprised? Thing's rigged, huh, Peter?

Nope.

One of the many things Peter James does not realize today, what he cannot know, his head still heavy, cloudy, thick with last night's storm front, is that the laws of probability are religiously and cruelly fair. Like any game of chance – Black Jack, Roulette, the roll of a die, the flip of a coin, like beauty and light and fate – a Coffee Time promotion is only ever fixed against the gullible, blind, and self-absorbed. One in every twelve cups does win. Really.

Remember, just because a coin comes up tails a hundred and one times in a row, there's no reason to believe it doesn't have a thoughtful head.

It's just that Peter's never, well, rarely, one of the lucky twelve. Lately, it seems, he's not wanted at that particular supper.

For a month, on these hundred different occasions, give or take, the person who either preceded or followed Peter James to this particular Coffee Time counter received a cup with a rim that gently folded over the words: "Congratulations, you've just won. . . ."

Ninety-nine of these cups, containing an identical fifteen fluid ounces of one-to-nineteen-minute-old coffee – sometimes with a little sugar or Sweet'N'Low or cream or milk thrown into the mix because the world is filled with unique, beautiful individuals – offered the bearer of the product a free cup on the occasion of their next visit. Ninety-seven of them found their way into garbage cans, drained to the dregs, within a four square mile radius of the establishment in which Peter now sits. Yellow and red and cloudy and coffee stained and slowly decaying in various dumpster and landfill sites, their rims unrolled.

That's a hell of a lot of free coffee just, well, going down the drain. Isn't it?

Damn.

Two lucky stiffs, an elderly woman with a pair of monstrously fat cats and an improbable nine-year-old budgie named Buddy, and a thirty-three-year-old schizophrenic homeless guy who hadn't bathed in at least ninety days, did, in fact, roll up and win.

More odds, more probabilities: only about two percent of the folks out there bother with the stupid contest. Coffee Time, Peter, banks on this the way Colombian drug lords bank on the voraciously deviated septums of Miami and New York and L.A.

Both winners, of course, saved their lucky cup. And each fully intended to take Coffee Time up on their kind offer. In the case of the widowed grandmother of three, the cup found its way to the top of the refrigerator, where she wouldn't miss it the next time she left the upscale retirement condo for a coffee and a bagel with her friend Maureen. Well, Maureen had the stroke three days later, so that put things off. And then, the next day, exactly one week ago, one of those darned cats – the black one, a four-year-old mischievous fellow named Timothy – climbed up on top of the fridge to get a better view of his little buddy, Buddy. Excited, his tail fidgeting back and forth, he knocked the cup down into a warren of happy little dust bunnies hiding behind the major appliance.

Buddy noticed, of course, and tried to tell Muriel. And so did Denny, the older, gargantuan tabby. He, in fact, mewed and rubbed his Buddha belly about it for three quarters of an hour.

But Muriel didn't quite get it. And, annoyed as she'd ever get at something she loved so much, she simply fed her big fat baby again, adding just a little more to love to his twenty-seven pound frame.

Details regarding the whereabouts of the other cup are necessarily a little more sketchy. The guy is, after all, homeless. And paranoid. And schizophrenic. Hell, some folks – most, in fact – call him nuts. Many simply say he's a crazy motherfucker. Anyway, the mendicant left with his coffee, and, as always, returned to his spot in the fire-exit doorway next to a heating exhaust vent by one of the big office towers just around the corner. Drinking his damned fine cup of joe and winning big, he was, naturally, sitting on his ratty, stained sleeping bag, happy as a pig in shit. Oh, and he had every intention of returning later that day for his freebie. A big splurge. But, as luck would have it, a conscientious citizen, who'd taken it upon himself to deem this guy a human fire hazard, managed to convince the good folks down at the psychiatric hospital to send the kind of ambulance that carts you away whether you like it or not. This was twenty-three days ago, and since that time the homeless bum has been reunited with an old friend: a regular dose of his prescribed anti-psychotic medication. His condition, his psychic disposition at least, improved dramatically: he no longer barked at people, "Give me a quarter you goddamned masturbatin' sonsabitches." No, now he says, "Hello, sir." And, "How are you?" Sometimes he'll go: "Nice day, huh?" And he does it on his own, meekly and politely, without even being prompted.

"A complete recovery," the fresh-faced resident marvelled. So complete, so utterly miraculous, that at this very minute the undertrained, overpaid young pill-pusher's clicking the top of his pen to sign the man's release form. In less than an hour, the rehabilitated and heavily medicated paranoid schizophrenic will be a full-fledged citizen, set free, once again, into the streets of the fair, good city, the whole city, he calls home. Of course, technically, he's still homeless. And friendless. Even blessedly family-less – because, jeez, if you only knew, Peter, if you only knew. Even without the benefit of a year or two of psychiatric training, yeah, even you'd say he's better off without *those* particular goddamned masturbatin' sonsabitches.

And oh, one more thing, he's still without any possible means of paying for the medication he needs to maintain.

Oops.

The rehabilitated winner'll get a new second-hand set of clothes and some shoes though, a gift from the Salvation Army, and he'll cut a fine figure as he wanders, shaved and shorn of a snot-smeared beard and madcap dreads, sane and happy and aimless for the rest of the day. He might be homeless and penniless, but he's got his health now. And that's all that matters, right? Besides, sitting on the edge of his narrow psych-ward bed, he has that free cup of coffee to look forward to, doesn't he?

Well, er, no. Not exactly.

"Of course," he's told as he's discharged, "we've had to incinerate your old clothes. And, ha ha, gee, I'm very, uh, sorry, but it seems we've misplaced the shopping cart with the rest of your belongings."

So, there's another fifteen ounces – and about thirty-five pounds of worldly possessions – you'll never see again.

There has been one other winner, just ahead of Peter in the Coffee Time prize cavalcade. It happened earlier this morning, in fact. A jumpy, vaguely familiar, sporty dude with money – the kind of money that wears you. A little older, good jacket, short, darkish spiky hair, flashy blue shirt, nice yellow tie, the guy with a briefcase bought his large coffee the same way Peter takes it, two creams no sugar, to go, looking something like Early Grayce in *Kalifornia* and that bald-headed dude, whatshisname, in *The Phantom*. Peter waited, a bit impatiently, for his second cup as the dude lingered at the counter, fumbling through the mechanics of picking out and purchasing a green Bic lighter and pack of Winstons, no, Dunhills, no, Camels, no, Dunhills. Thrown off his game, Peter momentarily considered speaking, wondered whether or not to ridicule the guy's bumbling with the tough-looking, bored, gum-cracking teen with olive skin behind the counter. But then he lost himself again in the crude ballpoint diamond tattoed just above her watch, and decided against it. Nothing much to say. Right? He mumbled, "Another," or something, and watched the guy shuffle off while he waited. Instead of leaving, the guy sat down, close to the front door, and sipped tentatively at his piping hot beverage through the convenient plastic splash-proof tab you fold back and latch onto the lid. After struggling with and biting at and finally removing the cellophane that locked all the fresh tobacco goodness inside his deck, the man cracked it open, heated and removed the backing from the tinfoil, balled it up, put it into his pants pocket, then proceeded to chainsmoke and theatrically nurse his coffee. Two or three times he removed a cellphone from his briefcase and punched in a few numbers. He never pressed send, though, never made the call. Instead he just put the thing back in the case, snapped the snaps, smoked some more, sipped loudly, and mumbled to himself.

After a while, Peter got bored with trying to figure out how he knew the guy. He looked like someone he'd seen in the Coffee Time before, a few times, but that guy didn't smoke. Maybe somewhere else? The Rail?

Fuck it.

Anyway, Sporty nursed his coffee until Peter had gone for his third and sat down to unroll. Dude caught his attention just before the moment of truth, delaying Peter's favourite game for a second. He watched as the guy put his smokes and lighter into the briefcase, snapped the thing shut again, then got up to leave, saying "Man, oh Man, oh Man."

Jesus. Freako.

And then Peter went back to his rim, played himself a little mental drumroll and, ta-da: Sorry. Please Try Again.

Sitting there, one for a hundred and one, one step closer in his futile assault on absolute zero, Peter smoked his smoke, flicked his ashes into the tiny, dry aluminum ashtray, and turned up the volume on his walkman. Judas Priest and Rob Halford's operatic Harley of a voice, "The Ripper" from *Unleashed in the East*, the first live album, made his head bob as the ponytailed girl in her crimson and lemon apron and the saffron and candy apple visor picked up the half-full cup the guy had left behind and dumped his ashtray into a large old tomato juice container. He watched and mouthed: "Oh hear my warning, never turn your back. . . ." She wiped the dude's vacated tabletop with a blue J-Cloth and then walked back behind her counter, pitching the now half-empty cup into a large green Glad-bag-lined garbage can.

The girl, thoroughly dark-haired and eighteen with a small, sharp, perfect nose, a clear, olive complexion, and a crude blue-green tattoo – a whole world outside Coffee Time ahead of her – never even considered the guy's rim. And why should she? An employee of the company, she's not eligible to claim a prize, so no biggie. It's all just garbage to her, a stupid annoying promotion. Besides, why the fuck does somebody order coffee to go when they've got no intention of leaving, or even playing, huh? Think of the fucking environment. And oh yeah, buddy, there's trash cans all over the place. Ain't nobody ever taught you manners? Pick up after yourself. Or are you too fucking good to toss your own shit? No, she doesn't give a rat's ass about some guy who looks like a stand-in for someone in *Thelma & Louise* or a bit player in *Tombstone*. Not about him or his goddamned unrolled rim.

But Peter? Or the dude himself?

Well, they'll never know, will they? So why bother ruining their day by telling them what they've missed out on? This ain't *Wheel of Fortune*. Right, buddy?

Not quite.

It's better that they never think about the yacht one of them could have had, sinking deeper and deeper into the flotsam of Coffee Time's sunbeam-dappled somekind of red and somekind of yellow and somekind of tawny refuse.

· · • · ·

Despite all the tricks of light and colour preying on him, feeding off him, and despite the almost perfect string of random Coffee Time misfortune that's playing him for all the dupe he can be, Peter's as amused by all the rims in his past, present, and future, as he is by the tabloid sports section he's thumbed through since he planted his ass in his red and yellow and cream-coloured chair.

The appropriated paper, the contest, the coffee, his smokes, and the homemade hardcore and metal ninety-minute mix in his Aiwa all serve the same purpose: they get Peter through the worst part of the day, every Monday through Friday, from the moment he wakes until 10:45.

Peter orders his coffees to go and plays into Coffee Time's little game, even though he'd actually prefer to be drinking out of a cheap crimson and orange-embossed china mug, simply to keep his mind off, well, thinking. Everything he does before a quarter to eleven on a weekday morning is about secrets and fears and passing the time.

Coffee Time gets Peter James to drinking time. To Bud and Jack Daniels and tits and ass time. Coffee Time gets Peter to The Rail.

The Rail, of course, takes Peter away, far away, from all the other Peters of this Peter's day. That's why he keeps going back for its bad medicine: a familiar face, oblivion time, a different kind of pain. The Rail hides, comforts, and protects him – from versions of himself. From the guy who's mocked by billboards inscribed with the names of the young men who, depending on his mood, either fucked him over or succeeded despite him. From the fuck-up who can't hold a job. From the man who barely avoided killing a young Black paperboy in a Bulls cap, while driving lost and aimlessly and laughing and drunk, early, very, very early one morning, by swerving into a light pole. From the Peter who sat through his first and only AA meeting, oblivious, pissed out of his tree. From the Peter James who hurt the only women he ever cared about because . . . because he believed, briefly, occasionally, and however misguidedly, that the pain of others might make him hurt less.

And from the dead father he can't, won't, face – because the face is so goddamned familiar.

The minutes between 10:45 and 11:15? They pass themselves. Easy minutes, they fly by with a little soothing magic and deep breathing – a little help from an equalizing friend.

Now, contemplating spending his fourth dollar on his fourth large coffee and another chance to roll up and win, believing that he's pretty much broken the hump of his down time, that his getting up and shuffling out and walking up the street time nears, Peter's fishing in his front left pocket for his scratched, waterproof blue and silver plastic Quemex while reading about Boston's questionable goaltending.

Byron Dafoe?

Like, whatever. I'm a questionable fucking goalie, too.

The well-stretched and fading black denim in this clean, Tide and Downy-smelling pair of pants has receded a bit because Maria's just washed them.

And ironed them, too. Jesus.

It pisses him off, of course, but he's undeterred: when it comes to drinking time, the last vestige of something ruthless and sober in Peter knows enough not to trust the Coffee Time clock. He feels his pager there, totemic, and his keys, the two-inch plastic square framing Greg Ginn and whatsisname, the guy before Henry Rollins, Dez something, exploding on stage, performing *TV Party*. He leans and twists awkwardly to fish his whole hand into his pants until his wrist pops through the tight denim and the mouth snaps shut. Blunt, dyslexic fingers nub at the stuff, explore dumbly. Tight confines, only so many possible hiding places, no holes.

No watch.

Wait a minute. Now, that ain't right. Is it?

A creature of many habits and compulsions, Peter's mostly undeterred. Discrepancies are rarely apparent, for this man, because they're generally irrelevant. Still straining and fishing, however, something in his neck pops – brings another brief moment of wide-eyed clarity to Peter before, post-pop, the chain-saw rip cord inside him gets pulled by something vindictive in his central nervous system; it snakes through his spine and snaps and whips around his neck and his head's cleaved and pulped. Evidently, even after his paper and games and three cups of fine Coffee Time coffee, Peter James finds he can, once again, feel worse.

Much worse.

His thoughts belch, convulse – a plump sponge, they soak up a broken manful of bile.

Ughh. Where's my fucking watch?

Trying to remove his hand from his tight pocket while righting himself on his chair sends his stomach lurching. His relatively clear blue eyes go milky, even more grey, shot through with crimson and something almost jaundiced.

Coffee Time, for Peter, has gone very bad.

It happens. When you don't want to give in and just be a hopeless drunk – when you want to be a perpetual, functioning drunk so bad you take every precaution against killing yourself with the alcohol that's keeping you alive – you regiment your life and starve your body and play little games with it. You almost take care of yourself, keep relatively clean and lie consistently, evenly, to keep yourself in the game, to maintain. And it's a precarious balance, one that's always shifting, measured in microscopic increments, precise calculations and adjustments. An act of ferocious will and constant compensation that, sometimes, gets away from you.

It happens, though; sometimes you lose control.

Peter believes that he *cannot* drink before 11:15 – even though he understands he *must* be drinking by 11:15, and no later. He believes this because if he didn't he would be drinking from the moment he woke to the moment he passed out. And that would be bad. He turns twenty-five tomorrow and as his many, maturing, operating systems know – even if he won't, or can't, articulate it – that if Peter gives in, completely, to his most demanding and reckless passion, two things will happen. First, he will become a hopeless alcoholic – the terrible, pitiful kind, one who does not maintain. And then?

Well, then Peter will die.

So, working together for once on this – his body's capacity to keep going, to continue drinking is their favourite plaything, their primary concern – his mind and his addiction have come together to make these kinds of decisions for Peter. He might be pitiful, almost hopeless, but he's all they've got. And neither is willing to let Peter get away from them. At least, not yet.

No, a death in this family would be very bad for business.

Still, it does happen. Sometimes – despite all the best efforts of your unconscious and your addiction, despite all their cunning and miraculous, selfless teamwork – you really do lose control. Badly.

Between the pain in his head and stomach and Coffee Time-coloured eyes and his wobbly body and distractingly free but timeless hands, an unprecedented and horrible confluence occurs. These things, real and physical, wrest control from Peter's mind and addiction: they take over and toss Peter, spinning him high in the air and out of sorts, like college football players tossing a freshman cheerleader on a taut beach blanket after a particularly gruelling and debauched kegger.

Now there's a whole lotta lurching and rocking and jerking and rolling going on.

So, Peter farts: a loud, slow, wet emission. Simultaneously, acid rockets from the bottom of his guts to tickle his tonsils; many different muscle groups spasm, all kinds of sphincters, all over his body, go haywire. Approving of the melee, the room spins for him in counterpoint: a red and yellow and creamy kaleidoscope. Atavistic impulses and fears take over, put all kinds of terrors into his head.

Oh no. No, I couldn't. No way. Could I? Please tell me I didn't shit myself.

And, wait. Wait for it: OhmygodImgonna....

With quicker reflexes than he's ever demonstrated at a high-paying assembly line job interview or as one of Rent-a-Goalie's numerous thickly padded employees, Peter bolts from his chair to the Coffee Time can.

He hurls open palms at the door marked with a little man, but they spring back stung, repelled.

No, Jesus, no. Locked. Occupied.

No time to be choosy, he takes a step to the left and punches the little woman. She gives, throws herself open to him.

Peter doesn't hear the second Coffee Time employee, the older woman, forty-five, maybe fifty-five, in an identical visor and apron, who's dropping a chocolate chip muffin into a blood red and ochre paper bag when she turns her head, startled by his flight, yell after him.

"Hey, you can't go in there! That's the ladies!"

What he does hear, instead, is the amplified echo of the taupe and greenish contents of his stomach, hurled with incredible, automatic force from his belly through his throat and tinkled off his teeth, splashed against piss-coloured water and cold porcelain. Peter's fallen to his knees in one of two filthy stalls, his long black hair almost caressing the rising offal in the bowl. There was no time to raise the seat or flush, so his hands, firmly gripping the plastic there, reverential, are stung by the backsplash. Worse, his palms are wet, and it's not from puke seeping through his grip.

102

No, somebody's pissed on this particular taupe Coffee Time seat. A crispy sliver of bacon winks up at him – yup, that's right, Petey, that's piss – from the toilet paper lifeboat it's found itself captaining.

He heaves again, partly because he's still a bit sick, and partly because a reeking toilet and piss-covered seat demand nothing less.

His tongue dances around his mouth, trying to wriggle free of the wretched sweater it's been forced to wear. It's either jigging an unrealized laugh or ululating a silent scream, but whatever it's doing it's flopping all over the place as his lips try not to touch the words, "Arghh! How does a chick piss all over a fucking toilet seat? Jesus. I mean, Jesus, right?"

Yeah, so, it happens. And then it's over. So what?

Peter recoils at the stench of his vomit mixed with bleach-smelling piss; the dampness of his palms only makes things worse. He can't turn his head to get away – there's no away to get to in this cubicle – so he does the only thing he can do: rear straight up and back.

This movement, of course, for a man in Peter's condition, is far too complex. His mind and his addiction have regained the upper hand, but they still don't have that kind of control. Besides, what do they care if he's embarrassed? That simply doesn't concern them. So, instead of getting up and backing away from the mess he's made, Peter flops, shaking like jelly, down on his ass. The heels of his hands, at least, help break his fall.

The Coffee Time woman's not angry any more. Alert to the many sounds of gastric trauma, well-versed in the pathology of morning sickness and food poisoning, she's knocking politely on the door, concerned: "Hey, you okay, son? Everything alright in there?"

Mortified, his bruised ass standing in for the omnipresent pain in his head for a moment, Peter mumbles, "Sorry, flu. Couldn't wait. For men's. Locked. So sorry."

"It's going around, darlin', that's fine. Take care of yourself. But try to hurry up, if you can. Okay?"

"Uh huh."

"Poor dear," she mock whispers, actually quite loudly, to her younger co-worker, shaking her head as she walks back behind the counter to empty the remains of another nineteen-and-a-half-minute old batch into the stainless steel sink. "The flu. Same one I had probably."

The other girl scrunches up her nose. "Yeah, maybe. But, damn, Vera, I'm not cleaning it up."

Everybody else in the place buries their disgusted heads in their papers, or they stare dumbly at the coffee cups in their hands, oblivious to their own uncertain stomachs and the fickle temperament of grace.

Right, Vera, they're all thinking. Don't be so naïve. Listen to your partner, she knows the score: the kid's obviously terribly fucked up. Jesus.

Peter is laughing now, very, very quietly, stretched out awkwardly on his ass and hands, laid out on the filthy fire engine red and amber Coffee Time bathroom floor tile like he's reclining at the beach.

I am *so* fucked up. Jesus.

Funny though, his handlers, the addiction, and the automatic unconscious functions of a mind that act as guardian angels in this case, are beginning to convince him he's lived through the roughest patch, that things from here will get better.

Hey, his monstrous desire for another drink reminds him, they couldn't be much worse. Right? Pull yourself up, son, we've got the whole beautiful day to look forward to yet. God's bounty.

Obedient, Peter staggers to his feet and makes for the sink. He's fine until he notices the yellow and brown-stained square of toilet paper stuck to his palm.

Oh Jesus, that's sick. Fuck. Ohmyfuckinggod. Flush would you, huh? Jesus. Fucking disgusting pigs. Christ.

He pulls the sticky square from his piss-soaked and possibly shit-smeared hand and, standing between the cubicle and sink, burps up bile. His throat squawks out a cack and his stomach lunges and jerks around a dry heave. Acid's burning at his sinuses, his legs are weak, and he's still unfocussed. Peter's almost afraid to move, afraid of the strange girlpiss or worse on his hands finding its way to other parts of his body. He can't remember something important: did I wipe my lips after I puked?

That's the natural thing, right? You run your hand across your face. Through your hair even. Jesus.

Which hand? Let's see: I'm right-handed so. . . .

No, I couldn't have. Could I?

Shuddering, his left hand balls the toilet paper into its fist: automatically, he pitches the brownish bauble at the tiled wall inside the cubicle. It sticks to a burgundy square, begins its slow descent down to the pumpkin tile below. It'll be hours before it reaches the creamy one below that.

Mad, confused, disgusted, but also recovering, Peter punches up the lever for the tap with a contaminated palm. The water's lukewarm but the pressure's good and he dangles his piss and shit-covered hand under its stream, still horrified, visions of an army of grinning bacteria, Green Berets, marshalled and advancing up his arm, preparing to assault his lips and nose and hair and eyes.

If they haven't already.

Like a TV surgeon, in the manner of Noah Wyle or Ed Begley Jr. or Mike Farrell, Peter scrubs; he's covered himself, both hands and forearms, in the pink industrial soap he's maniacally pumped from the plastic bubble dispenser to his right. It's an obsessive-compulsive pattern, hands wringing, rubbing, scrubbing up to the elbows and back down. Between each finger, pushing circles into his palms and rubbing the scales off his knuckles. Foamy suds are everywhere. Lather, rinse, repeat.

The action's calming, his senses are returning, and he figures he's got this nasty bit of biological warfare almost beat. He's about to move on to his face when the Peter in the mirror looks the one frantically washing his hands in the eye.

You're disgusting, soldier.

Peter sees the vomit swinging from a free chunk of his blue-black bangs, painting his cheek in delicate wisps of greenish brown. He freaks.

Great gobs of pink goo are pumped into his right palm, mashed into his left, and swirled around his face. His eyes are stung shut and the detergent breaches his lips. Peter's tongue, inevitably, washes his own mouth out with soap. He's blind and gagging and still reaching and pushing more pink stuff into his palms: he rubs his pockmarked cheeks raw — rawer. Water now, cupped in his soapy hands, lots of it. He drenches himself with it, and his black t-shirt becomes a makeshift splatter sheet, rose scented.

The process doesn't end until Peter's got his whole head under the faucet, wringing more soap through his locks, washing that vomit right out of Miss Clairol's hair. When he feels done, clean, safe, Peter manages to open his eyes.

Okay. They don't sting.

That's a start, right? Better?

Yeah, better. Couldn't get much worse.

Wrong, actually. They do sting. Badly.

What the blinking Peter in the mirror sees strobing now is a quiet battlefield, rivers of soapy remains. Water, water everywhere. And, a drenched Peter: shirt soaked, pants stained from the waist to the crotch so he looks like he's pissed himself.

Fuck. But at least there's no pissy, shitty creepy-crawlies all over me, right?

Who's kidding who? What makes you think, aquaboy, that Coffee Time would spring for anti-bacterial soap? Besides, there's nothing in nobody's piss or shit that's gonna harm you, you drenched little maggot. Christ, you got eyes, look at yourself and think about it.

Try. Consider what you do, touch, eat, drink – on a daily basis.

No, a little piss, a little crap? They're the least of your worries. Your immune system's a regular fucking genetic miracle.

It's like you're bulletproof, soldier. Relatively speaking.

Okay? Okay. So, dry yourself off and get back out there. Drinking time, son, is just around the corner.

His eyes returning to normal, Peter removes his shirt and wrings it out, his acne-scarred neck and back already beginning to dry clammy in the processed Coffee Time air. He walks to the door and locks it, modest now that he's stripping down to his harshest insecurities in a public place.

And then he takes off his pants.

He's still worried, of course, that he's shit himself – it feels, well, damp down there, kind of sticky – so he reaches, tentatively, into the back of his Jockeys to check. His hand comes out like it went in, pink, smelling like a rose.

See son, things are looking up already. Now, get a move on, maggot.

He punches the hand dryer's silver button ten or fifteen times before he slips back into his jeans and pokes his head and arms into his damp but toasty shirt. It's the drone that messes him up, takes him back to the time that takes him to Coffee Time – Uncle Joe and lying and riding in the Olds time.

· · • · ·

The idling engine is gunned, gears shift into reverse before Peter can slip fully into his jacket, his second skin, and slam the door. His tape's still driving him through the mushing punishment of today's hangover.

"You're late."

Motörhead done, the Aiwa's cutting to the opening hammer and pull of *Paranoid*: Black fucking Sabbath. The religion he got from Black fucking Flag: heavy metal's cool again.

"Pete! I said, you're late."

Peter's head bobs. And then he's punched in the arm, hard.

"What the. . . ?"

"Turn that fucking shit off, boy, I'm fucking talking to you here!"

Stunned, screamed at so loud even young, thin Ozzy's overpowered, Peter yanks at the rubber wires running up to his ears.

He looks and scowls at his Uncle Joe, but Peter sees his father, ten years before his death, and he becomes a scared teen all over again. Almost a man. Not quite man enough. No, not nearly man enough.

"Don't look at me like that, you stupid little pecker! I'll kick your stinking teeth in if you've even got the notion of giving me any of your crap. Smartass. Look at you, for chrissake. Shaking in your boots, ain't ya? Fucking chickenshit little prick. Jesus, you're Grade A fucking useless. You know that? Probably pissing your pants right now, ain't ya, son? Ya little maggot-faced freak. Ha."

Narrowing his eyes to really see his uncle, Peter backs off from the confrontation he believes he can't win. The fireplug of a man beside him – seven inches shorter, forty pounds lighter, and twenty-six years older – has been dying for the chance to kick his ass since all of this started, more than three months ago. Peter knows he's bigger, stronger, and younger; he also vaguely remembers that he himself is a fearsome, ugly, vicious brawler. Actually, more of a particularly, stupidly fearless, psychotic drunk. Under different circumstances, when he'd managed to achieve and maintain the correct ratio of blood to alcohol, he'd never be afraid of any fucking grey-haired dude with a square jaw and brushcut. Ex-military, Marine Corp? Who gives a flying fuck? The fact is, the guy's just too old and small to ever really scare him.

Except for one thing: his uncle, like his dead father, can be a mean and crazy sonofabitch. Completely fucking unpredictable. And even a stone cold waste case knows that in an unfair fight, mean and crazy's always the great equalizer. Yeah, his uncle *would* kick his stinking teeth in – and relish every second of the demolition.

"I'm sorry," Peter says.

"Listen, jarhead, if I wanted an apology I'd look it up in a fucking dictionary. Now shut your stinking hole and start listening to me. I want to talk with you."

Oh Christ, another sermon from Uncle G.I. fucking Joe. All the way from the driveway to the hotel. Hell and gone. Twenty-two minutes across town – if they make all the lights.

Joe pulls out and asks, quietly now: "Pete, how's your mother?"

Well, that's unexpected. Unusual and unprecedented. Sobering, calming almost. The ride to work's primarily the time when Peter's made to understand, in graphic, screaming detail, why he is, and will always be, a useless failure – just like, God bless him, Robert, his father.

"Uh, okay, I guess."

"You sure? She's taken all your trouble hard, son."

"Yeah."

"And you know the money's tight. Your father hadn't planned things, well, too. . . . Hey, let's call a spade a goddamned spade. He fucked everything up."

"I guess."

"You guess? Yeah, I fucking guess you guess. I know you, kid, you got

107

your bit and figured that's that, right? You guess. Fuck. Fuck you, Pete. But I guess, then, son – I guess you've been helping out around the place. Since you've been working, right? I mean, you've been paid by now, right, so you're helping out, at least, with the groceries and things?

"Uh."

"And I'm also guessing you're not blowing your goddamned money on booze and whores and whatever the hell else you're doing, right? No more dope. Right? Am I correct in assuming this, young Peter Alexander James?"

Peter nods his head in affirmation and then lets his eyes roll and drift out the passenger window: liquor store.

His uncle leaves the wheel to his left hand and uses his right to rap knuckles against Peter's mercilessly un-numb skull. "Hello? Christ, any-fuckingbody home? Pete? I'm over here, Pete. Look at me when I'm talking to you, son!"

Peter looks back, eyes lowered, and reaches into his leather jacket for his smokes.

"You see, Pete, and correct me if I'm mistaken here, I'm also assuming you're not hungover every fucking morning when I pick you up, right?"

"Uh."

"Well?"

"No."

"No? *No!* Fucking-A you're not. Am I right?" Uncle Joe slams on his breaks just in time to avoid running a red and killing the bicyclist who's already tearing through the intersection.

Peter, not wearing his seat belt, cracks his elbow off the dash in a spastic, dilatory effort to brace himself. His cigarette's cradled in his hand, unlit and unbroken, and his shamed, withdrawing mind panics for the words: "I mean, I'm trying–"

"Listen, asshole, I don't give a flying fuck about you. You're a worthless drunken piece of goodfornothing shit, just like your old man. I accept that. Look at you. You can't fucking help yourself. One in a long fucking line of lost causes: the sorry bastard who was your father, my hopeless fucking old man. If none of you ever had the sense to quit, to get to AA, well, that's embarrassing, but so be it. Right?"

Peter squinted and turned his head as the first of the three *Roadwolf* billboards on their daily route sped by. His uncle, knowing both the cause and the timing of these facial distortions all too well, automatically flipped down the passenger-side sun visor.

"Light sensitive, poor baby," he said, and laughed. Then, straight-faced again, deadly serious, he continued, more hellfire and brimstone. "Pete, you know, I don't give a rat's ass that you don't respect me, though God knows I deserve that from a little pukefaced punk like you. But the one thing I won't accept, the one thing I don't ever want to hear, is that you've been fucking over your own mother. You got me?"

"Yeah, Joe."

"What did you say?" Joe screams as he squeals the tires, making a sharp right onto the waterfront freeway onramp.

"Yeah, I mean, yes. Yes, sir."

"Okay. Fine. We understand one another, right?"

"Yes. Yes we do."

"Good. So, what this means is that you're going to be doing everything in your power to help your mother unload that goddamned money pit you've got yourself nested in. Am I right?"

"Sure."

"And then you're going to use your share of that money from your father's insurance, and what you're making now, to find your own goddamned apartment and give your mother some peace. Am I correct?"

"Well, yeah. That's—"

"Of course you are, Pete. Of course. And another thing: you're not going to fuck up this job, are you?"

"No."

"No, you're not. I mean, I got you three fucking interviews, didn't I, Pete? And fine. That wasn't good enough for you. Eh, boy? No, you don't need old Joe's help. Fine. Now it doesn't matter that you were too fucking stupid and lazy to actually get those jobs. What did I expect, right? And I'm not saying you should worry your fat head about how that made me look after I pulled those strings just to get you into those places. No, I don't expect that, either. It's not your fault that you were too drunk to get past the fucking reception desk at the autoplant. No. No, you still had to deal with your troubles then, right? Who could blame you, going on a bender like that? Your old man dead, just being fired from your job and all, fresh out of fucking jail – your drunk ass still fucking quivering and sore and clenched so goddamned tight...."

"But—"

Peter's stomach lurched as his uncle swerved to avoid the cab cutting them off from the left. His head split as Joe rode the horn and screamed: "Asshole! Ignorant fucking foreigners! Who taught you to fucking drive, dickhead!" In the reprieve Peter scooped out his lighter and lit his smoke. Better, feeling better. Yeah, well, no. Not really. I mean, hell, things couldn't get much, I mean, like, worse.

"I mean. . . ." Another *Roadwolf* billboard. Number two.

"And Pete, listen. I don't hold it against you, even though you think I might. Who knew a kid like you could be so goddamned uncoordinat-ed? You know, you shameless little sonofabitch, it almost broke my heart. There I am getting an old war buddy to do my nephew a favour and give him a unionized job on a mindless fucking assembly line, a job that any trained fucking monkey could do and still rake in enough money to feed a family of four, and I'm talking a big fat fucking family of four, Grade A porkers every fucking one of them, and you. . . . Well, who knew you couldn't get those pudgy little fingers of yours to push the right fucking buttons. Couldn't tell left from fucking right. Ha! Red from goddamned green. Go figure, right? All those fifty-fifty odds and you come up bust. Ha ha."

"Hey, Uncle Joe—"

"No, Pete, hear me out. You just suck on that goddamned cancer stick and listen to me here, son. Okay? This is important. I want you to know this, too. I wasn't even mad when you insulted my friend Jerry — a guy I've known since I was half your age — by telling him that you'd need more money to feel 'comfortable' working for him. No, son, that was fine. Him phoning me up like you were the biggest jackass in the world? Fine. We laughed. Great. After all, you had a few of your dead Daddy's bucks in the bank. And I'd paid for all your legal bills, right? You prob-ably even made a grand or two off that goddamned car you cracked up. You were sitting pretty, weren't you? Living large and rent fucking free off your mother's tit like a spoiled goddamned kid. So why would you want to take a job that offered you three dollars more than the minimum fucking wage for answering the phone a couple times and booking serv-ice appointments?"

"Joe, look, I'll pay you back for everything you've—"

"Shut the fuck up. I've told you, I don't want you to pay me back. I bailed you out and I paid for that goddamned lawyer and I squared things with UPS for you so you wouldn't have to do time. Sometimes though, you know, sometimes, son, I wish I had let them put you away. I mean, I don't know if I did you any goddamned favour. Jesus, what were you thinking? Did you think no one would notice? I mean, Christ: forgetting to make the 'odd' fucking delivery. Having the stones to actu-ally say that to the cops when there were maybe forty fucking pieces of undelivered shit in your fucking trunk. No wonder, you lazy fucking alcoholic bastard, no wonder they thought you were a fucking thief and not just another DWI. Jesus. And no, I don't want a fucking cent of your money. I did all of it for your mother and the memory of your sainted fucking grandmother, not for you, you little shit. And not for your fucking old man, that's for goddamned sure. No, there's only one thing I want. And that's for you, Pete, for you to let your fucking mother get on with her goddamned life. Alone. So, what I'm telling you . . . what I'm asking here . . . is this: tell me you're not fucking up the job at the hotel. Just tell me that. I don't give a fuck about you or your fucking life, but tell me you're not fucking this up, too. Because if you are . . . if you are, that's it. I can't fucking help you any more. Got me? Not with jobs. Not with lawyer's bills. And not with meeting the terms of your fucking suspended sentence. Got it?"

"Yes sir."

"So?"

"So what, Joe?"

"So, tell me you're not fucking up. You *are* still working, am I right? How you managed to get this job, I don't even wanna fucking know. I mean: who, Pete? Who did it for you? Who'd ya have to blow? Aw, fuck. Forget it. But just tell me: you're not planning on quitting or getting fired, are you?"

"No sir," he said, the vision of a hazy young blonde, rolling her eyes, flitting through his head.

"You're sure?"

"Yeah."

"So we understand each other?"

"Yeah."

"I've made myself clear?"

"Crystal."

"Don't get smart with me, funny boy. You definitely ain't Tom Cruise and I'd kick the shit outta Jack fucking Nicholson. Just like I'm gonna kick the shit out of you, son, for real, if you fuck with me again. Got it?"

"Yes, sir."

And then Uncle Joe pulled the Brougham Sedan over in front of the hotel. Peter grabbed his walkman and his brown bagged lunch, opened the door, tossed his butt at the curb and swung his legs out.

"Kid. One more thing. Where's your fucking uniform at these days? You can't tell me they let you do security in jeans and running shoes."

"Uh, Joe, you know. I, uh, I leave them in the office. Yeah, see, that way I can get the hotel laundry to take care of things. Don't have to bother Mom."

"That right?"

"Yes, sir," Peter says, staring wistfully at a freckle that stands in for his watch on his left wrist. He's tired, sick, and diminishing. His disorienta-

111

tion tells him he's behind schedule already: exactly a minute-and-a-half late for the true beginning of his day.

"Honest?"

"Yes, Joe."

"It better fucking be."

Joe James smiled then, sighed and shrugged his shoulders and pointed up the street. He stabbed at the third *Roadwolf* billboard with the perfectly manicured nail of his right index finger. His voice modulated, became a different kind of avuncular, without malice at all. "Look how it could've been," he said before pulling the passenger door shut, revving his big engine, and peeling out, tires squealing. "The boys have done alright. Call 'em, son. Pete, look how it could be."

"Fuck," Peter mumbled, squinting again, turning away, dying for a drink. "Fucking asshole. Christ, who the fuck does he think he is?"

9:43 AM

BUDDY'S SWEET, DOWNY HEAD TWITCHES, jarred by the dull, old needle cracking and popping and jumping forward and back in a dusty, thick, vinyl groove. Through the thin, tarnished bars of his very old cage, the budgie's right eye is trying to focus on the perspective that unfolds and mushrooms out from his world. A gentle, steady pulse of clean fall air, fresh with just a hint of electric and tantalizingly sharp, chilling trouble, combs his feathers, calls him. And then there's another skip, and then the jerk comes.

And then the movement is reversed, repeated. Again and again and again and still another skip and again and now.

In the few seconds he has before the electromagnet sound wrenches him away once more, he can only see, can only process, a limited, finite distance. Closest to him, everything begins just past his cage. It's here, in these few short, important inches, that his impossibly complex bird brain begins compensating for the metal bars, the obstruction to his vision. This fuzzy point is the small, business end of his quickly expanding visual funnel. At its farthest point, outside, what Buddy manages to see deliquesces at the outlined edge of the large potted houseplant he knows sits on the lip of the porch. Sometimes, out there, a leaf will rustle in the same breeze and poke reassuringly into view.

Sometimes not.

In between these two points, the alpha and omega of a tiny, tender guy's annoyingly unstable, skittish universe, a fascinating still life is balanced on a precarious threshold: set up for inevitable collapse, for what seems like an eternity now, five maybe six hops and skips and pops, the old guy's remained motionless, wooden, completely absorbed. Surveying the scene, Buddy knows it cannot maintain. He wonders if he'll see the change come before he's taken again.

And yes, Ed Harrison's little fella, Buddy the fourth, does.

It happens just as the needle works through the final turn of the last fat groove of the 78 spinning inside the enormous, forty-year-old, teak RCA Victor combination console. Five-and-a-half feet long by two-and-a-half feet wide, three-and-a-half feet high on removable four-and-a-half inch legs, the 130-pound box houses a trade-marked phonograph, and a fancy AM radio with big dials and a nifty red station pointer. It also has built-in, state-of-the-art speakers and a storage unit large enough to house the collection of any modern audiophile. The transformation, Buddy notices, occurs at the precise moment when the blunted point of sound is silenced, concerted into a simple, sharp point of rising metal, popped up to begin the short, innocuous arc of its flight backwards in time by its unavoidably illegible contact with a small disc of heavy paper.

In the fermata of this moment, the six-year-old budgie really learns to grieve. He's not mourning the three other Buddies who've lived in this cage before him – fellows nicknamed, in turn, Buddy Boy, B.B. Junior, and Sweet Bud the third, he knows their singular, unmistakeable scents, yes, but he's never had the pleasure of their acquaintance – because he does not understand that their tiny colourful bodies have long ago decomposed into the loam beneath the flowerbed behind the white ash which lies out there, just beyond the large, mysterious, potted plant.

Of course, if he had met the guys, or knew of their fate – really, they were a great bunch, just super – he would be disturbed, a bit weirded out.

But hey, that's life. Right, Buddy? Right?

Yes.

Um, well, no.

No, instead, his strong little budgie heart gets stuck, breaking, in his tiny perfect budgie throat, because he knows he cannot work his small claws around the latch and open the goddamned door to this stupid cage. No matter how much he wants it, wills it, he cannot leave his perch and fly through the tin bars and through the bars of dust floating in the sunbeam that comes in gridded through the open screen of the back door. Buddy cannot spread his powerful wings and glide and arc up and to the right. And he cannot descend. Cannot land, gently, ever so gently, on the old man's bare, age-freckled shoulder. He cannot do this, and he cannot whisper and sing, so softly, so gentle: I understand, my dear old friend. It'll be alright.

Buddy grieves because he is lost; for himself, because he's helpless, hopeless. It's so damned selfish he thinks, my pain for yours. But it hurts. Damn. And I cannot make this better.

Not for you, my friend.

Not for me.

And so, in the timeless moment before his sad eye was closed by the force that's twisted his small-boned neck so many times now, Buddy watches, impotent, as a tear forms, hangs suspended, and falls upon the brittle yellow newspaper clipping in his friend's still hands.

· • • ·

Now that's something you've never actually seen before. And won't see again. Sure, you know time's infinite and encompassing, all things are possible. But it's also devious, cruelly limited. Nobody wants to think about that, do they, Buddy? And then there's the small matter of your personal history. Admit it, there are lacunae, things you might not know. Hell, you're still a young fella. Your predecessors could tell you otherwise, might have other information. But again, what's it to you? All you've got to go on is what's happened outside these bars since you've been here. Exactly five years to the day now, since he brought you here, a gift for his wife. What you've accumulated, though, a world of experience, tells you this is disturbing shit. Alice, sure, she'd let go once in a while. That'd happen. But, wow, what's gotten into Ed today?

The budgie watched a still, tough old guy cry for only the second time in his adult life – and he was embarrassed for his pain, and there was nothing he could do.

Sorry, Buddy.

When the bird's head was his own again, and the throbbing subsided, and he could slow and unscramble the jigging blur of his eyes, nothing was the same. Ed Harrison was composing himself, his back stiffened, his hands wiping dry the salty dampness furrowing his stubbled cheeks. He'd returned: a man simply moving through a beautiful morning, a man moving on.

· • • ·

Peeking into the back room from the hallway, framed by family portraits, homemade and mounted snapshot collages of the kids at every age – Ted playing ball, cold arena shots, Belle graduating from high school, her first day of college, both of them driving the car for the first time, and countless Christmases with Ed's family – Alice Harrison stands stock still in a faded blue chenille housecoat. Craned so she can see around the tarnished old birdcage, she's watched her shirtless husband shuffle through the rest of the past she believes is better left in storage now. Her own name greens and fades in his tattoo heart.

Ed sits crosslegged and hunched, his strong back bent, on aged and worn taupe broadloom, in front of the horrible old mauve couch and ottoman, amidst piles of photos and letters and kiddie heirlooms he's pulled from black, and pink, and blue and yellow and green paisley hatboxes as old as their marriage.

Oh, and in his lap, that old photo of them dancing. The one from the paper.

Alice also knows better than to interfere. It's that kind of day now, that kind of mood. Fine. He's trying, but when Ed gets like this you can't tell him anything. So she watches her husband of fifty-three years – tomorrow at eleven AM it will be fifty-four – in unblinking, red-eyed silence.

The silly old bugger's gone and worked himself up over ancient history, and if she dared she'd tsk him sharply, snatch up that filthy bit of newsprint, march over to the hi-fi, and break that damned record over her knee.

That song. Again.

Lord Jesus, when did she come to hate that record?

Recently, right? It had to be quite recent.

Many, many years had passed – easy, busy, thoughtless time – and that song was so simple, just a sweet part of a very nice memory. Something they'd remember and laugh about once in a while, that she herself would play, occasionally, when she was dusting or fixing a cup of tea in the kitchen and Ed was at work and Ted and Belle were at school.

Sometimes it would leave her flustered, even when she was alone, flushed, knowing how silly it was. She'd catch her reflection in the toaster or the sink, her distorted lips happily, mindlessly chirping along with the words, and she'd be embarrassed.

Our song. Right.

You've got to be kidding. Alice, your poor tormented mother – no matter how mean-spirited, pigheaded, and wrong she might have been in her own right – did not raise you to be a fool. Not even a fool in love. It's all just too, well, corny. Think about it. Look at you. Look at Ed.

But it *was* their song. And another month or two would fly by and she'd find herself removing the newspaper from the bottom of Buddy's cage to clean it – she found herself regretting, now, that she hadn't lined the thing with that damned photo of them years ago – and she'd see her lips moving in the metal there. And then she'd hear herself: "Then you came and caused a spark, that's a four-alarm fire now. . . ." And then her face would flush again. Only this time she'd think of her man, his gorgeous eyes and arms and the soft hair on the nape of his neck and she'd be positively blissful.

Blissfully happy. Happier than she'd ever been.

Lovestruck and beginning to see the light.

She was still seventeen when the memory was fixed, made indelible and inescapable by that song and that clipping. It was the day before her birthday. Tonight, more than five decades ago; my God, the fall of 1944. Ed wasn't nineteen himself; they were back in Cape Cod, and he was on leave. In two days he'd be getting his orders, probably to join his brothers: the twenty-one-year-old who's already gone over, Francis, and the twenty-year-old corpse, John, who's buried or blown to bits on one of those tiny South Pacific islands. Not even islands – improbable, floating graveyards.

They had passed the evening dancing in the ballroom of her parents' private club. Her father was there, too, and he certainly did not approve. Mom wouldn't have either, but even then the folks spent every waking minute moving as far apart as humanly possible, politely maintaining only the public semblance of something like a marriage. Mrs. Berard would get a report, though – the spectacle warranted at least a memo, if not an awkwardly full-blown civil conversation.

Each time they left their table to hold each other while the band swung through another number, her father's mood grew darker. He glowered at them from the bar where he sat mumbling beside that ridiculous little bastard Reggie Colter. Funny, Daddy falling to bits in the outrage with her tormented, frantic ex.

If he only knew.

She remembered seeing them every time she was turned back that way, and to this day she wonders what Ed thought of the pair as they danced, two habitually inscrutable men, uncharacteristically ill-at-ease in their evening suits, getting shamefully drunk while they waged their own private battles.

Did he know what was going to happen? Could he possibly have known what she was thinking?

Her family, like Reggie's, was quite wealthy – actually, they were very, very rich. And Ed. . . . Well, Ed wasn't. He *was* handsome, distinguished in his uniform. But back then everyone looked sharp, didn't they? Still, the first and only other time her father had met him, when she'd invited him to dinner two months earlier, Max Berard was, of course, gracious, excessively polite. He smiled and shook Ed's hand warmly, feigned interest in the war, Ed's training, the Harrison family. And then her father had taken her aside and absolutely forbade her from seeing him again. Alice crinkled her nose and stamped her heel when he said the boy was beneath her and called him trash. But she'd learned many valuable lessons on the skirts of her mother, who shamelessly flirted with Ed in the garden while this lecture was taking place – he might not have been good enough for her little girl, but he was a damned fine, red-blooded dreamboat. She knew without a doubt that Daddy's bullying obsession with propriety, his manipulative, tyrannical insistence on maintaining a spotless family image, only actually extended to what other people might think. In truth, he didn't give a rat's ass about what she or the missus did – as long as he didn't find out about it from one of his friends or associates, and as long as it didn't cost him too much. So, she bit her lip until he finished and resisted the indignant tantrum. And when it was over she faked a little crying jag and sighed and gave in and promised.

No, she wouldn't see him again. Because, yes, Daddy, okay. You're right, it's probably for the best.

Of course she saw Ed the very next day, and night, and the next. And for the next eight weeks, maybe fourteen or fifteen other times that late summer and fall, she'd tell her parents she was going out with a girlfriend and sneak off to a club or a show with him whenever he could leave the base.

That night, *the* night, was different.

Just a few hours earlier Ed had learned that his platoon was finally going to be mobilized. He said that they hadn't been told where the transport would take them. It didn't matter, she understood. Wherever they sent him wouldn't be pleasant.

And then Alice saw the carefree little smile beneath his hard, doomed eyes, and also knew that this man was too brave for anyone's good – he simply wasn't smart enough to be afraid enough to come back alive.

She still remembers, feels actually, the staccato of her exact thoughts. Damn. Poor boy. He really is nice.

And jeez, he really is sweet on me. So shy, too. And nothing like Reg. Not at all like him.

There wasn't much she could do, right?

Alice took his hands and drew him to her, just the way the movies tell you to do it. She held him hard and said what she was supposed to say, smiling the way she was supposed to smile: "Well, Mr. Eddie Harrison, if this is your last leave for a while, then we better do it up right."

Then she told him to pick her up at the house at seven-thirty. That she knew the perfect place.

And so, there they were. Together at what was shaping up to be quite the do. Eating dreadfully good food and running up a very large bill on her father's tab. Listening to a relatively famous band – famous enough that two different press photographers had been snapping away all evening. Dancing, quite romantically, at a very fancy club.

To hell with anyone who thinks there's something wrong with that.

To hell with Reggie Colter.

And to hell with her father. Oh, he was slick, courteous, and magnanimous when he saw them, strolling over with a hand in one pocket and a cigarette in the other, waiter in tow. He grinned and grasped Ed's shoulder, pumped it with a familiar squeeze, and made a sweeping gesture with his Marlboro.

"I want you to make sure my daughter and this brave lad are taken care of."

Ed returned the smile, rising out of his seat. "Thank you, sir. Thank you. This means the world to me, Mr. Berard. Will you join us?"

"No, I don't think so, son. You two enjoy yourselves. I wouldn't dream of interrupting."

When the waiter asked Ed if they'd like a cocktail before seeing the menu, he was distracted long enough for her father to shoot her a look that was part disgust, part malice.

And then he walked away.

Through the years Alice looked back at herself sitting there, watched her mouth draw tight and an eyebrow rise, saw the precise moment she began thinking damage control.

She waited a moment, then excused herself, telling Ed that she'd be right back. "Get ready to dance, darling, I just want to thank Daddy."

Her father was already at the bar, already finished his first scotch. She sighed, shook her ringleted auburn head, and tried to assuage him.

"I'm sorry, Daddy. I know. But you don't understand. He leaves in two days and–"

His open palm and the viciousness of his scowl stopped her. There was no use. He wouldn't listen.

Berard whispered: "You're an embarrassment, Alice Berard. To yourself, to your mother, to me." That was it. End of discussion.

Two-and-a-half drunken hours later, clearly the only thing preventing Max Berard from blowing his top was his horror of causing a scene in public. That, and the fact that he could be reasonably certain in his belief that when and if his baby next saw her young soldier it would be in a nice, solid, airless pine box.

Reggie Colter, though, was just beside himself with jealousy. And Alice would have been the first one to admit that she loved it: watching *him* squirm suited her just fine.

She'd been dating Colter on and off – okay, it was more on than off, for her at least – since she was fifteen. In fact, they'd been close since they were kids. Reggie was two years older, with a family wealthy enough to pull the kinds of strings that, at the time, kept a boy far away from the war. Anyway, it was like they had always been a couple. For years their folks, even their friends, had put an ampersand between their names like it was inevitable. Alice & Reg: when you said it, it sounded predestined, a mutually beneficial merger.

Alice enjoyed the arrangement. Older, popular, good-looking, as rich as she was – everybody knew Reggie was a catch. Her friends, the rich ones and the very rich ones, the pretty ones and the homely ones, envied her; her parents were content that her life was set and, basically, left her alone.

The way she tells herself she remembers this part, now – living an acceptable version of the story, the one she's convinced herself she can live with – life was perfect. Sure there was school, and then the war and all those boys dying. And her parents had always been monsters, but so what? She'd always have Reggie. Never worrying about whether some guy liked her, never even considering the exquisite torture of waiting for somebody she liked to ask her out, Alice was the rarest creature of all: a blissfully happy, incredibly well-adjusted teenager.

It's not that she was a saint. No, she was as devoted as the next girl, but when they were apart for months at a time, being educated and finished, what did you expect? She was very pretty and very popular and exceedingly rich and she'd be damned if she'd sit around pining while uglier and awkward and poorer girls were having fun. So yes, there were other dates – many others. But nothing serious. There really wasn't anyone else who made her happy.

Yes, at seventeen Alice Berard was in love with Reginald Colter. Or, at least she thought she was – to the best of her recollection.

Despite his stupid name. *The mean little rich kid.*

They were going to be married, you know? Okay, they hadn't set a date or anything. And Reg was still reluctant to make those kinds of plans. But he was wearing down – honestly, you could tell.

So that's why she'd lead him, by the hand, deep into his folks' topiary maze. Why, when they got to their favourite remote spot, she'd ease down his pants.

Other boys could kiss her. The really swell ones could even, maybe, sometimes, feel her up.

That was it though. She had a steady and going further just wasn't right.

Reg was different. She went as far as she did with him because making her guy happy made her happier. Also, the truth was, when it was her turn, well, she was pretty happy, too.

Happier than happy.

And happier was, is, you know, so damned good.

So damned good that that's what they called it: getting happy.

The problem? Old story, right? One day Reggie got it into his head that he wasn't happy enough. That he could, in fact, be even happier. Extra happy.

At least twice as happy.

The stupid bastard.

It was a gorgeous mid-June Saturday on the coast of Massachusetts when Alice Berard discovered she was less-than-happy with her boyfriend. They had arranged to get together that afternoon, hadn't they? And when Reggie didn't show up at the appointed time – he was only a bit spontaneous, a tad erratic, generally quite punctual – Alice wondered if she'd been mistaken about their plans.

Her mother swore she'd mentioned that she'd be going to the Colter compound for brunch a few days earlier, so, chastising her scatterbrained self, Alice begged her father to drive her up the street.

Max sighed, reluctantly pulling himself away from the financial pages of the weekend edition, but shrugged his shoulders "what-the-hell" because he wanted to get out anyway.

After kissing Daddy goodbye and asking him for money, Alice met Reg's mother at the front door.

She tingled all over when the hard, angular woman said, "I'm sure I wouldn't know, dear. Try the maze, perhaps. I believe he was heading in that direction earlier."

My, what a happy surprise.

You remember, right? What it was like? You're seventeen and horny and pretty good and innocent for chrissake. Thinking: Oh, what a romantic, happy, plan.

Only it wasn't. Not for Alice. And certainly not for Reg.

Well, he had been happy all right. Very, very happy. He'd probably never been happier.

Happy enough, anyway, that he didn't hear her approach as she made her way along the impossibly intricate but hormonally memorized pathway.

Unhappily, that's just how she found him: exceedingly happy, in their secret happy spot, in the centre of the sylvan labyrinth.

As she had hoped, Reggie was quite prepared, naked from the waist down, for all the teenaged ecstasy to come. Only he wasn't happily alone. No, as she turned the corner of the last large hedge she found him, already largely, blissfully happy, with one of the girls who worked keeping his mother's house.

Rather plump and remarkably homely, at that moment a nineteen-year-old domestic she once called Sally, a slack-jawed cipher of a girl shock and anger and the sucking void of memory have renamed "the Cow," effectively ruined Alice Berard's improbable teenaged happiness.

She saw what she saw and it wasn't pretty: that thing, on her knees, in front of Reg. Worse, the Cow's mouth was obviously making him happier than her small, perfect-boned left hand ever had.

Oh.

Jesus.

. . • . .

As they danced, Ed's large right hand delicately supported the small of Alice's back, guided her through the new, pale yellow *crêpe de Chine* that perfectly draped her slender 110-pound frame. The dress was one of many gifts, pathetic acts of atonement, Reggie had presented her with since the unhappy incident. Now, Ed was slowly turning her clockwise while the band played her favourite Nat "King" Cole tune, and when she opened her eyes she saw Reggie and her father float by again and smiled.

Mortified, terrified, Reggie hadn't even tried to follow her when she marched back out of the maze.

You couldn't blame him.

The Cow had been startled, you see. And there'd obviously been a stampede of twenty-nine or thirty tiny, yellowed, decaying teeth.

Oh.

Christ.

Now that's rich. Good, for a start. But not quite good enough.

Just before Reg let out the wonderfully sharp, loud agonized series of yelps triggered by the cud-chewing comedy of him toppling the Cow in a ripping, wet plop as he fumbled to grab the slacks at his ankles, the new, happy couple noticed they had company. Oops.

Her eyes had narrowed. She'd stopped the scream deep in her throat, so the first sound she'd made was more of a warning growl than anything that might've registered as shock or pain. But then she gathered all her resources and muttered, with all the menace and power her family's name and reputation conferred, the kind of thing everyone between the ages of seventeen and seventy always dreams about saying in this very situation: "Son-of-a-bitch. I'll ruin you for this. Ruin you both."

At the time, of course, she'd never meant anything more.

Better, both the Cow and Reggie knew that she probably could carry out her threat. And that she probably would. Neither realized how simple, swift, but exacting her revenge would be.

Gulp.

"Ow! Ow! Ow! Ow! Christ, oh my God! Jesus! Ow!"

Firmly in control then, from that very moment, through the following weeks, she'd timed her complex series of emotional responses and subtle machinations perfectly. Stony-faced, she left the maze in record time, without breaking into a sweat. Ten yards from the last turn before the labyrinth's entrance – and from Mrs. Colter, who was all concern as she hurried, with her gardener, towards the disturbing cry of what sounded like a small, wounded, effeminate animal – Alice simultaneously broke into hysterical tears and a reckless, pale-faced, blind, hyperventilating gallop. Calculating her trajectory perfectly, the avenging angel exploded into the porcelain arms of Reggie's blue-blooded and positively pious mother.

Lucky? Sure. But the best of the best always take a few risks, make their own luck.

A frantic seventeen-year-old in her arms, Mrs. Colter became even more translucent as the gardener bolted into the maze and toward the now only slightly less-frequent bleats of anguish.

"What is it, dear? My word, what's happened?"

Sobbing into the woman's dress, heaving and shaking in wild fits but actually wondering how in the world such a rich woman could be wearing such a rank perfume, Alice delivered the most satisfyingly sweet *coup de grâce*: "It . . . it's. . . ."

"What!"

"It's . . . oh my God . . . it's disgusting!"

"Girl, calm yourself. Tell me what's happened. What was that noise?"

"It . . . it was Sally. And him! It was . . . Reggie. Reg and Sally . . . doing . . . oh my God!"

Composing herself, wiping away the crocodile tears and straightening the pale blue ribbon that swept back her hair, Alice listened intently as Mrs. Colter wound her way through the maze towards her son, desperately calling, "Reginald!" while the gardener guided her with shouts of "This way, ma'am! Left, turn left! Then your second right! Over here!"

Alice clasped her hands together delicately and nodded to herself when she knew the woman had found the gardener who had already discovered her compromised, injured son.

"Reginald Alistair Colter! Sally! Oh my God, no! What have you done!"

Ow.

Now, that's gotta hurt.

But Alice wasn't finished with the sonofabitch yet. Not by a longshot. The fun had only just started.

After church the next day it was Reggie's fat and awkward and stammering father who took Alice aside to apologize for his son's shameful behaviour.

She'd expected this.

"Horrible. Poor girl. Alright, are you?"

"Yes."

"Coping, eh? Good. Now. This. A most unfortunate situation. An embarrassment to us all. Truly."

"Yes."

"Surely you understand, discretion and all that."

"Yes."

"Yes, well, well. Discretion. Yes. Of course, that would be for the best. The boy's mother's devastated. We all are. He, we all, all of us, ask your forgiveness. Absolutely scandalous."

"Of course."

"Well then. Good. Awful stuff, this. Dreadful. He's broken-hearted. Really. That tram– that woman is no longer in our employ. You know he's a good boy, led down the garden path, so to speak."

"Yes."

"Know how you must feel. I do. My word. Quite. Shocking, terrible."

"Yes."

"Please, find it in your heart. He wants to. There must be some way. Amends and all that. At the very least hear his apology."

"Certainly."

"May he, then? Apologize, I mean. Now? I'll just get him, shall I?"

"No."

"Pardon?"

"Mr. Colter, my parents are waiting for me. You understand, surely. They're not pleased."

"You, you've told your father, then? Your mother?"

Colter was reeling, his corpulent frame close to bursting with fear: My, my, terrible stuff, this. Very bad. Awful. Very bad for business. Alice waited a moment before answering.

"No, sir. Not yet."

"I see." Colter thinned a bit with relief.

123

"I haven't decided what to tell them yet."

"No?"

"No," Alice replied. "I haven't. But, of course, sir, they do know that something is wrong. And why wouldn't they? I won't lie to you, I was in quite a state when I returned yesterday." Alice blinked prettily and mentally crossed off another item on her *How To Teach Him a Lesson He'll Never Forget* list; in truth she was perfectly composed when she returned home, and her parents suspected nothing. "It was the worst moment of my life."

"Well. . . . Well, yes. Quite. Poor girl."

"You understand, I just can't bring myself to see him right now. That will take time, Mr. Colter. Time. He will have to wait. Time must pass. This wound must heal. Maybe next Saturday. Yes, then, perhaps, I will be ready to listen to what he has to say. Please tell him this, sir. And tell Mrs. Colter that the Berards accept your apology."

"As you wish."

"Oh, and Mr. Colter?"

"Yes, Miss Berard?"

"Is there still much pain? For Reg, I mean. Is it bad?"

He blushed. "Oh, dear. Poor boy. It's healing nicely, but still quite terrible, I'm afraid."

"Good."

The following weekend Reggie was at her front door with a gorgeous bouquet of roses. Mommy, who she'd manipulated and whined into a completely unrelated, but nonetheless terrifyingly foul mood, informed him, curtly, that Alice was unwell.

"Quite unable to see anyone. She suggests you meet her Wednesday. After her lessons. Goodbye."

"Yes, ma'am," she heard him say from where she lay on the couch in the parlour, "I just wanted to say—"

"Reg, I'm very busy. Please. Wednesday. Now, goodbye."

"Yes, ma—"

The second half of his last syllable was sucked up by the door shutting in his face. Good, that's another check.

"Mommy, I'm sorry. I'm feeling better now. In fact, I think I'll go for a walk. It's such a beautiful day. Was that Reg? My, what beautiful roses! For me? He's so sweet."

"Honestly, child. I've just sent that nice young man away. Are you sick or not?"

"No, Mother, I'm better. I'm feeling much, much better."

On Wednesday Alice saw Reg cradling a tiny, beautifully boxed, and delicately ribboned gift, nervously shuffling and kicking at the dirt by the

124

long wooden fence. For a while she pretended not to notice him from where she stood brushing her horse. She waited, again knowing exactly what would happen.

It was Evelyn Abbot, one of three or four best friends she'd ridden with since she was twelve, who set the scene in motion.

"Alice, your boyfriend's here."

Alice waited a beat, allowed the colour to drain from her contented, sunkissed cheeks, moaned, "Oh my God, no!" and burst into tears.

Immediately, four fabulously wealthy teenaged girls and one rather large unpredictable horse were all over her in support, petting her, asking her if she was alright, cooing at and consoling her, hating Reggie Colter's guts.

Frances Drummond went first. Somebody had to ask, right?

"What's wrong?"

Evelyn knew, and answered the obvious question for her: "It was him, wasn't it?"

Alice cried harder.

Prince the horse snorted, rolled his majestic head around his powerful neck, and narrowed his inflamed eyes.

Dorothy Tisdale wondered: "What has he done?"

Grace Addison guessed: "The bastard. Another girl? It must be!"

And then Alice collapsed into their collective ministrating arms and bawled even louder.

Prince stamped, his left fetlock bristling with terrifying equine rage.

Playing her part, Alice let the girls steady her pitifully weak and devastated body for another minute.

Then she looked up and over at her currently off-again guy. His face red with shame, he turned away from her mad, hysterical gaze.

There, that's another check.

She knew that Reggie now believed, even if he hadn't actually heard, that every important, eligible young girl from Boston to the Cape would, within hours, think he was a disgusting beast.

Did you hear about Reginald Colter? Shocking. With the *help*, no less. Jesus. . . .

So then Alice composed herself, and tentatively, haltingly, said: "It's just. . . . No . . . I . . . I can't . . . I just can't . . . let him see me. . . ."

"Why? What's wrong? C'mon, you can tell us," three of the four demanded.

"I . . . I think. . . ." Alice sobbed another sob.

"I think I'm getting fat." Snort, wipe, and then another full-blown crying jag.

"He can't see me.... Don't let him see me. Please. Not, not like this. I'm disgusting. He must think I'm fat!"

"Alice!" Evelyn rolled her eyes and hugged her best friend hard. "Silly." And then, all seriousness, she asked the others to leave them alone for a minute.

Frances, a truly heavy girl, laughed softly. Thinking her best friend spoiled and insane, she patted Alice's pretty red head and walked back to her own perpetually overburdened mare.

Dorothy, who'd spent the last two years binging and purging, decades before anybody decided there was something actually quite fucked up about that kind of behaviour, nodded her understanding and mumbled, "I know how you feel darling, but it's not true. You're not. You're just not fat." She walked away from her best friend in a daze, thinking: You think you've got a problem, honey. Just you thank Christ you're not me.

Disappointed there was no scandal, Grace, as remarkably, stereotypically bitchy a best friend as a fabulously spoiled, wealthy young girl could ever have, walked away bored, barely occupied with the question of who to mock the scene with first.

Cooling down, his bloodlust abating, Prince nuzzled at Alice's riding pants pocket: Look, lady, I'd have killed for you.

Alice herself laughed then, tickled by the horse's nose and a plan well-executed. She pushed Evelyn away gently, wiped at her eyes with her left hand, and fed Prince a sugar cube with her right. "I'm sorry. I'm such a stupid girl. Really, I'm sorry."

"That's okay, darling. I understand. Are you better now?"

"Of course. I'm sorry. How embarrassing. Of course I am."

"Sure?"

"Yes. Thank you."

"You really are my best friend, you know that?"

"C'mon. You'd do the same for me."

"Yeah. But, Evelyn?"

"Yeah?"

"Evelyn, I'm not fat? Am I?" she asked, always willing to see things through till the end.

"God, no. You're perfect. Disgustingly, beautifully, perfect."

"Really?"

"Really."

"Okay. Good."

"What?"

"Oh, nothing. Do you think Reg saw?"

"Yeah, probably."

"Is he still there?"

Evelyn looked over her friend's shoulder. "Uh huh, he's against the fence. He's looking away, though. Not at us. And it looks like he's got something for you."

"Really?"

"Alice, you're so damned lucky, you know that? He's wonderful."

"You think so?"

"Yeah."

"I know."

"Don't you dare ever let him go."

"Oh, Evie, don't worry, I won't."

"You better go see the poor boy now. He looks so confused."

"Really? I mean, I'm sure he is."

Her arms folded over her chest, Alice walked up to Reg without looking at him. She stopped five feet from the fence he still nervously leaned against.

"What do you want?" she spat, sullen.

Not wanting to set her off again he spoke soft and slow: "I think we should talk. I want to apologize. There's things I need to say."

"It's a little late for that, don't you think?"

"Alice, please. I'm so sorry. I never meant to hurt you. Honestly."

"Right."

"Really, I never meant for this to happen."

"You mean you never meant for me to find out."

"Alice, no. That's not true. I know how it looks, but. . . ."

"You have no idea, Reg. You have no idea how it looked."

"Okay, Alice. Okay. You're right. I don't. But I never planned it, I didn't want it to happen. Honestly, you have to believe me."

"You're saying the Cow forced you? Is that it? Made you do it, against your will?"

"Well. . . ."

"Well what, Reg? Well what? How could you do this to me? How could you do this to us?"

"Alice, God Alice, I feel so, so terrible. Please listen to me: I'm sorry."

"Yeah, you are. You really are. You're as sorry as that piece of trash you were with, and you're not good enough, definitely not good enough to be with me. So, I'm going, Reg. That's it. Okay? We're through. You've apologized, now beat it. I never want to see you again."

"No Alice, no." It was his turn to cry now.

"You're pathetic, you know that?"

"Alice, I'm sorry. Please, please, forgive me. I don't know what I'd do without you. I'm sorry. Don't leave me."

"Too late. I'm already gone."

And then she started to walk away.

Frantic, he sobbed after her, "Please, don't go. Alice? Alice, please. I love you, Alice. I need you. I love you and I can't live without you. I want to be with you. I want us to be together for the rest of our lives."

She stopped in her tracks. That's it. He'd finally been broken. He'd finally said it.

"What did you say?"

"I said, I love you. I can't imagine being without you. "

"Funny way of showing it. Did you love *her*, too?"

"No, Alice, no. God no. She's nothing to me."

"Why should I believe you?"

"Look at me, darling. I'm begging you."

"Well, that's the least you should be doing, isn't it?"

"Honestly, I love you. Look at me. I'm destroyed."

"Too bad."

"Please, angel. I need you."

"Why, Reg? Why? You didn't seem to need me a week-and-a-half ago."

"Look, what can I say? Tell me. Just tell me. What can I do?"

"I don't know, Reg. Really, I don't."

He composed himself a bit then. Looked her in the eye for the first time.

"I do love you, Alice. Look, I've got something for you. Open it, and you'll see. You'll know how much I love you."

She knew exactly what was in the box but feigned reticence. As good as she was, Alice could barely hide her pleasure.

Check.

"No, I don't think so Reg. I should go."

"Alice, please. Just open it."

"Why, Reg? Why should I?"

"Because this is something I should have given you a long time ago. Because it's meant for you. And when you see it, trust me, you'll know. You'll know how I feel and you'll know that I've changed. Trust me, just this once, Alice. Try."

"Oh, Reg."

"Go ahead, Alice. Please."

It was his great grandmother's ring, the prized heirloom of the Colter family's first fortune. Alice thrilled at the thought of his mother's bitter resignation, prying it off her cold, bony fingers. In her possession now –

finally where it belonged – the brilliant, perfect, massive diamond danced in the light, crowned with all its perfect babies.

Check.

Well, that's that. It's all over but the shouting. Now, if you just make him wait, make him really work for this, earn back his happiness. . . .

Oh, alright. Yeah, go on and train him.

After trying on "Mrs. Reginald Colter" one more time for good measure, Alice reaffirmed that for now, given her options, she could do a hell of a lot worse.

Boys will be boys, right?

Alice, girl, you've got the whole world in the palm of your hand. A very, very valuable hunk of it, at least. And he's certainly not going to screw up again. Not for a very, very long time.

So, with all the casual, dismissive reluctance she could muster, she told Reg that she'd be willing to give him one more chance.

It was crazy, she said, but she wanted to believe him. If, over the course of the next six months, he could demonstrate that he was worthy, well, she might consider his proposal. It would take time, though, for the wounds to heal. And they'd have to start off slow. Casually. Rebuilding trust. She'd need time to make up her mind. And entertain other notions.

Was he willing?

Like any condemned man, offered the faintest hope of a full pardon, he took the deal.

A New Year's engagement, she thought. Announced to friends and family around the fire. That would be perfect.

By the beginning of August the breaking of the playfully horny Reginald Colter was almost complete. When he'd paid the appropriate penance – his offerings filled her closet and drawers and dressing table and vases – she finally agreed to the occasional social outing, the odd date. Of course, Alice took pains to point out that they still weren't going steady again, that she still wasn't sure. A good boy now, he assured her he understood.

· · • · ·

Ed's left hand was damp, and the paper moon was fading as he guided her around the room for what would be the last time. Hearing their damn song – not the one they danced to, but the song the band played next – skipping now, five decades later, watching him wipe his rough, leathery cheeks dry while he shuffled through another small envelope of photographs, Alice thought of the look in his eyes.

That one moment, dancing, was the only time she'd ever seen anything like it.

It was the only time Alice Berard Harrison could ever remember her husband being that way. So absorbed. Like he didn't even know she was there.

Ed's eyes: the deep, fearless blue had gone milky, grey, afraid.

But that was understandable. Considering where he was going, right?

She was going to tell him that he had nothing to worry about, that he'd be okay.

She was going to lie.

And then the burst of harsh light washed out his face – the photographer's flash – and then she watched him blink.

And then, maybe. Maybe what? Maybe then, she started to fall in love.

Funny, though, she'd never really put it all together before. How all the accidents of that moment changed everything.

But at this moment, from the hallway of the home they'd shared for the last forty years, still with more than half a mind to shake Ed by his naked shoulders and tell him not to be such a big baby, she realizes that the faraway expression, preserved in that yellow clipping, and now replaying itself, skipping back and forth, over and over again in her memory, was not the look of a man preparing to die.

No, it was the way a strong, supremely self-confident man looked when he found himself challenging everything he believed about the world and himself, a man on the verge of asking a very difficult question. Of someone about to put their life, their happiness, in your hands.

With each new skip of the record, Alice is drawn back to that expression. She watches it form on Ed's face, and then her mind races, and then it's blinked away. "It's Only a Paper Moon" skips as well, and Ed just manages to turn her to face her father and Reg again, and his head pivots and his eyes open wide and his lips part and he's just about to speak. And then the moment hangs, suspended. And then it begins again.

In the suspension, standing so still, watching her husband from the hallway, she's amazed by her own life, all the little ironies.

My God, anyone could see that her happiness has been amazingly unlikely.

On a sweltering early August Saturday fifty-four years ago, the Colter and Berard families were both dining on the terrace of the very same club pictured in that photo. Looking at her ex, seated three tables away with a mother and father still terrified that her own parents would hear of the scandal, she decided it was time to begin the final phase of Reg's rehabilitation.

And that, of course, was why she ended up dancing with Ed.

She'd needed someone, you know. She needed to date some guy, for just a little while, to really make Reg jealous.

With lunch over, and her parents ignoring her and each other, Alice also decided that she'd much rather have Reg falling all over her heels, walking her home. She excused herself, announced her plans, and approached the Colters' table to inform him of his responsibility.

Alice told him that she'd wait outside, on the corner – for precisely five minutes, no longer – while he finished his lunch.

She couldn't have planned what happened next. Completely accidental, it was also too perfect.

When she exited the club she knew that Reg was close behind. She smiled at the doorman as he swung one of two large finely worked brass doors open onto the street. The sun was low in the cloudless late afternoon sky and the way its orange pulse burst over the buildings and through passers-by distracted her. She squinted, momentarily blinded, and tripped on the one low step and fell – right into the broad back of the soldier who stood talking to a middle-aged man and his young child.

This is how Alice Berard met Ed Harrison.

How Ed fell for her.

Because of her.

Pushed from behind, the soldier stumbled. He had to scoop up the kid before he could steady himself, and actually staggered forward and to the left a step or two with the boy, ice cream and all, pressed close to his chest. Because Alice had to cling to his back to keep from toppling herself, he had to become part human Eskimo Pie, part flying Wallenda – with enough cool and grace and equilibrium for three.

"What the hell? Watch it, buddy."

Her feet back under her, Alice disengaged. Her cheeks were already crimson, "Oh my, I'm so sorry. Forgive me, please."

Ed turned to face the most angelic voice he'd ever heard, a confused blond-headed six-year-old still stuck to his shirt. He peeled the boy off and returned him to his father. Ed's head tilted on his shoulders and his eyes narrowed, the vein in his temple still pulsing. For a moment Alice believed he was sizing her up, carefully choosing the best way to cut her down. The man was huge, intimidating; his muscles testing the limits of his uniform, set to snap.

And then he smiled, the temper of his eyes, his hard, jutting jaw, dissipating, giving way.

What an odd boy.

Ed, of course, *was* sizing up the beautifully clumsy girl. Already carefully choosing, preparing, shaping, the words he believed he'd be speaking to her for the rest of his life.

"Now, miss, like I always say, no harm no foul, right? It'd take more than a little accident to ruin such a beautiful day. Of course, that's nothing new I'm telling you, is it? I mean, you've got your Ovid says as much and more. Right? Again and again and again and inside out, am I right? But you, miss, you took yourself quite a spill there. I'm just sorry I wasn't facing the other way – so I could've, you know, caught you. I mean, why else's a tree got branches, if not to make sure the most beautiful birds don't fall from the sky. Aw, anyway, what I mean to say is, I'm good. Just great, miss. So, what about you? Tell me, now, you alright?"

Her gaze darting from Ed's happy eyes and purplish lips, down his shirt and just below his belt buckle, then down further to the little boy who looked like he might cry, holding the stump of a cone that would never again overflow with a cornucopia of thick, sugary white, and up again to the kid's father, who was caught between wanting to laugh out loud at Ed's rambling and feeling duty-bound to console his sticky, bereft son, Alice was dumbstruck.

Her mother and father barely spoke that much to one another in the course of a week. And this just isn't how polite, meaningless, accidental small-talk is supposed to go. I mean, I've never heard anyone talk like that. Who does he think he is? And the things he says. Is this guy for real?

"Miss, can ya talk? You alright? Maybe you should set yourself down on the curb here, you look a bit stunned."

"Sorry? I mean, I'm fine. Really. Thank you. Just startled."

"You sure, miss? Miss?"

"Of course. I mean, Miss Berard. Alice Berard."

Ed bowed his head slightly and his right hand brushed against the top of his pants, then his left swung out to gesture graciously while he spoke. "Miss Berard. Miss Berard. Well, Miss Berard, this here's my buddy Jack and this fine young man is Albert, his little boy. And I'm, well, I'm Ed Harrison, Miss Berard, and it's been a pleasure bumping into you."

Ed's massive right hand shot out now, in her direction. She stared at the creamy goo running down his thumb and over his wrist.

"I'm afraid, Mr. Harrison. . . ."

"Now, miss, call me Ed. Everybody just calls me Ed. Some day, maybe, if you're good, I'll introduce you to Mr. Harrison, but as far as I can see he ain't here. Right? My old man, that is."

She still hadn't taken his hand, and it looked like she was actually going to laugh. It was his turn to blush.

"Well, Mr. Harrison. . . ."

He was almost hurt: "Ed. . . ."

"I'm sorry. Ed. . . . Well, Ed . . . I'm afraid I've made a complete mess of you. . . ." She pointed to his shirt, politely trying not to look lower, then to his outstretched hand. And then she did laugh, bending down to look upon Albert's vanilla-smeared face. "Of both of you."

Ed smiled and wiped his hand on his thigh. "Well, that's no good, is it? Look at me, making a jackass of myself. Nothing new there, right? But don't you worry about a thing Miss Berard, a little ice cream never hurt no one. Right, Al? Am I right?"

He ran his sticky hand through the boy's shock of hair. The kid still didn't know whether to cry and darted behind his father's leg.

"Please, Miss Berard," Jack said winking, knowing her family's name and reputation, sounding a little nervous, too, impressed with just making her acquaintance, "don't worry yourself. The boy's fine. Actually, you can't tell the difference – he was wearing most of the stuff to begin with."

"Come now, this is all my fault," she said, looking directly into Ed's startling eyes. "I should have been paying more attention. Please, the least I can do is have those things cleaned for you. I feel just terrible. Let me just run back inside and speak with my father – he'll write you a cheque."

And then Alice tensed, supremely self-aware: Reg had skipped through the door, out of breath, just at that moment. He'd pulled up shy, dumb, utterly confused, behind her. She could tell: he was more than a little ashamed at the thought of her talking to a man in uniform – a suit his father had spent a great deal of time and effort and money making sure he'd never be fitted for.

Meekly, he said, "Alice?"

Everybody ignored him.

The soldier spoke to his girl: "Now, Miss Berard, I wouldn't dream of taking one red cent from you or your father. Listen, this little mishap's nothing that a little soap and water won't fix. Am I right, Al? Sure I am. Jack?"

"Sure."

"So I'll not hear of you worrying your pretty little head. No, don't you worry. Anyway, why'd you think the army dresses us all alike? It's so a mess like this doesn't trouble no one."

"Please Mr. Harrison . . . Ed. I insist."

"Sorry, nope. And that's that."

"At least let me get Albert another treat. They've got wonderful pastries in my club. . . ."

"Now, miss, again, I figure little Albert's had just about his fill anyway, right Jack? And if anybody's gonna get him another cone it should be me. Just for the honour of this young man's company."

"Are you sure? I really would like to do something to make this up to you, for the bother."

"Well, Miss Berard, now that you mention it," Ed said, "there is something you could do."

"Anything."

"You sure?"

"Well, certainly. . . ."

"Good. Okay Miss Berard, I figure you letting me buy *you* an ice cream should make us just about even. How 'bout that."

This was perfect. She could feel Reg's gaze boring through her, his blood boiling. "Well, Mr. Harrison, I'm not sure. . . ."

"Oh, c'mon. Call me Ed. And everybody loves ice cream, right? Besides, you said it yourself, you have to make this up to me. Can't say no, now, can you?"

"No Ed, I guess you're right. So, I'd have to say that I'd love to."

"Fine. Perfect. I'll tell you what, I really should get cleaned up. But I'm on leave all weekend, so how about tomorrow? I could come call on you. You just tell me when and where."

· · • · ·

Following sullenly behind her, Reg didn't say a word for most of the walk home. Shocked, hurt, speechless: Alice decided she liked him like this, liked him very much. All he had to do was behave himself now, demonstrate the right blend of ardent terror, humility, and patience, and she'd let him marry her.

Of course, when he finally did speak, he wasn't happy. And sure, he came on strong, wanting to know "the meaning of this" and telling her she "can't be serious." The look she shot him, and the palm of her open left hand, stopped him in his tracks.

"Remember," she said. "You still have to prove you can be my friend, Mr. Colter. And friends, I say, don't treat friends this way."

Reg lowered his eyes, then, flushed and puffed his jowls with a gust of breath, and kicked at the dirt. And that's how he was for the next eight weeks — carrying that hangdog look around the city like he invented it.

Once, it was maybe the third or fourth time she'd met with Ed, and they'd gone for a harmless afternoon walk, Reg actually managed to confront the two of them together. He'd obviously followed them into the park, had probably planned it for an entire week after Alice had mysteriously evaded and then declined an invitation to the annual ocean-side picnic his family always made a big deal about hosting: "No, Reg," she'd finally said, "I won't be able to make it. I'm afraid I've already made plans I just can't break...."

"You're kidding, right?" He almost whined. "Alice, you know I have to be there. And you should go, too. I mean, how's it going to look? We've always, you know, gone together."

"Sorry."

"So what's so important? What is it you'd rather be doing?"

"I don't think that's any of your business, Mr. Colter."

His face found a deeper shade of crimson than usual, and he bit his lower lip, hard enough to leave a worried grey line in the pink there, but he didn't press her further. Then, when he was supposed to be across town enjoying himself, probably playing touch football with some of those handsome boys who came over from Hyannis Port every summer, he magically appeared, trying to look casual, like he was simply out for an afternoon stroll. It was funny and pathetic, Reg strait-jacketed by the stiffness he'd inherited, thinking he was doing a fine job of acting both surprised and relieved to see her, but botching it terribly. And while he desperately wanted to carry off something like a smirking diffidence, it was all he could do to keep from tripping and spitting all over himself and avoid looking Ed in the eye: he was that intimidated.

Ed, of course, was both friendly and perplexed, unsure of what to make of the mixture of disdain and envy and terror emanating off Reg when he took his small hand in his meathook and said, "Pleased to meetcha, buddy, Ed Harrison."

Reg stammered, but managed to get out enough of a lie that Ed felt obliged to give him a moment of privacy with Alice: "Mr. Harrison, yes, yes. Alice has told me all about you. Yes. But, but if you don't mind. I mean, I really need, I'd like, a word with her. I've been sent, you see, and it's rather urgent. Family business. You understand. I believe her presence is requested."

"Ah, yeah, sure pal, sure."

So Ed nodded to Alice, walked away discreetly and hovered out of earshot before spreading himself out on the steps leading up to a gazebo. Alice scowled, shook her head, and lit into Reg.

"What the hell's going on?"

"So this is why you're missing one of the most important get-togethers of the summer. And with him. C'mon, Alice, what are you doing this for?"

"Reginald, I thought I'd made myself perfectly clear: this is none of your business."

"No Alice, it is my business. It is. Listen, I can't take it any more. You're making a mockery of yourself, of us. Tell me – tell me you're having a good time. I mean, look at him: he's a yokel, Alice, a farmboy. You've got nothing in common, and, quite frankly, darling, this demeans you."

"Shut up, Reg."

"I hate saying this, Alice, but the fact is you know I'm right."

"You couldn't be more wrong. Do you understand me, Reg? I have a very nice time with Ed."

"Oh please, he's not even an officer. I mean, what do you see in the guy? What is it about him that would make you snub Bobby? You know everybody's been asking for you."

"You don't want to know, Reg. Really."

"But I do, Alice. It's driving me crazy. So, tell me. What do you see in the guy?"

"You really must know? Is that it?"

"Yes, I think you owe me at least that, now, if I'm to continue putting up with this charade."

"Fine, Reg. Fine. I'll tell you. See, Reg, this is about happiness. That's right. My happiness, for once. And let me tell you, Reginald Colter, and I suggest you take a good look at that *man* over there, he knows how to make me very, very, happy."

Well, of course, all of Reg's summer colour drained from his face right then. Positively pasty, he looked like he was going to be sick. She could tell he had all kinds of horrible images dancing in front of his eyes: payback, tit for tat.

Jesus. His little girl? With him? No way.

Oh my.

"You wanted to know, Reg. And you wanted the chance to win me back. And all of this is what it's going to take – you've got to accept the fact that a girl in my position has learned, the hard way, that maybe it really is best to shop around. Do you understand, Reg? Yes, I think you do. So, Reg, maybe you should just run along. What do you say? I can tell you one other thing, you probably don't want to get Ed upset. . . ."

"So what are you telling me, Alice? Are you with him now?"

"I'm not telling you anything, Reg. Nothing. As far as I'm concerned nothing's changed. Not yet. We're still trying to be friends. I'm still giving you the benefit of the doubt, waiting to see where it all might lead. Ed, well, Ed's just another friend. You know? But don't push me, Reg. Don't make me go and decide anything right now. Because I'm not sure you'd like what I'd have to tell you."

"Fine."

Reg sidled away uncomfortably, carrying an agonizing, impotent stitch in his walk. He was, and would remain, emotionally flensed.

When Ed returned, he wanted to know if everything was alright.

"Why, yes dear. He's an old, silly friend. That's all. Unfortunately he just doesn't know that when a woman says something's over, she means that's it."

Before she'd finished saying the words she saw the transformation taking place. The thought of Reg simply annoying her, on its own, was enough to push him to what for all the world looked like psychosis.

Jesus.

"I mean, our families, you see," Alice said, recovering quickly. "Well, we used to have dealings. Our, our mothers had a falling out, so to speak. He's constantly trying to repair that rift. Wheedling at my father. Me. I think he's concerned about what it looks like, socially. But who has time for that kind of thing, in this day and age? I mean, honestly."

Ed calmed himself, all the sharp edges softened. "Oh, yeah, sure."

"Yes. Silly, isn't it?"

"You sure that's all it was, Alice? I mean, he wasn't bothering you? It looked, well, if you don't mind me saying so, I figure it looked a damn sight more personal."

"Oh no, Ed, I'd tell you. I swear."

"You sure?"

"Uh huh."

"Okay, angel. Okay." Ed shook his head again, and they both watched Reg skulk off in the distance, his body broken with the agonizing weight of a terrifyingly uncertain and carnal new world suddenly dumped upon him.

· · • · ·

And that's still how Reg looked in the shadows of the paper moon. As if watching her dance with Ed was crushing him, compacting his ego into a sullen little ball.

Alice has moved and the new perspective means she remembers that evening with such perfect clarity that it's as if she's seventeen and spinning clockwise and in that dress and being held by a man in a crisp, clean uniform. Looking into Ed's raw and expectant and vulnerable face as it was exposed by the flash, she could feel his powerful back through the military's fabric as clearly as she can see Ed now, standing bare and barrel-chested over the old stereo, finally lifting the goddamned needle.

Please, darling. Ed, please. Just turn the damned thing off, okay?

Really, my head's throbbing. Just turn it off and sit back down here with me and let's clean up this mess.

But the needle drops from fingers that have become a little less deft of late, as if the small, fine muscles of Ed's hands no longer know what to do with all that power. The new hiss of white noise that pours out of the speakers disturbs the air into forgotten undulations, causing the sparse white hair of his knuckles to sway and give.

It's starting again. The song.

Oh please, no. Ed? No.

Buddy shivers and ruffles on his perch.

Look Ed, you're freaking us all out.

But it's no use, is it? Even if she could bring herself to say these things, the way he is now, he wouldn't listen.

And then she knew that it was about to begin again, the song, that night. So, one more time. She let herself go.

· · • · ·

She remembered wondering how long it would take before Reg stood up for himself, how far he could be pushed until he'd screw up the courage to try to win her back. But while she and Ed danced she found herself praying, with all the faith she could muster, that she might get through the night without having to deal with Colter: Please, God, let him wait, for just a little while longer. C'mon, Reg, take it easy. Relax and tomorrow everything might as well return to normal.

Seeing him every time Ed turned her that way, though – how drunk he was getting with her father, how ridiculous he looked clenching his delicate fingers into a small, uncertain fist – she was afraid she'd finally pushed too hard.

Daddy, the way he was – so poisonous now, and egging the boy on – didn't help either.

Damn. Tonight, of all nights, Reg had, clearly, been pushed over the line that separates shamed disbelief and unbridled jealous rage.

For the first time since her ex and the Cow had ruined her happiness, after all the small, pleasant, happy, perfections of her subsequent plans, things weren't going her way. It's not that she regretted anything. She'd done what she'd had to – and who could blame her? But now she wanted it to stop. She had Reg where she wanted him – but she also really wanted this night to pass uneventfully, to let Ed have his last dance.

If only Reg, or her father, had known her better, maybe they'd have realized that there was nothing to worry about. Honestly, what did they think she was going to do? She liked her soldier, okay, sure, but anyone could see that's as far as it went. He was fun, kind of exciting because he was so different – the way he talked, his big arms and shoulders, his large, rough, weathered hands – and especially because, for the last couple of months, he wasn't Reggie. Ed was a great big sweetheart, and he treated her like a princess even if he was coiled, so hard and intimidating. But that's all he'd ever be, right? A sweetheart? I mean, the guy really was from a different world. And the fact was, she just wasn't going to fall for him. Not that way.

But then the flash went off and she saw all the uncertainty in Ed's face absorbed in its uncompromising clarity, disappearing, instantly, swallowed back up into his self-confidence. And as she heard the words "It wouldn't be make believe if you believe in me" for the last time, Ed stepped away from her gently, looked into her eyes and spoke and told her and asked: "I love you, Miss Alice Berard. I know that's a fact like I know my own name. And what I need to know, what I'd like you to tell me, because I'm gonna be away for a bit, is just this: would you be against marrying a guy like me? 'Cause if you said you'd have me, I swear, Alice, I swear I'd make you happy."

Okay. It's like this.

There are hundreds of reasons to turn down a marriage proposal. Probably more. But find one that works. Try it, see how excruciatingly hard it is. How impossible it seems when you've got to be the one to do it. When, like Alice, you need to open your mouth and produce the simplest little word – the most exquisitely pure statement of both intent and rejection – and you can't.

You can't because all you can think about is how trite it's going to sound.

How painful. How wrong.

Of course, you know *what* you've got to say. And that your reasons are good reasons, the best maybe. But do you really think you're just gonna say it?

Nope. No way.

And so, in the silence that hung between exhaustion and expectation between the end of "It's Only a Paper Moon," as some competent and semi-famous bandleader gulped at his drink, patted at his brow with a handkerchief and took a deep breath before announcing that he had a very special treat for the crowd – that Helen Forrest herself was in the audience, and would actually be joining the boys for their next number – this is what Alice was up against. She stood there, alone, in the centre of the dance floor, feeling like a spotlight and every eye in the place was on her, looking up into Ed's hopeful face, wondering just how she should, could, say, "No."

Oh my God, Alice. Girl, you didn't see this one coming, did you? This guy's happily going off to war in a couple of days, probably to die, and here you are about to kill him before he even steps onto the transport.

At least, that's what she was thinking then. A half century later? Well, that's different, right? A woman starts looking for signs. That's what time and memory do for you. Perspective, retrospection, whatever. I mean, nobody falls in love with the guy they're using to make the man they want to be rich and powerful with, and happily married to, jealous. And certainly not just because that guy beats your man to a bloody pulp right at your feet. Especially when the beating's that horrific. When the guy kicks your man's stinking teeth in, literally.

A girl just doesn't do that, right?

Well, no, not always. Not some girls.

Because, sure, if you want to look at it that way, put such a fine point on it, that's precisely what Alice Berard Harrison did.

But after watching her husband sitting on this ratty old broadloom, kicking the shit out of himself now, dredging up all those old memories, listening to their song, going through those yellowed letters, delicately handling the curling edges of those black and white snapshots, and cradling this damned clipping in his lap like he was still holding her on that dance floor, she also knows that it was so much more. It wasn't just a look, or a beating, or a decision. And it wasn't about disappointment, or rebellion, or embarrassment, or realizing the stuff you thought you liked about someone just wasn't the right stuff, not real, important stuff at all – though after fifty-four years you, well, you consider and accept all of these things. That maybe they all played their own little part. No, at this very second, watching Ed, having him move her beyond words, again, rubbing his salty beard as he waits for their song to transport him back, and forward, into another eternity, she realizes that until those few brief moments on that dance floor had passed she knew absolutely squat about passion and honour and conviction.

And, even less about love.

It all happened so quickly.

As Helen Forrest took the stage and the band launched into the long, beautiful intro to her trademark version of "I'm Beginning to See the Light," Reginald Colter decided he'd put up with quite enough. For such a puny little fellow he'd done a fine job of drinking himself big and mean, so why not follow the usual script and do it up right?

Um, bad decision, Reg. Very, very bad.

Alice was so lost in Ed's vulnerable eyes, her mind racing to keep up with the ruthlessness of the rejection she was trying to find the word for, that she didn't see Reg approach. When she did see him he was practically wedging himself between them. The "No" she'd started to say with a shake of her head – the word that would have begun a long awkward sentence that went something like, "No, I don't think that would be a very good idea Ed, I mean, I like you, you know, as a friend, but . . ." – changed direction, shifted its lone vowel so very subtly, and levelled itself at her interloping rat bastard of an ex: "Nnn . . . not now, Reg."

"Look, Alice," the drunk managed, "I've had just, yeah, just about all . . . all I can take." And then he actually tapped his foot and glowered, his tiny fisted hands balled deep into his very deep pockets.

"Reg, please! Sit down. I'll come over and speak with you later." .

"No, Alice! You! You go. Come! You come with me now!" He was screaming, of course, because he was angry and smashed and because the band was in full swing then. And then one of those little fists sprung out of its pocket, clawed and grabbed her by the wrist.

Helen Forrest had just begun her first line when Alice screamed back. No one in the place was paying any attention to the singer any more.

"Damn it, Reg! You're drunk! Look, I told you, I'll talk with you later!"

He was undeterred: "Nah! Nope, I'm total, total, completely clearheaded. Lessgo. Now! C'mon."

Ed spoke then, and he was the only one who wasn't yelling. Instead, his voice was eerily calm and low. But it was also clear, so razor sharp it seemed to cut through the music. Looking at him, Alice saw a man she didn't recognize, pale – dead almost – but wild. He gently poked Reg in the chest with his right index finger and said, "You better listen to the lady, pal."

Reg let go of her arm and actually seemed to stumble.

As drunk as he was, Colter believed he could still confuse the rube with reason and logic, that his parents' wealth might still convey some power and make the guy back off. He foolishly leaned closer to Ed so he wouldn't have to yell as loud.

"I know, sir. Now I know this about that. I know, for example, that you know nothing about this situation. And this, this's not your fault. You lack *in-for-mation*. S'sad. Yep. Okay? But I think she – Miss Berard here – she's been leading you on. Alice? *My* girl. Everybody knows that but you. Fact, *pal*, she's gonna marry me. *My* ring: she wants. *Mine*. Yep."

Then he grabbed at Alice's hand again and said, "So, c'mon, Miss Berard. We're gonna talk." And then he pulled her by the wrist. Hard.

Too hard.

"Ow! You're hurting me!"

A man's pupils shouldn't disappear. Lips shouldn't thin to translucent piano wire. A jaw shouldn't set that hard, and muscles, normally, just can't move a pair of arms and legs that fast and produce that much impact.

But when Reg Colter hurt Alice Berard, as Helen Forrest hit her best note, all of these things happened to Ed Harrison.

It took ten, twenty seconds tops.

Reg never saw Ed's fists ball or fire.

The first left broke his nose and he staggered forward.

Ed then fluttered this hand down to Reg's shirtfront and used it to keep him on his feet, standing nice and still and straight.

Before the blood could flow past his upper lip, the first right broke Reg's cheekbone.

The third punch simply dropped him.

Ed's polished black shoes cracked and dislodged teeth, opened a hairline fracture in his jaw, concussed his drunken brain so badly that Reg was rendered blissfully unconscious.

And then Ed's pupils reappeared, and his lips plumped, and his jaw softened, and his muscles ground to a halt.

And then the song ended.

And more flashbulbs flashed.

And then Ed shook like it was forty below.

Over the years Alice has had to find ways to forgive Ed many, many things. Drunken nights, sometimes entire weekends, with buddies and with complete strangers, dubiously fast friends; the occasional holding cell and having to make bail; getting canned – in the early days – from more jobs than she cares to remember. Bar fights and black eyes and split lips and busted ribs and a broken hand and many, many "You-should-see-the-other-guys." Pigheadedness and screaming arguments, terrifying rages that would dissipate only moments after they began. Even more terrifying silences that seemed to last forever. He'd cut off buddies for even the first hint of betrayal; he'd indulge wild, manic sprees that sometimes threatened to leave them homeless. Ed would give the shirt off his back to a casual acquaintance in need; more than one old friend fought off the DTs on that beaten old couch. He spoiled the children rotten, fostered wilful little monsters in their unfettered hearts. Taught them, by example, to desire and dream and take no shit.

And then he turned on Belle when the drugs really got her – right after she quit school. Stealing from them was bad enough, but when she started stripping, and *worse*, to put that stuff in her arms. . . . Well, that was it.

Ed Harrison would not forgive his daughter, told her she was dead to them, that they'd all learn to live with a dead daughter.

Alice tried to reason with him, wanted to get Belle help. They fought. Once, they almost came to blows. Ed raved about Belle being a disgrace, lost, a drug addict and a whore. Raised his hand, scared the budgie half to death. She'd have none of that.

Belle wasn't any better. Worse, in fact. Even more volatile.

Now they hadn't spoken – not a word – in almost twelve years.

But it was as much her daughter's fault as her husband's. More maybe, the things she said, to both of them, the lies she told, and the things she did.

Alice tried to see her, to help her, but it was no use. Belle turned on her, got violent herself.

Just like the old man – it's just that drug, you know, had robbed her of sense. Her restraint.

Alice never told her husband about the slap. The shove. She wasn't hurt – but of course, she *was*. Anyway, it was like Ed knew.

No, Belle never tried to put her life back together. Never apologized. She just gave up. Even as messed up as she was, she was still a Harrison. Stubborn as stubborn can be. Treated them like they were dead, too.

Some things are unforgivable, right? Aren't they?

Stubborn fools sometimes, the Harrisons.

Yes. Fine. Living with a Harrison, with Ed, was often a trial. But, still, Alice always forgave....

Because sometimes he couldn't help himself. Because of the sorrow he felt. Because of how he beat himself up.

Because *he* forgave *her*. Because he taught her that.

Looking down at her dress, watching floret hearts of her ex-boyfriend's blood blossom in beautifully soft *crêpe de Chine* while Ed was being restrained by almost every man in the club who wasn't her father, however, was one thing she never had to forgive him for.

How can you forgive someone for making you fall in love?

And so, while the police detained and prepared to cart away her bad soldier, and the medics milled about Reg discussing and treating his terrible injuries, and the photographers took their sensational pictures, and Helen Forrest left through the kitchen in an outrage, and the band argued about whether they should pack it in for the night, and her father tried, as drunk as he was, to spirit her out as well, ever mindful of being linked to a scandal, all Alice Berard could do was look around the swimming, teeming room and shudder at her culpability and feel bereft.

Not because she'd toyed with Reg.

But because she'd used, and lied to, Ed.

She'd repaid a pure, uncomplicated devotion with the meanest, most common sort of betrayal. And then Ed's honour and passion had beat some sense into her, shown her that up until that moment she really didn't have a clue what love actually was.

But without him – so what?

In cuffs, surrounded by Massachusetts' finest, Ed still shook: his eyes were heavy with such a palpable mortification that Alice believed it was more her betrayal, than the violence, that tore him up. Just as she was beginning to see the light, she was sure, he was plummeting out of love. Again, who could blame him?

Then, with her father tugging at her arm, making for the exit and mumbling all manner of nonsense about the poor Colters and court-martials and having to buy off the tabloids and "Army boy" and how he'll "rot in hell forever if I still have any say in this town," Alice pulled away and ran to Ed. An officer tried to block her path but he was too awed by her radiance to restrain her.

Ed was dejected, disgusted; he could barely make eye contact. The cop behind him cinched his grip on the prisoner's wrists even tighter.

Alice could only begin the words she felt she needed to say: "You must hate me. This is all my fault. I'm. . . ."

And then Ed's eyes flashed and his face flushed and he stopped shaking. "I forgive you, Miss Berard. Water under the bridge, like that sonofabitch Faulkner says. So, miss, lets us never speak of this again. Okay?"

"But—"

"But nothing. 'Cause now I know you'll never lie to me again. Right? But I still believe there was a question you were going to answer. Truthfully. Something difficult you were about to say when we were so rudely interrupted."

"Really, you still want—"

"C'mon buddy, we ain't got time for this." The cop was now shepherding him, forcefully, toward the door.

Without resisting, Ed craned his neck back to look for Alice's response. She stood motionless on the dance floor again. He yelled: "What's your answer?"

"Yes," she said. "Yes, Mr. Harrison, I'd be honoured to be your wife!"

Ed couldn't see every head turn to her as she accepted his proposal, but he felt the astonishment of a crowd of strangers. He did watch Max Berard collapse against the doorframe, however, as the cops hustled him through it. The man's face was crimson and confused and burying itself in his hands.

Ed laughed himself into the paddy wagon.

It doesn't get much better than this.

· · • · ·

Alice Berard Harrison took the leather-bound copy of that Faulkner book from her father's library on the morning she left home. She even had folded in one of his many new beautiful, white silk handkerchiefs. These things and the very copy of their song that Ed's been listening to this morning would become the presents she gave her groom. Three small gifts, one bought and two appropriated, were, along with Ed's freedom, her dowry.

Her family was worth a million bucks and she came to Ed with nothing but her love.

Daddy and Mommy – no kidding – did not approve. They both wanted Ed to be dropped behind enemy lines with a target drawn upon his back. Failing that, at the very least, they believed he should rot forever in some military prison. And, of course, the Berard name was powerful enough to make that happen.

Fine, she said, she'd be the wife of a convict.

They forbade her, of course, threatened to lock her up as well. So she left with just the clothes on her back, the book and a few bucks in her purse. Went and bought the record. Silly. All she could think of when she handed the clerk the last of her money was: I have to do this, because it *is*.

Our song.

Purposefully, Alice then made her way over to the courthouse, where Ed was being transferred, juggled actually, between the hands of civilian and military justice. When she finally found him, her soldier was joking with two others, telling them about the dance and the fight while being marched over to their truck. Ed saw her and beamed, proudly told the boys, "This here's my fiancée. The reason, I figure, I'm in this scrape today."

They approved.

And then he convinced the MPs a quick little detour to the home of a minister he knew couldn't possibly mean any trouble – from him or for them.

So what the hell?

Mischievous romantics, softened by those troubled times – they were all, well, they were all aw shucks and golly gee.

And just like that, by noon that early October day, Alice found herself married to a man she watched, from behind a barbed wire fence, get carted off into the army's makeshift stockade.

One of the MPs then came over and handed her a newspaper. "You've probably seen it already," he said, "but I thought you might like to have it anyway."

She looked at the shot of her and Ed dancing: it was their only wedding photo.

Now Mommy and Daddy really had a reason to be pissed, didn't they?

But it was done, she was Alice Harrison. It only seemed like forever, but before the sun set her father did the only thing he could do. He went down to the military base and pulled every string his wealth could pull. Within hours a senator had been contacted, and money changed hands, and the Colters were hushed, and Ed was discharged, and the fallout was contained.

Oh, and Alice was on a bus, for the first time in her life, wide-eyed and married, heading north out of the great state of Massachusetts with her new husband, disinherited.

In this way, Alice Harrison started the first day of her new life as a poor woman. Not just relatively poor, dirt poor.

Pecuniarily shunned. Effectively orphaned.

With just a dress, a book, and a song, Ed brought her to this city, to this utterly foreign place where being a Berard, for the first time in her life, meant absolutely nothing. Even he had no idea what they were going to do. His cousin, he figured, might be able to fix him up with some work, give them a place to stay for a while. *Might*.

Somehow, though the years had become a blur now, they always made do. It was a struggle, more often than not, but so what? Her mother even came around a bit, sent her a card once, and a huge shipping carton full of clothes that were no longer in fashion or even practical. Hell, the damned hatboxes that surround her? They were *in* that carton.

Strange, isn't it?

Life?

So damned precious. How it ties itself back up into neat little packages just when you least expect it, in an old record or a photo.

Or in that same old leather-bound book she'd given Ed more than five decades ago. *As I Lay Dying*. Yeah, that one. She'd tried for a year to get him to get rid of it.

At least put it back on the shelf, hon. Don't keep it laying around on the bedside table.

But he wouldn't listen or kept forgetting – on purpose. For memory's sake. For love. It was the same thing when they heard Daddy died. Jesus, it must be forty years ago now. She didn't expect to get anything from the will, and if there had been much Ed would never have accepted it. But when the amount was so embarrassingly, insultingly small, well, he couldn't complain. No, he just shook his head and rolled his eyes and said, "Yup. What did I tell you? Typical. Damned typical. Eh, Alice? Mr. Fuckin' Fancypants. Typical. Jesus. Sure I'll spend his goddamned pitiful little absolution. And I hope the SOB turns in his grave when I spend it making his little girl happy."

And that's how they raised the downpayment for this old house. It wasn't much, not even then, but she adored the place. Because it was their place.

Anyway, the way they lived was probably for the best, right? Because for the most part their struggles had always been very, very happy ones.

Not a bad life. Not bad at all. Yeah, I'll take it. Suits me just fine. And that's always been what she's thought, for better or worse, whenever she's looked at her husband.

Looking at the newspaper clipping a soldier had given her fifty-four years ago. Looking at the man Ed was then. Looking at him now, as he closes his eyes and runs a big paw through his white hair when the music, the long intro before the first words of their song, begins again. Watching his cheeks puff with air, and hearing him sigh, one word, softly, "Alice."

Richer or poorer, deep down she's always thought: "I never saw rainbows in my wine – but now that your lips are burning mine, I'm beginning to see the light."

Just like their song, she thinks. This song.

And then the phone rings and Ed lifts the record player's arm and shuts off the stereo. It rings again and he shrugs his shoulder and walks into the kitchen.

From in there she hears him say: "Hello? What's that? Hello? Speak up. Krys, my darling! How's my little girl keeping?"

Neither Ed nor Buddy can see it, but Alice still smiles from where she sits. And then she moves, follows her husband yet again. That's better, she's thinking, maybe they'll bring her by. That'll perk up his day.

9:45 AM

HIS THUMB PUNCHING THEN PINNING one of three down buttons between the bank of elevators in the Hilton's plush gold and burgundy and marble-floored lobby, Scott Venn is vacant and confused and lost and stupid and furious: a psychological oddity, a one-man freak show of conflict and indecision, he's an all-too-human encyclopaedia of the many miraculous levels and states and degrees of fuckedupness.

Uh-uh. No way. The elevator's not coming, not for him.

Scott removes his thumb on a whim of tricky benevolence, then stabs at the silver button repeatedly. Maniacally. His gouging weapon pummels the thing, hurting itself to a purpling swell, smushing the arrow, obliterating it. He finally notices its light redden: Alright already, stop, please, stop it, don't push.

Dropping his briefcase to his feet, Scott looks up at the floor numbers above the elevator, the movement of lights there. The thing's not coming to get him. It's moving higher, running away. He looks back down at the button. There are actually two of them.

And, yeah. That was the wrong one.

Looking around, feeling a thousand eyes on him, five hundred pairs of lips peeling back into five hundred vicious vampiric smiles, he blushes as crimson as the down arrow. He wants to find these assholes, tell them all to fuck off and mind their own business.

He knows, of course, that he's alone in the lobby. And that even if there were a thousand eyes on him right now they'd just see a man standing before a bank of elevators. A man with his arms folded over his chest, sighing. A casual, well-dressed man. A guy on his way up.

He pushes the up button, gently, and waits. And then Scott shakes his head and cracks wise with himself: You're losing it, Captain.

Captain?

· · • · ·

By 9:40 AM the cab had pulled out and followed the curb of the Hilton's circular front drive for precisely twenty-three feet. Then it stopped, paused, and parked with its flashers on. Frank and the kid were already walking back to their posts, two small podiums – eight-inch platforms with boxy, panelled, painted pressboard lecterns, really – that served as the frontlines of a modern and unnecessarily complicated arrivals and departures co-ordination nerve-centre. As the kid reached his post, and as Frank prepared to forge on to his identical lectern, they both stopped to stare at the twitchy guy with the white stain down his pantleg.

Scott pulled at the cold filter of his bummed smoke; he was sucking on air and hadn't yet realized. His eyes were closed and when he popped the butt from his lips he inhaled a lungful of nothing, deeply. As he exhaled he burbled smokeless monosyllabic nonsense: "Man, oh Man, oh Man."

And then he opened his eyes and looked between the perfectly manicured fingers of his left hand: the heater long gone, he held a paper-wrapped tube of cotton. He dropped it at his feet and stomped it with a fancy deck shoe.

"Shit, shit, shit, shitty, shit."

Frank nodded and cracked one corner of a tiny budding smile.

Then, of course, Scott started patting himself down again, searching for a very well-concealed weapon. Instinctively the kid covered his heart with his hand and thought: Whoa, dude, don't fuck with me.

A reborn and raving nicotine addict, Scott Venn was desperate for one last link. He needed to complete the chain before heading upstairs and throwing himself to the lions: before he heard fucking Kate Smith sing. Pocket to pocket to pocket and back, always the jock he thought: It ain't over till it's over, buddy. This is your two-minute drill. Your goalie's pulled for an extra attacker. Time for the Hail Mary. The long bomb. The half-court prayer.

The passenger door of the cab opened, and the guy in the purple Benneton sweater and red Roots jacket jumped out, flustered, saying: "Look, it's upstairs. No, it hasn't been stolen. This is a five-star hotel. It's on the chair. I remember putting it there when I changed my pants. I'll be one second."

From the back of the cab his wife, sounding like her eyes had rolled into the back of her head, said: "Well! Just hurry. We're late as it is!" And then to the cab driver: "We're so sorry." And then nasty again, to her husband: "Hurry! Now!"

"Look," he said. "Look. We're not getting anywhere without my wallet. Are we? Huh? Are we? And how about you checking your bag? You're always picking the damned thing up!"

Scott looked at him then, watched him blushing to anger. Yup.

Francis and the kid had watched, too, but they'd processed the scene already and were quite a bit more fascinated by the freak still in front of them. Especially the kid.

Hell, you see nasty little domestic dramas like this every day. But a bona fide public wanker? Jesus, that's always too good to miss.

And then Scott realized he was being stared at. Unnerved, still unable to remember what the hell he'd done with his smokes, his Winstons – no, Dunhills now, they don't make you impotent – and the big green Bic lighter he'd just bought and named Greener because he'd grown very fond of the moniker. Christ, there's still three-quarters of a deck, I just bought them a half hour ago. Think. Then he furtively checked his watch, forgetting, again, that he wasn't wearing one. Exasperated, he called out to the book-end valets: "You guys got the time?"

They both checked their wrists. Frankie looked at the kid, winked.

The kid said: "Yes, sir."

Unorchestrated, spontaneous, the beat, the pause, really was funny. To them.

Not to Scott. To them.

"Well?"

"Sir?

"The time?"

"Well, Captain. Yes," said Frank now. "The time. Let's see, Captain, it's.... Damn that can't be right, can it?"

He shakes his wrist dramatically, then taps at the crystal.

"What time you got, kid?"

The kid shows Frank his wrist.

"Damned if it ain't. Well. Time flies, eh Captain?"

Scott nods. "Yeah...."

"Well, Captain, it's exactly 9:42 in the morning. More or less."

"9:40? Already?"

"9:42, Captain. Niner. Four. Two."

"Perfect, that's perfect. Christ, there's no time. Damn."

"Captain?"

"Look, can I buy smokes inside?"

"Certainly, Captain, definitely."

"Where?"

"Well, there's the piano bar. But that doesn't open till eleven."

"Damn."

"But there's also the gift shop. Now she's open at six."

"Great. Thanks," Scott said, picking up his briefcase, ready to bolt into the hotel.

"But...."

"But? But what?"

"Well, Captain. The gift shop's run by Charlene on Fridays. Now, the poor girl's had a spot of trouble, death in the family. Hasn't been around all that much lately. In since Wednesday, though. But she's called in sick today, I hear. So they're waiting for Krystal. She's the little relief girl. Cute as a button, too. Won't get here till ten they figure, Captain. I'm sorry."

"Perfect. Just fucking perfect."

And then Scott remembered: "Hey kid, you wouldn't be able to help me out, eh? One more smoke, maybe, for the road?

The kid, who had at least another half a pack on him, shook his head no. "Sorry, sir. That was my last one I'm afraid."

"You sure?"

"Yes, sir."

"Not your day, eh Captain?" Frank asked.

"No. No, it's not," Scott said as he slapped the glass of the revolving door and entered the lovely Waterfront Hilton.

Ten paces behind him a furious husband and stepfather, carrying a Handicam and wearing comfortable sports slacks, an open Roots jacket, and a sweater, keenly fake-jogged back to his hotel suite. He was stopped dead in his tracks by the high voice of a pre-teen girl yelling out of the back window of a cab: "Hey, Rick! Rick, I'm using the cellphone! Okay?"

"What?" he barked over his shoulder, his run-for-it defeated.

"Mom says I have to ask if I can use the cellphone! I've gotta make a couple calls! Now! So, like, I'm using it!"

Rick waved his hand in bored disgust, mumbling, "Fucking little spoiled bitch." Slowly, nodding to the kid with the zits as he passed, shrugging as well in fact, he sauntered up to the revolving doors.

"Good day, sir," the kid said.

"Um-hmm. Bee-you-tee-full. Just fan-fuckin'-tastic."

Back at his lectern Frank checked a logbook, made an entry, then dug at a sharp, crusty bit of dried snot that had been driving him crazy all morning.

"Hey, Frankie!" It was the kid from his perch.

"Yup, that's me."

"What's up with that? You know, all that Captain shit?"

"You got it, kid."

"What?"

"Aw, c'mon. You saw. You got eyes, right? Twenty-twenty? You know."

"Know what?"

"Well, kid, you saw Cappy's shoes, right?"

"Yeah, so?"

"Fancy goddamned deck shoes, right?"

"Yeah?"

"Captain. . . ."

"Oh, sweet. I get it."

"Do you? You sure, kid? What about that white shit all over his pants?"

"Yeah, what's up with that? Totally, like, you know, freaky-deaky, you know?"

"Huh?"

"Whaddya think that was?"

"Birdshit, kid. And that fucking fancy-assed bastard was none other than Captain fucking Birdshit."

"No shit?"

"No, no shit. And not just any old shit. Just Captain fucking Birdshit."

. . . . .

Inside a mirror-walled elevator he's stabbing again, finally, fatally, twisting in the blade. This time the number twenty-seven on the control panel gets it. And then, before the doors close and he's carried up and away to whatever awaits, he sees the father from the cab – Jesus, the guy's actually whistling – ambling up. Scott punches the hold button. Waits and thinks: Small reprieve. I don't want to be too late, but hey, it's not like they'll start without me.

Jesus, the guy's taking his time about it. "Going up?" Scott asks, when he's still fifteen feet away.

"Yup. But you go on ahead. No rush. I'm gonna take in the scenery for a second. I'll get the next one."

"What? Really? You sure?"

"Uh huh, positive. Thanks, though, thanks a lot," Richard says, sneaking another glance at Scott's pant leg, thinking: Do I really wanna get in there with that lunatic? Nah. . . . Besides, fucking Andrea will be good and pissed that it's taking so long. She'll be late, all right, and it serves her fucking right."

"You're sure?"

"Yup."

Releasing the hold button, the door closes with a smooth glide, then the car lurches into motion. Somebody's tucked today's paper, the sports and business sections anyway, the important bits, into the polished brass handrail.

Looking around to make sure nobody will notice, he picks up somebody else's garbage. Yes, he's alone. And yes, he's still got enough of his wits about him to feel silly.

"Jesus, Captain, stay cool. Just you here, anyway. And it's just a paper. People pick up papers all the time. Nobody ever really owns a newspaper, right? You buy it and read it and forget about it. Somebody else takes it for a while. They circulate. Get thrown out eventually, then it starts again. There's nothing wrong with it. Keep your head. You're cool."

The black and white pinhole camera hidden in the standard hotel fire detection system at the top of the elevator – the one that's captured seventeen quickie blowjobs (five female, twelve male), nine instances of explosive drunken vomiting, six slaps or punches to the head, three pissed university students who couldn't or wouldn't hold it, two heart attacks, two strokes, and one conventioneer's half-baked and overly dramatic suicide attempt, in its first six months of operation – records everything: a man, with an obvious white stain down one pant leg, furtively folds a newspaper under his arm with his free hand while he slaps his briefcase against his thigh. He then scratches vigorously at his head with the same free hand and begins talking to himself.

Because there's no sound to go with these gizmos, the fat, sweaty hotel security guard monitoring fifty-nine other tiny monitors displaying black and white video feeds from all the other hidden cameras placed strategically throughout the upscale hotel, ignores Scott, takes a bite of his hotel breakfast cart cinnamon Danish, and returns his gaze to the two middle-aged maids in the hallway on the twentieth floor.

His job was better once, a month ago. For three days the hotel had given him a partner: a longhaired loser with a faceful of craters. A friend of his cousin's, he reeked of booze and was nothing short of useless, hungover for all twenty-one-and-a-half hours of his employment. But he was a good guy – company anyway. Somebody to talk to. A wiseass, for sure, but another set of eyes. Someone to have a laugh with. And, well, he'd bring in good coffee and donuts.

On the Wednesday morning of his partner's first week of work, all hell broke loose. The guy, James, a real character, comes in looking worse than usual, half an hour late. He can't drive any more and he's missed his ride. Anyway, he's not really in uniform, just the jacket, wrong pants, no tie, and he's lost his walkie-talkie. On most days: no big deal, right? Except, for the first time since they got the system up and running, the hotel manager chooses to inspect the station. Busts in just as James had doubled over the black plastic wastepaper basket. Down on one knee, a literal fountain of vomit exploded from him and into the empty trash.

The Hilton security guard was sitting there with a smirk on his face and a chocolate glazed on his desk. The manager looked at him, then at his partner, then down to his shoes. Goddamned backsplash. Bad timing. The whole nine. Anyway, the boss's got puke on his leather uppers, little bits of multicoloured candy sprinkles setting everything brown and syrupy off nicely, and James has got a lot of explaining to do. He retches once more, wipes his lips with his jacket sleeve, and mumbles something about bad donuts, food poisoning.

The hotel manager shook his head, overwhelmed by the alcohol smell coming off his employee so strong it's cutting through the puke, and said, "So I see."

James managed to throw his shoulders back and offer to clean the boss' shoes.

"No, that's fine, I'll do that myself," he said.

"You sure?" James asked.

"Yes. You just make sure you're feeling better. Okay?"

"Sure. And, I'm really sorry."

The manager was actually walking out the open door when he fired James, without looking back. He said it loud, so everyone would hear, the bellhops, the kitchen staff, the switchboard people. Yeah, he just did it, simple as that.

"By the way. You're not in uniform. You're through. Leave the premises immediately."

So that's a done deal, right? And they never get tubby another partner. Downsizing.

The fat, sweating, and still gainfully employed hotel security guard is wondering what the crazy kid's up to and taking another mouthful of his wretched hotel coffee. He coughs a little of it up, and some – not much, but some – dribbles onto his Hilton tie, when one of the maids, a surly white woman who'd been with the hotel for fifteen years, begins counting out a small roll of large bills with her friendlier Filipino partner: one hundred for me and one hundred for you. . . .

Scott's unmonitored elevator stopped at the second and third and fourth and fifth floors. Each time the doors opened to an empty hallway. When the doors opened again at the sixth floor he discovered three panting preteens, a boy and two girls, laughing and running for the emergency stairwell. He punched the twenty-seven again, then said: "Little shits, where's your goddamned rich fucking folks, huh?"

Because the elevator hangs open for longer than he'd like, he pops the door closed button for good measure. Thinking he's probably got the hooligans beat now, he stops talking, drops his briefcase, and pulls the paper from under his arm. Scanning the sports headlines, touting Philly and Detroit and Colorado as the teams to watch this season, he cracks the paper open to the opening night roundup.

Boston Bruins: projected finish. . . .

He gets that far and then drifts, unable to read. As the elevator inches up, carrying him past the seventh and eighth floors, it comes unbidden: he doesn't know what to feel as he remembers it – why he, Scott Venn, a valued subscriber, is reading this particular paper, somebody else's paper, instead of his own.

· · ● · ·

Just ten feet from the strange, messy bed, Amanda Venn sits naked at the kitchen table, bathed in a jealous ray of light.

It feels – my God, it feels divine.

Knowing she's delicious, Amanda glances up, kittenish, pulled to the liquid fire seeping through the bank of old leaded windows. At another time she might have seen the blue and black and grey of the sky or water.

Not now, not this morning.

But in the burning orange and yellow and red of her infidelity, a mass of white sits perched on the ledge. And see, the prick of two black eyes.

Hungry and ugly, the worst gull stares.

Stupid bird.

In the only other room in the whole spacious, desiccated fourth floor loft, the new man in her life sings, ridiculously, that Alanis Morrisette hit in a fake French accent: "Is she per-ver-ted like mee? Will she go down on you in-a-thee-a-terr?"

The remarkable acoustics of the shower stall give the tune a lithe, taut body, miraculous reverb. Thick walls of brick and mortar and metal and 600 square feet of concrete floor sustain it just for her.

Amanda lowers her forehead to the cool newsprint of her new man's paper and tries to stifle her laugh. She thinks: Oh, yes. Yes, she will. She certainly has.

Then she blushes.

He really is young, isn't he? Kinda dumb, too.

But Jesus, he's so sexy. At least. . . . I mean, Jesus. Is he big or what?

My God, the boy's almost twice the guy Scott is – I mean, seriously. You know, I haven't felt anything like that since college – no, in fact, seriously, never. And you just know he knows, don't you? He's not all like, you know, tell me. Not like Scott. Not, all like, you know, wanting you to tell him it's, well, um, big.

Amanda wants to stop thinking about it. Its soft contour, the way it twitches and sways in anticipation. The strangely exotic surprise of catching it unaware, the ridiculous caul.

She wants to, really.

She wants to be righteously pissed with her husband. For creating this situation. At her new man, too. It's his fault: letting her fall asleep. Falling asleep himself.

Oh, you. . . .

But her new toy's a peacemaker, the purest Ecstasy, a magic fucking wand.

Radiating, powerful, insatiable, Amanda can't remember what she was just reading. There's a field of bone and gore, the decomposing corpses of women and children lying flat and inky beneath her. A long black eyelash arches its back and purrs because the light's working tantric fingers into her neck and shoulders; the tiny hair twitches and rakes – a supple scalpel, squeaking down a length of sun-bleached femur.

Jesus, now that's a godawful sound: she snaps her head back, blinks rapidly.

Oh. Oh yeah. Kosovo. Where *he's* from.

Her new man had returned from answering the door confused, distant, surly, and Amanda decided she didn't really want to be bothered with those kinds of complications.

Besides, I've got a real fucking problem here now. So, no offence, but fuck off, kid. Scram and lemme think.

Fucking Scott. The lying little prick's gonna be freaking. Jesus, falling asleep. Here. And now your fucking hissy fit. Damn.

He'd growled something about his brother and being late, looking for sympathy. She rolled her eyes, bit into her lower lip, and said nothing.

Uneasy with her distance, her cool, calculating focus on all the possible variables presented by the day at hand – too young to appreciate a beautiful, naked, thirty-five-year-old woman sitting on his bed, arms wrapped around calves, fingers interlocked, chin resting on perfect knees, deep in profound, vengeful thought, skillfully orchestrating seamless damage control – he became embarrassed, solicitous, fawning. He sat beside her and stroked the small of her back, made silly little whispering jokes which she ignored, told her she was really fucking hot.

None of his manipulations worked, of course – Amanda had no practical use for him.

But then he leaned behind her and, propped on one elbow, kissed the small of her back. A soft, wet butterfly; the tiniest little lick.

Her mood brightened considerably.

He thought everything changed with that single, exquisitely romantic gesture, just like it's supposed to.

Yup, no matter how you cut it, chicks are easy. Yeah, you know, erogenous zones and all.

Anyway, she let out the cruel sigh of pleasure he'd intended to produce, and her new man, Stephan is his name, seized the moment to bounce up off the bed thoroughly pleased, utterly convinced he'd regained control. Feeling magnanimous and powerfully validated, Amanda's new guy picked his coffee up off the floor and handed it to her, grabbed the sports section from the paper, said, "I'm going for a quick shower, babe, and then I've gotta run," rubbed his hard, hairy, rippled belly through blue terrycloth, and then padded off to the can.

Watching his ass wiggle away on muscular pins, just hidden by the hem of his robe, Amanda sized him up immediately and knew precisely what he was thinking. She decided to let him believe that a sloppy, stubbled peck, there, could push her buttons.

Okay kid, whatever.

Of course, what really happened had more to do with bug-eyed incredulity, the mesmerized, Pavlovian jaw-dropping of the newest winning ticket holder in the great physio-sexual lottery, than with *Cosmopolitan* romance or the new *Chatelaine* sensuality. Because no, Stephan's cold purple lips hadn't rocked her world. When he'd leaned back, however – Jesus.

Even the intensity of her focused, angry, matriculating glare couldn't stop her – despite being so annoyingly peripheral – from noticing that her new man's movement had parted his robe.

And – oh my God – what a cock.

I mean, seriously, the fucking meat on this guy.

So now she sits, naked and illuminated, golden, at his rickety kitchen table, drinking his coffee and reading his paper, amused with the puzzlingly essential familiarity of morning rituals: boy scratches something and takes sports section to the bathroom; woman reads hard news and thinks about making a little bit more of the world all hers.

Chumps.

Amanda wants to focus harder on the real life horror story in front of her face: the words are rudimentary, levelling, primal; the picture's iconic, a perfect, democratic piece of the larger one that's always in her head. Together they are, in fact, exactly what she is at this very moment: redemptive, chaotic, vindictive, and perverse.

But that thing. That thing, she thinks, comes from there. That's where it was made.

When she first met Stephan, seven weeks ago, his cock was like every other cock: an inconsequential biological assumption. A functional necessity, neither large nor small. The drug store he worked for was one of the many branches belonging to the huge corporation that had just become her new client. As the new regional head of sales and distribution, she was making the rounds, meeting the managers who'd buy her father's pharmaceuticals.

Amanda arrived at this particular PharmaPlus at just before eleven on a Friday morning; she was a half-hour ahead of schedule, and hoped to quit early, get a head start on the weekend. The manager was in another meeting.

It was a large, muscular boy – Stephan/Assistant, his blue and white name tag read – who looked at her and smiled and offered her a chair, actually an Obusform display, while she waited. He smiled harder then, watching her from behind the counter. She sat and self-consciously spun her wedding band and engagement ring in counterpoint and tried to avoid his gaze.

Christ, he was staring.

Perv. What the hell're you looking at?

A squat, red-faced, and bald dumpling of a man ambled up and cleared his throat nervously. Grateful, Amanda looked away while the guy whispered to Stephan/Assistant. She heard him sigh and then she heard the squeak of his Vans as he walked from behind the counter. He floated by in a cloud of musk with the embarrassed little man shuffling behind and she looked up and watched as the two of them disappeared down the aisle marked: Eye Care/Feminine Hygiene/First Aid.

Fucking guys.

As soon as they'd disappeared one of the three women who were still behind the counter whistled low, said, "My, my, my, what unbelievable buns," and chuckled. Amanda looked up at the huge, pink-faced blonde and, triangulating where her hound-dog gaze dissipated, knew she was talking about her younger co-worker. The blue of her name tag read Bonnie/Associate Pharmacist and she was a few pounds – okay, at least a hundred, she jiggled as she laughed – over the ideal medical body weight for a person of her stature. Her skin was stretched into something like a youthful glow, so Amanda couldn't tell precisely how old she was. Fifty? Sixty? Old enough to be the kid's mother, anyway.

"And Jesus, Lord, what a package," Bonnie/Associate Pharmacist said, wheezing, slapping a downright ugly grey squirrel of a teen, who wore the name tag Krystal/Jr. Assistant, on the back. "You seen it, didn't ya, Krissy? Didn't ya?"

Krystal/Jr. Assistant puffed her soft fuzzy cheeks, squinted the beads behind her purple glasses, and then grinned from ear to ear. The huge pink woman looked Amanda over and decided she was okay.

"What about you, hon? You get an eyeful when he walked by, or what?"

Oh God, Amanda thought, now she's talking to me. She shrugged her shoulders, pretty much thoroughly bored, and fought back the words: Shit, lady, you are one fat fucking horny old broad, you know that?

Still, Amanda smiled the polite smile you smile in these situations, the smile that says: Yes, whatever, and now, please, fuck off.

The other woman behind the counter, small, prim, and silver-haired, huffed and shook her blushing head. "Excuse me, ladies, but I'm going to get change," she said as she stormed off.

Amanda watched this name tag – Mrs. James/Assistant – speed by purposefully as Bonnie/Associate hectored the retreating little woman who wore an impeccable white lace blouse under her starched lab-coat: "Oh, don't be such a stick-in-the-mud, Maria! I've caught you looking, too!"

Actually, Amanda realized she didn't notice; it never even occurred to her to look for – at – that.

Why? I mean, what's the point?

But once the idea was planted. . . . Well, she couldn't help herself. Who could? So, when he returned. . . .

There's a hell of a lot of truth to one of the little life-lessons Amanda overheard Bonnie/Associate giving Krystal/Jr. Assistant that day: "It's not the revenge fuck that's gonna blow your rat fuckin' bastard of an old man's mind – it's when you tell him, casually, about the extra five fat fucking inches."

Smiling to herself, Amanda hears Bonnie's voice now, remembers how she licked her lips when she looked at her squirming against the backrest, shook her head, and said: "Any less than that? Girl, it's not worth your fucking while, is it?"

She lowers her head again, rubs it "No" against the newsprint killing field, and stifles another laugh.

No, it's not.

It doesn't matter that the bloody grey newsprint torso of a child has seeped into pores hidden amongst her eyebrows, or that shrapnel from someone's grandmother's fatal bullet wound is smeared, when Amanda sits back up in her chair and sips at her coffee and rubs away a dribble with the back of her hand, around the petal of her luscious mouth. The day and the sun love dirty faces, and in this light Amanda Venn is just like every other earthbound angel: utterly terrifying and terrifyingly wrong.

Until this morning the revenge she'd been exacting had taken the form of subtle, well-hidden little time bombs, measured and tiny, but deadly in their precision. She thinks of it this way: Scott's childish obsessions grew exponentially, from haunting fucking strip clubs, to stalking that French bitch, Colette, to fucking Margaret motherfucking Chisholm. Therefore, she realized, in order to level the emotional playing field, she would have to hurt him slowly, methodically, and in kind: tit for fucking tat.

A month ago, when she discovered the note in the way she discovered all his pathetic little secrets – by opening a bottle, pouring herself a nice glass of wine, and leisurely snooping through his desk drawers while he was out throwing twenties at nineteen-year-old lapdancers – she came to a series of quick, ruthless decisions.

The square of yellow legal paper read simply: *Hilton / meet / Friday 10 AM / Margaret C. v. Me!!!* And of course, that was enough.

His shorthand? That cunt Chisholm, "visiting" him in a hotel room, obviously.

And three exclamation marks?

Oh, she's fucking him all right.

Fine, okay? Fine. So here's what I'll do. First, hey, accept no responsibility. None. Not for this. Then, get as much of the money out of him as you can. Set yourself up for the future. Find yourself the stud that's gonna rip his guts out: younger, better-looking, bigger. One that's not too fucking impressive, not too smart or successful or anything, 'cause this is all about you, hon. Just make sure he's a ripped, sexy motherfucker, and way more studly. An obvious, glorious funboy. A huge, hard, wonderful toy. One who worships the ground you walk on.

Then, finalize everything with the kind of unbelievably luxurious escape that's gonna make the sonofabitch green. And, oh yeah, don't forget to sweet-talk Daddy – make sure he's good and pissed, too, and that the fucking barracuda he calls a lawyer's retained and loaded for bear.

Now, at her new man's kitchen table – the delicious boy she remembered and picked out, and up, the day after she discovered Scott's pathetic exclamation marks – Amanda thinks: It was almost done, almost perfect. All over but the shouting.

Reading this particular copy of a newspaper that was also delivered to her home, accidentally camouflaging herself with the very same, but, oh my, such very different ink, everything avenging and angelic in her means only she understands how tragically funny this all is. It was this newspaper, after all, that caused Scott, finally, to crack – turned everything pitifully banal and immature about him inside out, pushed his obsession over the edge. He might have been a pig before, bone stupid, lazy, even occasionally frightening in his temper – but he was always predictable; a low-maintenance husband, you could count on his shortcomings, know his limits and limitations, and trust in his essential loyalty. For some reason, Amanda knows, indulging fucking Colette and his newspaper paranoia gave him licence to explode his life. Their life.

Well, uh-uh, no way, José. Not in my airforce.

And until last night she'd taken care of business, hadn't she? It was this close to being done, and Scotty didn't have a fucking clue.

All I had to do was get home by three, but fuck, no, whatshisname let's me fall a-fucking-sleep.

I'm here and I shouldn't be and everything I've set up for myself's gonna be ruined by this pair of idiots.

Even Scott will have figured this out. Right? Even he's gotta realize he's being played. No matter how drunk he was after the fucking stag. When he finally stumbled in and discovered I wasn't home he would've listened to the message and figured I was at my folks. Figured something was up. He'd know that I know and he'd freak. He would've called, tentative and apologetic. But Mom would give me up; say, no, I wasn't there. She'd be cold and not let on too much, but she'd say she was worried. And then he'd freak even more. So then he's probably phoning everyone I know. And when he couldn't find me? Total paranoia time. He'd start looking for other clues. Oh yeah, he knows now, and he's royally pissed. Fuck, he probably started checking the joint account first thing this morning. Yeah, my Scotty knows, Christ, that a lot of our scratch has gone missing.

Fine, it's not ideal, but it's gotta be today.

Amanda rolls her neck and her body thrills at the warmth there, then balls up her fists, rubs her eyes a little more grey than they should be. Okay, this is it. She braces her hands flat on the newspaper in front of her, pushes herself back in the chair, and stands.

The sudden movement doesn't give the sunlight enough time to react and it's unable to follow her. She's left a little cold, in shadow, and her glow falls away. Amanda shivers, walks to the bed, snaps on her thong. The sexy little black bra.

Outside, the worst gull squawks its delight as she pulls last night's tight little blue dress over her head. Amanda looks beaten, raw, filthy. My, she's just a little ugly, uglier, now, in this light – isn't she?

In the shower, Amanda Venn's other man is still singing. She's more than a little irritated, tousles her smoky hair, sneers. Tell me again: what's he good for?

That's it, perfect – yes, yes, this is the light. Hold that pose. The bird nods, clucks satisfaction, approval: a sick old master who chooses models very, very carefully.

She shrugs and picks up her other man's cell phone.

Damn, I said, hold it.

It's always darkest, Amanda thinks, and then punches in her number. The singing's stopped and so has the water. Her other man starts the hair dryer. She picks at the patch of dry skin on her elbow while the phone rings: tell me it's not the eczema coming back.

Scott doesn't pick up; she's pacing a very small circle while the message plays, deciding she'll cop to everything and end it now, for better or worse.

And then she crosses into the path of the sunbeam and everything changes, back to the way this glorious day's supposed to be.

Warm, beautiful, thoroughly angelic, Amanda Venn presses the star key and enters her password. She sits at the kitchen table again, smiles. And, yes, she listens to Scott's message.

Man, oh man, he really is a stupid boy, isn't he? He really hasn't figured anything out; he's just whining, terrified, his big fat paw stuck in the cookie jar. Dupe. Can you imagine? I mean, seriously. How does anyone get to be that fucking dumb, that wrong?

She erases the message and hangs up, completely in control again, deliciously happy as her other man opens the bathroom door and walks toward her, swaggering, tumescent. He grabs the back of her head firmly, but moves it gently into his hard abs.

"You are beautiful, my angel," he says, stroking her hair.

She feels him pulsing through the fabric of her dress, and thinks, Jesus.

"And I want you now, angel. I do. But I must go to work. I'm sorry, but you understand. I'll call somebody to take you home."

Amanda wants to say: Whatever. You go. Just leave that thing with me, alright? I mean, you're not using it, so what the fuck? She snickers against his belly and pushes him away; she narrows her eyes as she looks up at him, pouts cruelly. As she speaks the light dims, a cloud distracting her secret admirer.

At least the gull's happy.

"Listen, get dressed," she says. "And hurry up. You're gonna take me home first."

"What? What about your husband?"

"Him? Forget about it. He's probably not there anyway."

"But what if he is? What about the neighbours?"

"Yeah, so? Listen, Steve, you'll take me home. I mean, even if he sees you drop me off, so what? You're nothing but another cab driver, lover. You're nothing to him."

Stephan Vlastic says nothing as he's pulling on his Joe Boxers. Amanda recoils slightly at something she smells. What is that? Is that me?

And then her light returns, the cloud's dissipated.

No, it's him. It's him on me. Yes, she thinks, mmmm, that's just about right. That's just about enough. Maybe it's time, maybe this is as good as it gets.

Yes, maybe it's perfect like this.

"I'm ready."

The memory already much more impressive than the real thing,

Amanda's drifting. Hoo ha. As good as it gets.

"Amanda?"

"Huh? Oh, okay, Stevie," she says, almost laughing at him, "your first fare's ready."

"Yes, of course, Amanda." She doesn't notice his tone darken when he adds, "I'll take you home."

· · • · ·

Unbidden: the memory of her and what he'd done.

Fucking Colette.

It had happened so fast, so incredibly automatically, that for the last hour Scott had completely forgotten the incident.

He was out back, at home, when he heard the cab riding its horn. Steady, purposefully, he marched around the side of the house, eyes levelled, staring at the ground before each of his steps.

As he pushed open the unlocked high side gate he saw his ride and waved, actually began to pick up his pace so the guy wouldn't disturb the whole neighbourhood. And then his pretty damned athletic peripheral vision caught it: there she was, furtive, on the Venns' front porch like a rabbit caught in the Plymouth's headlights.

Colette. His thirty-eight-year-old next-door neighbour. Colette, the painter. From France.

Now, Scott normally thinks of himself as a pretty neighbourly guy. When the old dude, whatshisname, two doors down, had his coronary Scott offered to mow his lawn. Once a week he did it, too, all fucking summer. Signing petitions, shelling out good treats for the little local kids at Halloween, sponsoring bike-a-thons for this charity and that, inviting the neighbours over for barbecues – he weighs in, every time. And, for the most part, Scott enjoys his neighbours. They keep to themselves, pretty much, don't get in the way. Nice folks, generally. So, since he and Man have lived in their house everything's been pretty smooth, neighbourly without being intrusive. Except for one annoying little thing.

Twice a week, on average, for the past three months, somebody's been stealing Scott's fucking newspaper.

Look, at fifty goddamned cents a pop, who'd do something like that? No one, right? You figure? Not in this neighbourhood.

Well, that's what Scott believed, too. In fact, at first he blamed it all on a kid he called "the shiftless little paper fuck." The first time it happened twice in a week he phoned the circulation and delivery desk and complained.

"Look, I'm not getting my paper. The kid's just not delivering it."

They promised to investigate and remedy the situation. Assured him that it wouldn't happen again. Later that day, another copy of his paper was hand delivered by a guy in a truck, neatly tucked into a blue plastic bag. Inside, neatly folded and signed by the acting circulation manager, there was an apology for the disruption of his vital service, and another promise that the matter had been resolved.

Next Friday: same deal. Scott gets up, goes to the porch, no paper. He was miffed, but too busy to do anything about it. And then his big Saturday edition went missing in action, as well. Outraged, Scott called again, threatening to cancel his subscription if they didn't provide him with a more reliable delivery kid.

Three-and-a-half hours later the kid, maybe thirteen but probably eleven, a wary, sweet-faced black child with his Bulls cap in his hand, is ringing Scott's doorbell. Next thing he knows the kid is apologizing, super politely, and swearing that he'd had that morning's paper on Scott's doorstep by seven AM.

"Sir, maybe somebody's stealing it?"

At first Scott thought: Yeah, right. Listen, you little bastard, who'd steal my fucking paper? I know these fucking people. They're my fucking friends. But then he saw how upset the child was, that he'd been reamed out by his boss, and he knew the little guy was telling the truth.

Well, I'll be damned. Shit on me.

Next few days, Scott's up early enough to get the paper. Actually intercepts the kid at the door for almost a week, sweat pouring down his serious face from under that Bulls cap. Each day he sees him hauling a bag of maybe a hundred more of the things. Actually bowed under the weight, in this heat. Scott feels bad, realizing how hard the boy's been working. And for what? Like, nothing, right?

And I, shit, call him a little prick. Rat him out without knowing who the hell he is. What a bastard. Shit.

Then he decides to perform a little test.

Next day, he's up and watching the kid from behind the curtain. Yup, he puts the paper where he always does, there on the porch.

Then Scott goes into the kitchen for a cup of coffee and some cereal. Takes his time, maybe half an hour tops. Finally, deciding he's given it long enough, he heads for the front door. Sure enough, the paper's gone.

Jesus. Somebody *is* stealing my fucking newspaper. One of my neighbours, in this fucking neighbourhood – one of these white middle-class bastards – is actually ripping me off.

It was so difficult for Scott to believe that for almost an hour he couldn't get his mind around the idea of trying to figure out who it might be.

Christ, I'm good to these people. Right? Good enough, anyway. They like me. Right? We say good morning. Hello and shit, right? I help 'em out when I can. Me and Man know everyone around here.

We're like them, for chrissake. They're our kind of people. Everybody. Except that French bitch, whatshername?

Colette. Colette something fucking unpronounceable.

Colette had moved in eight months earlier, rented a place from the woman who'd lived there for the last five years. Nice, quiet lady. Filmmaker or something. A five-year-old daughter. Missy? Crissy? Krystal? Something. Nice kid, too.

Anyway, she gets a gig in England, working a documentary, and she's gone for a year. So she leases out her place to this freaky painter chick. Some big deal thing in Europe that's gotten a big fat endowment cheque to allow her to work here for a year. And she's always filthy, covered in oil and acrylics, usually babbling away to herself in French in the back yard while she works. Painting the fucking beach, the birds, the water. Goddamned ugly paintings. Don't look like nothing, mostly birdshit grey and brown. Sometimes a black and white photo glued on here or there, then covered with all kids of muck. Paint just slapped all over. No picture at all.

When she moved in, him and Man, well, they tried to be nice. Right? Invite her to a barbecue even. Offer her a glass of wine in the yard. How about a Grolsch?

And the bitch mumbles to herself, doesn't even acknowledge them. Treats him and Man like they're fucking scum.

Well, fuck you, lady. Fine.

Whatever, right? They just ignored her, the whole neighbourhood did – counted the months until she'd be gone and the filmmaker'd be back.

And then his newspapers started disappearing.

So, on that day, when he'd confirmed that someone was ripping him off for a buck and change a couple times a week, Scott decided it had to be Colette.

Day after day he'd try to catch her. Obsessed, he'd sit at the door, staring at the paper like it was bait. Anticipating the confrontation, he'd dream about reaming her out. Hell, some mornings, if there wasn't too much on his plate, Scott would actually put off heading in to work and just sit and wait and imagine all the things you never think of when you need to say them. He'd talk to himself, rehearse his anger. Add to and edit his tirade. Yeah, he'd sit and wait for the thing itself to skulk up the porch. Of course not every day, but often. Too often.

But he never could catch her. It was like the Roadrunner and fucking

Wile E. Coyote. You know, inevitably, Man'd call him into the kitchen. Or he'd have to piss, or the phone would go. And the paper would disappear without him finding out who was doing the stealing. Other days it would just sit there. For hours. Until he finally gave up, brought the damn thing in and read it himself.

Soon the weeks had become two or three months of this shit, and, well, Scott's life had changed. Radically. More drunkenly. Criminally.

By the fall he had more time on his hands, but had to look much busier. There were other, more pressing, much more dire concerns. So he gave up on the hide and seek, amateur stake-out shit. He forgot all about catching Colette. Man had even noticed, and she was almost worried at first. Then she chalked it up to an improvement in his overall mental health and began to indulge new, wilder, ridiculous suspicions.

"Scott, are you having an affair?"

Funny.

"Jeez, Man, no. You crazy? Me? No way."

Then, today, on the worst Friday morning of what had become his whole shit-for-luck life, without his house or car keys, late for an important meeting, for his own fucking funeral for chrissake, waiting to be hauled off to jail, waiting for a cab to ferry him to his doom, a car horn honked and he pushed, completely oblivious, through the stained pine door that led to his back yard.

Today, of all days, he caught his thief. He saw her: Colette.

So, who could blame him for blaming her for everything?

Crouched on his porch, wearing a fuzzy pink robe, with his newspaper in her hand, Colette something unpronounceable, the new neighbour, froze and stared at Scott. He did a double take and stopped and stared back. She looked like a kid with her hand caught up inside the trap door of the big prize candy machine.

Uh-oh.

Scott did three things then. First, he gently placed his briefcase down on the grass. Next, he waved at the cabdriver, raised one finger and shouted, congenially, "One minute!" And then, finally, he went fucking ballistic.

Before she had time to move he'd bounded across the lawn and up the steps of the porch, right in her face. And before she had time to formulate anything resembling an excuse in her terrible English, or even a cogent, remorseful apology or explanation in French, Scott was screaming the vilest abuse. He raged words that, even if she could've really understood his language, were more hateful than any others she'd ever heard in her life. Louder and louder, more and more aggressive, his anger, his beet red face, pushed her back until she was pinned against the Venns' front door. Her toes trembled in her idiosyncratically mismatched, but bizarrely similarly paint-spattered, fuzzy pink and baby chick slippers; she shook so bad that she caused the fibres of the Venns' welcome mat to pogo in sympathy. And still Scott came on.

"You fucking thieving cunt. What kind of stupid fucking bitch steals a guy's fucking paper?" Scott's foul, smoke and beer-loaded spit bit into her shamed face, and then he got louder. "You think I was too fucking stupid to notice? Is that fucking it? You fucking bitch!"

"Mais—"

"What? What! Speak fucking English, you fucking piece of shit frog skank thief!"

"But—"

"You cunt! You're fucking lucky I don't call the fucking cops, you know that?"

"Je suis—"

"What the fuck did you call me? What?"

"I . . . I . . . I—"

"You goddamned ugly fucking cow! You make me wanna fucking puke! Shut up! You can't even read fucking English, can you? So why're you stealing my fucking paper? Cunt! You ugly, stupid fucking cunt! Now! Get the fuck off my fucking—"

"But—"

"Shut the fuck up! Or, I'll fucking shut you . . ."

"I am—"

". . . up myself!"

"—apologies."

"Fuck you!"

And then Scott snatched the paper from her hands. Left her there, trembling, and stormed off to the cab. Of course, even in his anger he realized he'd forgotten his briefcase. He turned, still a rageball, and stormed back. He was vibrating too now, the smallest thing might make him do something, well, something, probably, regrettable.

Her small, terrified voice again called to him, mustering all the English she had. "I learn. The English. News. TV. Paper. Apologies. I thought . . . free?"

Disgusted, galled that she'd even dare an excuse, Scott really screamed now. Neighbours peered through windows. The cabby looked up from his paper. Deep inside the house, even, the budgie hid his head under his wing.

"How can one woman be so fucking ugly and dumb? You poor

pathetic bitch! Learn? Free? What-fucking-ever! And fuck you! Go fucking home, you stupid fucking frog ho. Get off my goddamned motherfucking porch!"

And then Scott did it.

He took the rolled up Friday newspaper in the electric fist of his right hand. And then his whole arm reared back, fluid, automatic. And then it moved forward, fast, accurate. And then he let go. And then, a very capable pitcher, he followed through.

Colette didn't really even see it, though she instinctively turned her head before it struck.

· · • · ·

There's a ping and the doors glide open. Scott's arrived. The twenty-seventh floor. He looks up from the paper he's not reading, and hurriedly stuffs it back under his arm. Picking up his briefcase he sighs and takes a step, to the left, out of the elevator.

Whoa, Captain. Stop.

There are two cops, in full uniform, standing very close to one another, whispering, right outside the door of the meeting room he's supposed to enter.

Oh fuck.

One of the cops glances over at Scott, then turns back to her partner and laughs.

Oh fuck fuck fuck. Stay cool.

Scott walks toward them, maybe ten feet, then turns to face a mirror on the wall. He puts down his briefcase again, then runs his hand through his hair and adjusts his pale yellow tie. His right eye watches his left eye twitch. And then something to his right, to the other side of the elevator, demands his attention. His peripheral vision, again, thank God. A brass pole, such a familiar object, one of the so very many he's known. This one, though, is supporting a square sign instead of tanning-booth brown and crossed and spinning legs.

The sign makes everything just about as okay as it's ever going to be. It reads: "Morality seminar."

Good. Yeah. Right. Fine. Okay.

Not for you, Captain. They're just cops. Cops who happen to be here. In fact, there's, you know, cops everywhere.

Not always just for you.

He looks at his arm again, checks the white oval in amongst the slightly tanned skin and bleached-brown hair. No help there, of course.

Am I late? Early?

168

He sighs and turns his head to assess the cops. Considers them. Considers asking.

He looks back to the mirror: Buddy, what're you gonna do?

Hell, at least I look together. Relatively speaking. Good shirt, nice tie. Great jacket. Hair's alright, too. A little red around the eyes, a little unshaved, but it's a fine, relaxed look. Right, Captain? One Amanda likes.

Oh Christ, Man. What am I gonna do when you call?

Scott Venn sighs, resolves to confess everything to his wife. To ask for her forgiveness, to admit he's in trouble and that he needs her help. He swears to himself that he'll make it better.

I love you, Man.

But first, there's the small matter of Margaret. Of being fucked. Of jail and bail and however that works. Should have paid more attention to that criminal stuff in school. And I'm gonna need an attorney for sure. A better one than me. Much better. But Jesus, Man, I love you. We'll get through this. Don't be angry, I'm sorry. Baby, I'm sorry.

"Hey, you guys got the time?"

The cops look Scott up and down and then look at each other. The woman makes to check her wrist but the guy beats her to it.

"Ten, almost."

"Thanks a lot."

"No problem, buddy."

Scott picks up his briefcase, rolls his neck and walks past the officers. He stops in front of the first door behind them, takes the handle, and turns it. Inhaling deeply before putting on his best smile, he pushes the thing open and walks through just as they begin to laugh.

· · • · ·

Drinking the last dregs of his stale, cold cup of coffee, the fat, sweaty security guard intently watches the monitor which features a slow-moving middle-aged guy who's carrying a wallet and wearing slacks and one of them Roots jackets and a nice warm purple sweater. You'd have to say the guy's, well, he's still sauntering, heading back down the hall towards the elevators.

The security guard had already followed this guy into his room. It was a two, three minute wait before he reappeared, wallet in hand. What the fat, sweating toady in the control booth had been dying to find out was, simply: would he bust out freaking?

He can't see them now, but he knows the maids have already moved two and three rooms down. He also knows the doors will probably be open. Yup, they'd definitely be suspects. Hopefully they hadn't totally cleaned him out.

Oh Christ, he thought while the guy was still in his room, this might ruin my morning.

Wait, there he is. Okay. A slow, happy bounce to his step. Sauntering.

Nope. I don't think he's noticed. Fuck it. Not my problem.

He watches the guy until he gets back into the elevator. Then he switches to another monitor, another fire detection spycam, just to make sure the guy's not playing cool and really heading down to his station to report something. He even watches him put the wallet he'd been carrying into his back pocket.

As he's getting up, about to leave his post to ostensibly get another coffee, but really to avoid any possible hassle, he notices the guy's smiling and, Christ, whistling.

Dupe. Ha ha. Fucking chump.

Sweating less that he's outside now, about to cross the street and head for the 24-7 donut shop because thinking of his fired, fallen comrade has made him crave sprinkles, the amateur voyeur, professional security guard looks back to see old Frankie and the kid watching the sweater guy getting into a cab.

As the passenger side door of the cab opens he hears shouting from the back: "Rick! What took you so long! Do you know what time it is! It's already after ten!"

And then the sound is cut off by the slamming of the door. Frank and the kid look at their fat friend and chuckle. He shrugs his shoulders and shuffles, no, saunters, out between traffic, thinking: Large, double double. Raised Hawaiians and crullers. Crullers, yeah. Maybe a box of 'em.

· • • • ·

Pulling out of the Hilton driveway, the improbable song on her Sony CDman turned up to eight to drown out Rick and her mom, Krystal sees the hint of a fat, sweaty security guard's ass crack as he's shuffling across the street.

Look at the child, grimacing and closing her eyes and escaping into the voice, the chords. But what should be "Wannabe," or liquorish All Saints, or a crushing fondness for the Backstreet Boys – even an outcast's pathetic reclamation of throwbacks, the Eurythmics and the like – doesn't drain up through the fancy gizmo and out into her sweet little gold-studded ears. Somewhere, someone's turned her on to the hard stuff, and the girl's already got herself a nasty habit. She relaxes with the hit, and Marilyn Manson sings.

"Sweet dreams are made of this. . . ."

Thinking about just what to pierce first, she shudders and curses her father, her real one.

Why, Ted? Why are you doing this? If you can't, how the fuck can I?

10:44 AM

COFFEE TIME. Still Coffee Time.

Peter's whispering a monosyllabic apology to the two women behind the candyapple counter he's staring at but trying not to focus on. Tiny scratches in the Formica confuse him, make him seasick. Too soon for this kind of detail, not good.

"Sorry, flu. Thought I was over it. Better now."

The younger one rolls her eyes and pops her gum as she walks away, telling her partner as she goes to check on the delivery of the next batch of donut bits, "Vera, just remember, it's your turn to clean the can."

Vera touches Peter's scrubbed pink hand, keeps her voice low so only he can hear: "That's okay, darlin'. Feeling better, really?"

"Yes. Thanks. Thank you. Another, another coffee, please."

"You think that's a good idea, sweetheart? You still look sick. I think you should be home in bed."

"Can't. Appointment, quarter past eleven. Please, coffee?"

"Okay, darlin', okay. Just take it easy on yourself is all. You know, you remind me of my Ralphie. Oh, he's only fourteen, but he's big and shy like you. You Ukrainian? Can't tell, you know, your hair's so dark. He doesn't stop for anything, you know? Never lets his illness run him down."

"No. Coffee? I mean, please. And, uh, what's wrong with, uh, him?"

"Pardon, darling?" Vera's pouring him another large cup.

"Your boy. You said he's sick."

She's very sombre now, drifting herself. "Ralphie? Ah, he's got a liver disease. It's bad, but we make do. Doctors say a transplant might work and he's on the list. So, you know, we pray. And wait. Yes, we wait and we pray."

"Oh." Peter lifts his eyes from the blurred counter but has to look away from the greying, ponytailed woman who's staring at him so empathetically – and even, sorta, rapaciously.

Jesus.

Fishing in his right pocket for another dollar's worth of change to pay for his coffee, Peter hooks five quarters and a dime and his watch. He

171

picks out the buck with his left hand and closes his fist tight around what's left: wait, that's wrong.

Vera's still devouring the man she hopes her boy might live to be and smiling. She doesn't notice that he can't look at her. "Darling," she says, "this one's on me. You just get better, okay?"

Peter half-hears her, thinking, trying to, at least: How'd my fucking watch get over there? He manages, or something directs him, to say, "Uh, yeah. Thanks."

Happy, frail and red and yellow, Vera walks the length of the counter to the back room. When she opens the door and stoops to pick up a bucket and a mop, her younger partner asks: "Did you kick him out, at least?"

Vera shakes her head. "Who? Oh, no dear. Why would I do that?"

"Jesus, Vera. Why not?"

All the rest of Coffee Time's patrons, listening keenly to this exchange, shrug their bowed and heavily-weighted shoulders: You got no argument here, kid.

But it's Coffee Time, right? Not time for righteous indignation.

And since Vera's putting up the red and yellow plastic Out-of-Service sign, the one with the cute little man in a construction hat, holding a mop, they collectively lose interest. The scene's over. Craterface stays.

Let her deal with the mess if that's what she wants.

Peter's shrugged his shoulders, too. Not because he's sent a woman with a terminally ill son into a very small room, ripe with the smell of soap and piss and shit and his vomit, but because he's been squarely confronted by one of the many, many things that he will not fully comprehend today. And so, as he's walking back to his red and yellow and taupe chair and table, to his paper and smokes and his Aiwa, he's forced to do more work than he's physically comfortable with. Yes, as shaky as he is, he forces himself to reconstruct the events of the last three hours of his life.

Before sitting down, Peter places his watch and one dollar and thirty-five cents in change on the table, then empties the contents of his front left and right pockets and places them, also to the left and right, respectively, around the first pile.

From here what Peter concludes is based more on belief than fact. Belief, primarily, and a logical proof based on comparison. If X is true, Y must also be true.

Seated and sipping his coffee and staring at his piles, Peter establishes certain fundamental truths. He believes in the resolute convictions of his various obsessions, and he believes in the uncanny self-preservation of his instinctual accounting.

Of course, Peter does not know these things, even if he does believe them. He understands, he *knows,* nothing. Not any more.

No, now he just believes. And what he puts his faith in, what he believes, is that for three months at least, probably longer, he's kept the same things in the same bulging pockets. A superstition, a ritual, whatever, it's the one constant.

What he also believes – though again, he does not know exactly why he should believe it – is that for at least the same period of time he's always been able to believe he had a certain amount, an exact amount, of money. He's believed this to be true and he believes he's never been proven wrong.

If I believe I have twenty-two dollars and thirty-seven cents, in four fives and change, I do.

Peter believes this because he believes that something within him has kept a running tab; he also believes that this entity is a ruthless, exacting mathematician. Finally, because he believes that his belief has never been undermined, he believes that something has gone drastically wrong somewhere between sleep time and Coffee Time.

To test his belief Peter performs a simple enough feat, though for him it takes a Herculean effort of concentration and will. Telling himself not to give up – not to go ahead and indulge and roll up the rim and lose and put on his walkman – he counts his change. There is, of course, the dollar and thirty five cents in the centre pile with his Quemex. Okay.

To the right, from his right front pocket, his pager, his keys, two quarters, seven dimes, four nickels, and eight pennies. So, what we have here, in total, is a long dead pager, nine keys on a Black Flag key chain, eight of which unlock nothing anymore, and one dollar and forty-eight cents.

Now, what do I believe?

Peter believes that when he left with Joe this morning he had exactly five dollars and eighty-three cents in his right front pocket. And let's see, this is his fourth large cup of Coffee Time coffee at exactly one dollar a pop. So, he should have, if his belief in his belief is correct, precisely one dollar and eighty-three cents left.

Staring at more than two bucks in change his faith is just about shattered. And then he realizes: Wait, I didn't pay for that last cup.

Rearranging the money into one new pile, he slowly adds it up. Yes, there's two-eighty three, exactly. He even pulls out his wallet to double-check: he's right, except for his bank card, two bus tickets, a scruffy baby blue pack of Zig-Zag rolling papers, and his useless driver's licence, it's apparently empty.

That settles it, conclusions can be drawn. We've firmly established that Peter—

"James, you look like death warmed over. Christ, hard times, son?"

Distracted, everything ruined, Peter looks up into the round pink face of a fat, sweating man in black. The guy's holding a large cup of coffee in one hand and something within Peter momentarily envies his rim; he quickly imagines rolling porky for it, taking him out back and beating the snot out of him, then dismisses the image: too fucking weird. Instead, he watches the guy's lips jiggle as his greeting trails off.

I believe they're sugar-sticky.

Yes, he's got a box of donuts wedged into his flabby side with the same arm, and a half-eaten cruller in wax paper in his other hand. I believe I can smell double chocolate. And candy sprinkles.

"What?" Peter resists adding: Do I know you, tubby? And: Fuck off.

"Jeez, James. All that shit. You look like a guy down to his last nickel," Peter's thoroughly forgotten former co-worker says, pointing at his piles.

"Nope. Just trying to prove something. That's all."

The security guard gets a whiff of rose petals and coffee and cigarette smoke and vomit and backs up a step. There's a confused, awkward silence. Peter's red-rimmed blue eyes have glazed over again, funny little donuts.

"Yeah, sure."

Peter drums thick stubby fingertips into his table top and says: "Damn straight."

"You okay, James?"

"Yeah." Who the fuck does this guy think he is?

"Really?"

"Yup."

"See Jennifer around?"

"Yup." Nutjob.

"Well. . . ."

"Well?"

"Good seeing you, James. You take care of yourself, you hear? Everybody still thinks about that day, you know, when it happened. And, well. I guess they think you got a raw deal."

"Yeah?" What the fuck? What's this fucking pig saying?

"So, anyway."

"Yeah, anyway."

"All right. Back to the saltmine. See ya."

"Yeah. See ya." Not if I see you first. Jesus. Freako. I mean, what the fuck?

Peter shrugs his shoulders: not for anyone's benefit, but because he's seen enough films to believe that's what you're supposed to do after a run-in with someone who's relatively harmless, though demented nonetheless.

Where was I? Oh, yeah. Okay.

Getting back to matters at hand, Peter looks down at his piles and retraces the intricate steps of his unique personal beliefs. He's reassured, finally coming to the same conclusion he would have drawn when he was so rudely interrupted: his belief in his psychic accountant, he maintains, is justified.

So?

Well, for Peter, this affirmation means that it also follows that all his other obsessions should be in their proper, obsessively assigned place.

His watch, in the first pile, for instance – okay, fine, he doesn't know, precisely, where that came from anymore.

He's moved the change, hasn't he?

So, fine, he's not sure if it came from the right pocket, where it's supposed to be. Okay. Fine.

Fine. That may be true, but he still believes, rightly, that the piles to the left and the right came from the pockets on either side of his body.

And so that's how he puts it all together.

I believe my pager should be in the pile to the left of my watch. It is not. Therefore someone's been fucking with me.

"Fuck," he says.

I also believe, therefore, that my watch was not in the correct pocket: again, proof that someone's been fucking with me.

And then his complex system of belief does something to shatter his Coffee Time – to essentially ruin his day.

I, Peter, believe that I also had one plastic-and-foil sealed condom, purchased from a strip club toilet vending machine, and approximately one eighth of an ounce of dope, wrapped in household tinfoil, in my front left pocket.

Oh, Christ, they're not here. The foil ball. The condom. Lucky blue and my dope.

Where the fuck are you?

Wait now, Pete, wait. Don't freak.

I also believe I wasn't wearing these particular pants yesterday. And I believe I got mad this morning.

Shit. My mom.

Mom, I believe, washed these jeans.

And I believe, despite the coffee and vomit stains, that these pants are very clean. Fuck.

I believe she's fucking with me.

Checking the time on the Coffee Time clock against the time on his Quemex, Peter picks up a quarter in his left hand, just to test his belief. After stuffing the correct pockets with all his other stuff and putting on his leathers and stuffing its left pocket with his smokes and his red miniature Bic lighter, he clipped his Aiwa to his jeans and shoved the headphones into his right jacket pocket. Rising, Peter walks to the Coffee Time phone believing he's left exactly two dollars and fifty-eight cents on his table.

Passing a fire engine red and brownish garbage can, he pushes his brown-bagged lunch, his lovingly-made salami sandwich and the cookies and banana, through the swinging plastic lid. Deep in his back left pocket, under the protective fold of his wallet's black cloth lining, a livid purple bruise swells on the black and white face of a kissing girl in sympathy: I'm afraid for you, be careful.

When the young, terribly tattooed Coffee Time employee picks up and pockets the tip Peter's left for Vera, the first tip any employee at any of Coffee Time's many locations has ever received, she's too furtive and almost guilty to, indeed, perceive that he's correct. Instead she just snickers and spits, softly: "Asshole. Fucking drunks. What a moron bastard."

· · • · ·

Maria James stands at the gleaming, sun-dappled sink washing her son's breakfast dishes. She's staring out the window and humming happily to herself, a melody she can't place.

Her son would know, it's the song he sings, warbles, drunkenly, late at night, when he believes no one's listening: "Jesus . . . don't want me . . . for a sunbeam. . . ."

In the apple tree that Robert planted with Peter on his second birthday, the light plays and tricks on the turning leaves and the last heavy fruit: green and gold and red and beautiful. My God, it's beautiful.

Closer to the house, on the back porch, the big tropical plant stretches monstrous leaves after a taste of this light.

Maria thinks, I've really got to get Petey to help me bring her in.

And then the phone rings.

"Peter, dear. I was just thinking about you, angel." Maria's ecstatic, thrilled by her boy's simple kindness, a call she never expected; he hasn't phoned her in months, and when she heard his "Mom?" she decided they had quite a lot of catching up to do for two people who live under the same roof, for a single parent and an only child.

"Oh darling, you're so sweet; giving your old mother a call. You know

176

that, Petey? I know you're working hard and you don't have a lot of time. You on a coffee break, son? You must be. How's work? Listen, I've got to leave in five minutes myself but I'm just so glad to hear from you. Isn't it a gorgeous day, Peter? Isn't it? Getting a bit warmer, I think. Isn't it? My God, the sun today! Anyway, I'm working until seven tonight, honey, but I was hoping. Well, I was hoping you'd stay in for a change. Maybe come home after you've finished work, and we could have dinner, and, well, talk. For a change. If you can. Can you, dear? I hope so. You've probably made plans for your birthday tomorrow. So why don't I cook a roast tonight? You'd like that, a roast. . . ."

Maria's been speaking so quickly, so cheerfully and freely, that she hasn't heard her son muttering, growing more and more impatient.

"Mom. Mom. Wait. Mom," he says. They're hoarse but hypnotic words, spoken low and over and over again.

She does hear him, finally, lose his temper; though what she hears is more rabid bark, more feral, than human: "Maria! Shut up."

Oh, I see, it's like that.

Again.

For the next minute she says nothing, only really half-listening to Peter's venomous tirade. Letting her eyes drift outside she watches the tree fall into shadow, a vague greyness, gloom. Her cheeks glow, mortified, as if slapped. The window she looks through becomes yellowed, smoke-tarnished, a barrier that will not be breached, something to keep in everything unclean. Behind her, she thinks the budgie has taken up her song, that he's answering her call.

. . . don't want me . . . for a sunbeam. . . .

Pretty, pretty boy.

The part of her that's not listening to her boy doesn't really hear him says the words "bitch" and "Jesus fucking Christ" or even "cunt." That part of her has never heard those words.

At least, not since the first year of her marriage, eighteen months before her son's birth.

When Peter's slammed the phone down, hung up on her rudely, violently, Maria tries to tidy up: she clears away her son's shit because that's what she's always done for the James men. Hell, she's good at it. So, all she actually remembers – and it's not that bad, right? – is, "Are you messing with me? Did you? Did you throw out my stuff?" That, and, "What gives you the fucking right? Who the hell do you think you are?"

The bird still singing, the receiver replaced, Maria takes up the dish towel and mechanically dries a plate, a black, Disney corporation coffee mug, a fork, a frying pan, and a knife. She looks to the kitchen table and acknowledges her purse and car keys; she straightens her white blouse and brushes a crumb off her navy blue polyester pants.

When she looks out the window, one last time before leaving for work, she sees the light has returned, that it really is a beautiful day. Of course, Maria doesn't notice that something about the tree is different. Or that her sink sparkles again. Or that her window is crystalline once more. She doesn't even notice her budgie – that he stopped singing the moment the sunbeam returned.

Maria doesn't notice these things because she's trying not to notice that she's trembling, almost spasming. Shaking uncontrollably. And crying.

No, Maria James doesn't notice anything because she's trying so very hard not to think about it, to forget.

She does not look out through her beautiful window, through the gorgeous sunbeam, at her husband's and son's redolent tree and think: The apple doesn't fall far, does it?

And she forgets that she also believes she heard her son say: "Fuck, you know, sometimes I want to fucking kill you. I mean, really, who the fuck do you think you fucking are, you fucking cow!"

And she forgets her dead husband's wild eyes the last time he screamed those words, just as she forgets the fire the back of his hand once spread across her face.

Instead, Maria sees and remembers the majesty, the bounty. She looks outside and then turns and picks up her purse and car keys, checks the time on the old cuckoo clock and dries her eyes and sighs and smiles. And she says, to no one in particular, thinking about the tree and her little bird's song, all of this world's beauty, "Ah, the good Lord's in the details."

The sunbeam and the budgie call after Maria as she leaves for work: No ma'am, sorry, He's not. Damn. Sorry. No, He's not. Not this time. He's not.

As she's getting into her car, the sunbeam leaves the tree to follow her. It does this because, well, because Buddy the budgie can't. Before it skips off, however, and dazzles this woman through the front window of her Dodge, it tips its cap to the bird and jumps down onto the James' back lawn.

The bird, watching this, sings goodbye, too. He notices, undeniably, exactly what has changed, what Maria would never let herself see. An apple has fallen from the tree. Rotten, wormy, pock-marked, disgusting. The sunbeam, perched on it, makes it all too clear: Maria, Buddy calls out, it has fallen. And it's fallen very close by. Very, very close by.

Some things will not be slipped through a mail slot. Not easily, not intact.

Oversized envelopes and small parcels are always a problem. As are large, humorous greeting cards, and tax forms, and newspapers, and those novelty cheques the actors who play sweepstakes winners always get.

Local and long distance directories; product samples, like those environmentally friendly light bulbs or deceptively unfriendly detergents; the plain-wrapped, imported S & M mags and videos stamped with the name of some bogus fundamentalist Christian outfit from Tulsa?

Forget about it.

Borrowed tools, garden equipment, or household appliances?

Come on, buddy, get real.

Then there's body parts – vibrant or otherwise – sight lines, and intent.

We all know the rule of thumb here, it falls under the rubric of the sixth Commandment: Do not fold, spindle, or mutilate.

Receiving any of this stuff at the very least means participating in another commanding act of faith: Thou shall not covet or steal the crap left at your neighbour's front door. Often it requires face-to-face, human contact. Sometimes it's pleasant, exciting even.

Other times, well, other times it's tricky. Awkward. Embarrassing.

Much, however, thankfully, *can* transpire through the breech.

It *does* happen. Every day.

Just this morning, in fact, a little less than an hour ago, Buddy spun on his perch like he always does when he hears the mail push through the small swinging metal flap and sift and scatter into an uneven heap in the entranceway. As usual, he cocked his tiny, perfect head and strained to watch Ed Harrison diminish a bit as he padded down the hall. Then there was the familiar pop of the knee, the little sigh at the twinge in Ed's back: Buddy's shudder of concern.

A few minutes later the budgie could hear his old friend in the kitchen, blowing on his coffee, talking. He'd forgotten to pay the damned phone bill again. Complained about not trusting those fancy bank machines anyway. Wondered how in the hell they expected him to change now.

"After so many years. Eh, darling?" Like having a teller do their goddamned job was too much of an imposition.

The pension cheque was in, though. Both of them. "And that's always a good day. Right, hon? Right?"

And then he heard the slit of a knife passing through an envelope and Ed saying it was a letter from Ted.

About Krystal and Andrea and him.

About the boy feeling real bad about not being able to make it.

Hell, there was even a cheque inside. For the flowers.

Sweet, ain't it?

"Oh, he's a good one, our Ted. One of the best. You sure as hell did a fine job with that kid. Darling, it says here he's sorry. That he would've given anything in the world to be able to make the trip himself. And you know that's so. That's just the way it is, isn't it? Since the divorce. But Jesus, why's he sending money? We know he's thinking about us.

"Christ, poor kid. Sometimes, well, sometimes it just gets to me. The way that tram— that woman, treated him. But I still say to him, whenever I get the chance, I say, 'Son, it's not your fault.' No, he's a fine boy, he really is. It's just little Krys I'm all broken up about. Being uprooted like that. Her mother living in another goddamned state. That's just not right. A girl that age, well, she needs her mom, doesn't she? Not that Andrea's any bargain. No mother's day contest winner, not by a long shot. No sir. But that's the whole damned point of them Greeks, ain't it? Sophocles and such: you can't choose your folks.

"Am I right?

"But what the hell was the woman thinking? Christ, it's not like she's a flighty little prom queen. A goddamned middle-aged idiot, that one is. Up and leaves, takes our son for everything, then remarries and decides she can't handle the kid right when Ted's trying to get a leg up on a new job. So she's sitting pretty and worry free with Mr. Friggin' Mutual of Omaha, pardon my French, while our son and their goddamned kid are living in a tiny apartment in the Cape.

"What's his name, anyway? Dick? Rick? Rich, probably, the sonofabitch.

"I mean, Christ. Now you tell me, is that fair? Eh, darling? Eh? I mean the only thing I like about this is that the Harrisons have finally gone full circle. You know? Still struggling, but finally back home.

"Yeah, he's a good kid. He'll show 'em. Mark my words, darling. He will. At least that Andrea condescended to bring her own daughter up for a visit. It says here whatsisname, Marlin Friggin Perkins – sorry – is in town on business.

"Oh, I know, hon, I'm ranting. Sorry, doll. I mean, it's not like you don't already know all this. But Christ, she's having a hell of a time already, poor sweet child. You could hear it in her voice, even through that ridiculous little portable phone she was yelling into. Just terrible, the reception. Jesus. Give the kid a quarter. I mean, I'm an old man, but I'm not deaf yet.

"Did I mention I told her I'd meet her tomorrow morning, then bring her back here for the day? Yeah, sorry, 'course I did. Alzheimer's, eh? Too bad though, them dragging her to hell and gone today. I hoped, you know. For more time. Ah, well. What do you expect?

"Imagine it, hon, travelling up here with a pair of idiots like that. Might as well be on her own. Not that they'd consider having her stay by us, though. Not when they can keep her cooped up in some godforsaken hotel. Of course not. I guess the place just ain't good enough. Eh, darling? Christ. What, are we just supposed to be grateful they're bringing her by at all?

"Jesus. I guess so.

"She's a trooper, though, making the best of it, it sounds.

"Yup, she's a Harrison all right. Don't have no use for a couple of fools, our Krystal. Still, her mom's her mom, right?

"So, what're you gonna do?"

Buddy shrugged his wings and thought: Not much, I'm afraid, not much.

And then he watched Ed reappear in the hall and pluck his cap and the orange and black jacket Ted had sent last Christmas from out of the mess of scarves and envelopes and shoes and newspapers surrounding and piled upon the old telephone chair by the door. When he'd put them on he patted his back pocket looking for his wallet.

Over here, old buddy, on the coffee table.

Ed remembered and walked toward him and passed under his cage. He picked up his wallet and opened it, reached into his pocket and pulled out the two perfectly halved pieces of paper. Staring into the little plastic window that opened to the right, he mechanically stuffed in the folded cheques and sighed and said: "Well, it's the bank first, I guess. Then maybe a little walk before heading back to get this place fixed up."

Good idea, buddy. Yes.

"Okay enough day for it."

Beautiful, it looks.

Ed just sighed again and started to shuffle, the wallet still open in his hand, back toward the front door.

Buddy chirped.

Hurry home, friend. I'll miss you.

And then he stopped. Abruptly. Shocked.

Wait. Don't go. Not now. There's something else coming through your door. Something bad. Very, very bad. You hear it?

Ed had one hand on the door knob and was closing his wallet, shaking his head.

You hear it, right? Through the mail slot?

"Still doesn't feel right, though. . . ."

It's not. So stay.

"Does it, Alice?"

Don't. I mean, what? Alice? I mean, sorry buddy, I thought you were talking to me.

"No, sweetheart, it sure doesn't."

Oh, God. Ed, listen to me. Don't go. Okay? Ed?

And then Ed opened the door and walked out into it, right out into the street. For a moment the noise that had crept in, bent all out of shape, through the mail slot, became deafening: the horrible, malicious cry of a demented, terrible gull. The worst Buddy had ever heard.

Please, don't go.

And then the door closed and Ed locked it.

The screeching died slowly; only stopped, completely, when Ed had gone far, far away.

Buddy hopped down from his perch and paced the bottom of his cage, thinking: That's one fucking evil bird. You watch your back, Ed. I mean it. I know about these things. Take care. Don't take no shit. And don't lose your head, okay, buddy? Okay?

· · • · ·

When the broken old man walked out of his house and into the awful light, the worst gull beat its huge, chipped and torn and fouled wings and pierced up and into a still blue sky marred only by one large, angry cloud.

Too easy, right?

Maybe?

No. No mercy.

It circled counter-clockwise and screamed, in lazy but purposeful gyres, while the old man waited in the shelter.

His black eyes narrowed when the man stepped up into the trolley.

The bird followed the car, hunted it, attacked its roof as it made its fitful, impatient stops. And when the old man finally reappeared, the worst gull followed him away from the lake and up the long busy street and prepared his attack.

He's wearing a hat. Get him in the neck. In the back. The worst gull cackled, slowed, sped up, popped its talons in anticipation as it flew.

The old man shuffled, paused unpredictably. Stared off through blinding storefront windows, teetered on, and then stopped, briefly, to babble with the younger, shiftless men who played chess on one busy corner.

Now?

Not yet.

The old man looked at his wrist, raised his arm, waved and carried on up the longest, busy street. He was steadier now, his pace consistent, determined.

The worst gull closed in.

I've got you, you old bastard. Three. Two. One. Now.

· · • · ·

Krystal's coming and Alice's birthday and our anniversary and Ted and Andrea and Cape Cod and the army and my dead brother and divorce and Belle and the goddamned phone bill and I really need a drink but I shouldn't but I do. Who's it gonna hurt, who's it gonna hurt, who?

Lost in thought, walking up the congested circus the old strip has become, for a while Ed didn't notice that he was only a few paces behind Miss Johnston, the dancer he'd sat and drank and passed the better part of last night with. When he finally did recognize her in her pale blue sweat suit, carrying her green and yellow gym bag, he decided, impetuously, to speed up and say hello.

But then, Ed being Ed – the man he was confronting, the man he'd become over the years in the light of the man he is now – he turned over a number of things in his mind that all told him it really wasn't a very good idea.

First, well, out here, on the street, in the middle of the morning, he felt unusual, awkward. Maybe just a bit embarrassed. And, of course, he conceded, it's not like I'm gonna make her day. Just what she needs, right? An old man following her. Besides: Alice wouldn't approve. Definitely not. So it's probably not the right thing to do, is it?

Finally, there was the small matter of getting himself into the bank. The way things had been going lately, he was liable to get halfway across town before he remembered. Christ, who knows what the line-up might be like. A man could spend hours running one little errand.

Yeah, forget about her. Leave the poor girl alone. Go to the bank. The bank. Jesus H, *that* was the bank.

Just about to pass the doorway to his day's only truly necessary destination, Ed Harrison snapped to attention, stopped on a dime and executed a perfect one-quarter turn. Goddamned military precision.

As he did this he noticed a big, ugly seagull, maybe three feet above him, and a half foot to the left, whizzing past and dropping its large payload. Christ. It almost hit Miss Johnston. Just missed that sweet young girl.

Alice always hated those damned things, he thought. Probably the only living creature she couldn't find a use for.

No fucking wonder.

And then he went inside and sighed and got in line and waited the bank line-up wait.

· · ● · ·

His wallet still open and the phone bill finally stamped paid and shoved into his coat pocket, Alice Harrison watches her husband count out the eighty dollars in twenties, tens, and fives that he hasn't deposited from the pension cheques. Looking up into his solemn face, from this angle, patiently waiting while he methodically counts and recounts and orders the bills the way he always has before putting them in his wallet, he looks just about as handsome as he ever has. Sure, he might be in his seventies, and his hair's white, but look at that face.

Still not an old age wrinkle – just a few more character lines. Those eyes. Still fierce and dreamy and commanding. Still smouldering. Eyes he has only for me. My happiness. Oh my.

And then the teller, a funny little man in a yellow sweater, probably still a teenager for godsake, clears his rude little pencil-necked throat and spoils everything. He's obviously impatient with her husband's ritual.

This pisses her off. Imagine, the nerve.

Ed, of course, finishes his business in his own time, refusing to allow the interruption. But when he looks up, Alice sees him flash the kid a look she hasn't seen this closely for more than fifty years. Funny, the kid even looks a hell of a lot like poor old Reg Colter.

Watch it, son. Not when he's like this.

Reg, they'd heard, had been killed in a plane crash not far from here in '72. Coming home from a business trip. His luck never got better, did it?

Ed was obviously considering whether to spend the eighty and buy the kid a ticket to join him.

Faced with the look her husband was shooting him, the teller's survival instinct kicked in. He pointed to Ed's wallet and asked: "Your wife, sir?"

"Yeah."

"Well, sir, if you don't mind me saying so, she's beautiful. You're a very lucky man."

Wow, Ed. Life, eh? Again. You just never expect it, do you?

Alice watched the fire behind Ed's eyes subside. He lost focus, averted his gaze like he was about to blush. His shoulders went slack and then he popped his teeth and sighed and said to the kid, "Yes. Yes, son, she . . . is. And . . . and I am. Thank you, son. I am."

"You're welcome, sir. Is that it, then? Anything else I can do for you?"

Forget about it, she thought. Go on home now, Ed. Go back and forget about it. We shouldn't be out today. But then she watched something dark and terrible and utterly bereft – something she had never been allowed to *see* before – tremble across his lips.

"Sir?"

"Hmmm? Oh, sorry, yeah," he said. "I've changed my mind. You better let me have another hundred."

Oh, Ed. Don't do this.

And then the money changed hands and Alice Harrison's husband counted and recounted and ordered and stuffed in the bills. And then the wallet closed.

· · • · ·

There are also other things, of course, that will slip through a mail slot, occasionally even pass under a door, with ease. Careless, thoughtless ease.

Lunatic confessions from lunatic confessors, cut and pasted abominations that torment the ever-present parents of missing children. Motel room Visa slips fastened with paper clips to nude Polaroids of cheating spouses. 1,600 tabs of your teenaged son's best friend's acid. The first intrepid roach. Even the frantic, insistent, reverberating knocking of a clean, rehabilitated, repentant child.

Or, a hastily scrawled note, written in red ink on a single baby blue tissue.

About twenty minutes after Buddy's warning was ignored, at exactly 10:51 AM, just such a simple passage transpired through Ed Harrison's front door. Buddy knows exactly when it occurred because he's that conscientious.

At first the knocking was tentative, barely audible. Easy to miss. It grew bolder, but still wasn't self-assured.

Sorry, nobody home. Come back later.

Bolder still.

Sorry, go away now.

The doorbell rang. Once. Twice. Then, an impatient, rapid-fire volley.

Hey! I said he ain't here.

And finally, through the mail slot, a voice. Loud, pleading. A female voice.

"Dad? It's me. Annabelle. . . . Dad, are you in there? It's Belle."

The mail slot squeaking open. A worm of a finger wiggling through. Lips almost visible. Moving.

"Dad, if you're in there and you're ignoring me, stop. Please, stop. Don't be ridiculous.

"Dad? Ed? Ed Harrison, are you in there?

"Look, Dad, if you are in there and you're mad or something, I'm sorry. That's why I'm here. I know I'm the last person you expected. Hell, even I don't blame you. But it's different now. I've changed. So please Dad, let me in. Dad? Listen, I'm here to apologize. To make things right. It's been too long. Too, too long. I didn't write, or call first, well, because I needed to do this in person. To make amends. All that stuff, you know? I needed to see your face. Look you in the eye and tell you I'm sorry. For all the pain I've caused. That I'm clean. I'm better, Dad. Clean for almost a year now. Oh Christ, you're probably not even in there, right? But if you are, please forgive me. Okay? I want to make things right now. I want to see Mom. I need to, Dad. I'm sorry. Dad? Dad, I'm home.

"Dad?

"Oh shit."

And then Buddy saw it, a slip of blue, tipped through the breach. It drooped and slipped, down at first, the red scratchings upside-down and indecipherable, and then it caught an updraft and bowed and flipped and hung in the air. He could just make out the words and numbers before gravity reasserted itself and twisted the Kleenex, sending it off course, back down, and to the left. Doubled upon itself it feathered onto the mess piled around, and under, the telephone chair.

It said: I've come home. To apologize. I'm sorry. I love you. Belle.

Good thing I got the number, too, Buddy thought. He's never gonna find it there, even if I point the damned thing out.

Wonder who that was? Who the hell's Belle?

Now all I got to do is get you to listen to me for once. Right, buddy?

· · • · ·

The worst gull watched and waited for the old man to reappear. Where the sidewalk dropped into the asphalt, it had made its stand. Oblivious to the bicycles, trucks, and taxis that hurtled behind, it pecked at what God always provides: fries, slathered in ketchup; the carcass of a stupid domestic house pet.

There's always litter and carelessness, always something killed in the traffic and left to rot.

Budgie guts.

Waiting and feeding and defying, the worst gull marked and annexed its territory with vicious eyes and a puffed chest. Sharp, imposing explosions and massive rearings of its terrifying wing-span. Homicidal lunges of its razored black beak.

Mine, it said, darting at calves. Women's bare ankles. And the sea of ugly freaks parted. Stupid people.

Disgusting light, the burning blue of the sky, peeled off the glass door when it swung open. The old man stepped out into the street. Stopped. Looked confused. Blinded. Stepped forward, closer. Stopped again. Looked left. Right. Up. He took off his hat and ran a hand through his white hair. Closed his eyes and swallowed and shook his head, "No."

From below the worst gull cawed and raged at the old man. I'm down here.

A gull lunged at his feet. Dangerously close. Reared back to strike again.

Everything good in Ed's struggling, haunted head gave up on him in that instant. Important synapses shut down in unison, old ones re-established dead connections. And then his foot shot back, sharp. Then fast. Hard. Forward. Out.

His toe caught the bird square in the breast while its wings were spread wide, as it hesitated, briefly, before darting at his leg.

The "Fuck" he spat when he kicked, and the gull, screaming and writhing as it tumbled back, haywire, into the street, and the wild follow-through of his powerful leg made everybody else on the sidewalk stop, stare, afraid.

"Get away from me, you stupid bird," he said while the worst gull, wounded, scrambled and shook and raged into the air to avoid the traffic that meant to finish him.

A teenaged girl, a runaway probably, a street kid with dyed green hair and an army jacket and a lip ring, shrieked: "Hey, asshole, what the hell do you think you're doing!"

Ed turned to the voice, pasty, vacant. His chest heaving.

The hood beside her held a squeegee, a shock of limp blue mohawk fell over the spider web tattooed above his ear. He stepped forward. "Yeah, Christ. What's wrong with you? Who kicks a defenceless animal? Jesus."

Ed stepped forward. Stopped. Crossed his balled-fisted arms over his chest.

The crowd stepped back.

He stared down the kid. "Fuck you," he said, quiet, low. "Fuck you and the whore you rode in on. And buddy, believe me, you'd best shut your fucking hole. Or you're fucking next."

THE PEELERS ARE ARRIVING. Punching in. Undressing for work.

They're slipping out of something comfortable and into stilettos and thongs and prickly garters. Lingerie for breakfast, eyeshadow and lipliner. Pink Lady Bic razors at all possible, delicate, dangerous angles. Lee Press-On Nails.

Lap towels and Miracle Bras have been laundered, blankets and teddies dry-cleaned. Change has been made.

The DJ's drinking a Starbucks non-fat venti latté, wearing shades, playing a *Sandbox* and Ween mix low so the boss won't freak, chainsmoking Gitanes and re-reading *Less Than Zero* or a photocopy of a story called "Home," or the new Julie Doucet, or the third edition of Sid Field's *Screenplay*. Occasionally, he scribbles something sinister with a Sanford Uni-ball Vision pen in a 200-page, black Brownline $9^{1}/_{4}$" x $7^{1}/_{4}$" ruled notebook. On the first page there's a single, speedy inscription: *I am what I play*.

The bartender's mixing bloody morning drinks, virgins, marking up the racing form. Circling Buddy Boy in the fourth, looking nervous, he drops a celery stalk, and plucks the MasterCard from the open wallet on the bar. The leather squeaks when it's moved: waxy build-up. He uses the bar phone to make a call: his bookie answers just as he's about to hang up.

In the manager's Naugahyde office, the owner's left hand is slipping between the thighs of the newest new kid while he casually peruses her ID; her dress is long and blue, she's already more than half-snapped — there's some pretty good ludes going around.

The day manager's outside the can at the pay phone, calling his mother, checking to see if she's remembered Dad's meds. She hasn't and that's bad. In a few minutes he'll need to leave, use another three days of his vacation time to arrange for state-assisted in-home care.

A waitress is writing her name with the owner's in a red heart.

The bouncer's on a VIP couch, taking a nap, squirming and damp with all the dreams eighteen months of patrons have let slip between the cushions.

The peelers are arriving, putting on their war faces, transforming, becoming appealing.

And through it all Scott Venn is smiling.

Actually, he's staring out the Harbour Hilton window at the red and yellow and cream-coloured yacht that bobs in the greenblue brown below, and smiling his dumbest, fat-lipped smile: *Coffee Time*.

Cool. Don't mind if I do, he thinks, and nibbles at the Styrofoam lip of his hotel coffee as he sips and grins and reads the billboard on the deck: *You Can Win!*

For the last five minutes Scott's been happier than he's been for months. Years, probably. Crazy, silly, goofy, happy. Irrationally buoyant. So happy that he's stopped paying attention and begun picturing himself in The Rail, drinking, buying his buddy Tony a beer and a shot and pussy galore.

It doesn't get any better than this. In his happy head he's trying new things, like saying: Hell, the next one's on me, everybody. It sounds the way he always dreamt it would. Feels just as good.

But because it's still a bit early – the doors don't open for five minutes yet – he's also been picturing the calm before the storm, opening night jitters.

That's what nobody ever considers.

They don't live there, the girls. They have to get up and shower and get dressed and go to work.

And the version of the beginning of another work day he imagines is, though of course he cannot know this, very, very accurate.

The peelers *are* arriving.

Getting off the bus, Cara avoids the hungry, cocksure gaze of a bearded, Birkenstock-wearing poly-sci doctoral candidate who's been staring at her for four stops, hiding his wedding band under his students' first papers.

Holly pays the cabbie while he idles in front of the fancy coffee and pastry shop four doors down from the club. Shannon's fallen asleep on her shoulder, and she looks so sweet, but she can be a real handful when you wake her up. The cabbie tries to look up her short skirt in his rear-view mirror; thrills at just a thought and whisper of pink panties. Shannon begins to drool.

Mistress Krystal Kupps, Christine Kupaceck, is on the phone in a hotel room three floors below where Scott sits. She's talking to her husband; their three-year-old son has the flu. She really wants to go home. Can't. Her manager's a dickhead. He's booked a pro-am film shoot in New York next Tuesday, the rest of the week in Florida, then back here, in yet another club, the week after that. She misses everybody, but it'll all be over soon.

Jules is a majestic, homespun tragedy. Always breathlessly tall on perfect, divine legs. Always bent. Cornfed and blighted. She's sleeping through her alarm again. Either that or she's stopped breathing. Nobody will know which until very late tomorrow – until long after it's all over and way past caring.

Janna and Jenna Jefferson have been fighting about "the delivery boy" again.

"He's a fucking stalker."

"No he's not, he's okay. Sometimes he's still kinda nice."

"He's fucking well not."

"He is. You just don't know. All he went through."

"He hurt you."

"Once."

"Once is enough."

"You think I don't know that? Fuck. That's why we broke up. But Christ, you know. He didn't mean it."

"He fucking well did. He hit you, for fucksake. I still want the piece of shit dead. He hurt you and he meant it."

"That's not really true."

"The fucking bruise was true."

"He didn't *mean* it. . . ."

"No?"

"No. He's not really like that. He's sorry. Changed."

"He's still a drunk. Still dangerous."

"Only to himself."

"What*ever*."

"Bitch."

"Skank."

Mercedes' boyfriend's buying tampons at the PharmaPlus. Tampax regular. The jumbo forty pack – the ones with the thing that's like a demented, ripping yellow Nike swoosh. He's also bought coffees and chocolate chip muffins and four packs of smokes – rented *Uncle Buck* and *Home Alone* and *The Breakfast Club*. She's called in sick. They'll do a bowl and have a John Hughes marathon and probably fight and cry and break up and pledge their undying love for each other. Maybe she'll give him a hand job, weaving fantasies about Molly Ringwald and Ally Sheedy in the precious little shell of his tiny perfect ear.

Sixty-something other girls, interchangeable parts in The Rail's machinery, walk through the shithole's heavy doors at various times during the next eight hours. Whenever they arrive, it might as well be eleven o'clock. All of them have similar – fake – names, many have peculiar Russian or French accents. It doesn't, and they don't, matter. None of this matters.

This is definitely not Cheers.

Only one thing really matters.

The boardroom clock reads eleven now. The peelers have arrived.

These happy visions of consumable, rentable, surgically augmented flesh, so completely devoid of thoughts of prison and his wife, are the product of Scott Venn finding himself in possession of surprising resources. New knowledge. Unexpected insight and power and control.

This is what happens when you learn you're merely a single corrupt man among many. Some even more twisted. Much more. This is what it's like to win. To dominate a game you never even knew you were playing. To be told the rules, after the fact, and to find out they were your rules all along. To have the other guy tip his hand and reveal he's been shitting bricks, too.

If only Amanda could see me now, Scott thinks. Well, okay, maybe not. But soon, right, Man? Everything's going to be right as rain. I swear. After today, I'm a new man.

Second chances and all that. And I'm not going to screw it up again. I just want to spend more time with you, baby. Do things together.

Amanda and Scott, forever. All over again.

Yup. Things are definitely looking up.

Yeah, Man, today's the first day of the rest of our lives. I swear. See, Man: *You Can Win!*

· · • · ·

Of course it's strange: just an hour ago, Scott's manic, fantastic mood swing was not even plausible. Not by any stretch of the imagination. Not to the casual observer or the mental health professional or the addiction counsellor or the criminal or divorce lawyer. Not to a sweet budgie or terrible gull. Not for the overdosing lapdancer or the cringing neighbour, the surly cabbie or the impertinent doorman, the obese security guard or oblivious cop.

Nobody dared to wish him well. That would've been mean, base – too much like rubbing it in, or tempting fate. Wrong, for so many reasons. Consensus was: things could only get worse. That's what he deserved. And what everybody believed.

But what's belief got to do with it? What's anybody – a painter, a pet, a fuck-up, or even a higher power – got to do with anything? No one gets what they deserve or what they wish for. Not precisely. Not ever. Complexity, probability, and chance? Always cruel, equally, always striving to outdo one another, to be the most perverse.

An hour ago, in fact, things *were* dire. Scott was fucked – screwed and being screwed over every which way but Sunday. Done like dinner, he could only open wide and take it, get ready to get fucked harder. Margaret Chisholm. Amanda. Accusations, many of them true. Prison.

Worse, he was just beginning to realize how hungover he was. Sick like a monkey, a whipped dog, tired past exhaustion, crippled with fear and rage and self-loathing and unnameable, shadowy humiliations, dying for a smoke.

The investigating lawyers and the Stooges were already in place around the big boardroom table when he walked past the cops and through the door. The first assault came as the eerie stillness of heightened formality, the silence of expectant yellow legal pads in the violent, relentless morning sun. When his eyes finished begging for bloodshot, photosensitive mercy, he saw the goddamned adding machine that had joined the lawyers' laptops, its white spool ready to itemize and summarize and punctuate the hardest, vaguest questions, the most brutal, deepest bottom lines. Where Chisholm usually sat there was a middle-aged guy with a nasty, bored grin. He looked like a sporting goods catalogue model but fiddled with the knobs and dials of the miniature DAT recorder attached to a moulded plastic gasmask contraption.

Holy crap, they want transcripts.

Scott placed his briefcase on the table, took his seat, turned his head, and stared, grim, out over the water.

Yup, okay. Now I'm fucked.

Everybody else wedged themselves into the tight, clean slacks of their mortification: Jesus, Venn looks like shit.

And then the Chisel walked in, her long thin neck and huge pointy head far back on the regal, powerful, hymenopterous shoulders that were as arrow-straight as her frightening spine, careful not to disturb all the chips stacked there. She'd beaten and processed her short wiry locks flat for the occasion; levelled and sculpted, they were pulled tight into a helmet so slick and severe and disciplined that her eyes seemed to bulge a bigger, even more predatory, vacancy.

Insatiable, Jesus. She really is a hungry little praying mantis.

Margaret nodded to the room and took her new seat, close enough to strike.

Everyone's eyes glazed and lowered when she cleared her throat, flashed her sharp little teeth and spat, and said, "Well. Here we are. Again. Let's get this over with, shall we? I'm sure we're all very busy. And I, at least, have clients to get back to."

Scott swallowed a month's worth of bitterness, a cartoonish gulp, ran a thumbnail under his rough chin.

Without looking at anyone, Shemp flushed; his lips made a fishy false start before the words got out. "Actually, Margaret, everybody, maybe we could hold off for a bit? I think we can wait another few minutes – if there are no objections. Uh, another one of the partners, I think, wants to be here for this. Something to add, I believe. Uh, I'm not sure. He called the office. Said he'd be here, at any rate."

"Look, Dave," Chisholm said, as she rolled her eyes, then looked down the terrifying slope of her nose, "I don't want to wait. And I don't see the point. Come on, we've all got enough to go on here, right? What you see is what you get. Venn engaged in collusion, basically stole money from his clients, fixed them into raw deals, robbed SSPR of its cut, and laughed all the way to the bank. Those are the facts here, and nothing's going to change these facts. At least, I hope to God it's not going to get any worse."

More still, awkward silence.

Margaret's voice became a bit more aggressive, sharper: "Right, Venn? I trust we know everything now. Or do you have any other little surprises you'd like to share?"

Scott glowered, felt his lips part and quake, the tremulousness before the rubbery jiggle, the stammering babble of guilty hatred.

I'm fucked, you fucking harpy. I get it, back off. You don't have to bite off my fucking head. Oh, yeah, I guess you do.

"Well," he said, "I . . . I'm sure that's, um, that you, Margaret, every-body. . . . Ah. . . . What it looks like. . . ."

And then he was arrested, mid-ramble. A familiar, serious, deep, thir-ty-seven-year-old voice cut through the room as the door shut forcefully behind him: "Please, everyone, I'm sorry I'm late." His grey eyes picked off everyone around the oval. "Gentlemen. Margaret." And then they fell upon Scott: "Mr. Venn."

His former co-worker, his friend, looked at him hard, without pity. With disdain.

Hey, what's happening here? Your message. . . . You said. . . . Hey?

You, too, Tony? You, too? Say it ain't so.

Tony Lewis shook his head, loosened his Ralph Lauren tie, removed his smart, navy Hugo Boss sportscoat, and rolled up his sleeves. Then he pulled out the chair between Scott and Margaret, sat down, opened his briefcase, and grabbed his Montblanc. After tapping the table top with the pen, he leaned back, put his hands behind his head, and sighed.

"I'm also sorry I was unable to make your earlier meetings. As you know, I've been out of the country. I assure you, though, I've familiarized myself with the matter and I understand both the urgency and the grav-ity. And I must say, well, frankly, Mr. Venn, I must tell you I'm shocked. Disturbed. Scotty, actually I'm disgusted. Jesus, buddy, why is this hap-pening? Ah, shit. Sweet merciful crap, I hate this. As many of you here know, we go a long way back, Mr. Venn and I. But, friendship aside, this is just too much. I can't look the other way here. Did you really believe, Scott, that you'd get away with this? What, did you think we were too stupid? Unbelievable. Unbelievable, hell, this is criminal. A criminal breach of trust. . . ."

The Stooges looked uncomfortable, and Margaret smiled at her surprising new ally, wetting her thin, permanently pursed lips. Her breathing quickened, and her hair threatened to writhe out of its slick: vengeance really is sexy.

Tony leaned forward now, his right elbow on the table, his hand supporting his chin and covering his mouth. Was he actually smiling while he began conducting his own speech, using the sleek black and gold tube as a baton?

"I'm surprised, in fact, that the matter's taken this long to resolve. It's time, Margaret, gentlemen, to put an end to this farce. . . ."

Scott's jaw literally dropped, his face had blanched as if he'd been speared, terminally winded.

Tony? Christ, Tones, what the hell do you think you're doing, dude? What about your message, man? Ain't it bad enough? Bud? Tony Tones?

The pen became a dagger, stabbed out the rest of Tony's outrage in Scott's direction.

"Everyone, it's obvious what Mr. Venn's intentions are. What they've been from the start. I don't know what sick thrill you're getting from making us jump through these hoops, but enough's enough. It's over, Scott. Okay? You win. The writing's on the wall. . . ."

He let the pen drop; it spun counterclockwise and stopped, pointing directly at the Chisel.

For the love of God, Tony, stop!

Wait a minute. *I* win? What the hell are you talking about? I *win*?

"Yeah, Scott, fine. You've got us dead in the water. It's obvious you're not about to blink. So, let's call it a stalemate and walk away. Nobody's got to lose their head here, people. Nobody has to do anything rash."

The silence became even more oppressive, not creepy now, just heavier, thicker, stunned.

No longer hot and bothered, really not feeling sexy at all, Margaret did lose her head: "Lewis, are you out of your freakin' mind? What the hell are you talking about? Jesus. This asshole, this, this Venn guy, has ripped off SSPR – that's you, Tony, and me, and all of our fucking clients – for hundreds of thousands of dollars. Christ, the only thing we're not sure of, is how much. That's why we're fucking here, Anthony. That's it. To add up the dollars and cents. To figure out what we've lost, not cut our losses. Other than that, you're right. Somebody is dead in the water:

your boy Scotty here. Jesus. After this, all we've got to do is call the cops. We should have done it weeks ago, but today's the day. And, let me tell you, I, for one, am looking forward to making that call."

Scott closed his eyes, tried to think clearly through the pain and dread.

Okay, this is good. But where you going with the bluff, bud? What don't I know? Where's your ace, Ace?

When the room and the lawyers and the Chisel and Shemp and the Joes blinked back into their low-resolution focus, Tony was laughing. He'd picked up his Montblanc, leaned back again, and sent the pen into the air, end over end. Just before it hit the table, his hand shot out and made a miraculous grab. The fluidity with which he brandished the dart at Chisholm was beautiful.

"That's funny, Margaret. Ha ha. Really, really it is." His demeanor changed then, became deadly serious. If he was acting, he was good; his pupils became gunmetal pinpricks. "But you know as well as I do, nobody here wants to call anybody. When I saw all those cops outside I was afraid you'd done something rash. Christ, you've been at this for weeks now. He knows. And we know. And he knows we know. And we know he knows. Jesus, this is stupid. Asinine. It's over, so quit the self-righteous crap. You're an agent, for chrissake. You're not fooling him, and it's definitely not fucking becoming."

Chisholm popped to her feet and raged over Tony. "I'm not taking this shit from you, dickhead! Not from you, not from your fucking thief pal, not from anybody! You don't know what the hell you're talking about. You're not making any fucking sense, you know that?" She turned and whined at Shemp, and Scott imagined her pointy head really flattened, turning the crank on a vice, poking her in the eyes: "Dave, do something. We can't sit here and listen to this idiot's crazy shit talk."

Shemp stopped being a Shemp then, rocked his head on his neck and sighed. When he spoke he was almost a Moe, definitely a Dave: "For the love of Christ, Margaret, sit down and shut up."

Chisholm did a double take: this wasn't supposed to happen, not how this part of her life was supposed to be consummated. Dave had become a senior partner again, and for the first time in a month she felt out of her league. She bit her lip and sat down.

Okay, Scott thought, this is good. I don't get it, but hey.

It's all good, baby.

Dave drew the knife edge of his left hand across his throat. "That will be all, Mr. Stayner."

The stenographer pulled off his mask; he looked disappointed. This was really good, really interesting.

195

"And please, you can leave me the tape on the way out."

By the time he was gone, ten dawdling minutes later, Margaret had found the courage to return to the offensive.

Scott was staring, happily, then, into the briefcase he'd just opened. Sonofabitch. There you are.

"Would somebody mind telling me what the fuck is going on?"

Scott looked up, feeling much better.

Good question.

The two Joes shrugged their shoulders and raised their eyebrows at one another, at Dave and the lawyers.

I'm not telling her, you tell her.

Scott shook his head knowingly though he still didn't have a clue.

You poor, poor dupe.

"Jesus. She really doesn't know, Dave? Jesus. What the hell were you guys thinking? And Margaret, can you really be that fucking thick? That naïve?" Tony laughed again.

"That's enough, Mr. Lewis. Fine. Margaret, I'm afraid I'm going to have to ask you to leave as well. In fact, I think it might be in your best interest if—"

"No way, Dave. You're not shutting me out of this."

"Actually, we are, Margaret. We have to."

"I'm not leaving."

For the first time, Scott spoke: "Why don't you tell her, Dave. I think she has a right to know."

And damn, I'd like to hear this, too.

"Wait a minute," Tony said. "What I want to know is why you guys took the risk in the first place? Why bring her into this if she didn't know?"

"Oh . . . shit." Dave loosened his multi-coloured tie. "You might as well know, Margaret. One way or another, I suppose, there's nothing we can do about it now. And Tony, the truth is, we were trying to kill two birds with one stone. The way the senior partners figured it, this was as much a test for Margaret here, as it was an investigation of Venn. Margaret, wasn't it obvious? We brought you in here to intimidate Scott, to push him to the brink with your goddamned self-righteous opinions, the way you bloody well blow everything out of proportion. We used you to provoke him into telling us how much he knew. Trouble is, you did too good of a job, went too goddamned far. You were even starting to scare me, for chrissake. And then he just clammed up. It got so we couldn't know if he was playing us, or whether he was just another goddamned greedy, stupid thief."

"Of course Venn was playing you, Dave. Christ."

"Actually, Lewis, I'm surprised you even figured it out. Our thinking was that the information had been contained within the ranks of the senior partners."

"Jesus, Dave, think about it. The guy's smart enough to figure out how to skim hundreds of thousands of dollars off the contracts of his clients. He knows enough to set up a network of conspiracy with dozens of owners and promoters. Then he launders the fucking money so it's basically untraceable. Did you really think he wasn't smart enough to figure out that the old bastards who run this agency had been doing the same goddamned thing for twenty years? It's not fucking rocket science, Dave-o. You know and I know SSPR isn't the only one involved in this. You think anybody believes that just because they got Eagleson things have changed? Jesus."

"You can see our position, Tony. We had to make sure."

"Look, Dave, I figured this out after reviewing the files for an hour. You sure as shit should have been sure. This isn't a game here."

Unbelievable. Scott looked from Tony to Dave and then back. Fucking unbelievable.

Margaret was up again, pacing behind him and Tony. "What are you telling me? What am I being told here, guys?"

"Mexican fucking standoff, babe," Scott smirked. He got it now. Thanks, buddy.

"Don't you even talk to me, you little shit."

Tony turned his chair away from the table to watch her stalk. "Margaret, calm down. Scott's got us. He's been bluffing all along. Waiting SSPR out. Why'd you think he agreed to your little inquisition? He knew we'd blink first. Of course, he can't have any hard proof, nothing on paper. The partners have done a pretty good job of covering their tracks. Better than him, anyway. But he knows enough to point somebody with unlimited resources, who can really investigate, in the right direction. And who know's what they'd find? Christ, we can't afford the risk, the fucking scandal. No one can. So, all I want to know, Venn, is do you want to end this?"

"I'd like that, Anthony. I want that more than anything."

"Fine. It's over. You've got what you want. I trust you can pay back the money."

Margaret freaked. "Wait a minute! What he wants? Hello, am I in the fucking room here? You can't be seriously considering offering him a deal, Dave. No way. He goes down, or I talk."

The lawyers looked to the Joes who looked to Dave. His eyes narrowed.

197

"Not a good play, Margaret. Not smart." Tony was smiling, shaking his head.

"Fuck you, Tony. I'm serious, Dave. Either he goes to fucking jail or I go straight to the fucking papers."

Dave brought both index fingers to his lips, blew the smoke from the barrel of that gun. "I don't think you will, Margaret. No, I don't think so."

She screamed again, walking towards the window: "You're all fucking crazy!" With her back to the room, she rapped her fist off the thick glass. "You're all fucking scum, you know that? Every fucking one of you. But you're fucking with the wrong person and you're not gonna stop me."

"I'm sorry you feel that way, Ms. Chisholm. I respect your position, and if that's the way it has to be. . . ." Dave was already punching numbers into his cell.

"Barry," he said, "this is David. Yeah, the Venn matter has been resolved. It's like we figured. Uh huh. We'll work out the details. . . ."

Margaret spun back from the window, her huge head cocked, defiant.

Scott stared up at her, through her. He mouthed the words: "I want to fuck your ass. I'm gonna fuck your ass and kill you."

She recoiled, shocked. Sickened. Terrified.

"And Barry, Ms. Chisholm no longer works for SSPR. That's right. See that you take the appropriate steps, and get a few of the girls on the phone to inform her clients."

Ha ha, Margaret, you're fucked now. Not me. You're the one who's fucked. Scott grinned and licked his lips.

"You can't do that, Dave! I mean it, I'll talk!"

Dave pushed the end button and flipped the phone closed.

"I can do it, young lady. And I have. And no, you will not talk. You will not talk because you have nothing. Nothing but conjecture. You have no evidence, honey. I thought you were smarter than this, I really did. But, just in case you weren't smart, Margaret, in case you began to behave selfishly, began thinking of yourself instead of the company, we made sure to prepare for this kind of scenario. So no, you won't talk. Because, Margaret, if you do, I think the police will find that the money's actually gone missing from your accounts. It's a miracle, Margaret, what a little creative book-keeping can do. And no, nobody will be suspicious about these meetings. Nobody in this room, in the whole company, will support you. Or, at least, you won't like what they say. No, you won't like it when I explain that the whole thing has been an elaborate ruse to flush out the real thief. That Venn here was actually part of a sting. It's over, Margaret. You've been stung. You can leave now."

"You won't get away with this." Chisholm was beginning to crack, her tight bottom lip twitching, her eyes going milky as she fumbled with her briefcase before storming out of the room.

"I believe I will. Oh, and Ms. Chisholm, you have until the end of the day to clear personal possessions out of your office. Your files will remain with SSPR. After that, you will not be welcome on the premises."

As the door slammed behind her, Scott sang under his breath, "Bye-Bye, bug eyes! Nah nah nah nah, hey hey, goodbye."

· · • · ·

With a shit-eating grin plastered to his rough, haggard face, Scott floated through the rest of the meeting. He wanted to hug Tony; hell, he wanted to kiss him. When they asked if he could pay back the money, he shrugged his now weightless shoulders and said, "What are we talking about here?"

Tony established the terms. "Listen, Scott, what you did is wrong. You haven't gotten away with anything. You got greedy, Scott. You didn't wait and play their game. But here's the deal. You give the cash back to SSPR and you can leave with a good reference and a spotless record. That's it. You can move to another firm and do whatever the hell you want. So, have you got the cash? What's the tally, Dave? How much did Scotty squirrel away?"

Dave looked to the lawyers, then down at the legal pad in front of him. He was becoming a Shemp again.

"Christ, Tony, you know, that's just the thing. So many variables. We can't be sure. It seems to add up to a little more than 350."

As blissfully worry-free, as mindless as Scott was, he froze. The wheels started turning.

Holy crap. They really don't know.

He heard Tony, but the words meant nothing to him. "Have you got the money, Scott?"

Holy crap. I'm rich. I'm free. They're thieves, too, fat old stupid ones. I'm free and I'm rich.

"Scott?"

"Yeah. . . ."

"Tell me you've still got the money, buddy."

"Yeah, Tony. Sure I do." The perverse, imaginary little guy – Scott Venn's personal motivation trainer, a tiny, fucked-up version of Tony Robbins – who sometimes murdered Scott's tiny angel and scared the bejesus out of his tiny devil, took its place on his shoulder, kicked its miniature legs, and whispered instructions in Scott's ear.

199

"But the thing is, no matter what, this is going to hurt. And you know, well, I think that my discretion – the hardship of this past month, what it's done to me and my wife – can only come at a price. I'm not the only one at fault here."

The room was perfectly still again. Scott waited. Finally, Dave spoke. "How much would you *like* to pay back?"

"Half."

Silence. A very long, heavy silence.

"Fine."

While the lawyers and Stooges bickered quietly amongst themselves, Scott grabbed Tony's pen and scratched out a note on a scrap of paper from his briefcase. He pushed them both back across the table to Tony when no one was looking.

The note read: *I owe you.*

Tony wrote and pushed his response back across the table as he rose. He put his jacket back on and snapped his briefcase shut, saying, "Gentlemen, if you don't mind. I'll leave you to work out the details." As he was walking through the door he turned back to his bud. "And Scott, you're a stupid, greedy bastard, you know that? And I'm not sure which is worse. Just don't ever fuck with me again."

Scott only feigned dismay, regret, now; he'd already read Tony's note: *Not cool to talk, dude. The Rail. I'll be there. Later.*

Feeling like he was about to laugh, Scott hid behind the top of his open briefcase and covered his mouth, ecstatic. When he was composed, he touched his cigarettes and lighter, considered just sparking up.

Greener, old friend, I've found you.

He didn't, of course. He just turned and stared out the window. Watching the boats in the beautiful harbour.

The peelers are arriving, he thought. Hitting the grind. Getting on with getting it on. The peelers have arrived.

See, Man, he wanted to say. *You Can Win!*

And so can I.

11:19 AM

JOE JAMES THINKS HE'S HIS FUCK-UP NEPHEW'S LAST BEST HOPE. The boy's a hardcore alcoholic. Deep in denial. A reckless monster. Just like his father, just like his grandfather.

Christ, it's all too much for Maria – the life she's had – to handle.

It's for this reason alone, for Maria and her suffering, that he's even

bothering to interfere, willing to get involved one final time. She's sur-
vived by suppressing, ignoring, shutting out what she can no longer bear.
Turned the other cheek, in blind faith and desperate hope and love, on a
hundred different occasions: only to have it hit, scarred, viciously, again.
First by her husband, Joe's brother. Then by his ghosts, his past and its
infidelities and carelessness. And now, horribly, by Joe's only other living
relative, her own son.

Oedipal fuck-up dipshit.

It's with remarkable restraint, then, that Joe sits, seething, parked in
his Olds across the street from this goddamned coffee shop. Reduced to
a fucking voyeur, he's sat and watched in disbelief for more than two
hours.

Peter sitting. Peter smoking. Peter fiddling with his goddamned coffee cup. Peter stumbling and disappearing in a hell of a hurry, holding a
hand over his mouth, the other clutching his ass. Peter returning, green.
More coffee. Peter putting on that damn hood's coat. Peter on the phone.
Peter shaking his head. Peter exploding.

And then, Peter still, always Peter, mumbling to himself, clenching
and unclenching sausage fingers into ballooned fists. Peter stumbling out
into the daylight, oblivious, tripping off the Coffee Time step. Peter heading to the right, then stopping, then to the left, then stopping, then
walking up to the bank machine on the corner.

Peter withdrawing money. Peter just barely pulling a punch that
would have shattered the ATM screen.

Peter hailing a cab. Peter getting in. The cab backfiring.

Peter heading back toward home.

The little lying prick.

Sonofabitch!

Joe had realized, somehow just knew, Peter was yanking his chain
when he pulled out of the Hilton driveway. The kid hadn't been able to
make eye contact for years, but even through the distillery urinal that
wafts off him like the cologne of every fucking waste-case he's ever
known, he could still smell the fear.

Christ.

So that's why he circled the goddamned block and parked at the
meter. And why he stopped that fat fuck the kid's supposed to work with
on the street. And that's how he found out – the donut chugging bastard
laughing in his face – that Peter hadn't been securing anything, not a
hotel or his own future, for a very long time.

Now Joe James starts the engine of his Olds, livid and curious. Pulls
out and follows that car. What the hell is he doing with himself?

Thinking about confronting the boy, even beating the living tar out of him, Joe already knows how the morning's going to play out. He'll tail his nephew until he discovers precisely how he's destroying his life, and then he'll catch him red-handed and lay down the law.

Joe knows he'll give the boy the choice, two fifty-fifty propositions. The bad news and the worse. One: either you tell your mother, or I do. Two: either you get help, or you go to hell.

And then Peter will, of course, fuck up. On both counts.

At least then, he thinks, it will end. Maria will have to open her god-damned eyes. She'd never forgive him for turning on her son, but the truth would be unavoidable and even she'd have to give up on the James's and save her goddamned self.

He could kill the little rat bastard for putting him, them, in this position.

Driving, he remembers. There used to be something there – a spark, something different about his brother's, no, Maria's, boy. A good, big kid. Lots of heart under all those scabs and the pus and boils. Joe knows how hard that must've been for a teenager. Oversized and uncoordinated. Weight up and down and up and down. Face like a fucking minefield. A rat fucking bastard for an old man. Knows too, that it was all part of Peter's rebellion: shaving his head like a fucking rooster or a goddamned Indian. The makeup and hair dye. Yeah, who could blame the kid for hiding behind the leather and chains and jeans and all that loud noise. Guys screaming a million miles an hour, worse than hippie shit.

Hell, Joe'd always tried to help Peter, encourage him, guide him in the right direction, offer him the opportunity to discover the life-long benefits of learning a little discipline. He'd always liked the little fucker, gave him something extra on birthdays and Christmas, decided to make himself available in ways that Robert, his brother, just never would.

Everything he did, you'd never figure the boy'd become more and more like his old man.

It was Joe who took Peter to his first hockey game; Cherry's Bruins were kicking the crap out of everyone back then, and that night was no different. Peter loved it: wanted to be Gerry Cheevers so bad after the one game that Joe suited the kid up and got him stopping pucks the next day. Made sure to get the same damned mask, the one with all the scars.

Poor bastard could barely skate – but he was as fearless as he was awkward. And eventually, not half bad.

Even Joe's friend Owen took a shine to the kid. Got him interested in film when he was thirteen, took him on commercial shoots – after one the kid came home smiling like a pig in shit, singing *Wonderful wonderful WonderBra* for weeks – and taught him about cameras, editing, video.

When Owen's blood turned on him a few years later, he left all his gear to Peter. Christ, his brother was so uncomfortable with it that Joe almost wrote the whole fucking lot of them off.

If it wasn't for Maria and the boy, he would have. Sometimes she made being a James bearable.

Yeah, his big brother Rob was a first class jerk: a drunk, a coward, and a hypocrite. He insisted, with real menace, that Joe keep his private life to himself; it was a probationary condition, he added, that would never go away. You never expect that kind of fear and hate and stupidity from family, but the younger James brother had spent most his adult life marshalling stoic resolve against institutional discomfort so he put up with it. Not that he had a problem copping to who he was – on the contrary, he was completely at ease with the intersection of the world at large with his private life – no, he'd just reached an age, and a point in his life, where he felt he'd earned his stripes and could put all the tough, small skirmishes behind him. So, when Rob said the kid wasn't to be told the truth about Owen's death, Joe James respected the ornery bastard's wishes. Rob *was* the kid's father, so he never told the boy a goddamned thing. After all, he'd figure it out eventually, right?

I mean, you can't grow them that dumb these days, can you?

Evidently, you can.

Joe was sitting on the battered old couch in Maria and Rob's living room when it happened. Four years ago, this coming Thanksgiving.

The boy had finished high school and, because his dad was such a fucking narrow-minded, lazy prick, followed blindly in the family's blue collar footsteps. All Rob had to say was: Don't even fucking think about more school, you stupid, lazy little fuck. And, yeah, Peter ends up working for UPS, too. Hauling brown packages, wearing brown polyester, driving an open-doored brown truck – greasy and sweat-soaked in a dirt brown sheen all summer, freezing his rocks blue, getting himself a little colour, one that wasn't shit brown at least, the rest of the year – just like his old man.

Maria tried, in her own quiet way, always barely maintaining – but Joe was the only one who really supported Peter in the film thing. When Robert wasn't drunk he ignored him; when he was, he ridiculed him. Or worse, knocked the kid around some.

It was Joe who convinced Peter to go part-time at the technical college, spend nights and weekends learning, making movies. It was Joe who popped for his tuition, praised his short films.

Jesus, they were fucking awful.

Banal and confusing, usually. Sometimes unintentionally hilarious.

You know, kid stuff mostly. Fake blood and monsters, bad buddy films, rock and roll.

Unbelievably, though, Peter and a couple pals raised the cash – a lot of it, thirty-five, forty grand – begged, borrowed, or stole the film stock, rounded up a halfway decent cast of young actors, and made a fucking feature film. A goddamned teenage road movie. They shot the whole thing during Peter's vacation that summer. Jesus, they even managed to get a relatively hot local director interested, amused probably, and he paid his editor to help them piece the thing together on weekends.

So it's Thanksgiving and Peter's partners are over after the family dinner. Damned if one of them doesn't blow Peter's mind by announcing that their director buddy's got them lined up to meet his producers next week; says the guys's talking, even, a possible distribution deal. For real.

Rob hears this from the kitchen, where he's fixing himself another drink, and laughs. Normally, you see, he couldn't give a flying fuck about his useless kid and his idiot friends, but he's been drinking all day and getting meaner by the glass.

Anyway, the whole idea tonight is for the guys to pop a tape in the VCR. The big premiere. It's for Joe's benefit really, because he kicked in a thousand or two himself. Yeah, they're are all proud and excited now, giddy as kids, and Joe's happy to give them the opportunity to strut.

Nobody figured Rob would plant his ass down, too. He never had before – always holed himself up in his bedroom, watching his own TV, drinking himself to sleep. Especially on weekends and holidays. Tonight, though, he was in the mood for a little fun. Something different.

Tonight he was going to explore his parenting skills. Show a little interest in his only son.

Christ, it was tense, Maria sat rigid through the opening credits, the guys eyeing Rob nervously. Peter's face burning beet red.

Joe figured his presence would be enough to keep his brother in line.

Fuck, he couldn't have been more wrong.

At first, it seemed like everything might be working out. Ten minutes in, Rob's head bobbed and his eyes narrowed. Everybody assumed he'd passed out, or at least was getting there. Maria and Peter visibly relaxed. Joe was able to focus on the film.

It wasn't the worst he'd ever seen. Not quite.

But Jesus, it really did stink.

Now, one of the big differences between Joe James and his brother Robert, men who were in so many ways identical – forget about the fact that one was sober and the other a drunk, and leave Joe's bachelor status be for a minute – was that for all his bluster and tough talk, Joe thought of himself as, and actually was, a kind person.

Just because Joe hated the movie he was watching, just because it was actually indescribably awful, doesn't mean that he'd have to go and say anything. He *knew* there were other people in the room. And, unlike his older brother, Joe was acutely aware of them. He knew they had feelings. Empathized. No, he'd find it quite easy to keep his mouth shut, smile, and offer encouragement. Find something to praise even.

Robert? Well, Robert wouldn't.

Robert had no empathy. No pity. No remorse. Stone cold sober, Robert James had no self-censoring mechanism whatsoever.

It was worse when he was drunk.

A third of the way through the film, Robert, who looked asleep, started breathing more deeply, annoyingly loud. Almost snoring. Distracting, yeah, but everybody managed to ignore him.

As pissed as he was, this probably spurred him on.

Next thing you know, he's fake coughing, clearing his throat.

That got everybody's attention.

So then his eyes are wide open, and his drink's in his hand. The last little shavings of ice swirl around the pool of whiskey before he raises it to his lips and makes everything disappear, effortlessly. He doesn't even swallow. His throat opens and the amber fluid, ice shards and all, just glides down into his belly.

Believing his own little dramatic debut is the best thing about the night's entertainment so far, Robert pauses, then raises the stakes.

"You gotta be fucking kidding."

Peter's red again, looking at his shoes. A year or so on the Acutane and his face, at this very moment, looks worse than ever. His buddies? Well, his buddies are trying hard not to look at anything.

Maria, tentative, wants to salvage things: "Honey, how about we go upstairs and watch *Frasier?* You know, you like that dog."

Robert ignores her.

"Jesus. This fucking stinks. This is the worst goddamned piece of shit I've ever fucking seen. It's a joke, right?" Robert's pointing at his son and laughing. "You can't be serious. Don't tell me anybody's gonna pay to sit through this."

"Robert, stop." Quiet but firm, it was all Joe wanted to say. As far as he wanted this to go. His heart was breaking for his nephew.

"Fuck, Joe. Not you, too? When'd the fucking aliens abduct you, huh? When'd they take your goddamned sense? Ha ha. C'mon, li'l Joe, you know as well as I do, this's a piece of shit. The boy's fucking useless. My son? You know he's always been useless. Right? So ya don't expect much. But Jesus. Seriously. I mean, what the fuck?"

"Robert. I mean it. Stop."

"Don't be fucking encouraging 'em, Joey. Say it, man, they're all a pack of fucking useless little fucks. I mean, you saw that thing. What's it supposed to be? Looks like a fat chick in a fuckin' hot fuckin' chocolate-coloured toilet tank cover to me. I mean, the whole thing don't make no goddamned sense. For instance, how's a bunch of idiot fuck-up brats end up stealin' a motherfuckin' unmarked cop car? And why're they goin' out to the woods, anyway? What fuckin' for is what I wanna know. Who's goddamned cottage is that? How'd they get the goddamned key? Somebody please es'plain it, willya? Okay okay, you say all that's possible. Fine. I'll even give you that. But a motherfuckin' werewolf, Joe? Jesus. Why? I'll tell you why, Joe: it's 'cause my son's a goddamned idiot. That's why. And you, you soft little freak, you're leading him on."

Joe glanced from Peter to Maria then. His nephew looked like he wanted to cry. His sister-in-law was already wiping her cheeks. Joe James had heard enough. He stood and glared.

Calm at first, running his powerful right hand through the stubble on his head, he said, "Pete, Maria, I'm sorry." And then he turned on his only brother. "Fuck you, Rob. Big fucking man. Fuck you. Jesus, you got some nerve. He's your boy, Rob. Your son. How fucking dare you? Yeah, yeah, you're drunk, Rob. You're a fucking drunk and a real fucking asshole. But you know that. And I know that. Hell, everyfuckingbody in the room knows it. And yet you talk."

Her voice small, almost broken, Maria tries, one last time, to minimize the damage, to contain and maintain: "Please guys, let's just watch the rest. . . ."

Joe's voice cuts through hers, swallows it up. "Yeah, you talk big brother. You've actually got the nerve to make fun of your only fucking kid. That's sweet, Rob. Sweet, but no surprise. Why? Because you hate the fact that he's trying to do something with his life? Is that it? Yes, that's it. You wanna shit on him just because you hate your own fucking life so goddamned much? Huh? You've fucked things up for yourself, so you gotta fuck them up for everybody. Right, Robbie? Yeah, right."

Robert James, now red-faced too, not shamed but furious, staggers to his feet. "How do I? Jesus, fuck. Me dare? How'd you, huh? Fuck! Fucking talk to me like that! In my fucking home. You're maybe my little brother, but I'll still kick your pansy ass six ways to Sunday!"

"Go to bed, Robbie. Get your sorry ass out of here. You're drunk, buddy boy, so yeah, fine. Fuck you." Joe's trembling with rage as he says this.

"I said don't you talk! Don't you. You! Fuck! Don't you speak to me in my house! Like that. Fucker. Fuckin' freak, talking to me in my house!"

"Shut up, Rob."

The brothers have moved within inches of one another now; no-one else in the room has flinched. Everyone's afraid to even sharpen their focus on the confrontation, knowing that even the subtlest movement could set it off.

"Get out of my fuckin' house, Joey. We don't want you here. Nobody! We don't want your kind here, Joey. Get the fuck out."

"Fine, Robbie. Fine. But you leave everybody alone tonight. You hear me? I'll fuckin'.... Well, you don't want to even think about what I'll do to you if I hear otherwise."

"Get the fuck outta my house!"

"Yeah, yeah, Rob. I'm leaving." And then he turned to his nephew and the boy's friends and said, softly: "Guys: I love it. Come to my place next week and we'll watch the rest. Okay?"

Hearing this, Robert James shook his jowly face and then lurched at his brother, finger wagging at Joe's nose, spit flying everywhere. "You're such a filthy fucking liar, Joey. I know you, you know that? I know. Oh yes, yes, Joseph, I do! And you lie. Fuck! Your whole fucking perverted life's a lie, you fucking sick bugger. And I've had enough. Pete's my son. Not yours. My son! I'm his father, fuck! And I say he's not going over to no filthy fuckin' fag's house, even if he's my fuckin' fag brother. You hear me, Joey? That's it! No more! Stay away from my son you goddamned sick sonofabitch!"

No one, not even Robert, saw Joe's right hand fly at the drunken throat that was attacking him. It happened too quickly. All anyone saw was Robert's slack body after it happened: immobile, pinned to the wall, his face contorted, gasping for air. All they could hear was Joe hissing.

"The boy'd be better off if he had no goddamned father! They'd all be better off if you were dead."

The livid splotch of Peter James's face evanesced at this moment. He went pale, grew heavy-lidded, grey-eyed, sick, and hungry. His acne and pockmarks coalesced, cast themselves in the weather of defeat – surrender and mortification. In the decisiveness of self-consuming rage and loathing, he rose to his feet and roared that he wanted a drink.

In short, he became his daddy's boy. Blood alcohol: thicker than water.

"Get off of him, you fuck! Get fucking off!" Peter screamed and threw a big forearm around his uncle's throat, locked it in and pulled the vice back. Joe just set his Ranger choke hold more firmly around his brother's larynx. The three men swayed as one.

"Let go, Pete. You heard him. He's had this coming for years," Joe managed, though sucking for air himself.

"Let fucking go!"

Robert was blueing. His eyes jigging vacant, unable to focus on his brother, his son.

Three ferocious, angry men, playing out this kind of stalemate? A little more pressure might have been applied, the principles of torque and leverage might have come into play. Something could have happened to change everything: life, as the James boys knew it, might have taken on a new, legal definition. Become part of a new sentence. Maria's plea, however, made sure that the only ramifications were subtle and emotional. And much more devastating.

Terrified, crying, she found the voice for only three words: "Please, Joe, stop."

And he did. Hearing his sister-in-law's pain and terror, all the anger in Joe James's body drained away. He went slack in his nephew's strong arms.

Robert sucked in a painful, squeaking, sputtering draught of air. Peter, who'd heard but not processed his mother's words, tightened his grip around his uncle's throat and spun him away from his father. Between the two men now, he let go and shoved Joe back into the couch.

In the calm seconds that followed, Robert's resentment of his only son grew. Still drunk, still disgusted, as he regained his strength and hollow composure he puffed with stupid, fierce pride: "I didn't need no fucking help from you, boy. Fuck! I'll take the fucking fag. I will. Fuck. You're just like him. You know that? Fucking soft in the head, the both of you! My son? Fuck. Fuck the lot of you, fags. Pussies! I don't need you!"

Peter cocked his head in his father's direction, narrowed his eyes. Shut down. His chest heaved with the exertion.

Joe hung his head in the cups of his hands and Maria cried harder, still mumbling, "Stop, please, please, stop."

"Shut the fuck up, Mom. It's over! I fucking well stopped it!"

"Petey, dear, calm down," Maria said, shocked to a meek reserve by hearing her husband's words, spoken in the voice of her baby boy.

"I said shut the fuck up!"

Joe raised his head, stared at his nephew in disbelief. "Pete? That's your mother, Pete. Don't speak to her like that. Calm yourself, son. It's over. It's over. My fault. Everything, out of hand. C'mon, calm down."

"You!" Peter shook and pointed, another spitting image, a distortion of his psychotic dad. "You shut up, too! You *are* a liar! You are. He's a fucking bastard, but at least he's fucking honest. You lie so fucking much, don't you, Uncle fucking Joey? Who the fuck am I trying to kid, right? This is your fault! You fucking fag, pushing me all the time! What, you wanna make me like you, fag?"

"Petey, no. Joe, he doesn't mean this."

"No, Mom. I do mean it. Everybody get out. Get outta my house. All of you, go!" Peter pounced on the VCR, ejected the tape, took it in his fist, then slammed it against the exposed brick wall. "Who the fuck do I think I am? Jesus, what an idiot! Making a fucking movie with a bunch of fucking fags!" He spoke to the wall, the pieces of plastic and the loop of magnetic tape that had showered down around him.

Terminally embarrassed, sickened by Peter's display, his buddies edged out of the room. One of them turned, spoke the words that had to be spoken because they'd all turned on him: "Fuck you, James."

Robert laughed then. Laughed at his son and brother and wife. And then he too stumbled out, shaking his head, mumbling, "Jesus H. A fucking embarrassing pack of fucking freaks. Whoa, sensitive. Touchy little fuckers. Ha."

Peter's disfigurement hung over Maria and Joe, even though he faced the wall, his forehead worrying itself to new agonies on rough brick.

Maria approached her son tentatively; her left hand reached up to his shoulder but stopped, repelled almost, an inch or two from making contact. It hovered there as she spoke. "Joe, I'm so sorry. Petey's sorry. He's just, just disappointed. But maybe you should go."

"Yeah, sure." Joe, still shocked, began to walk away. He stopped to look at his sister-in-law and his nephew, to check, almost, if this had really happened.

It had.

"And I'm sorry too, Maria. We've all ruined your holiday. The turkey was wonderful. I'm sorry." And then he addressed Peter. "Look, kid. This isn't right. I'm sorry. I lost control. But don't do this to yourself. Please. Look at me. Don't do this. We should talk. Fix it."

"There's nothing left to say, Uncle Joe," Peter whispered. "Just get out. Leave me. Okay? Leave. Christ."

"C'mon, Pete, you're not like this."

Peter turned then, and his mother backed off. He walked towards his uncle and stopped, looking down, inches from his face. "You're wrong. I am. I am like this." And then he too walked from the room.

Maria and Joe were left looking at one another but unable to see anything but their own, remarkably unique pain.

Petey? Pete?

In the kitchen Peter went straight for his father's bottle. Taking it and a large juice glass he walked up the stairs to his room.

The budgie called out after him: Hey buddy, don't sweat the small stuff. You know how the old man is. Buddy?

Peter James shut the door, firmly, behind himself. His mother had the window cracked open; a fresh, brisk breeze cut through the toasty smell of the gas furnace.

Peter shut the window, tight, walked to his desk and set the bottle and glass down. He popped *Sid and Nancy* into his VCR and punched on the TV. Then he cracked his neck, lit a smoke, poured himself four fingers of whiskey, and sat down on the edge of the bed. As the rim of the glass met his lips, he shuddered: not at the bite and burn of the alcohol – none had toppled into his mouth yet – but because something deep inside of himself said: It's about time. Thank you, and goodbye.

And then his throat opened, just like that. The contents of the glass disappeared.

They didn't really know what was happening, of course. Though both of them suspected. And at the very same moment, downstairs, Joe and Maria James turned away from one another and spoke, in unison.

"I'm sorry," they said.

Aware of a new balance, a new standard to maintain, in the house, in his life, but before losing himself forever in the whiskey and for a while in Gary Oldman's character, Peter reached out to the bedside table and turned over the framed photograph of his pretty, young, blonde, soon to be ex-girlfriend, face down.

"I'm sorry," he said over the sound of Uncle Joe's Olds coughing to life in the driveway. "I'm sorry. Christ, Jennifer, I'm so fucking sorry."

· · • · ·

Payback time. Whup-ass time. I haven't got the time to be fucking around like this time.

Not Coffee Time or walking time or drinking time or lapdance time or just one more time or closing time.

This is new time, unfamiliar and uncomfortable. Painfully unrehearsed, improvisational time. Time he hadn't planned on taking. Time his mind and addiction do not know how to account for.

Seeping and seething into the back of the piss and puke and pine and BO-reeking cab, Peter James was not happy about all the things that had gotten into his time. He chewed at a soapy lock of his blue-black hair and closed his angry red and grey blue eyes and rocked himself against the tension between the throbbing in his head and the farting car lurching forward.

Through teeth and damp hair, he managed his address.

The driver shook his head, laughed. "Rough night?"

"Ugh."

"That bad?"

Peter opened his eyes; his stomach churned.

Motion sickness: he had to find something to focus on. Picked the photo behind the headrest, the cabbie's licence.

The ugly square head of Goran Vlastic.

"You're not gonna be sick, are you?"

"Huh?"

"Not in my fucking cab, got it?"

Peter glanced up at the rear-view. Those weren't the same eyes. Not the same guy. He looked at the back of his head: younger. Maybe not quite his age.

"Uh uh."

"Good. Jesus, what the fuck did you do to yourself last night?"

Peter belched, clamped his mouth shut just in case his stomach had a mind to bail. Tequila and beer and bourbon and cigarette gas forced its way through his sinuses, escaped through all his cracks.

Feeling better. Couldn't get much. . . . Aw, fuck.

"Buddy?"

Peter managed a smile. Twisted and malicious, the curl to his lips came from nothing he knew – he still knew, understood, nothing. The smile was faith, demented fervent belief: it was how his body responded when his mind and his addiction decided they'd regained control. That, heading west, for home, they might maintain.

There was a drink there, right?

Peter answered the cabbie who wasn't the ugly, square-headed Goran Vlastic.

"The nights aren't so bad. But the mornings are a bitch."

"Okay. . . ."

Putting on his headphones, flipping the cassette, Peter asked the guy if he had the time.

"Yeah, just going on eleven. Five to."

Peter pressed play. His own cruel little joke – the sample before Henry Rollins growling about Black Coffee and Metallica ripping through the Mistfits' "Die, Die, My Darling" would put him at his own front door – threw faith back up into his scarred face. Sylvester Stallone in *Rhinestone;*

211

Sylvester Stallone, *singing:* "Budweiser, you created a monster. And they call him, Drinkinstein."

I believe that's funny, he thought. I believe, I don't know what to believe.

I don't know.

I don't know anymore.

Maybe it's not funny.

Maybe it's time for something different.

Maybe it's time for a new tape.

· · • · ·

A creature of so many habits, Peter James forces himself to sit down at the kitchen table and roll a joint before going upstairs to his room, to the bottle he believes will make up for lost time. He's not listening to "Ace of Spades" at nine on his walkman because he wants to – it's just what he does.

It's smoke time. I'm late, but it's definitely smoke time.

And this is how smoke time goes.

Licking the gummy edge of the Zig-Zag paper, automatically curling it over and into a perfect missile with his screwed up thumbs, he thinks nothing of this miracle of dexterity, the minute, Swiss precision his motor skills rise to, always, at this time.

Only at this time.

Instead, his thoughts roll clumsily, painfully, back upon themselves. Tighter and narrower and tighter.

Much too narrow. Way too tight.

He's been transfixed by the way the light burns in his tree. His father's tree. The kitchen is grey, gloomy; the window streaked with tar, lifeless; the sink tarnished, all used up – but out there a thousand thousand sunbeams dapple explosions of possibility on a thousand thousand dying leaves.

Out there, not in here.

No room to manoeuvre. No way out.

And then his thumbs stop and his thoughts collapse into two terrifying dimensions, horrific, inflexible linearity.

And the song becomes an accusation, gets stuck on its own hard indifference.

You win some, you lose some – it's all the same to me.

And then a single cloud passes overhead, and a thousand thousand tiny lights are extinguished, and his tree, his father's tree, becomes a dying, skeletal thing.

All vital signs are flatlining.

Peter presses stop, ejects the tape, and rips off his headphones. He grabs his miniature red Bic lighter, gets up and walks to the sink.

He sighs and thinks of his mother, of coming into the house and finding his dope in the laundry room wastepaper basket.

I believe she thought my tinfoil ball was garbage.

I believe she just wants to take care of me.

He nods to himself: some things never change.

I believe I hurt her.

Hurt her as much as the old man.

I believe that must change.

Hell, Pete, you *know* that must change. Don't you?

· · • · ·

Joe James is shaking, the shock and the shame and the pain and the rage have not yet receded. His left index finger sits heavily on the button that's disconnected the call he's just made on Maria James' kitchen phone.

The kitchen still reeks of pot, as strong as when he slipped into the house five minutes earlier.

The light in here is incredible; the bird sings happily, oblivious.

Everything changed so quickly. Got taken to a level higher, more dire, than he thought possible.

Good for nothing little fuckup. Maggot-faced puke. Worthless piece of shit — just like his old man.

Pete, you've fucking done it this time. I'm sorry, Maria, he deserves everything he's getting. There's no other way.

Fuck. He'll always be the same. Just like Rob.

There had been no answer when he'd rapped on the front door, already tense from playing out the confrontation in his head. Furious, then, he let himself in.

Upstairs, the stereo blasted. A morose, tuneless voice ghosting all sorts of pansy-assed denial: "The piano has been drinking, not me."

Yeah, right, buddy.

He'd followed the smell first, into the kitchen. Saw the kid's dope, dropped his car keys on the table, and rolled up his sleeves.

How could he do this to his mother? Jesus. She can't go through this, not again.

He'd hesitated at the threshold for a moment before storming into Pete's room, the kid sat at his desk with his back to the door: he obviously couldn't hear him approaching. On his bed, there were two Glad garbage bags filled with shit, a full bottle of whiskey tipped against one. His closet had been pulled apart, goalie pads sat stacked against a vacuum on the floor beside him. The kid held a framed picture of his old girlfriend: he was crying, the sick little bastard.

It was pathetic, just fucking pathetic.

Peter's tears had made him angrier.

As he dials 911, Joe tries to remember if he slapped Pete before or after he spun him around on the swivel chair and started screaming.

It all happened so fast.

Pete covering up and begging: "Stop, stop."

All the years of Joe's frustration, tumbling down the twelve steep steps of *his* rage.

All the hate, and abuse, almost incomprehensible. The wrath of outliving his father, his brother, and his lover; his powerlessness.

The kid on the floor, his crazy fist cocked high above his right shoulder.

Letting go but not hitting. Really wanting to hit.

Collapsing then himself, falling to the floor.

Saying: "Maria, oh Christ, Maria, I'm sorry."

Seeing the blood on his nephew's lip, the sorrow of thinking that's not enough, not even a start.

His chest hurting bad.

Watching Pete scramble away and up, a mean little crab, grabbing the bottle. Watching him run out the door.

Feeling, through the floor, him tear down the stairs.

Sucking for breath, fighting his pain, hand over heart.

Joe James sat on his nephew's bedroom rug for four or five minutes, thinking he was having a coronary. When he caught some of his breath and some of the crushing weight began to lift off his chest, he came to many interesting conclusions.

Today, for example, was not a good day to die.

His heart, at any rate, still wouldn't dare attack him – not quite, not yet. But he also knew he had to wake up and smell the coffee: he wasn't bulletproof, he wasn't G.I. Joe anymore. He also knew he deserved to get old, after all the shit he'd been through. Besides, Peter Anthony James just wasn't worth his while.

Tentatively, Joe got up and walked to the stereo. Turned it off. He ran the edge of his thumb along the dusty cassette case that sat open in front of it. In blue and green lettering it said: Jen's Tape. Under that there was a pink heart. And under that it read: Tom Waits.

Walking slowly down the stairs, holding the banister, he called out:

214

"Pete? You there? Listen, Pete, I don't give a rat's ass what you do anymore. Got it? I give up. You'll never change."

The sonofabitch, of course, didn't answer.

But now, after calling Maria at work and breaking her heart, sitting at her kitchen table, listening to her budgie sing, the emergency operator does.

"My car's been stolen," he says. "My car's been stolen, and I know the alcoholic sonofabitch who did it."

· · • · ·

Maria James knows she's her son's last best hope.

When Krystal/Jr. Assistant said there was some guy on the phone for her she lost count of how many painkillers she'd already separated from her little blue-grey hill.

My, was that twenty or thirty?

Oh well, just start again.

She was happy for the call: probably just Petey, wanting to apologize for being such a grouch.

It wasn't.

Now that Joe had gone and ruined everything, now that he'd called and told her and said he was going to have to phone the police, she hurriedly, hastily filled the prescription and told Krystal to ring in the customer.

Goran Vlastic paid for the fifty Vicodin he'd been prescribed for his bad back. The blue-grey bombers, lately, made the hours he spent in the car bearable. In two weeks he would rage about the fucking criminals who sold him only thirty-eight – it would be his way of reintegrating, of adding something useful. His way of saying: Thank you, I'm ready to participate in your polite society, to rejoin, if you'll have me.

After taking two fear-filled, conscience-plagued weeks off, he'd be welcomed back with open arms.

Maria James was on the phone again, doing the only thing she could think of doing, doing the thing she hated doing more than anything else.

Peter's mother was trying to find his ex-girlfriend, Jennifer. No answer at home or at her sister's, she tried that horrible place where she works.

The man who answered said, "You'll have to hold for a couple minutes, ma'am. Or call back later. I think she's in the middle of a dance. Yeah, I'm sorry, she is."

"I'll wait," she said, not wanting to know what really happened between her boy and the only woman he'd ever been with. She feared the worst, of course, but wouldn't allow herself to believe it – just as she

215

wouldn't allow her mouth to complete the phrase that's dying to get out: "I'll wait . . . for the *slut*." Instead, she said, "Please, if it's not too much trouble, I'll wait."

As she popped one of the many linty, baby blue Valium she'd snuck into her lab coat pocket over the years into her mouth and under her tongue, she realized her son would never forgive her. While it dissolved, she hummed along with Jon Bon Jovi and closed her eyes and convinced herself, yet again, to forget.

Some day he'll thank you. It's for the best.

Have faith, Maria.

God willing, some day he'll change.

TWO

Nobody knows what it's like
to feel these feelings
like I do . . .
and I blame you.

PETE TOWNSHEND
Behind Blue Eyes

And this gave me comfort. Thinking that
so many men were ready to make jubilant jumps
into oblivion, or to put tidy little holes in their heads,
with me, I was unable to view my own self-destruction
as anything but a trifling and dreary dream.

FREDERICK EXLEY
A Fan's Notes

SATURDAY, OCTOBER 4th

Everyone's forgotten. You cannot forget.

She's hurt bad. There's so much blood. Too much.

When you start you start with the outline of a woman like this. You can disturb nothing, so you're careful, take it all in. Do not move her. Do not hurt her further. Do not compromise her dignity.

You hover over her, inscribe her in the soft, fluid arc of your attention, a gentle swaddling, a white blanket in a cradle of down, the simple dimensions of purity and pity. This will protect and preserve her.

You can see it all, then and now, and you reconstruct and you remember. Over and over you hear your own breathing disturb the cool air in whispers of sorrow and you remember and reconstruct with each breath: he walks through the door and they argue and then something snaps and his eyes flash and die and his lips thin and he's electric and she's shocked and he strikes and she falls and he strikes and he strikes and he walks through the door. . . .

You've watched a thousand thousand thin bubbles draw all the light into tiny rainbows on a sea of crimson as they've risen and pushed at their seams and popped and fallen back into the gaping middle of her face.

You've seen the crimson starfish pulse and grow and spread from the shell of her ear: it keeps reaching, still, for something you cannot see.

A pulpy pink tooth still strobes behind her lower lip.

You've smelled the smells of mortification and mortality, of fear and trauma, the automatic smells of excruciating pain.

You've spasmed with the spasms, the darker blood and bile that birthed another creature, sent it off towards you, crawling, begging for mercy. Accusing maybe, monstrous. Released to hunt you down.

You've counted all the splinters, traced the contours of all the abrasions. You've recognized yourself, broken, there beside her on the floor. You've been blinded by her copper halo, awed by all the angels who've sung to her in the heart of your breath, and those who sing on the wire of cool night air. Gathered her, gently, so gently, in soft wings.

You've raged against the terrible angel who laughs.

You've heard the rattle in her, the buzz that should not be, an ocean of new sounds, listened to the drowning rehearse. You've cried and averted your gaze.

And then you remembered and reconstructed again. And then you watched. And then you waited.

You've measured eternity itself in the minutiae, the almost imperceptible rise and fall of her broken body, her one good lung.

You've said it a thousand thousand times, and thought it, and cried it, and fought not to collapse under the weight, the horror of it: Come back, buddy, come back. She's hurt bad, come back.

It feels like forever, this moment. Everyone's forgotten. You cannot forget. And then the moment passes. And then you cry, Buddy, you cry.

Breathe, goddamn it. Breathe.

LAST CALL

FRIDAY, OCTOBER 3rd

11:59 PM

Pussyswoggled.

The guy she's led over the hard, beaten, red and black carpet, through the amazing dark – weaving him, deep into the club, past small tables where other girls hang on the every word of whomever, past security, a dogleg right, up a step and through a narrow entrance way, stepping high and delicate and side-stepping around the high heels and calves and swinging hair of women contorted everywhichway – pivots and eases back, nonchalant, cool as anything, never breaking eye contact.

He sees himself this way: irresistible, formidable, quicksilver, his face hard and cold and perfect. His smile is coy and his jaw is strong; his eyes burn, transfix, draw her down into his lap. He could make her laugh or break her heart; she'd confess any wicked secret, say anything to win a moment more of his attention, admit weaknesses only he can kiss and make better – he fulfills her darkest, dampest fantasy.

This is all her doing, of course. And she's good, very good, at what she does.

He's feeling fantastic and when he feels fantastic he always wants to take out the new ones for a test drive: shower his magnanimous attentions, share all of his bad self. There's plenty to go around, baby.

And so he lowers his powerful, beautiful self, easy into the tight alcove.

Actually, no. He flops, this guy. Tries to plunk his drunk butt down.

She watches him – eyes spinning, red and white and blue, flying saucers – misjudge the edge of the black vinyl and red velvet backed booth's worn, plush, built-in chair. And she doesn't laugh when his elbows keep his ass from plopping on the sticky black vinyl tile below and his face contorts into a surprised puppy's disbelief. And she doesn't even flinch or sneer or break eye contact – she's seen and felt it all before –

when an arcing fountain of lager burps up and ejaculates out and over her right ankle. Squishing a bit, Molson Golden seeping under her heel, soaking into her black stiletto, dripping another five-and-a-half inches to the floor, she shifts her weight and spears a million foamy bubbles: all the tiny, dishevelled men in red neon and blacklight reflected and refracted there, this guy and the one in the next alcove and the one directly across and the one next to that, pop.

Perfectly strip-pokerfaced, she just thinks: Smooth move, Ex-Lax.

Scrabbling back like a baby turtle, he becomes a jellyfish on the imitation red velvet, flicks his ash to his left and takes a swig of his green-bottled beer. Goofy now, he wipes the excess with the back of his smoking hand.

"It's twenty, okay?"

His tongue draws left to right over the edge of his teeth and just under his rubbery lip.

"Okay?"

He blinks the only choice he has left, pulls at his casual collar, loosens the knot of his pale tie.

Jesus, he's so old.

She smiles and growls and tilts his head back by chucking his stubbled chin. He thinks of a million brilliant things to say, trolls his lovelines – they're all good. But he can't pull his eyes away from how pneumatic she is, can't stop thinking: Monsterbagos, huge fucking melons. So he says: "You're so fucking beautiful. . . ." And then he adds: "I like this song."

It's Prince. She crinkles her freckled twenty-year-old nose and shrugs. Whatever.

She produces a small beige towel from out of nowhere, drapes it over his lap.

Suave, he knows he has her now: "Don't know about the little freak's new stuff, though. Where you from? How you doin'?"

Not about to answer, she rolls her eyes and bends her knees, looks into his okay face and smiles vacantly, taps his hand. He butts out his smoke and she lifts his arm and lets it fall into his lap. She eases her ass onto the armrest. Puts her arms around his neck.

"You've been through the drill, right? You can't touch me. I touch you."

He blinks, stutters his soundless mouth around something pat to say next.

She helps him out: "What do you do?"

His head's swimming in the smell of her, baby powder and lilies and sweat and smoke. It's divine, his favourite smell in the world.

"What? Oh, I. . . . Um, contracts mostly, I make deals. . . ."

He nods and swigs more beer. The wheels turning, his nostrils flair.

It's the shrimpy Artist's last verse now. "Darling Nikki" almost done – onstage, Nikki Sin's bunching up the ratty duvet between her thighs.

She thinks: Just like she does every time. Every guy in the place trying not to look like he wishes he was that filthy piece of cloth.

Her new guy laughs, narrows his eyes. "You know, if you touch me, then I *am* touching you."

She shrugs again.

"So what do we do about that?" He thinks he sounds like the smoothest motherfucker, like butter, like silk. He's sweating beads of beer and Sex-On-The-Beach and Orgasms.

My new guy's a talker and he's smashed. Bad combination, good combination – depending on how you want to look at it. Okay. Fine. She plays the card he's thrown, uses a finger as a pointer and touches her wrist and shoulder, her knee, her elbow. Using her deep throat and the kittenish squeak she learned from Marilyn Monroe movies, she says: "Okay, you get to touch me here and here and here. And here."

Nikki's gone to light applause, drunken slurs and hoots – all the impossible noises guys learn from teen sex farces, even a couple Blur woo hoos. The DJ's doing his game show announcer voice now, his tenor rising in fake excitement to get a response from the crowd. The Steve Miller Band plods into its groove: fuck, fucking Krystal's first of three, overindulgent '70s shit, the stuck-up cow.

She runs her hand over the guy's short spiky hair and sighs – she hates long, moody dances, hates this fucking interminable song. Reaching over his lap to grab the other armrest, she swings her cleavage around his cheeks as she vaults her left leg over his right knee. He sinks deeper into red when she's standing straight up in front of him, her long-nailed, French-manicured fingers tapping at the snaps on her hips, her heavy tits braced in their pink-lace underwire bra.

His eyes race from the slope her left toe begins, up, and then down the other side of the perfect V and then back up again.

She unsnaps her magic thong and with a flourish pulls the cloth out from under the table she's set for guys like him. He follows the sleight of hand like he's supposed to, up across her taut tummy until he sees the pink cotton kiss the tattooed Balinese weaving that frames the body art of her belly-button ring. Ta-da!

Jesus.

When his eyes finally drift down, a soft honey brown heart has replaced the thin V of pink. The illusion's so perfect he doesn't notice the faint blue shadow of stubble, angry pricks of red. In fact, he's so entranced by the perfect symmetry of her, the miraculous fold and tuck of her genital disappearing act, that he doesn't notice her cracking gum as she defies gravity by unveiling her huge new breasts.

And then he does and he's very, very pleased.

Like, Christ. Pam Anderson and David Copperfield, rolled into one. So many illusions: like, in this light you can't even see the scars.

She's listing with the music and readjusting the hand-towel, taut, over his uncomfortable lap; he's squirming and blinking rapidly, taking off from the launching pad of her magnificent nipples, over her belly and between her legs again. Completely taken, he's thinking: Where does it go?

I mean, it's like she really is a living, breathing Barbie doll.

His jaw drops and he sucks in enough breath for an extra-point team's worth of drunk, horny guys. For a moment it feels like it's not enough, that he's suffocating, even his pants constrict him and he spreads his legs wider, looking for relief. His cheeks balloon as she shoots her index finger straight into her pubic heart. When he pops and hisses out the air, his eyes follow. The kick's up, and it's good! She smiles and shakes her long blonde hair.

Christ, I'm good.

This is the part she likes best, the stunned, stupid look of amazement a guy gets when he first falls for the miracle of her snatch. The pale look of disbelief that quickly becomes pure, blind desire; his new obsession, the beginning of a game of peek-a-boo that will end only when he's broke.

I don't care if his girlfriend or his wife swallows, I'd bet a thousand she won't, can't do this. And that means he'll keep coming back, to me, for more. The old guy's gotta have it.

She pivots 180 degrees and bends and touches her toes, grinds, slowly, down. He slides his hips even lower, charmed, to follow her lead. The bulge under the handtowel grows; it's tenting now, slightly peaked, aching closer. His tongue wants to snake across the salty small of her back, across the electric, thick black lines that fan out there in another tattooed V. She shimmies back up. Inch by inch, closer and closer, she comes. Soft, tiny white fuzz dances on the first hint of cold, sweet gooseflesh. She's moving closer to the immobilized man's laboured breathing, the fat roll of his hot wealth. His back bows and his neck strains forward: he's ready, this is it. She sinks the trick – still doubled over, the blood rushing to a head happily occupied with thoughts of the new stereo she's going to buy tomorrow – by running both hands up the insides of her spread thighs. His gaze skirts, from the pink rosebud in his face, up onto the track, the valley between her tanning-booth bronze hillocks, then sleds forward, fast along the Vaselined slick. His eyes crash to a halt against the padded tips of her two fuck you-fuck me fingers. The perfect nail on the right one wags: drum roll, please. She winks and she winks: Janus-like, one for an invisible audience and the guy working security, and one the other way, just for him.

The finger on the right does the honours, reaches all the way back to tickle her asshole, then dives into the track he will remember and long for, for the rest of his life, but never touch.

She draws the greased digit forward slowly and her lips part. A garden of delights springs out, and then, there it is, the rabbit out of the hat, the warren, the flower released from its sleeve, breaking ground.

The tiny, wet, perfect hood of her clit.

Jesus. Jesus, he thinks, I gotta see that again.

One hundred dollars later and she's hovered over every inch of him. This fallen angel's hands have spread out and pushed off his shoulders, the back of her wrist has caressed his cheeks, all of her lips have spilled intoxicating perfumes into his mouth, always stopping just before they kiss. Her naughty finger has grazed his lips before disappearing, deep, to the quick, between hers. Both of her thumbnails have raked up from his knees, up high on his inseam. They never got past the crease in his pants that folds over the place where his balls are cupped. Her head has dipped into his lap a half dozen times, long bleached locks have brushed the length of his cock.

He wants to explode.

He thinks he needs another drink.

He might explode.

He definitely needs another drink.

"Another?" she says, tired, bored, hoping for a clip of three-minute pop numbers.

"Uh, yeah. . . . Maybe." His cock's only half-hard now; he's lost some fuel, some lubrication, can't quite maintain. "But how 'bout I buy you a drink first? Gotta check on my buddy, too. You could come sit. Take a break. Talk."

She's relieved. She'll take his money and the drink, then move on to someone else, make him wait for her, for later, another time.

He'll be back alright. And you don't want to overload him, you know? Spoil the surprise?

Doing up the right snap of her thong, the lethal weapons she knows her breasts have become already holstered, she says: "So, um, that's one-twenty."

"Oh, yeah." He's lit another smoke and balled up the hand-towel. Doesn't know what to do with either. She relieves him of both and takes a crimson-lipsticked drag while he flops around, struggling for his wallet.

"Oops, not enough cash. Card, though. Right, put it on my card."

"There's a twenty percent service charge, you know."

"Whatever. And bring me an extra $200 and another Molson's, okay?"

"Yeah, but I'm not allowed to buy you a drink. Ya gotta go through the waitress, okay?"

"Okie-dokie."

Jesus, did he really just say that?

"Okay, sure, I'll bring your card and cash to you and you can buy me that drink. Where you sitting?"

"Watermelon row," he says, rolling a tiny foil ball between his free thumb and forefinger while he grins and smokes.

"Pardon?"

"Um, you know, watermelon row. Right up front. By the stage." His perfectly capped teeth flash from within an overplayed wink and nod.

"Never heard it called that before."

"Sure you have, it's an old nudie bar, burlesque kinda thing."

She lifts her razor thin eyebrows

"You know, like the Tom Waits song."

She cocks her head, sniffs, "Well. . . ."

"Jesus, ya gotta hear the guy, he's brilliant." He sings, froggy, bourbon voiced: *"Chesty Morgan and a Watermelon Row, raise my rent and take off yer clothes. . . ."* Coughing then, sputtering, he nods. "Watermelon row, you know, it's like the first row."

She purses her lips, almost amused: "Whatever. I know the song. But, like, I think you've got it wrong."

"Nah, I've listened to that album a million times."

"Well, it's rose. Rose, not row."

"Say again?"

"Rose! Watermelon Rose. It's a chick's name. It's about a girl. Some old stripper."

"Nah, no way."

"Uh huh."

"You're shitting me."

"Nope."

"Naw, you don't know what the fuck. . . ."

The conversation's over because she's stopped listening. You couldn't pay me enough, shitfuck.

She's just noticed the white stain that runs down the guy's leg. She must have missed it in all the goddamned black light and neon. Shuddering with disgust, desperately wanting to bathe, she turns and walks to the bar holding the guy's credit card far away from her body, as delicately as possible, between her right thumb and her magic finger.

Who knows what the old fucker's got all over it.

Scott Venn tries to stand, to follow the night's newest fine lady. The scold in his unevenly drunk head pushes him back down into his seat. He blushes, hoping none of the other peelers writhing on the laps in the adjoining booths saw that.

Many of them did.

Few care.

Scott burps, opens his mouth wide, and stretches it around the beer gas to make an envelope. Bitch, he thinks. I hate Tom fucking Waits.

· · ● · ·

Stop me if you've heard this one before.

Three guys walk into a nudie bar.

One, well, one's an unstable, middle-aging, thieving, unbelievably rich, oblivious cuckold. Right, for this joke, and hundreds of others, call him a lawyer. Actually, call him a lawyer covered in birdshit. The next guy? He's an unemployed, violent, crater-faced alkie who's just seriously fucked with the terms of his agreement with the local courts. Not quite an ex-postal worker – it's not that kind of joke – but close. The last guy's always talking, telling stories, going on and on. Today, though – hell, everyday – he's mostly talking to himself. He's, well, he just looks kind of mean and crazy, you know? And he's real old. A senior fucking citizen. But, you know, say he's just a real old guy. With all those old guy things wrong with him. Memory and stuff.

Whatever.

Anyway, these three guys walk into this strip joint and they spend the day drinking. And they're beside one another. Not together, but all your ducks are pretty much lined up in a row.

A waitress labours up to where they're sitting, for maybe the twentieth or thirtieth time, but goes through the motions anyway, to be polite. You know, she makes the effort, asks each of them, "What'll it be."

Shithead says. . . .

Scarface says. . . .

And Gramps says – he spins a whole fucking story when he says. . . .

· · ● · ·

229

Her hair is pulled back tight and even the elasticized scrunchie is irritating her tonight, edging into her scalp. She's been asked – okay, *told* – to pull a double. The place is packed. It's been a long day. About to leave the pick-up station, fully loaded, the hard leather backs of the new high heels she's been asked – yeah, fine, *told* – to wear are digging into the back of Veronica Addams' tender ankles. Blood has begun to seep right through the unsightly Elastoplast bandaids. Her unnaturally stretched calves ache and her arms are bone weary from balancing the heavy, wet black tray above her head as she's walked the obstacle course of tables and men and strippers again and again and again. Her ears ring from hearing the same bad loud songs over and over. The thick cloud of smoke, cigarettes, and putrid fucking cigars and dry ice is playing hell with her asthma. Even her glasses are biting into her, rubbing her nose raw, pinching the sides of her head, biting into the soft fold of her ears. Her skin feels dry and oily at the same time, she's flushed like she's overdosed on Caramilk bars, on the verge of flaking or breaking out. Physically, she's dead out there, completely done in. Emotionally, it's worse. It's hard to believe, the way her body hates her right now, but most of all she's tired of all the stupid guys. Guys who want to talk, about their kids and jobs and wives. Guys who ask her to send drinks to the other girls. Guys who think because she's working here it means she's. . . .

What's a nice girl like you. . . .

It's all a fucking joke.

And if she hears it one more time, she's going to lose her fucking mind.

Veronica sighs and heads toward the stage where Janna's doing a solo number; right now she's got her legs wrapped around a brass pole, twirling 'round and 'round. To keep herself from getting dizzy – unable to look away, Veronica sees the strobing girl reflected in the million mirrors of the dank place – to keep her stomach where it's supposed to be, she tries to come up with a punch line.

Christ, girl, maybe the punch line's you, you ever think of that?

No. Never think of that.

Just maintain.

Shithead says. . . .

Scarface says. . . .

Gramps goes on and on and eventually says. . . .

That's how it goes, this fucking joke. That's how it goes now. It'll all be over soon.

· · • · ·

"Three guys in a strip club were drinking, beers and a shot, watching some peeler go through the motions up on stage, having a conversation. Two of them were talking, bragging, about the amount of control they have over their old ladies. The whole time, the third dude doesn't say a thing. He just drinks his brew, stays totally quiet. After a while, one of the first two turns to the other guy and says, 'Hey dude, what about you? You keep your woman in line or what?'

"Anyway, this guy takes another swig, hoots at the peeler, then says, 'Listen, I'll tell you what, man. Just the other night, my bitch came to me on her hands and knees.'

"Like, the first two guys were amazed, right? Right. So, like, they asked: 'What happened then?'

"He shrugged his shoulders and polished off his drink. 'She said, Get out from under the bed and fight like a man!'"

Jenna punched him in the bicep, just below the sleeve of his black t-shirt, and laughed.

"C'mon, it's funny. You get it? Fight like a man? The guy's whipped, right? Under the bed. Like, he's hiding."

He just nodded and polished off another shot of Jack Daniels.

"You're a pathetic fucking SOB, you know that? I still can't believe you screwed up the job I got you, but, like, you know, that was still something fucking human. I mean, at least it was funny. Christ, I wish *I* could've seen cousin Porky's face. But you, you're so dead, Jesus, you didn't even see how fucking ridiculous it was. I liked you better – yeah, I really fucking liked you – when you still had a fucking sense of humour. At least you had that, Pete. At least that was something."

He cleared his throat and ran his tongue under his lip, still tasting blood there, stared into his glass, and then rubbed both his eyes with the stubby thumb and index finger of his left hand.

"Look, half the time you're dogging me to talk, and now I can't get a fucking word out of you. I don't fucking know who you are any more. So, what's up with that? Jesus."

"I'm sorry," he whispered.

"Yeah, you are," she said as she walked away thinking his hurt, his edges, his goddamned scary, motherfucking temper.

Maybe Jan's right. Maybe not. I'm sorry for his old lady, though. Crying and all. But what can I do? I ain't gonna be anybody's last hope.

Peter James didn't hear her parting shot, didn't see her shaking her head, because he was mustering all his focus on the mousy waitress. She was heading his way again, and he was rehearsing the words he'd have to get out to get another drink. Oblivion time, he thought. I believe maybe just a few more.

· · ◆ · ·

Cara's on the catwalk wearing knee-high black PVC boots, the ones laced up the back with a hundred leather X's. Her purple teddy falls in a soft caress over an itsy-bitsy canary G-string. She's leaning up against the mirrored wall – the seam between one pane and another pinch into her skin – stretching, ignoring everything that's happening below. Ten minutes ago she walked into the booth with a handful of CDs because she was changing her set. The DJ bitched – the way he always does – about her and all the new freelancers throwing off his flow. She only half-listened: something about nobody realizing how hard it is to programme the night and introduce the girls and keep the fish drinking.

Like he's some fucking artist.

Cara's getting loose, but she's psyching herself up, too. It's never easy, coming down the dangerously steep, vertiginous stairs, a flimsy-looking wrought iron grate that says The Rail, the only thing to keep her from pitching over and out into a sea of drunk men. On the way down her eyes just begin to adjust to the assault. From out of the darkness, the round red spots above the stage reflect off the disco ball, the eerie black lights cast glowing ghost shadows, the strobing yellows push epileptic extremes. Trying not to topple, carrying her blanket high so her heel doesn't spear it and launch her to her death, she's always attempting to bounce into her first song like she really means it. Actually, she hates this part of the gig more than anything. The table dances, the lapdances, okay. Fine, that's intimate. You can seek out the dark corner tables, the booths. She's always in control there. But getting on stage, in the centre of everything, with the brightest lights in the trickily dim place hot on her skin? Even when she's still got her clothes on she feels exposed. All those bored and drunk and distracted and horny faces, expecting something. Wanting to be entertained. She hates this part, she really does.

So, before she goes, she always breathes, stretches, puts herself through an athlete's paces, finds the mindset that allows her to maintain, runs through her routine.

I'll give them a fucking show.

There's about two minutes left in the Trickie beats some new Russian chick's finishing up on when Jason startles her from the top step.

"Packed tonight, Cara," he says. Under his tux, his cut chest and arms and shoulders take a break from bouncing, stoked tendons and veins recede.

"Yeah."

"Lots of dickheads. Some old fucker up front's talking crazy shit talk, kinda hassling some of the girls. Any trouble, you let me know." He pulls a joint out of his breast pocket.

"Uh huh." She looks down now, scans the pervs who line the stage.

"Wanna toke?"

"What?"

"Smoke? Before you're on?"

"Nah, which one is it?"

"Which one what?"

"Which jerk? The problem."

Jason lights his blunt with a gunmetal Zippo and inhales, "Oh . . . um. . . ." He clicks the lighter shut, exhales the sweet smoke, and points. "That one, the guy in the floppy cap and the black and orange jacket. Brown pants."

"Him?"

"Yup."

"I know that guy. He's alright, Jason."

"Tell that to her fucking majesty, Krystal. She wants me to beat the old fucker senseless."

The song's fading and the DJ's calling her: "Gentlemen, get ready for something new from Miss Cara Lott. She does, guys. So give it up."

"You're on, Car."

Catharine Johnston eases down the steps to the opening strains of her new first song. The Who, Roger Daltrey crooning: "Behind Blue Eyes."

From the moment she gets on stage, she never allows her gaze to leave Mr. Harrison.

He doesn't look at her, though, won't acknowledge her at all. He just sits and drinks and talks to no one in particular, looking wild. Something inside her shudders and turns, shuts a little tighter: it hurts, but Cara maintains, goes on with the show.

She lifts the teddy over her head, her back to the crowd. The way the klieg lights burn into the wall of mirrors she faces, all the men appear zombified. The opal in her nipple ring looks as dark as aortic blood.

. . . But my dreams, they aren't as empty as my conscience seems to be. I have hours, only lonely, my love is vengeance, that's never free. . . .

· · • · ·

Vengeance.

Its belly still aching for anything evil, the worst gull worries its damaged wing with pricks of its beak.

Swallow the pain, the pain feels good.

Preteens head south to the mall; businessmen cross west at the lights, scurrying back to their office tower cubicles after lunch, cocktails, massages, glory holes; suburban folks out for an evening on the town enjoy a long leisurely walk north to the subway after the Phantom lets out; high-schoolers and low-riders drag the strip in both directions once dusk breaks; hip young couples walk arm in arm towards the Midtown where they'll wait happily in the long queue to see the film that's being advertised by the huge, expensive billboard that looms majestic above them all. If any of them were to stop and look up, they'd see the image that had been all over the city for months: blood-stained claws ripping through a picture of four teens hurtling through the air, screaming, in an unmarked, portable cherry-topped police cruiser. Under the spinning tires, the familiar caption: *Roadwolf: To Hell and Gone*. And, of course, if anyone took an extra moment to read the huge fine print, they could silently work their lips around the phrases "The surprise blockbuster hit of the summer!" or "A camp masterpiece – two thumbs, way up!" Some might even be impressed by the slightly smaller line at the bottom of the two-storey poster, the one that says the flick's been produced in association with one of the country's hottest young directors. Others might even smirk with pride at knowing who the three unknown film students, the local guys who created the movie everybody's been talking about, are. These people, you can tell by the bounce in their step, have a subscription to *Movieline*.

One or two folks, the most sensitive ones, the ones with the keenest vision or maybe even some remote psychic ability, might also notice the cruel white shape perched on top of the billboard itself. They might see the horrible black eyes of a gull, fixed, staring down and across the street with contempt, utter malice.

This is how a day has passed, as all days pass, into night. The sun has moved up across the sky, burned harsh overhead, and then it's fallen. The passage was slow, imperceptible. But the fall was very real.

And from its perch, across the street and high above The Rail, the worst gull, injured and furious, has watched and waited and plotted. It's known all the dark, twisted secrets of every soul that's passed below and this has made it stronger. For twelve hours, it's sucked up the rage and hatred and pain, and it's begun to heal. Feeling better. Couldn't get much worse.

The worst gull's also picked out the two men, separated them from all the rest, who are the most worthy, the most fascinating. Who deserve all its special attention. It's watched them, and helped them – along with all

234

the others who might some day be worthy, some day soon – walk through the heavy doors of a place that holds enough pain, the most of what it needs.

And then there was another man, a third, who did not need its help: an immaculate conception, it marvelled.

So very, very rare.

But I'm here if you need me, buddy, it laughed when the disfigured boy entered. Oh yes, my child, I'm not going anywhere at all.

For twelve hours, it's waited and plotted and watched, staring at The Rail. It could stare and watch and think vengeance and wait a million more. But that won't be necessary. Because the worst gull knows the evil it knows, it knows that time, sometimes, is horrible and inconsequential. Blissfully terrible and fleeting. Sometimes time is empty, meaningless.

A malicious black eye blinks, and more than twelve hours pass. And nothing's changed.

Shuddering in the cold and stretching its sore wings, the gull laughs. Everything that will happen, has happened. Don't blame the bar or the booze or chance or fate or the past or coincidence or the seven deadly sins. It's not greed or envy or sloth or lust. It's not sex, or desire or adultery. Not turpitude, not flesh. They help, of course, The Rail and the alcohol and the accidents and the history and the poverty and the need. But they're symptoms, diversions, digressions. Amusements, the bonus prize.

They're not the disease. Disease is timeless, primary, automatic. The first fucking sunrise, the first fucking breath. It's me. And I'm in them. With them. A part of them.

I'm always and everywhere. And I'm in this place.

Like me. Yes, it's like me. Remember, buddy, a place, a situation, can do things. To people. Make them need to forget. Not want to know.

Like me.

Because I am the bar and the booze and chance and fate and the past and coincidence and all manner of sin. Base and debased, I am all your softest, most vulnerable, rotting places.

And I can wait and I can watch and I won't ever miss a thing.

Nobody will.

In that place? Ha.

Nothing new ever happens there.

Nothing really remarkable.

It's time and it's me and I have all the time in the world.

Out here. In there. It's the same.

Especially in there.

Everything everywhere is always falling apart.

It's me. The worst gull. Only me. Only I maintain.

Now, almost thirteen hours have passed since the old man walked through the door. Hundreds of minutes, thousands of seconds, a thousand thousand fleeting instants, and ten times as many heartbeats and glances and cellular suicides. The entire world has shifted and shifted and shifted again; completely unrecognizable, it's the same as it ever was.

Watching and waiting and plotting, the worst gull can reduce the experience of a million or a thousand or three men, inside The Rail, like this: drinking and pissing and desiring and spending and lying and puking and fighting and dreaming and laughing and failing and coming and hiding and cowering and abusing and manipulating and cheering and cheating and screaming and berating and selling and praying and preying and drinking and dying and drinking and dying and dying just a little bit more.

And from the blur of it all – from the moment the first drink was poured and the first piece of cloth fell to the filthy floor of the brightly lit stage, from the moment time collapsed upon itself – the worst gull has picked apart and devoured the choicest morsels of pain, the worst hunks of time.

It's grown stronger. The pain feels good.

Of course it has its favourite bits, scenes, and seconds it plays and replays and picks at and worries again and again. In all of the nothing that ever happens in The Rail, today, tonight, there have been sweet, insignificant moments that have made the gull feel good, very good actually, about being so very bad. Moments that, it knows, have already transpired. Others that, it also knows, are yet to come.

And still it watches and waits and plots and controls and maintains.

Closing time is coming, buddy. For you, buddy, and you, buddy, and for you.

The worst gull screams at the blueing moon.

And fuck you too, buddy.

No one below bothers to look up. They don't have to see the bloodied claws anymore. They all know they're there.

It's coming for you, buddy, the worst gull thinks. It's coming for me. And still its belly aches.

· · • · ·

Pussyswoggled.

Scott Venn's almost feeling bad, very bad actually, about feeling so very good.

Almost.

He's not about to let anything get him down.

And even if he could, circumstances, as they are wont, as they will and often do, conspire against him.

Don't dwell, buddy. Dwelling's no good.

There are so many diversions, digressions, amusements. A cornucopia of delights. So much time.

Think about it. Right now he's got a chick grinding her pierced twat into a long, tall pole just a couple feet away from his face. She's so close, in fact, he thinks he hears the tiny ping of impact, stainless steel on brass muffled by a light wet squish, with each and every labia-smushing hump. Even with the distorted but unbelievably appropriate Tom Petty she's got the DJ blaring, Scott thinks he hears this glorious sound and it makes him happy.

"Yes, I'm free. . . ."

Ping.

"Free fallin'. . . ."

Ping ping.

Of course he doesn't hear it, not really.

And he doesn't really get it – Scott's already *that* drunk.

He only thinks he hears it because he thinks he's fucking Superman and Jamie Sommers rolled into one. And, all things considered, maybe he is. A man's man, in touch with his feminine side.

His inner fucking mechanical six-million-dollar yoni or some fuckin' shit.

He's got his best bud Tony beside him – and as shitfaced as he is, too, the guy radiates goodwill, a prince of bud-dom. He's got a huge roll of cash in his pocket, and an even bigger wad hiding in the miracle of a couple pieces of plastic which access the three different local banks that feed like happy, blind little piggies off numbered Swiss accounts. And he's got all the expensive, chic beer and fancy, fiery shooters money can buy lined up in front of his pretty little kisser.

He's bionic and bulletproof and studly and on the fast-track to alcohol-enhanced ecstasy.

And? Well, there's also the fact that somewhere in the neighbourhood of six dozen of the finest, sluttiest pieces of tail in the whole goddamned city are hovering within a jampacked 1,000-square-foot radius. When you remove all the wasted space, the long bar, the tables, the male bodies and whatnot, that's like a hot and willing peeler every nine square feet – maybe not quite the most intense population density on the planet, but close. And yup, sweet merciful crap, Scott knows they all want a piece of him.

Like the little skank he'd thrown almost a bill-and-a-half at earlier. Tipped her even, another twenty. Chump change, and a little 'tude ain't gonna fuck with his head. Not today. Not now.

Not when he's on top of his game.

Ladies, please. One at a time.

And that's how they always come, one by one, one after another. Slinking by, running a casual hand over his shoulder, gently raking the tiny soft hairs of the back of his head. Whispering into his ear.

"Now?" Or, "Wanna dance?" Or, "Come back with me."

It's all good, baby.

But that's not the half of it. Nowhere near the best part.

Nope, the best part, for Scott, is that he's free.

You're the man, Tom fucking Petty. Baby, you are *the* fucking man.

"Well, yes, I'm free. . . ."

A spinning smush, another muffled ping.

Yeah, *You Can Win!*

He's gotten away with everything. Feels like a million bucks.

Christ, he has a million bucks. More maybe. Who can count that fucking high?

Scott Venn's gotten off, scot fucking free.

"Well, yes, I'm free. . . ."

I'm not fucked. The fucking harpy's fucked.

I'm not going to jail.

I'm stinking filthy fucking rich.

I'm not fucked. Hee hee.

Not yet.

". . . Free fallin'. . . ."

Watching Tony, as he's running his hand gently across the the small of the back of the compactly pneumatic new girl, a raven-haired pixie in a devil of a long blue dress, who's leaning close to him, trying to coax him to the back for a very special dance, only one nagging, annoying thought pricks at his swelling wealth of good feeling: Amanda.

Damn.

"Yeah, I'm free. . . . Free fallin'."

For chrissake, man, you've still got a wife. A pissed wife. And that's still a problem.

He reaches into his right pocket automatically, fingers the wedding band he always slips off before he walks into places like this. Then he lifts another shooter, a B-52 this time, to his lips.

You're still fucked, buddy. What the hell were you thinking back there? Losing your fucking cool like that in your own fucking home?

And then he's mercifully shot. Put out of his misery. The warmth of the liquor spreads through his throat, hitches a fast ride into his bloodstream and radiates to the far reaches of his body and up into his head.

Fuck it. Forget about it. She'll call, you'll lie and fix it like always. No big deal. There's a perfectly reasonable explanation.

Tony's phone call? Well, you see, hon, I wasn't allowed to say anything. Hush, hush. But that fucking bitch Margaret – you know you were always so wrong about her – well, she was ripping off the company. Yeah, they used me as part of a sting. Tones was away, didn't know. But fuck, we got her. Still, I dunno, you know. It was all pretty sleazy. I know you've probably thought I've been acting kinda weird. Obsessed, right? Well, fuck. It was, like, well, it was intense. So yeah, I was pissed and really just wanted to nail her. But hon, sweetheart, the whole thing's making me think maybe I should start out on my own or something. You know? SSPR's kinda slimy. And I could spend more time at home, with you.

Yeah, she'll buy that.

You're Superman, Scotty. Bulletproof.

Rebuilt.

Oscar – Mr. Fucking Goldman – thank you very fucking much.

I'm free and bionic and stinking filthy rich.

So yeah, fuck Man if she can't take a fucking joke.

Scott blinks his eyes shut, drifts in a senseless stasis, strip-club nirvana. No lights, no sounds; not even really fall down and go boom drunk. Just pussyswoggled and nothing and nowhere and not anything that even resembles human.

And then he slips off his elbow and time's collapsed and there's a new song playing and a new girl on stage, seriously thinking about popping out of her bra. He looks at his wrist and burps and smiles at the waving light brown hairs that shiver in the white, watch-shaped band of skin. . . .

· · • · ·

What the hell happened here? How long was I gone? Did I miss anything?

I don't have the time. Hee hee. I really don't have the time.

Aw, hell, buddy, you've got plenty of time.

All the fucking time in the world.

You are time.

And, see, the peelers are peeling. So, who cares?

He really is happy again, and completely unaware that he's had a sad little episode. And of course, he's already forgotten that he was feeling so bad about feeling so good. Unaware that sometimes twenty minutes evanesce just to help you out of a jam, his drunk mind rationalizes the new strangeness of his surroundings like this: Venn's first law of drinking – blackouts are fine. Part of the game.

Passing out's no good, though. Nope. Don't wanna do that.

Scott Venn is a sportsman who plays by the rules. And the rules are simple and the rules are necessary; the rules, he believes, keep him from becoming an alcoholic.

And so now, the alcohol-drenched sponge of his brain chides him, solemnly, with the second and third postulates of the laws that govern his alcohol consumption.

2: You reap what you sow, and so your head will hurt to remind you. Tough shit, dude.

3: You never *need* a drink, you only *want*, perhaps, yes, just one more, before you go. As long as everybody else is. . . .

Okay, okay – he shakes his wobbly, rubbery jowls, a berated little boy – I get it.

Inside his head a very private and very old argument rages.

I know, I know, jeesh. What do ya think I am, an idiot? How many times do you think I gotta be told? So shaddup.

See, Scott Venn is not an alcoholic. Really, he's not.

He never needs to drink. It's just that when he does – and he does quite often – he always drinks to excess.

And then his personality goes through more changes than seventy-two strippers in a 1,000-square-foot radius over the course of a busy fifteen-hour workday.

Many of these changes aren't very pretty.

But remember, okay? He's not a drunk. Whisper it with him as he blows a hurricane over the spindly forest of tiny hairs on the back of his wrist: "Whoosh. . . . Scotty, you're no alkie. Yup, you're good."

Because he's still very, very intoxicated, he's still quite amused by his watchless wrist. This amusement sets him off on another little scavenger hunt through his pockets, gets him jigging and squirming on his chair. Ass, thighs, breast. The sudden familiarity of the obsessive gestures recalls a humorous anecdote he intends to tell Tony.

Dude, you'd never believe the day I was having. . . .

That's how he's going to begin. And he opens his mouth and his tongue starts wagging, when his fist automatically pacifies him by sticking the long, green, soothing neck of another Molson's into his gaping yawp.

Not a good idea, buddy. Not funny.

His alcohol-soaked brain is berating him again.

I mean, it is. You know, funny. But it's like you're the fucking joke. Remember?

Your watch?

Nose pressed against glass, locked out of your own house, your keys and your watch and your last fucking smoke strewn all over the place, taunting you, shit on and electrocuted, early for your own fucking execution.

Yeah, right. That's funny.

And so, because the Venus flytrap of his addiction uses this sobering window of memory to set its jaws firmly into the pink flesh of his lungs, Scott quickly forgets to be happy about forgetting to feel so bad about feeling so good. And then he panics.

It's like he's Linda Blair, right? Head spinning?

Well, yeah, buddy. He *is* that fabulously smashed.

Now he believes he hears a horror movie voice: We've renewed old vows, dude.

Oh, it's the tar and nicotine.

You've got responsibilities again, so cough it up, pal.

Scott's eyes dart, frantic, the words ringing, echoing, in his head. His mind churls. No watch. No smokes.

No, Greener. Oh, Christ.

I remember. . . . What the fuck do I remember?

I remember a dark, dark time.

I'm scared, Greener.

He looks down at the thick varnish that covers the long stageside ledge. Jutting out a foot, eighteen inches below tiny, strobing runway lights, a blinking, cautionary yellow that mesmerizes and blinds and shows you there's no way out, the infinite plank is *his* table. What Scott sees is as terrifying as the voice he's heard: nothing but beers and shot glasses and wet drink rings, and his own dark, distorted, gaping, cigaretteless mouth.

Greener, where the hell's Greener? Where's my smokes?

His pulse quickens, his haywire head spins, and he's about to scream like Jamie Lee Curtis.

And then he looks at his left hand. Crazy, spidery fingers, jaundiced and strobing. The half-empty pack of Dunhills he squeezes with them.

Flipping open the box top, he blushes. The ridiculously happy drunk again, he laughs and says, loud, "Greener, my man! There you are." Jabbing a smoke between his lips, lighting it and inhaling dramatically, his body morphs back into tip-top shape.

"Dude! What the fuck?" Tony's spun away from the old guy he's been talking to heatedly.

"Huh?"

"You're back."

"What?"

"You were zonin', bud."

"No fuckin' way. I'm good. Look at me, I'm good."

"Dude. . . ."

"Fuckin-A. Not zonin', bud. In the fucking zone. I'm a fucking super-star."

"Whatever."

"Give me a smoke."

"What?"

"Gimme a smoke, ya fuckin' himey bastard."

"Ah, dude. . . ."

"Wassup?"

"You've already got one burning, man."

"Fucking right." Scott smiles and nods and starts to rock out, but his attention slips back away from his bud, back up over the ledge, onto the stage, over the eight-inch squares of black vinyl, up a black pump, a white thigh, through another, strange, fleshy V, onto the fractured slabs of mirror and up into the large strobing yellow lights on the back wall. He mumbles and sings: "Long time since. . . . I fucking love this tune. . . . *Tonight, we're on the loose.* . . ."

Fascinated with the pudgy brunette now that she's writhing and flexing and spilling all over, topless, Scott doesn't notice Tony turn back to the old man and resume their argument. He has the vague sense that it has something to do with hockey, the Boston Bruins.

"Look," he barely hears his best friend say, "Thornton's a bum and I should know. The lazy fuckin' little prick wants me to be his new agent. . . ."

And he definitely doesn't hear Tony add: "My man Scotty here's got a piece of the Russian kid, he's an agent, too. At least he was. Right, big guy?"

Instead, Scott Venn is keenly focused on a spot fifteen feet away, watching all the yellow bits of chubby stripper that rise and fall and writhe in all the different mirrors behind the whole woman who arches her back and lifts her right leg just three-and-a-half feet away from his face. He's grinning like an idiot because he's found pieces of himself under the sway and through the geometry of her. So pleased with making himself out, with his own studliness, he also completely misses the look on her face as she rolls over onto her belly, turns her head, licks her lips and fakes a moan just for him.

And then he misses her roll her eyes and purse her mouth: Asshole.

Deciding he looks damned fine, he lights another Dunhill and inhales, checking himself out one last time.

I look cool when I smoke.

He mumbles and sings, again, without any idea that he's repeating himself: "Damn, I love this tune. You never hear this tune. *Tonight, we're on the loose!*" And then he rests his cigarette in the ashtray to his left, right beside the other one he's got going, and knocks on his head with his right fist and tries to remember.

What were these guys called?

Toto? Poco? Styx?

Nope, nope, nope.

C'mon, you remember, you saw them open up for someone when you were a kid. They did this wicked thing with electronic drums and a suitcase and shit.

Remember?

He decides a smoke might trigger something. Lights another. Inhales and closes his eyes and thinks real hard.

When Scott opens his eyes he's still drawing a blank, but he hears an old guy, leaning over Tony, jawing right at him: "So I say, to your fancy fuckin' friend here, I say, well they're not my words exactly, but a little wisdom I picked up from Mr. Henry James, Esquire, himself, I say, 'You don't know shit from shinola, son.' And so, what I wanna know, Cappie, is how *you* figure Burns' boys are gonna fare this year."

"Huh? Wassup?"

Tony's laughing, chugging back the rest of his Heineken.

The bottle drained and slammed back down on the ledge, he points and says, "Earth to Dude? You okay, man? You were gone again."

"No way and who the fuck's this?"

Tony rolls his eyes. "World's biggest Bruins fan, I guess."

The old guy extends his right hand across the ledge. "You can call me Mr. Harrison, Captain."

And then his old cloudy grey eyes narrow, go black. He looks just past Scott, just over him, to his right, and barks, "What're you lookin' at, you scarfaced sack of shit?"

Tony and Scott both turn their heads, startled. Scott does a double-take, then watches some metalhead with long black hair and bad skin set his jaw, avert his gaze, and start staring deep into a shot of Jack Daniels.

How long has he been there? Scott wonders. Jesus.

And then the old guy smiles thinly, his hand still reaching for Scott, and repeats himself. "Yessir, Captain. I'm Mr. Harrison."

Scott stands and lurches like he's offended, but he's actually too fucked up to care. He doesn't take the old guy's hand but says, "Pleased to meechya – I gotta piss. Ha ha."

He turns like he's about to make for the can, then stops and turns back and squares himself.

"Question," he yells, pointing his index finger straight up in the air, "I just wanna know. Why's everybody calling me Captain all of a sudden?"

The old guy laughs and Tony joins him. Even scarface is smirking. The four of them are actually annoying everybody in the place now.

By the bar the night manager's scanning the room, looking for Jason, fingering the butt of the holstered pistol under his jacket. There's never a bouncer when you need one. If he's getting high again, or banging one of the chicks, I'll fucking kill him myself. Shoot him fucking dead.

Composing himself, the old man finally manages to make himself heard over the music and Tony, who's still doubled over laughing, beside him. "You don't have a clue, do you son?"

Scott shakes his head and tightens all the muscles in his groin. The pain – the pressure of all the beer and shooters threatens to work its way past the breach – is almost unbearably sobering.

"Well, if that don't beat all, eh, funny boy?" The old man slaps Tony's laughing, convulsing back. "You see son, you see, it's like I was telling chuckles here, I said to him, I said, 'You should be the one to tell the sorry bastard, 'cause after all he's your bud.' But what the hell, eh? I mean, take a look at yourself, son. You and your goddamned poncy little boating shoes and your goddamned fancy pants."

Tony sputters, his head between his knees, "Dude, you *really* do, you really look like shit."

"That's right, Captain. I don't know what you got yourself into, but take it from an old dog, that there's shit. Birdshit, son. Ha Ha. And you know, how's an old man to resist? So that's why I've been calling you what I've been calling you, shithead. And what're you gonna do about it? That's all I wanna know? Yep, I've been callin' you Captain fucking Birdshit 'cause from where I'm sitting that's what you are."

Tony rears up, breathing deeply and rubbing his eyes like he's wiping away tears. "Sorry, dude, but he's right."

Scott finally looks down, mortified.

Fuh-uck.

"I gotta piss," he says, holding his crotch and blushing as he turns and weaves around the corner of the stage, past the row of guys sitting at the bar. His head hung low, his body automatically navigates the dogleg left, then twists through the chicane, right, and down the stairs. Pulling up in front of the always unexpected door marked Women's – he's shamefully clearheaded now and not about to fuck up that bad – he hangs another right, strides past the row of three pay phones, and kicks open the men's room door. A couple of underage guys pissing side by side turn their heads nervously. Scott ignores them, moving quickly to a urinal on the opposite wall.

He unzips, bangs his head against the filthy white tile, releases a horsy stream and screams, "Fuck!"

The pressure beginning to ease, his mind sighs out the rage and slips back into the front car of its drunk and scatterbrained emotional roller-coaster.

Scott cracks up.

The kids finish and split, one of them whispering, "Psycho."

Scott jiggles his dick to draw a happyface grin on the back of white porcelain.

"Man oh man oh man. Jesus. Ha ha. What a day, eh, buddy?"

And then Scott laughs his heartiest laugh. He's talking to his cock and the little dickhead's a fucking hysterical mimic.

"Ha ha. What a day. Man oh man oh man. . . ."

Twenty minutes later, after scraping off the worst crusts of black-flecked gullshit and dabbing away the rest with cheap wet toilet paper, and after picking off many if not most of the little wet white balls that were left behind, and after washing his hands again and again and again, a smiling Scott Venn bursts out of The Rail's stinking men's room, still amused.

"Man oh man oh man."

No longer noticeably covered in birdshit, he's transformed himself into a different kind of captain. Now so pissed he stumbles as he heads back for the stairs, so off-kilter he has to grab onto the middle phone for support, the wet spots that dot the inseam of his lower leg make him look like a shitfaced Captain Morgan – a fancy pants cartoon who's been pissing into the wind.

Confident that he's cleaned himself up, that he looks sharp again, he's also become a new kind of oblivious.

Captain fuckin' Pissypants doesn't have a clue.

"Man oh man oh man," he says again, pushing off the phone to launch himself back to Tony and his beer and the girls.

His hand knocks the receiver off the hook.

Startled, rearing back, Scott watches the thing swing and dangle. Not a pink elephant, exactly, in the garish fluorescent light of the basement it does, all things considered, look a hell of a lot like a speed bag. He thumbs his nose, sniffs, jabs at it quick, below the belt, twice – then knocks its block off with a hard right. Too hard. Too square. *Realer than real deal Holyfield.*

Scott screams, demented, a machine gun staccato burst, *"Ow! Ow! Ow! Ha! Ha! Ha!"* He summons a ring announcer's voice: "Gene, that's gotta hurt."

As his knuckles begin their slow but inexorable inflation and angry, nearly broken discolouration, a great deal of the alcohol in his body is converted to powerful painkiller: field medic moonshine, home-brewed morphine. It also clears the path for something very like thoughtful remorse: That's not right, that's no good. What did the phone ever do to you, eh? C'mon, ya gotta be cool, Scotty.

"Man oh man oh man," he says as he bends and grabs for the receiver. He says it once more when he captures it with his good left hand, second try.

And then he laughs again, listing before he falls. "Man oh man oh man overboard." Hysterical now, he speaks into the receiver: "Man oh man oh. . . . Hello? Ha ha."

Scott Venn cracks himself up like this until he uses the dangling metal cord to pull himself back up to his feet. His call completed, he hangs up gently, still babbling.

"Man oh man oh man."

At this precise moment, Scott Venn's drunk mind finally returns him to the beginning of the ride: he's back in the place where he feels so very bad about feeling so very good.

"Oh man. Oh Man."

Oh fuck.

The phone.

Amanda.

This is not good. This is not right.

I'm fucked.

I still gotta talk to my fucking wife. I still gotta fix that marriage thing.

Telling himself he's got to get back upstairs, to his briefcase, and his smokes and Greener, and his cell phone, he finds himself there.

Yes, he's *still* that drunk. And yes, the ride's just about to start again.

Before it does he manages to notice that Tony's gone. His own stuff's still there, though, beside the old man in the Bruins jacket and cap.

"Did ya fall in, Captain?"

246

"Huh?"

"Thought you went down with your goddamned ship."

"Uh, yeah. Ha. Um, where's Tony? The guy I was sitting with."

"He gave up on ya, son. Lost at sea, we figured."

"What?"

"Went home, Captain. Kinda too pissed to maintain. Told me to tell ya, if I ever saw ya again, that ya bought us both another round of drinks. You can pay the one with the ponytail and glasses, she's bringing me one more now."

"Oh."

"And another thing, son."

"Yeah?"

"Your goddamned briefcase has been ringing off the hook, and I wish to God you'd make it stop. I mean, Captain, I'm almost embarrassed to be sailing with you."

Scott reaches under his chair and pulls the briefcase to his lap. Clicking it open, he reaches for his cell and checks the call display. He barely registers his knuckle's mocking, livid throb.

Amanda.

His lurching mind hurtles five different drunken ways at once. Terror. Pain. Arrogance. Annoyance. Lust.

I'm fucked. My marriage is over.

And then the Freddy Krueger fingers of his old ball-and-chain knife through him: Feed me.

He lights another smoke, shrugs his shoulders, and punches in the numbers to get his voicemail. Fuck it, he decides, exhaling a perfect smoke ring, then breaking it with his little finger.

I can take care of her, like that. His angry fingers refuse to snap.

The phone pressed against his ear, he hears nothing then realizes he's forgotten to press send. Crap.

The mousy waitress approaches with more beer. He fishes for his wallet. Tips her big. Too big.

Back in business, he punches in the numbers again, gets into the system this time. As he strains to hear his wife over Melanie, singing about a fucking brand new pair of rollerskates, his eyes drift across the tiny perfect squeak of a Tilley who lies, legs spread, on a new white blanket. It's the blue-dressed devil who wanted to dance for Tony.

Her pubes are cut very short.

He tries to focus on his wife's voice.

Hears her.

Honestly, he does.

Well, he gets the gist, right? Anyway?

He lifts the beer to his lips.

The raven-haired girl tweaks the nub of her big clit between the thumb and index finger of her right hand. Cups her ample right breast with her left.

Pussyswoggled, Scott Venn absently presses a button to replay Amanda's message.

You're so fucking beautiful, he thinks, imagining her leading him to the back. The way she smells as she eases down onto his lap.

Amanda's voice again.

Scott's not happy about what he thinks he hears.

He erases the message.

Oh fuck. He takes another long drink. I need a fucking cup of coffee. Somebody stop this ride. It's time. I wanna get off.

He sneezes all over himself, sniffles, wipes snot from his upper lip with the back of his hand. His sinuses throb in pace with his knuckles.

Shit, now I really am getting a cold.

There's something else I'm forgetting.

Oh Christ, Alex. Alex is getting married tomorrow. I'm the best fucking man.

He feels his forehead. It's warm.

I don't feel so good.

And then he polishes off the beer and waves at the mousy waitress.

Maybe one more first. And then a cup of joe.

And then the rage sets in. Excessively drunken self-righteousness, masking exceedingly pissed self-loathing.

· · • · ·

She was in a foul mood as soon as she walked through the door and heard the radio. The place was lit up like a Christmas tree.

"Scott?"

No answer.

"Scott, are you home?"

Nothing.

What the hell?

Shaking her head, taking her time, she casually reached to punch the four stupid numbers into the alarm.

Scott, you idiot!

The damn thing wasn't armed.

Her other man's cab peeled away then, still backfiring, and Amanda Venn, haggard, in last night's dress, stood with her hands on her hips, looked at herself in the half-opened mirrored closet door, and slowly began to take in the wreckage of a shiny new day.

Jesus, what the fuck has he done?

In front of her, on the floor, sand and birdshit-covered Oxfords were strewn about another shiny new pair. In the mirror, she also saw Scott's keys, lying beside the freshly chipped ceramic vase.

Fuck, I liked that thing. Scott never did.

Turning and bending, furious, to pick up her husband's keys, she noticed that the bench was off kilter. Down there anyway, she pushed it back, flush against the exposed brick wall. One of the legs was wobbly, like it had been kicked out of joint.

Christ, could he have been that drunk?

By the time Amanda had walked into her kitchen, of course, she had her answer.

Coffee grounds everywhere. "Red," her husband's childishly sacred coffee mug, in shards in the stainless steel sink. Coffee stains and sticky spilled coffee on the countertop and on the tile. One of Scott's Arrow shirts, coffee stained, and his Armani tie, ruined, also on the floor.

A trail of popped buttons led into the living room, and she hesitated before following them, afraid of what she'd find.

He really was that drunk.

Asshole: what, like, I'm supposed to clean up after the fucking pig?

The fine tip of a sunbeam cracked off the broken crystal of Scott's Swatch. When it bit into her eye she made a point of stepping on it and twisting into it with her heel.

I gave him the goddamned thing.

And then she followed his tiny white trail through the French doors.

Buddy peeped: Hey, finally. You're home. Jesus, you look rough. What're you gonna do about this place. Can you believe it? He was having a hell of a time.

In front of the stereo, Amanda rolled her head from side and cracked her stiff neck. Then she punched off the babbling DJ and sighed and said, "Must have slept funny."

What?

Buddy didn't know what the hell she was talking about and said so.

"Hey, Buddy. Who's my pretty boy? Who is he? You poor little guy. I'm sorry you had to see this."

You're sorry. Jeesh. Forget sorry. You don't know the half of it. And for chrissake, lady, I'm starving.

Ignoring the budgie, Amanda walked over to where Scott's sportscoat lay, in front of the sliding glass doors.

Fuck, and now he's smoking again. Jesus. He's a dead man, she thought, as she flopped onto the couch.

A split second later she was back on her feet: her bare arm had touched his overcoat.

Ugh. Christ, it's covered in birdshit! What a pig. I mean, Jesus, Scott, how pissed were you?

Pulling the disgusting thing off her furniture, flinging it on top of his jacket and last cigarette, Amanda Venn came to her last straw: she saw the butt that the dangling arm of the overcoat had spit out, blackened, by her left toe.

That's it. I mean, that's really fucking it. You little fucking moron, you could've burned the fucking place to the ground.

Resolving to finally rid herself, once and for all, of a lying, cheating, good-for nothing, alcoholic pussyhound of a rat-bastard, fire-hazard husband, Amanda Venn stormed out of her living room, through her dining room, towards the utility closet where she kept her vacuum.

Today, I'm cleaning house, she thought. Yeah, today, Amanda's cleaning up.

It wasn't regret or fear that stopped her in her tracks. Not memories of falling in love, or her wedding day, or the good times she and Scott once had, not even thoughts of her other man's massive cock. Nope, nothing could dissuade her now, she was in complete control.

The only thing that gave her pause was the tiny, blue-grey speck she caught, peripherally, below and to her right, as she raged. It was nestled snug against the leg of one of the dining room chairs.

Well, well, well. Doll, it's your lucky day.

She stooped then and scooped up the happy little pill.

By the time she was upstairs, changing into sweatpants and an old t-shirt, it had already dissolved and begun coursing through her blood. Neurotransmitters re-arranged, vacuuming and rubber-gloved scrubbing and throwing shit out time had never been so much fun.

It took her a few hours, because she was so thorough. But the hours, like Amanda, flew. Sucking up sand, dumping Scott's ruined things in big green Glad garbage bags, tying them off one by one. She hummed as she worked.

Buddy sang with her, and reminded her, constantly, that he hadn't been fed.

The lady's in a world of her own, he thought.

A preoccupied and numbed little busy bee, Amanda fed off her rage and the Vicodin: while she scrubbed the bathroom clean of Scott's filth; while she closed cupboards and dresser drawers, swept up broken ceramics, and glued bench legs and vase pieces; while she erased every trace of her own last night, throwing out an empty bottle of Chardonnay, clearing the dishwasher, throwing out the rotting Brie.

Manically, she worked herself ragged: turning off the lights Scott left on as she first finished off one room, and then another, and then another.

She even went out back and swept sand off the porch. Noticing a dollop of birdshit on the monsteria, she wiped that clean, too.

Buddy tried again, selflessly: Hey, bring that thing in! It's too cold out there. Hey, lady? Hey?

She just kept working.

Finally, standing in her sparkling kitchen, her mind racing, she peeled off her yellow rubber gloves, dropped them into a final big Glad garbage bag, and surveyed her work.

This is my house. My home now.

Remembering then that it was garbage day, Amanda Venn summoned the last of energy and hauled out the trash.

And then she returned through her front door, closed it, walked up the stairs, ran hot water into her shiny clean tub, and peeled off her clothes.

Naked, powerful, but very, very soiled, Amanda had a final, vengeful thought.

Fucking telephone company, fucking technological crap.

So, before slipping into a bath she feels she so rightly deserves, before even considering phoning her sorry excuse for a husband and putting him out of his misery, she decided to fuck with his head, one last time, before finally fucking up his life.

She strode proud and curvy and a bit chilled into Scott's office, reached for the Vista phone and deleted the list of callers.

Not just last night's callers. The entire list.

Just in case the retard gets half a clue, she thought, padding back into her bathroom. He'll never be able to trace a goddamned thing.

Remember, Scotty: you're the one that's been fucking with me.

I'm the innocent.

You started this.

And now you're fucked.

After kicking back and soaking, luxuriating in her long hot aromatherapeutic bath; after scrubbing every inch of her body with the gentlest, sweetest perfumed soaps; after washing her hair and gathering it up in a big, fluffy white towel; after caressing herself, everywhere, with another, equally fluffy white towel; she wrapped herself in a very, very, fluffy pink bathrobe and headed, barefoot, into her kitchen, opened a bottle, and poured herself a very refreshing glass of white wine.

Buddy, from where he was perched in his cage, could just look her over.

You smell nice, lady. But you missed a spot, right there, on your right temple. Lady? Hey lady, your face is still dirty!

Pleased with her bird's song, Amanda called back: "That's a good boy. Who's Mama's little baby? Pretty, pretty, Buddy."

Listen, lady, I hate to be the one to tell you, but I'm not your god-damned child. You're obviously very human, tragically so, from where I sit, and I'm obviously a fucking budgie. That's why we have such a bitch of a time, me and you and everybody else around here, communicating. I am pretty, though. Pretty fucking hungry? *Capice?*

"That's my good little birdie, yes. Sing for Mama."

Oh crap, he peeped. And then he shrugged his tiny wings and shook his wee head.

"Aw, is my Buddy tired?"

Yeah, lady, that's it. I'm very, very tired.

And then, wine in hand, Amanda grabbed the cordless phone and went back upstairs.

One desperate, final time, Buddy called after her, his happy little voice dripping with sarcasm: No, really, I'm fine. Seriously, I couldn't eat a thing.

Comfy in her bathrobe, warm and relaxed and content and pleased, Amanda sauntered, sexily, into her bedroom, and dove into the blue ocean of her downy, king-sized bed.

One hand behind her head on one of her six soft, perfect pillows, the other resting on her groin, waggling the phone like a thick and curvy blue-black dick, she laughed.

King-sized bed. Stephan-sized.

Definitely not Scott-sized. No, he's definitely more of a disappoint-ingly skinny, single kind of guy. Isn't he? Like, especially now.

Sighing, she turned on the cordless.

It's time. Quitting time. Down time. Putting the dog down time.

Time to end it. End it all.

She punched in the numbers and put the phone to her ear.

It rang, three, four, five times.

And then the message kicked in.

Fuck.

She punched the pound key and talked to the machine.

"Listen, it's me. I've been thinking. It's time we talked. There's things we need to discuss. I know, and I hope you know, we can't go on like this.

252

So, what I think you should do is this: come back here as soon as you can. I'll be here. So come as soon as you can, okay? Yeah, okay. Bye."

And then Amanda Venn hung up.

Before making her next call, a much more pleasant one, Amanda Venn smiled and said, "Fuck you, Scotty. Fuck you, too."

Beneath her prone, thirty-five-year-old body, under the plush fabric of her soft pink robe, the last trace of the worst night of Scott Venn's life, a wet spot of drool, and maybe tears, continued to dry into the vast, timeless blue of a duvet ocean.

By the time Amanda was roused by the knock at her front door, this last visible trace of her husband's unique guilt was gone.

· · • · ·

From his mirrored-in perch high in a crowsnest amidst The Rail's rafters, the DJ everybody calls buddy, not exactly with contempt, but, because his name is, well, Buddy – Hi Mom, Dad, and thanks a fucking lot and fuck you very much, he thinks, for the twelve-millionth time, for the goddamned Borscht-belt handle – shudders at the song he's just had to force himself, literally, to modulate into.

Really, he actually had to take his left index finger in his right hand and guide it toward the play button on one of his three CD players.

Saga. Can you fucking believe it? Saga.

It's quite possible – take, say, seven-to-two odds – that Buddy's talking as he thinks. Even repeating himself. Buddy never shuts up. Working fourteen, fifteen hour days five or six days a week means he's mostly annoying himself: good thing he's also a very, very patient, indulgent interlocutor.

Saga. Can you fucking *believe* it? Jesus.

The Rail's DJ has spent so much time alone, inside his head, telling himself stories, that when he's actually in the company of others he feels they can't understand him; sometimes, that they're not really listening. He's right of course, but it's nothing personal. It's just that he speaks in such a rush, unleashes such a torrent of words and ideas and rants with a self-confidence that borders on arrogance, no matter how filled with real concern those words may be, that he can make people so uncomfortable that they literally *can't* follow him. In the simplest terms the creepy little mother weirds folks out.

Sa-Ga! I mean, I've had to play some bad fucking tunes. But Saga?

Who *ever* listened to this shit? Tell me, who *ever* listened?

Buddy rises, lifts his pear-shaped body off of its comfortable chair, and cranes to see the pigeons through his two-way mirror. With this bird's eye view he's got the best seat in the house. Three of his special favourites – the regulars who make his imagination race to compose possible lives, even though his fear of both their envy and contempt means he never actually wants to meet the characters whose lives he orchestrates – for the first time ever, are actually sitting beside one another, stageside, front and centre. He knows this is coincidental, that in all probability it was simply bound to happen and just as unlikely to amount to much. In terms of his storyline, though, accidents are beautiful: pure pulp. The sporty guy, the alcoholic neurosurgeon played by Brad Pitt or Billy Zane in his movie, is punching his fist in the air and whooping.

"Tonight we're on the loose. . . ."

Jesus. Some of them, dupes, actually seem to like this shit. *Fucking cretins.*

Though he takes great pride in his work – Buddy is so exacting about the integrity of his mixes that he insists the girls notify him, in writing, of a planned change to their set at least three days in advance – surveying the scene he understands no one will ever appreciate his professionalism. Face it, the pervs don't come for the tunes.

The Rail's DJ is a veteran. And although he's just far enough past the tender age of twenty-two that he tells people he's almost twenty-three without irony, you can see, in the dark shadows under the sunken, beady black eyes that dart far behind the long sharp slope of his nose, that he's been doing this job for exactly, precisely, five years. The day he was hired, in fact, was the first time he'd ever fudged his age: he had to tell the lie just to get the gig. The deception, you know, added character, maturity; left a little grey just around the temple. It made him fit right in, didn't it? Having a little something secreted away. Five years ago tonight, Buddy took the job figuring the experience would look good when he eventually felt ready to hit up the real dance clubs for work. Somehow, well, somehow he just never got around to leaving: DJ Buddy Love's career as an internationally respected house-mix guru never took off.

Teenage torpor? A middle-class lack of motivation? Buddy's parents and siblings have berated him with this for years.

His answer: Who the fuck do you think you are? The pay's too damned good, and, occasionally, the perks, the fringe benefits, well, they're definitely worth your while.

Chicks always dig the DJ, even in a ripper bar. And ample-bottomed Buddy, who isn't tough or handsome or even really cute – well, maybe cute, the way ugly housepets are sometimes the most beautiful of God's many fucked up and improbable critters – likes the attention that occasionally comes his way.

Anyway, the gig's a cakewalk – he's like a machine up there, automatic for the people – and that means he has plenty of time to occupy himself with, you know, more important things. Like books and stuff, improving his sensitive, wildly improbable, and utterly twisted mind. Some kids get off on crack. Some like the taste of crystal meth. Buddy gets fucked up mainlining the mainstream.

And so, somewhere along the line, he doesn't remember when, after reading three or four years worth of other people's shit, he figured he could do it, too. A screenplay, maybe. A TV series, a good one like OZ. Or a movie. Whatever, he'd just write it. How hard could it be? Besides, where he works, there's, like, shitloads of material.

Look at the old guy down there – Clint Eastwood, maybe, if you can get him, or Coburn or even Borgnine if you're really pinching pennies – what's his life like?

Tonight, Buddy makes him an ex-cop, pumping the guy he's talking to for information, trying to break his last, big, unsolved case. A mob deal the owner's involved in. Of course you know the life-long bachelor with a heart of stone's banging one of the peelers. Fifty years his junior.

Yeah, The Rail oozes fucking stories, there's thousands to peck away at. All you have to do is look and listen; and if you miss something good there's always some little bird flitting in to set you straight. So, for maybe two years now Buddy's been drawing outlines, copying out great quotes. As a DJ, he knows the importance of starting off on the right note, the value of the perfect epigraph, guiding principles, the architecture of entertainment. He hasn't really written a word, but he has been, you know, like, sowing the fucking seeds. Storyboarding the whole goddamned thing.

Problem is, he's always being interrupted right when the juices finally start flowing.

By the fucking manager saying he's playing too loud, or not loud enough. Or that he's talking too much when he's introducing the dancers. Or that he's being too much of a smartass, baiting the pervs, always chirping. Or, too often lately, that he's both incomprehensible and sounding kinda bored.

And then there's the girls, popping in whenever they fucking well please, deciding they want to dance to some damned song they just heard in the cab on the way over.

And no they don't know the name, or the artist.

That's why he's developed his carefully controlled playlist. Why he's imposed the three-day notice rule.

Oh, occasionally he'll make an exception: nothing's that hard and fast.

Like if one of the chicks offers to do him . . . a little favour. Or if they get him high. Or if they make the effort to listen. Or if they actually bring in something that might make him groove, something that really smokes. Tonight, for instance, he pretended to give Cara a hard time, because she could be so goddamned standoffish, but he thought playing that particular Who song was pretty fucking cool.

Jesus, I mean, the way Townshend ghosts Daltrey's vocal when he's swallowing anything evil and sticking fingers down his throat. Yeah, no one knows what it's like, dude.

To be bad. To be sad.

Like him. A voyeur at the smoke-yellowed window of the human soul, Buddy shifts his focus to one of his other regulars. Bad and sad, with his fucked up face, the black-haired metalhead he always casts as an alcoholic on the verge of getting into recovery, reclaiming his life and getting back his girl – clean him up and tone down the uglies and Skeet Ulrich, desiccated and full of a night at the Viper Room, might be up for the role – stares into his drink, runs his hand through his hair and subtly shakes his head. Perfectly bad and sad. And jaded and faded and cold.

Stretching and sighing and collapsing back into his chair, Buddy savours it, the twist, the momentary respite from the monotony, all over again. Mostly he's forced to play the same old shit, shift after shift, week after week. Metal and hip hop and top forty pop. High decibel Sleep-eze. Worse, half the girls want to peel to the same tracks. Some days he has to play a tune six, seven times.

Occasionally, like now, in fact, he'll write himself into his fantasy and indulge his most morbid thoughts by setting his body swinging, by the neck, above everything, with speaker cable; or better, kill off one of the chicks and hang her, right there, from the fucking catwalk.

I thought I saw a . . . a ripper. Now that'd be a show. Yeah, a real show, that. So much for nine fucking lives, Pussycat. Swing baby, swing.

Another tune already lined up and ready to go, Buddy scratches his left breast through his homemade GBV t-shirt and scans down the next twelve songs on his master list, today's version of his bible.

Jesus, he thinks or says. There's no more art in this game. No art. Rippers have no fucking imagination, no sense of humour. Their minds have been ruined, these naked, sexy little lemmings. Ruined by how easy it's become to rip off pop culture.

And so they're always, like, yesterday.

The worst culprits? Poisonous, hip film soundtracks.

Buddy's stomach turns.

Particularly fucking *Trainspotting* and goddamned *Boogie Nights*.

Those two films, almost single-handedly, in the opinion of an old pro like Buddy, have ruined strip club DJ-ing.

Okay, there wasn't a hell of a lot to fuck with, but still.

Double checking that tracks twelve and eleven are lined up first – Buddy likes having at least a half hour's worth of discs stacked neatly, from the bottom up, at his immediate right, their jewel cases in the correct descending order to his left; his workspace is a meticulously tidy, cozy little nest, and he returns a just-played CD to its alphabetized position in the bins behind him as soon as it's in the can; when the stack of current CDs begins to diminish, he'll pull out the next thirty or forty minutes worth of music and create a third pile further to his right – he takes yet another moment to essay to himself, to expand and annotate, his theories on the ruination of scoring a good all-nude revue.

The songs that set him off, his mind or his jaw clicking, working wildly, are the last two numbers in Paige's set – part of this week's cavalcade of fresh meat, she probably drifted into town from up north somewhere – but they're also tunes he's played for dozens of other rippers over the last year: "Lust For Life" and "Brand New Key."

With a twitch and an exasperated, dismissive squawk, the nail of his right index finger tapping a silver disk, Buddy pokes at the musical corpses. Taken as they should be, far out of the context of this kind of place, both tracks are infectious, well-crafted examples of relatively original songwriting. He thinks "Lust For Life" is one of the best Bewlay Brother productions ever, a fine example of inspired collaboration. From the odd little rockabilly riff that kicks the song into gear, to the frenetic, bouncing guitar that's doubled by both the bass and the snare, David Bowie and Iggy Pop created a flawless protopunk masterpiece. The imitators are legion: can anyone say Violent Femmes?

Great music, funny, fucked-up lyrics, Iggy's voice – what a combination.

Worth a million in prizes?

Buddy's upper lip peels away, forces his face into a twisted grin.

Damn straight.

The bell of the DJ's ass shifts into the well-worn depressions of his faux leather executive chair, overburdened casters squeak for WD-40. He coughs, clears his throat to command attention, then continues.

In a totally different vein, "Brand New Key," written and performed by Melanie Safka, is one of those improbable miracles of pure pop. Verging into bubblegum terrain, its insouciance, Melanie's bubbly, folksy delivery over keys and guitars that Buddy thinks sound like they could have come from Arlo Guthrie, never stop surprising. The lyrics are simple, sometimes childish, but they're also sexy and sad. One good, open-minded listen, and he was hooked.

Awesome tunes. Really. Top of the line.

Buddy's knife-edged hand goes to his hairline, comes down sharp, hard, in a crisp salute.

Problem is, rippers are not the most subtle of choreographers. Their range is so damned limited, and they're easily influenced.

And so the reasons so many girls want to peel off their clothes and writhe and gyrate to these and other wonderful tunes are all fucking wrong.

It's stupid and depressing and, slumping, deflating, Buddy knows precisely where to place the blame: the complete lack of originality and imagination of most of the girls, home video, and a cultural inability to appreciate either subtlety or irony.

One day, a few years back, some ripper, somewhere, decided, after finally seeing the Danny Boyle screen adaptation of Irvine Welsh's reasonably captivating, gritty novel *Trainspotting*, because everybody else was seeing the flick, that dancing to the song that plays during the opening credits would be a fun idea. A fragment of a line struck her, this little Van Halen freak, as appropriate – "do another striptease" – and, bingo, the next day she walked up the stairs to her DJ's booth, hummed and butchered the guitar riff so it was completely unrecognizable, sang the one part of the one line she knew, and expected him to play it, immediately. Frustrated, to say the least, homicidal probably, this poor guy and this painfully headstrong and inscrutably stoned girl, would then argue back and forth for half an hour.

Pushing back on his exhausted seat, the DJ spins around once, counterclockwise. Dizzied, he gets up, stretches, and begins to pace the confines of his small squared cage. Buddies, many of them, almost translucent, palpitate and contort in the smoke and multi-coloured lights bouncing off the glass walls. His jiggling, elastic lips do the voices, low and high, sick and whining and bored, for both sides of the conversation.

Do you know who sings it?

Nope.

Do you remember anything else from the song?

Uh uh.

What kind of song was it?

Um, sorta fast. Hard.

Metal?

No. Not that hard.

Punk?

Maybe. Sorta. What kinda punk?

After eighteen or nineteen attempts at this game of Name That Tune/Twenty Questions, the generically exasperated DJ asks her *where* she heard it.

Um, in a movie.

And then they'd start again.

What movie?

Like, I don't remember what it was called.

No?

No.

They talked funny.

Foreign?

Yeah.

Subtitles?

Huh?

Writing? On the bottom of the screen?

I know what subtitles are, fuckhead.

You said it was foreign, you know, that they talked *funny*.

No. It was English, but, you know, with a funny accent. Strong.

In Buddy's head it goes on and on like this it, until, inevitably, the poor guy finally gets her to admit the film had something to do with drugs and trains.

Oh, he'd say. *Trainspotting*.

And then he'd sigh and say: Iggy Pop, "Lust For Life."

And she'd go: Whatever.

And then he played the damned thing and she gyrated and strutted and bounced happily, her implants flopping everywhere.

And then, Buddy maintains, his arms spread wide, operatic, dictatorial, it spread like wildfire, like a horrible, terrible virus: Blockbuster kept renting the vid to impressionable, youngish girls on their nights off, and they kept on deciding the song was perfect, that it was "their" song.

Soon every girl in North America would be ripping to the damn thing, ruining the tune for guys like Buddy everywhere.

And none of them, anywhere, and no one in any nudie bar audience, would ever question its appropriateness.

Christ, he sneers again, hopping back into his chair. It's Bowie and Pop, for fucksake.

That line about doing "another striptease"?

It's about a fucking guy. *He's* gonna do it. A dude.

And listen, will you? To *all* the lyrics. Iggy sings about getting it in the "ear" before. Now what do you suppose that means, eh?

Buddy's feathered hair shakes with his head. He lights a Gitane, inhales deeply, then uses the glowing tip like a sinister pointer, a branding iron.

So what the hell are they thinking, these girls? Quoting this movie? This horrific, heroin-sick version of the old descent-into-the-bowels-of-hell theme?

Ladies, and you, you drunken pervs: enough already. You just don't get it, do you?

People, this is not good. Not good for people.

The film itself? The Rail's dramatically smoking DJ believes it's a dark little gem. Ewan McGregor is, *inhale*, superfine, *hold it*, as Welsh's Renton, *exhale*, makes a career for himself, in fact, because of the squalid, track-marked role. But it's Robert Carlyle's Begbie who, *inhale, hold*, for Buddy's money, *exhale*, really steals the show. He plays the desperate, psychotic, alcoholic piece of violently manipulative shit so well that – admit it – you almost like the guy.

What a performance: of course, neither he, nor the flick, won an Oscar.

It's that good.

With *Boogie Nights*, the Paul Thomas Anderson-written and directed satire of '70s and early '80s porn, you've got a depressingly similar situation. Actually, Buddy argues, it's worse: as a camp masterpiece, *Boogie Nights* was all but ruined by a public who'd become inured to irony.

And when that happens, what's the point?

The fact is, *Showgirls*, the 1995 Verhoeven and Eszterhas collaboration released a couple years earlier, was just as good, in precisely the same ways: Elizabeth Berkely, Gina Gershon, even Kyle MacLachlan – all wonderful. But the pic was universally panned, loathed.

Buddy shrugs, butts out. You'd think the rippers want a piece of that action, too. It's like, so damned appropriate.

But no. No way.

Pearls before swine.

Like Jim Carrey's *Cable Guy*, *Showgirls* was just a few minutes ahead of the fifteen minutes it needed, just ahead of the time when "the public" would be in the right mood to go: "Ah, we get it."

The release of *Boogie Nights*, especially on video, however, was timed perfectly.

Burt Reynolds, fresh from being the best thing about *Striptease*, the Demi Moore piece of shit ripoff of *Showgirls*, was stunning as an old hardcore porn director. So good, he deserved the Oscar he was nominated for. *Really*.

Another groan fills the DJ booth.

Of course he didn't get it.

Boogie Nights' soundtrack is one of Buddy's favourites, as hilariously appropriate, he says to anyone who'll listen, as the film's costume designs. The late-'70s through early '80s done to a T. Whether it's Diggler's incessant cataloguing of his terribly polyester wardrobe, or the brilliant use of classic tracks like War and Eric Burden's "Spill the Wine" and The Commodores' "Machine Gun," or even the so-bad-it's-great scoring of songs like "Sister Christian" by Night Ranger and ELO's "Living Thing," the movie forces you to think when you consume and groove.

At least it should.

The DJ bites off his own laugh, spitting.

But no, the rippers got their hot little hands on Heather Graham's Rollergirl character – she's all like, wow, and blowjobs – and ruined everything. One after another they clamoured after her theme song: "Brand New Key."

For weeks after the film was released to home video, no fewer than eight different girls mixed and matched a couple of fads and took to The Rail's stage wearing in-line skates. To say the results were often disastrous is a wicked understatement.

Management finally put a stop to the nonsense when one chick lost her footing on the stairs and fell, clanking off six different slabs of metal, to the vinyl floor below. A concussion, a busted up-nose, multiple other abrasions, and a badly broken ankle later, and that was the end of that.

Thank God.

Lawsuits, you know.

They still want to grind to the song, though. Want all the pervs to unlock Pandora's box with the brand new key – the bank card – they keep in their wallets. And, in a way, it gives Buddy a perverse thrill every time he presses play: blood, in neon and black light, looks so cool.

Any day now, one of the chicks is going to walk in demanding that he play Motörhead's "Ace of Spades." She'll have just come from a matinee at the Midtown, thinking the way it's used in *Roadwolf* – and it is so fucking brilliant, the way the pudgy stripper helps those guys steal that cop car, them never suspecting that she's a fucking werewolf, too – is just to die for. And then they'll all want it and, well, another brilliant film will start to mean a little less.

Fucking animals. No respect. Not for music. Not for movies. Not for history or even fucking art.

And certainly not for me.

Buddy's snapped out of his little rant by the song timer that starts flashing a powerful ghastly red in the middle of his masterboard. He'd rigged the thing up a few months ago because more and more he found himself drifting, unable to focus on the girls and the music and what went on below. The light meant, mercifully, that there was only fifteen seconds left in the fucking Saga.

Slowly he begins to lower the lever that will mix the abomination into oblivion – at least until tomorrow. With his other finger he begins to pump up the volume of an equally odious tune: Motley Crüe doing "Girls, Girls, Girls."

He shudders again, still pulsing, utterly transformed in his red warning light. If anyone were to barge into his booth now, or during the next seven seconds that the light will shine, they'd recoil, terrified by the glowing face of a demon.

With Saga finally ejected, the light clicks off and Buddy goes back to scanning his bible, trying to pick up the threads of his "Lust For Life" and "Brand New Key" theories, but the train's derailed.

Instead he remembers that he has to make another alteration to his playlist: Jules hadn't shown up for work.

She danced to the Iggy Pop number, too.

At least that's a break, right?

Once he crosses out her songs with a big X, and after moving up in the order, with a looping arrow, the three soppy duets Jenna and Janna feigned their incest duo bit to, he pulls the *Trainspotting* CD from the bottom of the stack to his right and places it directly in front of himself. Then he fishes out a little origami square of paper from his left pants pocket.

Opening it, he delicately taps a good sized button of white powder from the paper onto the plastic that covers Ewan McGregor's face.

Taking the Saga CD, using it like a blunted, makeshift razor blade, he chops up the button and fashions it into a thin white line. Then, with the straw he'd snagged from the bar and kept on his control board for just such occasions, he snorts the coke.

Wiping his nose, then licking his finger and brushing the remaining white flakes off the jewel case and Saga disc, and then sucking the sticky powder off his finger, he laughs and rises from his perch and peers, once more, out over his crowd.

"Girls, Girls, Girls," he mocks, shaking his oddly-feathered hair.

Once the fit subsides, he hurries to put the Saga back in the S row of his bins, replaces *Trainspotting* to the bottom of the discs on deck, and prepares to introduce the next ripper.

Bathed in demonic red again, he summons his announcer's voice, turns on his mic, and says: "Gentlemen, give a big Rail welcome, to Candy!"

These words are delivered automatically; no one, as usual, is listening. Happily, Buddy's thoughts are elsewhere, focused on his coke. Where he'd gotten the wonderful little package. There was a delicious *Trainspotting*, *Boogie Nights* vibe to it all: he'd bought the drugs, last night, from Jules. She had little use for the stuff, and some john had "paid" her with it when he was a little short for a ride and she threatened to have him beaten to a pulp. Buddy readily took it off her hands, because she was so fucked up that she was offering it for less than half of what it was worth.

That's how transactions go down in The Rail, he thinks or says, watching, again, his regulars drink and watch and drink. Consumer goods offered, consumer goods consumed. Simple economics, bargain hunting. A constant exchange of wealth.

The club pays me to play records. The girls tip me so I don't fuck with their sets. Jules gets tips for dancing up a little extra. She sold me her tip, I paid her with mine.

And then she went out and used my money to buy herself a little smack.

Yeah, lust for life.

And what a cozy little life it is, eh, Buddy? Nice and easy and neat and tidy. Seriously, hope she's alright.

· · • · ·

Oblivion Time.

Please God, let it come.

Please.

For thine is the kingdom.

The power and glory.

Peter James believes he should be much drunker. Believes that he should be much more messed up than he actually is.

By any reckoning he's actually overfed his monstrous addiction.

Drinking time, today, when it finally started, had begun like it always does, like every other drinking time. He had planned and maintained his consumption carefully, spent the hours of his drinking time wisely, in anticipation of the moment.

This moment.

But drinking time, today, was not like any other drinking time. Today was a day like no other.

Today, from somewhere deep inside – call it whiskey-soaked circadian rhythm, call it an alcoholic's biological clock – Peter James felt he was just a little behind his time.

Early that afternoon he carefully maintained the correct balance, saturated his blood with just enough alcohol to make the final push past consciousness possible. Just like he'd done so many, many other times over the last few months.

The trick, as always, was not to approach the summit too quickly. Too much alcohol, and not enough blood, and you were done for. Sick as a dog. Ruined. And then you'd have to start all over again.

As any serious drinker could tell you, that's the last thing you want.

Peter, really, truly, believes this. Peter James is, after all, a seasoned pro.

He also believed he had enough experience with this matter to prove the point, logically.

After a while, however, an unfamiliar desperation took hold. It wasn't the kind of desperation he felt when he couldn't get a drink, when his addiction wasn't being fed. No, this was an entirely new feeling.

Like neither drinking nor drinking time were enough. Like it would never, ever be enough. Like there wasn't enough booze in the world. Like he'd never forget again.

Like there was no oblivion time.

And so, fearful, he increased his intake, believing, logically, at first, that his monstrous appetite for alcohol had suddenly grown, reached a new level, needed to be fed more, and more often.

But right now, he also believes that this logical assumption might actually be wrong.

I should be hammered. Much more drunk. Shitfaced. Destroyed.

Please. Please, God. Deliver us from evil. Lead us not into temptation.

Oh fuck. I'm not. Oh fuck. Am I sick? Am I dying?

He's not, of course. Not quite.

But something tricky and malicious has occurred, and it has influenced the addiction and the mind of Peter James. If you were a vengeful gull or a disgusted sunbeam or a card cheat or even a higher power, you'd laugh now. Hard.

The joke's on you, buddy.

Sometimes you lose, eh? Eh, buddy?

Peter James *knows* he's not drunk enough. In fact, he *knows* he's done the impossible.

Peter James has drunk himself straight. Stone cold sober.

Oh, God.

And so he's feeling everything. Hearing everything. Seeing everything.

Deep behind his blue eyes it's all pain.

He watches then, Jenna and Janna, one after another, slink down the stairs. He hears their first song, "Don't Go Breaking My Heart," begin to play. He listens to the hoots of the guys around him, the catcalls and woo-hoos. He watches the sisters disrobe one another, pretend to touch.

He believes he feels disgusted.

Peter also hears the old man, yelling over Captain fucking Pissypants beside him, telling yet another goddamned joke.

"Listen up, Scarface. You too, Captain. Here's another one. And this one's goddamned good. Told to me, in fact, by an old army bud, fifty years ago. Okay, maybe they're not his exact words, but a goddamned close, reasonable facsimile. Besides, it's as old as the goddamned hills, a goddamned classic. A timeless goddamned joke, told in every god-damned culture. Hell, in my mind Hemingway says as much in his god-damned stories. You guys know what I mean, right? Back from the first war? Anyway, it goes like this. . . .

"There's some guy walking down the road near a cemetery, and he notices this strange goddamned procession approaching. First he sees one long black hearse, and then he sees that the damn thing's being followed by another long black hearse — it's close by, maybe fifty feet back. Behind the second car he sees this solitary guy, dressed all in black, and this som-bre fellow's walking a big mean old monster of a mutt on a heavy chain leash. The thing's snarling and growling and almost pulling the guy along. Behind these two there's at least 200 other guys, not dressed for a funeral, mind, but still following the procession, walking single file. Anyway, the first guy just couldn't stand it any more. Curiosity gets the better of him, right? And of course, he has to ask. So, this guy bows his head and tentatively, respectfully, approaches the mourner walking the dog. Christ, we're talking a real hellhound here. Anyway, he says, 'Sir, I know this is a bad time to disturb you, and I'm really sorry, but I've never seen a funeral like this.' The guy just nods, so he asks, 'Whose funeral is it?' Well, the guy walking the dog doubles up on his leash and says, 'Uh, well, you see, that first hearse up there is for my wife.' 'Jesus,' the first guy says, 'I'm sorry.' But since he's still curious about the second car, and the dog, he presses on: 'What happened to her?' The other guy sighs and sorta shrugs and says, 'My dog bit her, and then she died.' Amazed, the first guy inquires further, 'Okay, but who's in the second hearse?' Sorta grinning now — a perverse, crazy kinda sorrow, the first guy's thinking — the man answers: 'My mother-in-law. She was trying to help my wife when it happened, and then the dog turned on her and bit her, too. And then, well, now she's dead, too.' The whole procession stopped at this point, the hearses getting further ahead. The first guy stands there, staring at the widower and his dog, all thoughtful. A moment of silence passes between them. But then the first guy can't resist. So he says, he says, 'Jesus, now that's a bitch. But, sir, I'm wondering, could I borrow that dog?' And you know what the guy with the dead wife says? Hey, Scarface, you listening? Yeah? Well, the second guy points behind at all the other guys and says, and this is the kicker, he says: 'Get in line.'

"You get it, kiddies? Get in line? Ha ha."

With this, the old man's busting a gut and slapping the suit beside Peter on the back; Pissypants – who right now really does look kinda like that kid in *Thelma & Louise,* a sloppy, fucked-up, dark-haired version who's so bombed he's been talking to his goddamned lighter and drinking both a faggy imported beer and a cup of terrible black coffee – is laughing cruelly, too; in fact, when the old fucker in the Bruins jacket delivered the punch line, Pissypants actually did a goddamned Hollywood spit take – spewing coffee or some green bottled brew up onto the stage. Some of the foul spit ended up all over Janna's ass, who, at that very moment, had her snaking tongue just inches away from her twin sister's twat. She turned and shot them all a look. Livid.

Peter blushed, felt his pockmarked face go crimson.

Waiting for the bouncers to descend now, Peter James stares at his two cronies, stone-faced. Incredulous.

But the bouncers don't come.

In a way, he's grateful. For both the joke and its aftermath. He pushes his seat back from his part of the stage ledge and stands on sturdy legs.

Erect, Peter James has just come to a surprising number of clearheaded decisions.

He knows, for example, that he cannot watch Jenna pretend to eat her sister, or vice versa, any more. Never, ever, again.

He knows that this hurts.

He knows it's both too freaky and too disgusting.

Just not right.

And he knows that he's simultaneously envious of, and appalled by, the old man and the yuppie. He knows he wishes he was as drunk as they are. He knows, sadly, that he's not. He also knows that it's pointless. He will not get hammered, destroyed, not even pleasantly drunk.

He knows he doesn't belong here. At least not in the front row.

He knows he's not happy.

Forsaken.

He knows he's a joke. That for months he's been making himself more and more of a joke. He knows he's got a problem. Many, many problems.

He also knows that this really is oblivion time after all.

And Peter James doesn't like it. It's no fun. Not funny at all.

And it can only get worse.

Finally, Peter also realizes that the Captain and the old man have stopped laughing. That they're staring at him.

He knows this is making him uncomfortable, standing there, solitary, for everyone in the place to see. The last thing he wants, flying so goddamned solo, is to be this conspicuous.

And he knows the old man is making fun of him, needling him in a way that would normally make him so furious he'd beat the living tar out of him, no matter how wrong it might be to punch the snot out of a man who's probably fifty years older than he is.

He hears and sees and feels everything: the insult, the menace, and the shame.

"What's your problem, Craterface," the old guy says, "you offended or something? Did old Mr. Harrison say something to hurt your sensitive goddamned feelings, you shiftless sonofabitch? Don't be getting holier than thou on me, son. Let me tell you, you'll regret it."

With this, Ed Harrison tips his Jack Daniels to his lips, drains it quick, laughs, slams it on the ledge, and polishes off the gesture by chasing the bourbon with what was left of a Budweiser. "Well, tough guy, you startin' something here?"

Clamping down his rage, clamping it down hard and deep, Peter shakes his head.

"Nope," he says. "In fact, I want to thank you both. It's been a slice. No, illuminating. Actually quite illuminating. I'm very glad to have met you, but I believe I need to stretch my legs now. Clear my head, God willing. You take care, though, Mr. Harrison."

Nodding toward Scott Venn, he adds, "You too, buddy."

And then Peter takes one last look at Jenna and Janna – their identical legs are entwined so crazily as they both spin around the same pole that it's impossible to tell whose long tanned limb is whose – and then he turns away from the stage and walks calmly to the end of the bar closest to the exit.

By the time Peter's sitting down, on top of the leather jacket he's draped over the last barstool, his sober eyes have become a more clear blue – not yellow, or bloodshot, or cold grey – than they've been, at this time of night, since his father died. Waiting for the bartender, he rakes a thick strong hand through his long blue-black hair. He's feeling terrifying, vertiginous things and humming the tune he'd heard earlier, when that scary one, with the piercings, started dancing a new set.

It was a great song. Be great to write into a flick. Maybe someday, eh?
My dreams, they aren't as empty, as my con-science seems to be. . . .
Yeah, maybe. Maybe I'll try.
"Hey, you're not at your usual perch. What can I get you, bud?"
Startled, Peter blinks at the bartender.
"Uh, coffee, I think. I think it's coffee time."
"Don't tell me my most rock-steady customer's pupping out on me."
"Naw, I just feel kinda funny."
"Oh, too much of a good thing, eh?"
"Not exactly."
"You ain't gonna puke at my bar, are ya?"
"Nope. Definitely not," Peter says, wondering why everybody's always wondering whether he's gonna puke.
That can't be good.
"Well, I'll kick your ass six ways till Sunday if you do. Got it?"
"Yup."
"It'll be a minute then. How'd you take it?"
"Right now? Black. Tonight I'm drinking black coffee."
While he waits Peter pulls out his wallet, fishes in there for a small bill. Something about the black light and neon combine to make him notice there's an odd ridge under the lining. He runs his thumbnail against his swollen lip, then uses it to dig.
Later, already on his second cup, Peter's in a world of his own, doodling on a napkin with the bar's pen, making notes actually, his stomach churning – not from the booze or the bitterness of the coffee, but from everything within him fighting for control. The fears of his mind and addiction, his sorrow and anger, the memories and regrets and loss and rage.
Confusion time. Feeling worse than he's ever felt before. Less than zero. Rock bottom.
His dad and mom and Uncle Joe. The cars. The crimes. The friends he's lost. The jobs. The passion. The girl.
Half a long-forgotten photo booth picture strip stares up at him now, from the bar.
It's already made him take a first, baby, step.
Beside the two photos, on a square cocktail napkin, Peter James is beginning to make amends, making his list, checking it twice.
At the bottom of the list he writes: *Roadwolf.*
And then a voice startles him: "Hey, Pete, what're you writing?"
Embarrassed, he covers the napkin and photos with his right hand, blushes and looks to his right. It's the mousy waitress, the new one,

Ronnie or something. She's sitting on the next stool with her shoeless left foot propped on her right thigh. She looks exhausted and she's rubbing her arch.

"Huh?"

"Don't be shy, I was just wondering what you were writing. I'm not used to seeing you over here. And you're not drinking. And so I was wondering if you were okay. You always used to be writing things, I remember. Jesus, what a night. I'm dead out there, pulling another double."

"Is your shift over now, um. . . ."

"No, I gotta close. Just sneaking a little break."

"Oh." He crumples the cocktail napkin and tries to stuff it, awkwardly, into the right front pocket of his clean black jeans with his Black Flag key ring and the little that's left of his dope and the keys to his uncle's Eighty-Eight Royale. The photos are left exposed.

The waitress stays his hand. "You okay, Peter?"

"Yeah. Look, I'm sorry. I don't mean to be rude. But do I know you? How do you know my name?"

She looks a little crestfallen, but doesn't let go of his balled-up fist.

"You really don't remember me?"

He shakes his hangdog head. "No, sorry."

"Think back, a long time ago."

"I'm sorry."

"Oh, that's okay."

"So, where do I know you from? Another club?"

"Nope. This is my first job in one of these places."

"Really?"

"Yeah. My boyfriend's involved here. I'm, um, helping him out."

"Oh."

"You sure you're okay? You look kinda sad."

"I'm fine, I think. But you still haven't told me how you know me. Christ, I'm so rude. I don't even know your name. And when did you ever see me write anything? I never write anything."

"You used to, Peter James. All the time. I'm Veronica, does that help?"

"Um. . . ."

"Veronica Addams." She squeezes his right fist harder.

Peter's expression is still blank, apologetic, but utterly blank.

She sighs. "We went to school together, you know. I wrote *you* a note once. I guess you don't remember."

Peter smiles.

"I had such a crush on you," she says, releasing his fist and gently patting his hand. "You were, like, the only punk in that place."

"No shit."

"No shit."

"Damn."

"Damn."

"Well, fuck me."

"You don't remember the note, do you, Peter? Aw, that's okay. Why would you? You were a grade ahead and probably didn't even know I was alive."

"I remember you now."

"Ha. Don't bullshit me, okay? It's fine."

"I'm sorry, Veronica."

"That's okay, Pete. That was a long time ago. We've both moved on. Maybe you never even got the thing."

"Maybe."

"So, you've got nothing to be sorry for."

"Naw, actually I do, Veronica. I've got a lot to be sorry for."

Sensing his mood darken, Veronica tries to change the subject. "So what's with the writing. You still dreaming about making movies, or what?"

Peter drops the napkin ball back on the bar, then rubs his blue blue eyes with his thumb and forefinger.

"Nope. It's just a list. You know, things to do."

Veronica snatches up the paper and unfolds it.

"Hey."

"C'mon, I'm nosy."

She only catches the word *Roadwolf* before he snatches it back, this time actually managing to wedge it into his pocket beside his pager.

"See, I told you. Movies, right? You always wanted to make movies, even back in school. *Roadwolf* is so cool. My boyfriend took me a couple nights back. It's so, I don't know, real. So strange and unbelievable that it's brilliant."

"Can I tell you something, Veronica? Can you keep a secret?"

"Sure," she says, readjusting the Elastoplast bandage and sliding her aching foot off her thigh and back into her uncomfortable black shoe.

"That's my movie. I helped write it. I directed it."

"No, it's not."

"No, really."

"Now why'd you have to start pulling my chain, Pete? We're having one of the first real conversations I've ever had in this hellhole, so don't lie. Okay? I hate liars. I've had my fucking hands full with liars."

"It's the truth, Veronica."

"Fuck you, Peter. I watched the fucking credits. I see the poster every goddamned day. . . ."

Peter cringes. So does he.

"And let me tell you, your fucking name is not, definitely not, up there. That, at least, *I* would've noticed."

· · • · ·

Although Veronica Addams was chastising her old flame, she wasn't really pissed. Yes, the lie was pathetic, but she actually felt sorry for him. She was only raising her voice, snapping at him, to make him understand that he didn't have to impress her.

Three other approaching vectors, who had been watching the developing situation closely from three very different vantage points and three very different points of view, saw things in a very, very different way.

While half-heartedly berating the drunk suit in the front row for interrupting her set, spitting on her sister, and ignoring the endless harangue of the old guy beside him, then inviting the obviously loaded preppie back for a lapdance to make it up to her – the least I can do is lighten his fucking wallet for him – Jenna's attention was actually divided between Peter James and Ronnie, and Jason, who was looking really pissed and making a beeline for the pair.

She gave up on the suit and walked cautiously to the bar.

At the same time the owner, a tall, thin Bill Gates of a microgeek, shoulderless and meek-looking, peered over the top of his little round silver glasses, saw his special waitress goofing off – talking with one of the assholes she knows they've been having problems with lately – and flexed an itchy finger around his hair-trigger temper. An outraged businessman who won't countenance anyone slowing down his fast track, and an enraged, extremely jealous boyfriend, he broke off the intimate conversation he was having with one of his new employees, a raven-haired, blue-dressed vixen who calls herself Paige, and advanced on the cozy couple with long-legged strides.

Jason and Jenna arrived almost simultaneously. The bartender leaned in: this might be interesting.

Jenna, protective, of herself and all meek, helpless creatures, let Jason speak first.

"Listen, buddy, I've told you once, I've told you a hundred fucking times. Stop hassling the girls."

"I . . . I. . . ."

Peter couldn't get another word out before Jason's huge hand was on his shoulder.

"What, you get fucking tired of stalking fucking Jenna or something? Huh, big man? After someone now who ain't got the guts to tell you to fuck off? That's it, you're outta here. Forever."

He picked Peter up by the collar.

Jenna was just about to beg Jason not to hurt him, when Veronica snapped, in a voice more powerful than any of The Rail's many employees could have thought possible: "Leave him the fuck alone, asshole!"

Jason released his grip, looked confused.

The owner was twenty feet away now, closing fast.

"What? Is this guy fucking with you? Or isn't he? Do I need to toss his ass out or not?"

"No. He's not. Believe it or not, buddy, we were having a conversation. Just talking. Okay? Am I fucking allowed to talk to somebody? He's a friend."

Furious, stopped just three feet away, the owner waited for things to play out, hoping that his bouncer would beat the fuck out of the guy anyway.

Jason turned to Jenna. "What about you? Has he been hassling you again?"

"No, Jason, he's stopped I think. He's been pretty cool for once. A surly sonofabitch. But he's not fucking with anyone."

"Fine. But listen, buddy, I ever catch you, ever, messing with anybody in this place again, you're goin' out of here in a body bag. Got it?"

"No problem."

"I've made myself perfectly clear?"

"Crystal."

Jason turned and walked away, cracking the muscles in his thick neck for show. Jenna sighed and relaxed, looking back and forth between Ronnie and Peter.

"You two know each other?"

"Yeah, old friends," Ronnie said.

Peter, mischievous, pursed his lips and added, "High school sweethearts, reunited."

And then he and Veronica Addams laughed.

Jenna smiled at the happy little idiots, relieved, but confused.

The owner, however, who loomed just behind Jenna, his white, goofy, college-boy face as red as the stage lights, pushed his glasses higher up on the bridge of his nose, moved Jenna aside, and screamed.

"What the fuck's going on here, Ronnie? What the fuck? Who the fuck is this guy? Huh? You think I'm payin' you to sit on your fat fucking ass you fucking cow?"

Ronnie cringed, terrified. Hurt beyond hurt.

"And Jenna, don't you have customers to look after?"

As tough as nails, she snarled, "I'm on a break. So fucking calm down, alright?"

The bartender backed away, turned, headed for the taps at the other end of the long stretch of mahogany, tail between his legs.

Ronnie looked like she was about to cry.

"You fucking skank," the owner sneered at Jenna. "Don't you dare start thinking you're gonna talk to me like that."

"Fuck you, Alfie."

"Look, bitch, I told you, I told all you bitches never to call me that! You call me fucking Fred! Actually, you call me fucking sir, or Mr. Fucking Escher! So shut your fucking hole, show me some goddamned respect, or you're done. Don't make that mistake, Jenna. I'll fire your ass so fast your head'll spin. Even you, darling, even you and your fucking sister can be replaced."

"Leave her the fuck out of this!"

"Get to work, bitch. And Ronnie, get the fuck away from this asshole and start making us some money. Both of you! Fucking bitches!"

He raised the back of his hand, menacingly, then gestured violently, with a sharp swing of his arm, to his bar.

Peter got up from his bar stool, slowly, non-threateningly, but purposeful.

"What're you looking at, asshole?" Fred said. "Get out of my fucking bar, and don't ever even fucking think about coming back."

It's funny how moments replay themselves, Peter thought, strange how things get into your blood and affect you. His eyes narrowed, still clear, but focused with an odd, but not wholly unfamiliar rage: *the strength to change.* His lip pulsed with it, too. It wasn't the evil of his father, and nothing like his own drinking-time dementia. Actually, it reminded him of Joe's violent indignation.

I believe this is acceptable.

Actually, I know it is.

Calm at first, running his powerful right hand over the stubble on his pockmarked face, he said, "Ladies, I'm sorry." And then he turned on the owner. "Fuck you, Alfie. Big fucking man. Picking on girls like this. Well, Alfie, you're a fucking coward. I know it, you know it, everyfuckingbody in this shithole probably knows it. And I'm here to tell you, Alf. Walk away. Don't fuck with these girls, Alf. Walk away."

Peter stepped closer to Fred, his right hand tensing to spring into the chokehold he'd forgotten his uncle had inadvertently taught him so very long ago.

Fred looked for Jason.

And then Veronica Addams spoke: "Please, everybody. Please stop."

Fred tensed, scared, though maybe even about to propel himself into his own ill-considered violence.

Jenna grabbed his arm then, and spun him towards her. Looking him dead in the eye, she said, "C'mon Fred. End this. It's over. Walk away."

He pulled away from her violently and Peter snapped.

A split second later he was crushing the skinny bastard's oesophagus, doubling him back over the bar.

Jason was there, suddenly, trying to pull him off, but Peter would not release his grip.

Veronica cried, "Please, stop, please. Don't hurt him. Peter, let him go."

And then Peter James closed his eyes, exhaled his rage, and let the scumbag go.

Jason flung him to the door. Stood, eyeing the surprisingly strong longhaired dipshit warily.

Fred sucked for oxygen, caught his breath, and wiped tears from his eyes. Hoarse, his scream was little more than a whisper.

"Get him out. Get out now. You're fucking barred!" And then he turned to Jenna, "And you, you fucking cunt. You're fired."

Veronica dabbed at her cheeks with the starched white cuffs of her shirt, fingered the unadorned gold cross that hung from her neck. Adjusted her delicate charm bracelet absently on her wrist.

Jason watched his boss skulk back to his manager's office, shook his head and thought: What a dick. Then he tossed the pockmarked kid, with new respect, his leather.

Peter walked out as Jenna screamed after her ex-employer. She didn't notice, absorbed, instead, in her bad movie line: "Ya can't fucking fire me, Alfie. You can't, you needle-dicked sonofabitch. I fucking quit!"

The entire club, at that point, was eerily quiet. The DJ had turned down the song Mercedes was dancing to, Alanis Morissette's "You Oughta Know," and even she was watching.

Everybody was.

The bartender.

Jason.

The night manager.

The DJ, Buddy, from his perch high above.

Girls in the middle of table dances.

Lapdancers peered from the back.

The guys in the front row swivelled.

And then the preppy beside the old man broke the strange calm. Began banging his beer bottle on the ledge. The guy who looked a little like whatsisname, Jennifer Aniston's boyfriend, hooted a Blur woo-hoo, and sparked up a smoke in his grinning lips.

As fucked up as Scott Venn was, he finally placed the pizzafaced rocker kid. The coffee shop. Hey, buddy, his beer and shooter and bad coffee-addled brain thought, *You Can Win!*

Beside him, the old man in the black nylon jacket and the cap raised his Bud to Peter.

Ed Harrison was saying, "Cheers."

And then Alanis sang about the mess that's made when somebody goes away and everything returned to normal.

The buzz of conversation buzzed. Drinks were poured and served and drunk.

A stripper stripped, kicking and jiggling.

Show's over folks, nothing left to see.

Jenna turned to Ronnie then, touched her arm. "You okay, doll?"

"Yeah."

"You shouldn't take his shit."

"Yeah."

"You should quit, too, you know. You don't belong here. He's such an asshole."

"He's my boyfriend."

"Oh."

"He doesn't mean it, you know. He's under so much stress. Let me talk to him. I'm sure he'll give you your job back. I can make him do that."

"I don't want it, Ronnie."

"No, I guess not."

"You sure you're gonna be okay? Ronnie, you don't look so good."

The mousy waitress just smiled. "Naw, I'm fine. Tougher than I look. And Jenna?"

"Yeah?"

"Please call me Veronica, okay? My name's Veronica Addams."

Jenna blushed. "Jesus, Ronnie . . . I mean, Veronica, I'm so sorry. You know, I didn't even know what your last name was."

"That's okay. Nobody knows who anybody is in here. That's the way we want it, right?"

"Hmmm. Maybe. But Veronica, I'm really glad to know you, you know. I'm pleased to finally meet you. . . . Properly. My name's Jenna . . . Jennifer. My real name's Jennifer Jefferson."

"Oh, I know."

"What?"

"I knew you from high school, too. Just like Peter."

"You did?"

"Yeah. I'm surprised your sister didn't tell you. I got a ride home with her the other night. We talked about it."

"Oh, she's such a bitch. Never tells me anything. Listen, was I a skank to you then? Back in high school?"

"Um. . . ."

"I was, wasn't I?"

"Kinda."

"I'm sorry, Veronica. I've always been a bitch. It's hard to change. But if you'll forgive me, I'd like to be able to call you my friend."

"I'd like that, Jennifer."

"Same here." She looked around the entrance way, expecting to find Peter standing there. He wasn't, of course. Instead, Jason stood in his tuxedo, checking the IDs of a couple of boys who really looked much too young. "Veronica, were you and Pete really a thing back in the old days?"

"No, he was just kidding. Besides, you should know," she said, picking the half photo booth strip off the bar and placing it in Jennifer's hand. "You went out with him. Look, Pete left these. How much you wanna bet I can guess who's got the other half?"

The stripper blushed as she looked at her young self in her palm; slowly her watering eyes rose to meet Veronica's gaze.

"I just had a little crush on him back then," Veronica said, kindly, "that's all. He was trying to make me feel good about it."

Jennifer sniffed herself composed and smiled warily. "Really? He did that?"

"Yeah. But really, I interrupted him. He was just sitting here, drinking coffee. Writing, looking at those pics."

After hesitating another moment, drifting off again, Jennifer said: "Um, I guess I should get out of here. Anyway, call me sometime, okay?"

"Sure."

"And quit this place?"

"Well, actually, I can't. . . ."

"Just think about it, is all. I know it's none of my business, but you're too good for him."

"Really, he's not that bad."

"Maybe. Maybe not. By the way, did you see where Peter went?"

"Um, no. Sorry."

Jennifer Jefferson called out to Jason, who had just ushered the underage kids in. "Hey, where'd the guy go?"

"Which guy?"

"Peter."

"Who?"

"My stalker."

Jason laughed. "He split, five minutes ago. Fucking guy patted me on the back on the way out, saying, 'No hard feelings.' And 'I apologize to you, sir.' Fucking alkies, eh? No figuring 'em. You should probably go, too, Jenna. I'm sorry, but you heard what the boss said. It'll be my balls next if he finds out you're still here."

Jennifer waved a small goodbye at Veronica and then scanned the bar for her twin sister. Janna – Janet – must be in the back with some guy. She'd make her quit tomorrow.

Telling Jason that she'd have to get dressed, Jennifer Jefferson disappeared downstairs. Five minutes later she was in her sweats and carrying her gym bag.

For the rest of The Rail it was like nothing had changed.

Veronica Addams was bringing another Jack and Bud to the old guy up front. Another beer and another coffee to the preppy.

Laps were being danced on in the back.

Cara was peeling up on stage again, her last set, the same as her first. . . .

"Behind Blue Eyes."

As she walked out The Rail's door for the last time, past the sign saying lapdances had been ruled illegal three years earlier, the sign everybody, even the police, ignored, Jason reached for her and grabbed her arm. He handed her a coaster that he'd hurriedly scrawled his number on. "I'm sorry about everything, Jenna. And if that guy ever gives you any trouble again, well, you call me, okay?"

"Peter?" she said.

"Yeah, if that's his name. Your stalker."

"Oh, don't worry about him. I'm fine."

"You sure, Jenna?"

"Yeah. And Jason?"

"Yeah?"

"I don't work here anymore. Call me Jennifer, okay?"

"Uh, sure, um, Jennifer. Look, if you, you know, ever wanted, maybe, to just get together sometime, well, you could also call."

"That's sweet, Jason. But I don't think so."

"Okay. Whatever."

"See ya."

"Bye."

And then she walked through the heavy brass door and out into the street. Peter James was sitting on the curb, staring up at the billboard. His jacket was draped over his lap.

She wasn't surprised.

She walked over and ran her fingers through the top of his long, black hair.

"It must hurt. To have to see that."

"What?"

"That poster. Every day you come here. Every day you must look at that thing. It must tear you up. You worked so hard on that movie, Peter. And no one knows."

"Oh, that. Well, yeah, it does, I guess. It did. Not anymore, though. At least, not now. I'm happy for them. Proud of them."

"Really?"

"Yup."

"Then how come you look so upset. Why're you staring at the thing?"

"Actually, I'm not. I wasn't even looking at the billboard."

"No?"

"Nope."

"Okay, I'm clueless, fill me in. What *are* you doing?"

Pointing, Peter said, "You see that white shape up there?"

"Where?"

"Up there. On top of the billboard."

"Yeah. What is it?"

"It's a seagull."

"Yeah, so?"

"It looks hurt."

"Oh."

"Yeah, it looks like it's in pain. I feel bad for it, I guess. There's nothing I can do."

"Jesus, Peter. When'd you get so sweet?"

"I'm not, Jennifer. You know I'm not. And I've fucked up again. I took my uncle's car. It's in the lot across the street."

"That's okay. I know. We'll fix it. Your mom called. Don't be mad. We'll all fix it."

Peter James began to weep then. For himself and his father and his mother and his uncle and Jennifer and mostly for the bird.

"C'mon, Peter," Jennifer said, slipping the photos into his hand as she pulled his right arm. "Get up. And put on your coat, you must be freezing. Now, give me those keys, I'm taking you home."

· · ● · ·

Catharine Johnston can't help feeling she's just made a big mistake. Five minutes ago, Veronica Addams had asked her if she'd seen Mr. Escher. Preoccupied with the guy she was trying to get to take her back for a dance, without thinking she'd said, "Yeah, I think he's in the manager's office, with Paige."

Veronica bolted then, and burst through the door.

For the next three minutes, there was screaming, obscenities, and a high, girlish whine. Whimpering. Paige had run out almost immediately, smoothing her long blue dress over her hips and legs as she scurried.

What the hell is going on in there? Cara wondered, slipping back, maintaining, deep into the daily bump-and-grind of The Rail. I hope Ronnie's okay.

· · • · ·

Veronica Addams was fine, thank you very much.

Alfred Escher, however, wasn't doing so hot.

When Veronica pushed open the manager's office door the first thing she thought was: Jesus, at least lock the goddamned thing.

The first thing she saw was her boyfriend Freddy's skinny little white ass.

The second thing she thought was: You fucking rat bastard.

The second thing she saw was Paige, lying on the desk, her long legs up over Freddy's shoulders, her shocked, open-mouthed face peering around his left arm.

The third thing she thought was: I'm gonna kill every last motherfucking one of you.

The third thing she saw was Paige, pushing Fred off, jumping down from the desk, adjusting her long blue dress, and bolting past her through the door. At the same time, Alfred Escher, her new ex-boyfriend, turned, blanched, and began to say, "It's not what it looks like. . . ."

The first thing mousy, straight little Veronica Addams did then was ball up her tiny right fist, rear back, and punch Alfie right in the nose.

Blood started flowing immediately.

The second thing she did, happily, joyfully, while her new ex-boyfriend clutched his bloodied schnoz and mumbled, "My nodze, my nodze," was rear back the sharp-toed shoe on her aching right foot.

And then she booted a field goal.

And then Alfie, the bad motherfucker, wailed like a little girl.

The first and very last words Veronica Addams would say to her new ex-boyfriend, the last he'd ever hear from her, before she turned and stormed out were an even crueler, lower blow, an even bigger score.

A goddamned touchdown.

"You're fucking fucked, Freddy. That's it. You're finished. I let you play the big fucking man, tough guy. I fucking made you, you geek. I even worked for you and let you treat me like shit, just because I didn't want it to look like you were playing fucking favourites. So all these fuckheads might actually think you were a real boss. Because *I* wanted to, Freddy! Because I wanted to be a bad girl and work in a place like this just to piss Daddy off! Well, Al-fred, you better start looking for a new line of work. Daddy gave *me* that money, Freddy. You think he would've staked you to a fucking strip club? No, Fred. You own shit. Remember, this fucking place belongs to my old man. To *me*, Alfie. It'll give him a heart attack, when he finds out. But when I tell him what you did with his dough, what you did to me, he'll recover. Oh fuck, he will. He'll recover and tear your stinking, cheating heart out and ruin you! You're fucked, Fred. Fucked. Forever and ever and ever. Fucked!"

And then Veronica Addams was gone.

The very last thing she did, as she exited The Rail as a waitress for the very last time, was walk calmly behind the club, to the private parking lot. Approaching a black BMW with a set of keys in her hands, it looked for all the world like she was about to add a little more insult to her new ex-boyfriend's injury.

But that's not what she did.

Veronica Addams did not disfigure the paint job. Did not take off one of her dangerous shoes and smash the tail-lights. She didn't even bend the antenna.

No, instead, she pressed the alarm button on her key chain, used the remote to unlock the car, opened the driver's side door, and slid behind the wheel.

And then she started the engine of the black BMW that her father had given her, the car she'd let her boyfriend drive so he could look like the bigshot he so desperately wanted to be.

Popping her favourite CD into the player, she rolled down the windows and cranked up the system: *Whitey Ford Sings The Blues*.

And then she drove.

· • · ·

Alice Harrison, in the dark of her kitchen, close to her stove, strains to see the time. She can't quite make it out. Anyway, the cuckoo's always wrong.

But it's late. Very late. Long after midnight. It's a new day. The anniversary day.

She moves to her hallway, still in the dark. She can barely make out the birdcage in the moonlight that filters in from the bay window.

Finally, she goes to her bedroom. There's a little more moonshine coming in through the crack in her handsewn cotton drapes. But not much. Barely enough. She can see the book. Still Faulkner. Still there: *As I Lay Dying*.

She misses her son. Her granddaughter.

She misses Belle just a little bit more.

She can't see Ed, anywhere.

It's dark and cold.

Too cold. Too dark.

Buddy, she says, tell me he's okay. Tell me he's coming home.

The tiny, perfect budgie, of course, is sleeping. Dreaming the terrifying dreams of those who'd slept in his cage before him. He shudders in his sleep. The nightmare voices of the dead.

Buddy? You okay?

He is. He will be. It's only a bad dream. A little guy named Sweet Bud the third's bad, bad, dream.

The old man, twelve years ago, yelling about his daughter. *Junkie whore!* This slightly younger Ed raving, the back of his hand raised. Not at anyone, but menacing, unpredictable.

Alice there, too: not cowering, not pleading. Her voice low, cold, precise. *Don't even think about it, buddy boy. Never, ever. I know you're upset, Ed. But I swear. I swear, Ed. I swear to God I'd kill you. I'd kill you and I'd leave.*

Buddy, Alice says again, are you okay? Is my pretty boy having a nightmare? Tell me, please, tell me you're okay.

He is. He will be.

And if he were awake, of course, if he heard her, he'd answer Alice Harrison.

Buddy'd do that, right? Probably? Maybe?

Maybe.

· · • · ·

"Last call. Can I get you guys anything else?"

Ed Harrison removed his Bruins cap, brushed imaginary lint from the big B crest over his left breast, swirled his teeth around his mouth, then ran his large, strong fingers through his shock of pure white hair. He said, "Yes, darling, I do believe me and the Captain here will go a final round."

Scott Venn held up his left hand in protest. "Naw, I'm good." The green bottle of his Golden is still half full, and he's still quite drunk. "Coffee, though, yeah, one more coffee."

"C'mon, ya dummy, you gonna drink with me or what?"

Scott shrugged.

"Yeah little lady, he will. One more round. And you, miss," he said, looking Catharine Johnston up and down, "you'll join us, won't you?"

"Um, sure. A G and T, okay?"

"Fine, now that's more like it." He smiled at the waitress. "Go on, girl, hurry back."

She shot Cara a look: Losers.

"Now, where the hell was I? Oh yeah, 1944. Anyway, so this guy Reg comes up to me, and he's obviously not a man who can hold his liquor, hell, he ain't half a man at all. Sorta reminds me of you, Captain . . . just kidding. Anyway, he comes up to me in the middle of this goddamned dance floor, in his fancypants clothes, stinking of the booze he shouldn't be drinking and all his goddamned daddy's money, and he starts making a play for my girl. Christ, I'm about to go off to war and I'm shaking in my boots, not 'cause of the fighting, mind, but on account of asking the most beautiful goddamned woman in the world, right then, right at the precise goddamned moment, to be my wife."

Catharine Johnston smiled, relaxed, gave away just a little bit more of her heart to Ed Harrison. She liked hearing this tough old man talk about the wife he's so obviously happily married to.

"And anyway, he's trying, the big shot he is, saying she's gotta go with him, and he's having to yell 'cause the band's starting up another number, and I'm thinking: Jackass. So then, then the sonofabitch turns to me, all uppity, and calls me a goddamned fool right to my goddamned face. Starts telling me, she's actually *his* girl. That they're eventually gonna get married. So I'm the biggest idiot there is, right? Thinking she's gonna say yes. Thinking she's gonna hitch herself to me? This woman, who's obviously too goddamned good for a guy like myself, with all the money in the world herself, you see, and I've only been datin' her for a few weeks, seeing her whenever I can get away from the base before they ship me off, this woman, she's seriously gonna accept my proposal? Hell, no. I see it all then and there, don't think I didn't."

Catharine leaned closer. Poor man.

"No, I knew. Yeah, that very second, standing there on the dance floor, that goddamned bitch was gonna break my heart."

Catharine reared back, looked at Ed's wedding band, embarrassed.

I'm glad, though, at least he found someone who deserved him. So many don't. So many like her.

"Man oh man," Scott said.

"Damn straight. No, I realized there and then – you gotta get up pretty goddamned early to pull the wool over old Ed's eyes – that I was being played for the patsy. Of course she'd been usin' me to make the rich sonofabitch jealous. Fine. Yeah, so I'm just about to walk away, you know? Enough's enough. Go out to a bar where I belonged, get hammered, pick up a little piece of something, and get myself laid. Christ, I was probably goin' off to get myself killed like my goddamned brother. Did I need this crap? No, I tell ya. No goddamned way.

"Like I said, I did *not* need that shit. I could feel it though, all the goddamned rage building up in me. More at her than him, but it was there, just begging to get out. Christ, you know, I was in love. And, well, yeah, the truth was she was not about to fall in goddamned love with me. Still, I fought that rage, you know, I respect a lady, always have, always tried. No matter what. But I'm thinking, I'm thinking, Ed, you have to say something, at least say something son, to save goddamned face here. And so there I was, just about to tell her where the cow ate the cabbage – to tell her how goddamned spoiled and stuck up and low and disgusting it was to do this to a guy in my situation, to lead him on – when Mr. Fucking Fancypants grabs her to pull her away from me. And he hurts her a bit.

"Now I know what you're thinking, you're probably thinking, well, she got what she had coming. All things considered. I mean, the drunken jackass just tugged at her the wrong way. And maybe you're right, maybe not. For me, anyway, it's never been cut and dry. Over the years though, and it's taken me a helluva long time to change my way of thinking about this, 'cause it takes a helluva lotta time to get over being used and lied to, and besides, he didn't really hurt her that bad, I think what I did, the way I responded, was right."

"So you walked away, right?"

"What's that, Captain?"

"I mean," Scott said, "you'd had enough. And what could you say. So, cool, you figured: you wanna be with the asshole, by all means, be my fucking guest."

Ed just stared.

Catharine, unsure of exactly who she was talking to now – he was different somehow, angrier, drunk – asked: "Is that what you did, Ed? Did you walk away?"

Ed turned to her, as if surprised, and offended, that she called him by his name.

His eyes darkened, his face blanched.

"What the fuck," he said, "do you two take me for?"

Catharine became Cara again, absolutely, definitively, Cara. Cara, sharp as a boxcutter, crossed her arms over her big breasts, and backed away in her seat.

Scott laughed, uneasy. "Hey there, Old Timer, no offense intended."

His eyes completely dead, his voice low, but forceful and calm, Ed addressed them, held forth.

"Fuck you, Cappie. Fuck you all to hell. No, kiddies, I'll tell you what I did. I did what any goddamned real man would've done. I swallowed my goddamned pride, balled up my goddamned fists, and proceeded, right there and then, to beat the living hell out of the pencil-necked little goddamned fag. Hurting a goddamned woman, Jesus! And you two think I'd walk the fuck away? No, I punched the motherfucker so hard that I had to hold him up to punch him again. And then I punched him even harder to get him down at my boots, down to where he belonged, in front of a guy like me. And then, and then, you know what I did then? Then, missy," he said, staring directly at Cara now, "I kicked the living snot out of him. I kicked him, and I kicked him, and let me tell you right now, I was going to, as sure as I'm talking to *you* now, I was gonna kill him. That, friends, was my intention before everybody in the place pulled me off the sorry piece of rich shit and the cops came."

The waitress hovered behind the three of them while Ed finished. She shot Jason a look over by the bar.

Could be trouble.

Jason pointed his left index finger to his right eye.

I'm watching, it's cool.

"Um, here you go. . . ."

Scott fished for his wallet one last time, paid for the drinks and gave the girl another big tip.

Cara snatched up her glass, and started to get up. "Well, guys, it's been, you know, um, real—"

"Sit down, Miss Catharine Johnston, I haven't finished the goddamned story. Or are you Cara now? Is that it, dear? Has Mr. Fucking Harrison, *sir,* scared you?"

"Hey—" Scott started.

"Shut up, Cappie. You're too fucking drunk and useless and late. Sit down, *Cara.* I'm just a harmless old man, who's always havin' too much to drink and gettin' too worked up about some things."

As angry as she was, Cara found herself easing back into her chair, clutching yet another sweating glass to her breast. Ed Harrison had her transfixed again.

Scott tried again, still drunk, to get the negotiator in him to rise to the occasion, wanting to mediate, maintain, bring things down a notch. "Listen, I know a story. It's funny. Yup. Listen. Okay, so there's this guy, this guy in a strip club. Yeah. And he's like, just staring at his drink, not paying any attention to the peelers, not moving a muscle. Anyway, another guy, a tough guy, sitting close by, notices him. And he decides he's gonna fuck with the little freak's head. So, this guy gets up from his table, walks on over to the sad sack, reaches in front of him, takes his drink, and swallows it. Drains the whole goddamned glass, man oh man, just like that. Astonished, the poor first guy looks up and then bursts into tears. The tough guy, getting more out of the dweeb than he bargained for, has a change of heart and tries to comfort him. 'Come on, guy,' he says, 'I was just joking! Here, I'll buy you another. For chrissake, you wuss, don't cry! I was just kidding.' And then you know what? Well, the bawling little guy looks up at this big, tough, mean sonofabitch and says, 'No, no, it's not that. Don't bother. You see, you just don't understand! This has been the worst day of my life.' So then the other guy goes, 'Look, I really am sorry. Tell me about it, what happened?' Completely fucked, the little guy decides, oh, what the hell. So he tells him, he says, 'Well, first I was late to work and I got fired. Then, I'm leaving the building, and I go down to the parking lot, and I find that my car's been stolen. And, of course, my wallet and credit cards are in there. Luckily, though, I've got just enough bus fare in my pocket to get home, you know, to call the cops and everything. Well, then. . . . Then I get home, right? But I'm early, you see, 'cause I've been fired. So I walk in, and you know what I find? Yeah, that's right, I walk in and I find my wife in bed with my best friend.' And then the little guy starts crying again. 'Jesus,' the tough guy says, 'Jesus, you really did have a bad day.' Well, sucking it up, and com-posing himself for a second, the snotty-nosed little loser looks up at the other guy then, and through his snot and tears says, he says, 'That's not the worst of it. You see, after I grabbed some money and things and left them, him still giving it to her – Christ, they didn't even have the decen-cy to stop – I come into this bar. And so, finally, finally I'm sitting here, staring at my glass, and when I think I've worked up the nerve to do it, to finally kill myself, you show up and drink my poison!'"

Cara groaned, but couldn't help laughing a little, nervously. "That's terrible," she said. "An awful, old joke."

Grinning, shitfaced, Scott was proud he even remembered the punch-line.

Ed Harrison just glowered, sucked on his Bud after draining his sixth or seventh Jack Daniels.

"You think it's funny, Captain Fucking Fancypants?"

"Um. . . ."

"You think that's funny? I'm telling you something goddamned important, something goddamned meaningful, about life for chrissake, and you have the goddamned nerve to interrupt me, you rude little shit, with that? That joke? Lemme tell ya, Cappie. That ain't goddamned funny. Not one goddamned bit. That's no fucking joke, you moronic piece of shit, that's a goddamned epic tragedy. That's goddamned Shakespeare, ya dummy. That story you just told, you fucking idiot savant, is *the* goddamned story. That story is fucking life. Yours. Mine. Everybody's.

"And you. Catharine . . . Cara . . . whatever your goddamned name is tonight. You're laughing, too? Tell me, why? Why did you find that so fucking funny? You like fucking funny stories, the two of you? Okay. Fine. You didn't appreciate the story I was telling you, fine. Okay. Here's a goddamned joke for ya. And this, judging by your sense of humour, this you'll find really fucking hysterical. . . ."

Jason watched Cara and the old guy and the shitfaced preppy carefully, ready to intercede.

"Me, the old sonofabitch you see before you now, me, Mr. Ed fucking Harrison, I've been blessed a million times over. No, nothing's ever come easy. I've never had a lot of money. I ain't famous and I ain't brilliant and I sure as hell ain't rich. But the good Lord blessed me just the same, you know? First, he gave me a beautiful wife, a woman who put up with me, who loved me as I was, not as she wanted me to be.

"And then? Then he gave me a son. My boy, Theodore. And Teddy's a good kid, always has been. Always will be. Too good for that bitch who left him to take care of our Krystal. My only goddamned grandchild. But she's perfect, too. An angel.

"And all of us – my wife, my boy, my granddaughter, my family – we've stuck together through thick and thin. We've made do. We've adapted.

"So, I've got everything a man could ever hope for, right? Right. I'm fucking blessed.

"Oh, I know, Captain Funnypants, you're wondering, yeah, you're wondering: Where's the goddamned punchline?

"Well, son, I'll tell you. The goddamned punchline is me. That's right. It's me who walked into your goddamned strip club, Belle!"

Ed Harrison turned to stare at Cara.

"It's me who comes here alone every goddamned day, not goddamned man enough to stop you from putting that goddamned poison in your goddamned arms, to stop you from throwing the body your goddamned sainted mother gave you at these filthy goddamned perverts."

Raging, Ed rose, pointing his finger, first at Cara, then hard into his own chest.

"And it's my fucking fault. I couldn't stop you, Belle. It's my wickedness in you, it's my wickedness that broke your goddamned mother's heart! And that's why I come here, and that's why I'm the goddamned joke. 'Cause I'm not man enough to drink *my* poison and be done with it, Belle! You see, the good Lord also blessed me with you, Belle, the most beautiful daughter a man could have, and I failed you!"

Wild-eyed, almost in tears, Ed will not let himself cry. He's not making any sense, to Scott, or to Cara. They're both terrified.

He's very, very drunk.

"And now you're a whore and a drug addict, Belle! And you're killing everything good in our lives. So finish it, Belle. For fucksake, finish me!"

Jason had heard enough; he cut in and restrained the raving senior. Ed collapsed in his arms, breathing heavily.

"That's it, old man, you're out of here."

Cara said, "Wait, wait a second, Jason." Her voice had become tender, but firm: "Ed, Ed Harrison, listen to me. I'm not Belle. Calm down. Listen. It's okay. I understand. I understand your pain. It's okay. Just let it go. Let it go, Ed. Calm down."

Wincing, Ed turned his drunken head, violently, away from her voice. His cap tumbled to the floor. Like a big white-haired child, he hid his face in his left shoulder.

Scott looked from Cara to Ed to Jason.

Cara continued. "Let him sit for a second, Jason. Sit him down. Don't leave. Just let him sit. He's old and he doesn't look too good."

Jason rolled his eyes, but put Ed, firmly, back in his place.

"Who's Belle, Ed?"

Nothing. Just heavy breathing. A sigh.

"She's your daughter, isn't she?"

"I have no daughter," he said, in barely a whisper. "Don't listen to me, I'm a foolish, drunk old man. I have no daughter. I have nothing. I don't even know what I'm talking about."

"It's okay, Ed."

"Yeah, Ed," Scott said, "we're all friends here."

Ed laughed then, another trigger pulled – aggressive again, waving his left arm in a dramatic, room-clearing gesture. "You think so, son? I may be a joke, Captain, but if you believe you've got a friend in this place then you're an even bigger jackass than I pegged you for."

Jason grabbed Ed's left wrist, hard. "That's it, pops. Sorry, Cara. He's done."

Ed responded by clamping his own right hand over Jason's right wrist, his grip vice-like. His stare was cold, hard: this is how it should end, it said.

287

Against his better judgement, his nature, Jason resisted nailing the troublemaker. Instead, he pointed to Ed's wedding band with the pinky of his free right hand.

"Go home, sir. It's very late. Go home to your wife now."

Ed shook his head, then slowly started to smile and release his grip. "Whaddya know about it, son? What could you know?" He laughed. "Aw, you're a good kid. But you know nothing. I'll tell you what, though, you're right. It is time for Ed Harrison to get the hell out of here. Time for me to go home."

And then Ed stood, straightened his Bruins jacket, and winked at Scott. Before he turned to leave, he grabbed Scott's last Molson, still mostly untouched, and drained it in one long swallow.

"Hope that wasn't your poison, Captain. Or maybe, maybe I do."

Everybody's eyes followed his slow shuffle out.

At the door, he stopped to look back and yelled, loud enough to be heard over the music and din, "People, in the words of old Oliver Cromwell, almost 350 years ago he spoke 'em, and these are the exact words, mind, his exact words to, ha, the *Rump* parliament – and isn't that fitting, ha ha – I'd just like to tell you all, my dear, dear *friends*, this: 'You have sat too long here for any good you have been doing. Depart, I say, and let us have done with you. In the name of God, go!'"

And then, following his own advice, Ed Harrison did.

Jason looked at Scott then, and put his big hand on his slouching shoulder. "You, too, buddy," he said. "It's just about closing time. I can't take any more. Do me a favour? Just leave. Now. Tomorrow's another day, eh?"

Scott nodded, still looking at the door Ed just passed through, saying, "Man oh man oh man."

Cara got up, backed away from Scott and the ledge and noticed Ed Harrison's hat on the beaten red carpet by Jason's feet.

"Oh damn, he forgot his cap."

"Don't worry about it, Car, he'll be back for it tomorrow, if he even remembers. But, guaranteed, he'll be back."

"I don't think so, Jason."

She picked up the Bruins cap, and not even considering the fact that she was still wearing her fuck-me heels, a teddy, and a G-string, ran after the old man.

He hadn't got far. In fact, Ed was just outside the door, leaning against the entrance to the club next door, where all the horny house-wives stuffed bills down male G-strings.

"Hi," she said. "You okay?"

"Yeah."

"You forgot your cap."

"Oh. Thanks."

"Look, you want me to call you a cab?"

"No. I'll manage. The buses run all night."

"You sure you're okay?"

"Fine. Go on back in. You'll catch your death out here."

"Yeah, it's getting cold, eh?"

"Yup."

"Okay then."

"Okay."

"Bye, Mr. Harrison."

Cara pulled open the brass door and was about to walk back inside when Ed said, "Wait. I'm sorry. I'm sorry, Miss Catharine Johnston. I really am an old fool. And I didn't mean to take all of this out on you. I'll never bother you again, though. I swear."

He offered her his hand.

She didn't take it. Just stared at him, trying one last time to figure the old man out.

"Well, goodnight then, miss," he said, embarrassed.

And then he turned and again slowly shuffled off, eyes on the sidewalk, heading south.

"Sir, wait a second."

He stopped but did not turn around.

"The story you were telling in there. The first one. About the fight and that woman. Tell me, how did it end?"

"Oh," he said. "I forgave her. It only felt like it took forever, but I forgave her, instantly."

"Really?"

"Yup."

"Why?"

"Well, Miss Johnston, no matter what, I guess I loved her."

"Yeah?"

"Yup."

"What happened to her?"

"I guess she lost her mind."

"What do you mean?"

"Well, she up and married me. Fell in love with me, then and there. Got my ass out of jail, gave up everything, and married me the very next morning."

"Really?"

"Yes, Miss Johnston. And today's our fifty-fourth wedding anniversary."

"Congratulations, sir."

"Yeah, I'm a lucky man, Miss Johnston."

"No, sir, she's a lucky woman. Actually, I think you're both pretty lucky."

"Maybe. But Miss Johnston?"

"Yes, sir?"

"For chrissake, call me Ed, okay?"

"Goodbye, Ed. Happy Anniversary. Go home to your wife now."

"Yup."

And then Ed Harrison began his very long, slow walk to the bus, to home.

· · ♦ · ·

The peelers are leaving.

The worst gull laughs out loud and blinks its black eyes, delighting in its pain.

From its cold perch high above The Rail it's watched them go, one by one. The immaculate disfigured boy and his girl have driven away. The old man is still waiting for his bus. Even the one it had marked has stumbled down the street.

The worst gull shivers into its damaged wing, tired and cold and deliciously hurt above the billboard.

It closes its black eyes tight.

It's dying or falling asleep.

It doesn't care which.

Snickering softly it thinks: The peelers are leaving. Everybody's going. That's what people will never understand, buddy, what they will never face. No matter what, every last one of them, *everybody*, has got to go home.

Sometime.

THREE

It's an early bird matinee
come back any day
getcha little sompin
that cha can't get at home
getcha little sompin
that cha can't get at home

TOM WAITS
Pasties & a G-String

SATURDAY, OCTOBER 4th

H<small>E PICKED UP HER MESSAGE</small>, stewed and made her wait. Made her wait a long time.

He savoured it. Wanted it that way.

I'm in control here.

The black and orange cab stopped in front of the beachfront house again, the same station playing, the same late night DJ throwing to another late night song.

"Whatever gets you through the night, my children, with the late Mr. John Lennon. . . ."

He nodded to the driver, slammed the orange and black Plymouth Colt's passenger door shut, and walked toward the house.

He looked back, once, shrugged, shivered against the cold. With his gloved hands he zipped his jacket tighter to his neck.

The driver lit a smoke, sighed, the engine still idling, listening to the song. He mouthed the words in thick, accented smoke clouds, getting them all wrong.

· · ● · ·

Okay, here's what I know. She was up in the bedroom there, when the knock brought her down.

She must have fallen asleep waiting. She rose slowly, I could hear her stretching. When she got to the hallway she was still rolling her neck. She looked disoriented. A bit fucked up.

She took her time. He kept knocking. He didn't ring the bell. Or use his key.

She yawned and opened the door.

He stood in the doorway, backlit by the sideswipe of a cab's headlights.

"I thought you weren't going to come," she said, still kind of sleepy.

"Sorry."

"Well. . . ." She drew her robe tight around her neck, flipped her hair, and smudged a little trace of dirt closer to the lower lid of her right eye.

"Well, are you going to ask me in?"

"Um, sure. The taxi. . . . Is he waiting for something?"

"Forget about it. He'll leave."

"Um, okay."

She sighed and closed the door, but didn't lock it. Then she led him down the hall, through the dining room, past the kitchen, and into the living room. The sliding glass doors were cracked open a bit. It was cold.

She shivered and pushed them shut. Set the locks.

I shivered, I watched.

I remember him lighting a smoke. He was still wearing his coat, his tight, snug-fitting gloves. Thin, but probably warm.

She said, "Please. At least not in the house."

He just shrugged, and blew a smoke ring.

It was so beautiful, hanging there . . . for . . . forever.

He butted out then, right there in his pack. Then he shoved his smokes back in his pocket.

She asked him if he wanted to take off his coat, his gloves. He shook his head. Said he was fine for the time being.

And then he said, I remember, he clapped his gloved hands together and said: "So, you wanted to talk. Let's talk. What's on your mind?"

He sounded funny. I remember that, like he'd been drinking. Happy, confident, you know. But his words weren't clear. Not quite slurred, but not like other times. I don't know, maybe he was nervous. Maybe he had an idea about what was coming.

She cleared her throat and began reasonably enough. Firmly, you know, not worried at all.

He just nodded and smiled. Like he was taking it very well, actually. I thought it was all going just fine.

I was happy for her. This was a good thing she was doing.

She explained how they just weren't right for one another. How they were such very different people.

He nodded some more, and maybe pursed his lips a bit.

I can't be sure. It was subtle, you know?

Anyway, she told him she still cared for him. But in no uncertain terms laid it all out.

He tried to reason with her. Said he understood how she felt. But that they were right for each other. That she'd see it, if she gave it time.

And then he offered her a candy or something. A pill maybe, I'm not sure.

She took it from his gloved hand, put it in her mouth. Said thanks. This was hard. That kind of thing.

And then he started to rub her leg through a small opening in her robe.

I could hear the soft leather on her skin.

She pushed his hand away.

She said, "You're not listening to me."

"C'mon, baby," he said. "We can make it so good again."

"No," she said. "Stop. I think you should leave."

"I know you don't really mean that, baby," he said.

"I do," she said. "And, I think you better leave now. For good."

And then all hell broke loose.

He started screaming.

Who the fuck did she think she was, that kind of thing. Too good for him? That type of shit, you know?

She screamed back.

I was terrified.

And then. . . .

And then something in him – I felt it – changed.

He didn't like being screamed at. He hit her. Hard.

And then she fell.

And then he was screaming louder.

And she was hurt and crying and calling his name.

Only it wasn't his name she was calling.

She was moaning, "No, Scott, no. Scotty, no."

And this enraged him even more.

And he hurt her more.

He kept hurting her and screaming – I remember the exact words – "You ugly, old, stupid, fucking cunt!"

"You stupid fucking cow, you stupid cunt!"

Screaming and hurting, he kept on and on, worse and worse and worse.

The clock exploded. Buddy, there, he went flying. Poor bird. Splinters everywhere.

And then the door burst open.

The man in the cab must have heard all the yelling.

I remember he was ugly; he was greying, older, he had an ugly, square face. Wearing gloves, too.

It was cold, you know.

He sounded funny, when he screamed, horrified, he sounded funny.

"Jesus," he said. "Jesus, Stephan, what have you done?"

And that's it, guys. That's it. Then they left. The ugly guy grabbed the guy who was hurting her and pulled him away and they left through the front door and then they got into an orange and black cab and then they drove away.

That's it.

I didn't get a cab number. A licence plate. It was too far. There's something wrong with it, though. Made an unholy racket. They guy's name is Stephan. Dark hair. Early twenties. Been here once or twice before.

Guys, are you listening?

· · • · ·

One of the homicide detectives, his head throbbing with the beginnings of what was going to be a terrible migraine, walked over to the budgie's cage.

"Please, buddy, please. Give me a break, okay. Stop your goddamned singing. My head's pounding."

His partner laughed.

"Too bad it ain't a fucking parrot, eh? Maybe he could tell us something."

"Fuck that," the first cop said. "I already know all I need to know."

Buddy peeped again: No, you don't, buddy. You really don't have a fucking clue.

BUDDY, CAN YA SPARE.....

SATURDAY, OCTOBER 4th

3:30 AM

Maria James stood in her driveway, a terrible sadness tugging hard at the corners of her wise, pretty mouth, running her hand over the cooling hood of her brother-in-law's Olds. She'd spent the better part of the day with him, at her place, at his place, at the police station.

She had, in fact, just dropped him off at his apartment

They hadn't spent that much time together since Rob died. Since well before he died. In the end everything was fine. But it hadn't started out too good. No, at first it was bad, very bad. Couldn't get much worse.

She had to leave Krystal alone in the pharmacy, and that didn't sit well with her boss. Stephan was coming in later, though, for his half-day, so they let her go.

She drove home and walked in and the cops were already there. Joe looked like hell. She was worried, the police wanted to call an ambulance, thought he might be having a heart attack.

Just like Rob.

He was telling them he was okay, waving them off.

"Just take my goddamned statement," he said.

Maria tried to intercede, to get him to stop. He just shook his head, wouldn't listen.

"It's the only way, Maria. I'm so sorry. He must be stopped."

The police wrote down what he had to say. They said Peter and the car would turn up, they'd have people looking. It might take a few hours, but they'd find him.

Joe thanked them and they left.

Maria called the realtor and cancelled the showing. And then she cried, and he tried, really, to comfort her. But he kept saying it was for the best.

Buddy was singing, she remembered. The sun in the kitchen was so beautiful.

And then she drove him home.

He knew she was upset, and invited her in to talk. She hadn't been in Joe's place for years. She cried again and said things, told Joe things that she hadn't told anyone. Ever.

Things about Rob. About how he was.

He made her tea and she told him more. He made some dinner and she told him more still, things about herself. Her dreams.

She never talked about herself.

She told him about Peter. Things Joe never knew. Things Rob had said, and done. How much pain she knew her boy was in. She told him about her dreams for him. Her hopes.

His cruelties.

Joe told her how he once thought of Peter as a son. How he'd lost his Owen. The disease. How that hurt.

And she cried again.

And then Joe James broke up, too.

She begged him, one last time: Don't make the police arrest my child. He's all I've got.

He said it was too late.

She said: "Joe, maybe not."

She drove to the station.

He didn't want to do it, she could tell, he looked so angry. But he did. He said it had all been a misunderstanding. A terrible mistake.

The desk sergeant knew he was lying.

"C'mon," he said. "You're sure?"

"Yeah," Joe said.

"Yeah, right."

The paperwork took a while to file, but Joe changed his statement. The sergeant said they'd stop looking for the car.

He asked one last time: "You sure that kid's not driving that vehicle? That, Mr. James, that alone, is a crime."

Joe bit his lip, breathed in deeply and lied: "No sir, I was mistaken. No he's not."

"Whatever," the cop said. "But it's your ass, too, now, if he is."

And then Maria drove Joe home. He was silent the whole way.

She must have thanked him a hundred times.

He grunted, and finally said, "Maria, I'm afraid we're both going to regret this."

"No, Joe," she said, "we won't. God will provide."

He grunted again.

In front of his apartment she said, "You know, Joe, He really does work in mysterious ways. . . . He will provide."

Joe James opened the door and stepped out of her car. Before closing the door, quite gently, he said, "I'm not so sure about that, Maria. But for your sake, and for Pete's sake, Christ, I hope so."

· · • · ·

"Petey?"

Maria James stood in her hallway listening. The house hummed, glowed, pulsed with all manner of circuits thrown open. An un-Maria-like disarray everywhere: the place looked like a bomb had hit it. Garbage and garbage bags everywhere. Music played low from upstairs.

That sad song again: "Jesus . . . don't want me . . . for a sunbeam."

Oh, no.

"Petey, are you here?" she asked again, louder this time.

From the kitchen Buddy peeped: He's in the back. C'mon, you've gotta see this. He just went out.

Ignoring the budgie, Maria walked cautiously upstairs, towards Peter's room.

Saucer-eyed, she thought she'd made a terrible mistake.

Not my house at all.

But it was Peter James' room: the curtains were open, the window, too. A nice, fresh, cool breeze blew in from outside.

A virtually empty room. An old desk. A bed. A stereo. Her vacuum, warm to the touch.

No Peter.

She shook her head, confused, and pressed stop and ejected the tape. She read the side of the cassette. Nirvana *Unplugged*.

I like that.

She turned to leave, hesitated in the doorway before snapping off the lights.

I think . . . I think I hear crying.

Maria walked back down to her kitchen, still tentative. There were empty bottles everywhere. Some of them smashed in her stainless steel sink. A dust pan lay on the floor beside a sticky wet broom, a mop, and a bucket. Glass shards in the dust pan, too.

The bright lights made the place look yellow and ugly, she could bare-ly see out of the smoke-stained window.

Please God, she thought, let Joe be wrong.

And then a slow movement caught her eye. Outside, a dark shadow by the base of the big old tree. She walked closer to the yellowed glass but still couldn't make out the shape: too many lights, keeping everything in, her own reflection obscuring her view.

She moved to the back door, pushed aside the yellowing curtains there. Still nothing.

Buddy warbled again: Go on out. It's okay.

She opened the door a crack.

"Who's out there? Petey, is that you?"

A sob. She thought she heard a sob.

"Peter James, this isn't funny. Is that you? You're scaring me."

A whisper, more sobbing. A groan.

"Answer me, whoever you are. I'm going to call the police."

"Don't. It's okay." A girl's voice, familiar.

"Who's there?"

"Jenna . . . Jennifer, Mrs. James. I'm out here with Peter. It's okay."

Rotting apples disintegrating under her tired feet, Maria James walked out into the dark, toward the tree, that girl's voice. She stopped when she was close enough to see her only son, curled and crying like a baby in that slut . . . that woman's arms.

Jennifer Jefferson looked up at Maria and smiled. She whispered shush to her new, maybe ex-ex-boyfriend and said, "It's good, Pete. Your mom's here now. Everything is going to be okay."

"Petey, what's wrong, angel?" Maria asked, stepping closer, kneeling and squishing yet another rotten apple.

Peter James sobbed again, more loudly, stuttered and fought for words: "Oh Christ . . . Jesus . . . Mom . . . Mom . . . Mom, I'm so sorry. Fucking so sorry."

"Shush, Petey, shh."

She brushed back her only child's long black hair from his weeping eyes, ran her right hand down his scarred right cheek.

"What is it, darling? Don't cry, everything will be alright."

"No . . . no . . . Mom . . . Uncle Joe . . . I. . . ."

"I know Peter, it's okay."

"No. . . ."

"It's fixed darling, I've fixed it. The car's safe out front."

"But—"

"Shhh. . . ."

"No, Mom," he said, composing himself, looking up at his mother, actually seeing her for the first time in months. "No, Mom, it's not. I'm broken, Mom. It's me. I need to fix me."

"I know, son. I'll help you."

"No, Mom, you don't understand. I have to. I have to start right now.

Now, Mom. And I have to start like this: Mom, oh God, Mom, I'm sorry."

"It's okay, Pete."

"No, it's not, not yet. But it will be. I am sorry, Mom, I'm sorry I hurt you."

Maria James kissed her son's scarred forehead. "I know darling, I know."

Jennifer hugged him tighter, smiled at Maria again, and said: "Maybe we can go inside now, eh, Pete? How about that?"

He shrugged and slowly, gently disengaged from her embrace.

The two women each took a hand and helped him to his feet.

"I'm sorry for all the mess, Mrs. James. I brought Peter home and we started cleaning up. Don't worry, though, it won't take us long to get rid of it."

Maria looked hard at the girl she'd never liked, the high school sweetheart who'd stolen her son's affections. Who'd become a stripper and dumped him and broken his heart. "I don't understand," she said.

"I'll try to explain, but really, lets get inside. It's so cold."

The three of them walked back into the kitchen. Maria sat her son at the kitchen table, and found him his favourite ashtray.

Jennifer put the kettle on the stove, took two tea cups and the Black Hole mug from the cupboard.

She turned then and looked at Maria. "Mrs. James, Peter's going to move in with me for a little while."

"What?"

"We were cleaning up his things, getting rid of his junk."

"Jennifer, I still don't understand."

Peter lit a cigarette, inhaled deeply, then flicked his ash into the dry B of Bahamas. "It's time, Mom. Moving out time. I've got to get on with my life. And I've got to let you get on with yours. You're never going to get rid of this place with me here."

"That's not true, Petey. I don't want you to go. . . ."

"I know, Mom, I know. But I think I have to. That's why all this stuff's out. All the mess. Don't you have people coming to see the place tomorrow? Today, I mean."

"Yes, I did, but. . . ."

"Well then, we better hurry up and get rid of this stuff and let you get some sleep."

"Peter, you don't have to do this now, they can come another day. I left a message to cancel–"

"No, Mom, today's the day."

And then Peter butted out, picked up two garbage bags, and took out the trash.

"Jennifer," Maria said, "why? Is this what you want?"

"For a while. Peter's taking, you know, the first step. He knows he needs help, now. He can stay with me until he gets a job, or a place of his own. Or maybe he can just, you know, stay. Whatever, we'll see."

"So you're back together?"

"I don't know, I really don't. Would that bother you?"

"Well, no. . . ."

"Good. Anyway, maybe Peter and I can find work together."

"What do you mean? I thought you had a, um, job."

"Nope, not me. Seems it's a good time to look for a new line of work. What do you think?"

"I think it's about time. I mean, sorry, Jennifer, I'm happy for you."

Jennifer laughed. "That's okay. And yeah, I'm happy, too."

"So."

"So."

"How's that tea coming, dear?"

"Oh, sorry, right."

Jennifer Jefferson turned to the boiling kettle, picked it up, and poured the water.

"Jennifer?"

"Yes, Mrs. James?"

"Maria, dear."

"Yes, Maria?"

"Why were you two out there in the dark?"

"Oh, that. Well, we were upstairs, and the stereo was playing, and I guess something about the song upset him. He ran outside to the tree."

"Why?"

"It was hard to understand, Maria. He was crying. But I think he was talking to his father."

"Oh, I see."

"And he was also saying something about cutting it down. I told him to forget about it, that it's such a beautiful old tree."

"Actually dear, I think that might be a very good idea."

"Why?"

"Oh, I don't know. I've just never liked the fucking thing."

"Maria!"

"Well, it's true."

"Really?"

"Yes. Really."

"Really what?" Peter was back in the kitchen for more of the garbage.

"You want tea, Peter?" Jennifer asked.

"Um, no. Coffee."

"Okay, I thought so."

"Really what, Mom?"

"Oh nothing, really, Peter. I was just thinking out loud, that's all."

"What?"

"Well, since you're doing all this work cleaning up, I was thinking, maybe, we should really do something to help get this place sold."

"Like what?"

"Well, I was just saying to Jennifer that when I found the two of you back there I finally realized what an abomination that darn apple tree is. A real eyesore, you know?"

"Yeah, I know. . . ."

"So. Well, why don't I call somebody later today and see about having it taken down?"

"Yeah, maybe that's a good idea, Mom."

"Yes, Peter, maybe it is."

Peter James grabbed another two garbage bags then and headed for the door. He stopped before leaving the kitchen, though, looked over his shoulder and smiled. "Mom?"

"Yes dear?"

"Thanks. And Happy Birthday."

"Oh, sweetheart, in all the commotion I forgot. I guess it's already your birthday, isn't it? I'm so sorry."

"No, Mom, don't apologize. I wasn't being sarcastic. I was thanking you. That's all. You know, for having me." He looked awkward, sheepish. "So, well, fine. Happy Birthday. And thank you, Mom. Thanks."

10:59 AM

AND THEN *PRICK* ACCUSED ME of stealing his money, Grampa."

"Krystal, sweetheart, now don't you be calling him that. Even if it is true. The sonofabitch, pardon my French, is still your stepfather."

"Okay, then *Rick* said I took his money."

"But Andrea . . . your mother, I'm sure, set him straight. Right?"

"Well. . . ."

"You're kidding me?"

"She didn't really believe him, I guess, but she asked."

Ed Harrison, walking slowly through the grass in the glorious sunshine with his arm around his granddaughter's shoulder for support, shook his aching head in disgust.

"I can't stand them anymore, Grampa."

"You know, darling, I feel the same way. How's your dad?"

"Okay, I guess. Sad, since Mom left."

"He misses her?"

"No, it's not that. It's just he's lonely sometimes, I think."

"Oh, he's got you, angel. I'm sure he's fine."

"Grampa, you know what I mean. He needs a girlfriend."

"What do you know about it, young lady?"

"I know plenty, Grampa."

"I guess you do."

"He's sad, too, you know. About not being able to come."

"I know darling, but at least I have you."

Krystal Harrison, her little fashionable legs easily matching her grandfather's slow, tentative steps, her hair pulled back tight in a scrunchie, the beautiful bouquet of red, red roses he'd given her clutched to her chest, was staring at Ed Harrison's serious, sad face as they walked.

"Have you ever been lonely, Grampa?" she asked.

"Me? C'mon, girl, don't you be worrying about me."

"You sure?"

"Yeah."

They continued a little further in silence, both of them listening to the wrens in the trees, the occasional cry of a gull, dying leaves rustling in the light breeze, and then Krystal asked: "How much further, Grampa?"

Ed smiled, his granddaughter's voice, the little unintentional whine, reminded him of his own children, their young voices, so many years ago.

"Not much further, Krys. Just up over the crest of this here hill."

Before they reached the very summit, Ed suddenly stopped.

"What's wrong, Grampa?"

"Nothing."

"Why're we stopping? Are we there?"

"Almost."

"Why don't we go on then?"

"Shhh, angel. Wait here for a minute. Just wait. And darling, shhh, I'm sorry, but be quiet okay?" Ed Harrison was speaking in hushed, but forceful tones.

Krystal spoke in kind: "Why are we whispering?"

"Shh, darling. All in good time."

Ed stared out in the distance, at a figure, a woman, who stood holding a single flower, her head bowed.

"Who's that, Grampa?"

"Don't know. But, let's leave her in peace for a spell, okay?"

Krystal, a little anxious, a little confused, a little bored, felt her grandfather's hand take hers and squeeze, firm but not hard.

His eyes were narrowed, his jaw jutting out, teeth grinding.

He looks so sad, she thought.

· · ● · ·

The delicious sun warmed Alice Harrison's smiling face through the glass. She watched the branches of the St. Stephen's trees sway, the delicate movements of the grass in the breeze. The last mow.

A rose so perfect. So beautiful. My God, *she* is so beautiful. Thank you, darling. It's good to have you home.

· · ● · ·

Krystal had knelt and laid the bouquet in front of her.

Ed Harrison stood just behind, stock still, his head bowed, his cap in his hands.

He still looks so handsome, Alice thought, so strong. His hair's getting a bit too long, and he really needs a new pair of shoes, but he still looks fine.

Krystal whispered to her, "I love you, Grandma," touched her face, and got up. Went back to Ed and touched his hand where a sunbeam played gold on his untarnished wedding band.

She really has grown.

I love you too, Krys.

Ed spoke then, his voice hoarse, "Darling, would it be okay if I had a moment alone with your grandma?"

"Sure," she said, and walked back up the hill.

Ed balled his cap up in his fist, stuffed his other hand deep into his pocket and sighed.

"Well, Alice, what do you think of her, eh? She's shot up like a little weed. Jesus, it's hard to believe she's still so young. The way she looks, and the way she talks, you'd swear she's an adult. She's a great kid, Alice. First rate."

Alice Harrison looked up at her man and smiled her beautiful smile.

"We brought roses, darling. Your favourites. And Ted, well, Teddy's so sorry he can't be here. He's sent these other flowers, too. And this one, I guess, well, I guess you know."

Ed knelt then, before his wife's grave.

"I miss you, darling. I miss you so goddamned much. I'm so lonely,

Al, I miss you so goddamned much."

It's okay, Ed; it'll be okay. I miss you, too. But I'm always with you darling, always. I need you to feel that, Ed. Feel me.

Ed Harrison pulled his fist out of his pocket. He was clutching a white handkerchief.

Oh Ed, I remember, I gave you that . . . when? Years and years ago.

He touched the small square of cloth to his left cheek then reached out and wiped at the glass that covered the small photograph of his wife he'd had set in her headstone.

"You've got a little smudge there, angel. Here. That's better. I want you to see everything darling, see how beautiful this day is."

Oh Ed, I do. I always do.

The sunbeam warmed, caressed her cheeks, hardly dissipating through the glass.

Ed stood.

"Fifty-four years," he said, composing himself. Getting his voice back. Smiling. "Fifty-four years ago today, Alice, you made me the luckiest, the happiest, man in the world."

Oh, Ed. . . .

"And one year, Alice. One year ago today, the good Lord decided he wanted you back. Oh, I don't begrudge Him none. How could you blame Him? His sweetest angel. I was a lucky, happy man, darling. But ya can't blame me for wishing, can you? I wish I could've had a few more years. Of happiness. Of luck."

And then Ed turned to go, whispering: "Happy anniversary, angel. I love you. I love you, Alice, I do."

Alice called after him.

Wait, Ed, there's still things we need to talk about.

He stopped for a moment, stiffened, and put on his cap.

Go to Belle, she said. It's time.

I watch you always, Ed. I'm always watching. From every photograph, darling. I'm always there. With you.

Can you hear me Ed? I'm watching.

Ed? Will you go to Belle? Twelve years, Ed.

Ed, it's long enough, too long.

Ed?

But Ed had already gone, his tall body began to disappear – feet, legs, hips, shoulders, cap – as he crested and descended, his arm around his granddaughter again, the green hill.

· · • · ·

"Are you okay, Grampa?"

"Yeah, Belle. I mean Krystal. . . . Sorry, darling. Ha. A touch of the Alzheimer's, eh?"

"That's okay, Grampa, even Dad does it sometimes. You know, sometimes, he'll call me by Mom's name. Once, when he was upset with me, he called me Belle, too."

"Yeah?"

"Yup. It's natural. Just means you've got something on your mind, something deep inside that's trying to get out, the way I see it."

"Yeah?"

"Yup."

"When'd you get your PhD, huh? How'd you get so damned smart? Must be from your grandmother. Certainly not from your old Grampa. No sir."

"Aw. . . . Grampa?"

"That's me."

"Who's Belle?"

"Nobody, darling . . . just somebody the family used to know."

"That's just what Dad said. But really? Really, Grampa?"

"Yup. Your father was right."

"You sure, Grampa?"

"Yes."

"That lady. Back there at the grave, before us. Was that Belle, Grampa?"

Ed Harrison coughed and stiffened and squeezed his granddaughter closer, but said nothing.

"Shouldn't we try and find her, Grampa? Wasn't that Belle?"

Ed stopped then and knelt to look directly into his granddaughter's eyes, his hands on her shoulders. "Listen to me, Krystal. Do you know how much I love you?"

"Yeah."

"Good. And do you know – God, I hope you know – that your Grandma loved you very, very much?"

"Yes, Grampa."

"Your dad?"

"Yeah, but. . . ."

"Good."

"But what about Belle?"

"Angel, that wasn't Belle. Belle left a long, long time ago. Right around when you were born."

"Oh."

Ed tried to smile, then, tousled his granddaughter's hair.

"Who was that then?"

His lips thinned.

"I don't know, darling, I just don't know who that was."

"Maybe you just didn't recognize her, maybe it was Belle."

"No, darling, no. Belle's gone, too. Like your Grandma. Like I said, darling, I said, a long, long time ago. Too long."

"Oh."

"Yeah."

"Do you miss her?"

"Your grandmother did. And your father, I guess."

"But what about you, Grampa? Did *you* miss her. Did it make *you* sad?"

"Oh darling, what should I say? Yeah, maybe; maybe some. Some days. Sometimes. Like I said, I really just don't know."

11:00 AM

I'M FUCKED. Cops everywhere. I'm going to prison. I'm fucked.

Amanda.

I'm fucked. Fucking Colette. Fucking Chisholm.

Amanda.

They won't listen to me. Why won't they listen?

I'm fucked.

Amanda.

Oh fuck, I'm so fucking fucked.

Amanda's dead.

Cops everywhere.

I'm going to prison.

Amanda.

I'm fucked.

They think I killed her.

Man oh man oh man. Oh Christ, Man, Man. Man!

· · • · ·

Spiralling down, from out of the sun, burning with rage, today's worst gull screams its hate. Black eyes, blacker heart. A vector, shearing evil, skimming the water, then pulling up into a terrible gyre.

In lazy circles the worst gull laughs, at the sun and the sky and the men outside the house. It watches and waits. They stretch yellow tape everywhere.

310

My hate is better, it screams. And I will kill you.

Below, a lazy beat cop, tired, the first one on the scene, is having a smoke on the Venn guy's back patio. He's reading the sports page of Venn's paper. Thinking about the tickets he has to tonight's home opener. The fucking Bruins.

He's tapping his ash into the soil around the big, ugly tropical plant, hoping none of the detectives notice.

Boring, stupid crime scenes.

From inside, Buddy calls: Hey, buddy, what the hell're you doin'? What did she do to you? And Jesus, ain't there evidence out there?

The cop ignores him.

Stupid fucking cops, why won't they listen?

And then, from out of the blinding hot sky, the cop is struck, twice, in the back.

Gullshit.

Through kevlar, he doesn't even notice.

Buddy, as fucked up as he is about everything, can't help but laugh.

Nice shot, you evil fucking bastard. Nice fucking shot!

· · ● · ·

"Okay, let's go over this again. You say you got home at . . . when was that, again?"

"Like I said, around 3:30. I'm not sure exactly. I told you, I fucked up and forgot my watch. I mean, what's it matter? I was kinda fucking freaked, wasn't I?"

The detective winced, rubbed at his temples.

"Easy big guy, easy. Okay, right. Actually, the 911 call was placed at twenty past four. Now, you say you left the strip club around last call. Just before two in fact. But it takes you a couple of hours to get home. Fine. You say you walked to clear your head, 'cause you had too much to drink, weren't sure what you were in for. Now, I'm a reasonable man. I can buy that. But all the way here? From The Rail? That's too much of a walk for a guy in your condition. And buddy, it was freezing. You said so yourself. So you say you stopped into an all-night donut hole and grabbed a coffee or two to help clear your head. We checked there, Scott. Nobody remembers you. Then you say you flagged a cab after a while. Somewhere by the hotels, down at the waterfront, before heading east. Fifteen, twenty minute ride. Of course, you don't remember the cab number. Who remembers those kinds of things, right? And you don't even remember what kind of cab. Or what the driver looked like. We can check the companies, sure, maybe somebody'll alibi you. But if it was a gypsy, well, then, you're shit out of luck, right? I mean, they never keep records; hell, we don't even know who half of them are. Anyway, you say the cab drops you off and you approach the house tentatively 'cause you and the deceased had been having marital difficulties. Hmmm. Well, okay. Yeah, I get that, we've all been in that doghouse, buddy. Anyway, you also say you were afraid of waking her because you'd locked your keys in the house earlier. Again, fine. So you approach the house and knock on the door lightly. And then, it just pops open. So you're scared then, right? Yeah, something might be wrong. And you call out. No response. And then you, tentatively again, walk into your own home, which may or may not have been violated, you don't know, and then you find the deceased. You find the woman you're married to. You find Amanda. Your wife. Lying there. On the floor. In a pool of her own blood. And then, of course, you bend over her, freaking out, because, hey, she's your wife, right? And then you touch her and check to see if she's breathing. All that shit people do. So that explains how you got her blood all over you.

"Anyway. You finally call 911. We've got your prints, in your wife's blood, on the phone. Yeah, buddy, of course we do.

"And you start pacing all over the place. Waiting for our squad car. I understand. You're flipping. Who wouldn't be? Seeing their wife brutally, viciously, horribly dead and all. I mean, wow. Right buddy? Worst fucking moment of any man's life.

"Anyway, you just can't take it anymore, being in the house with the woman you love – dead – so you go out on the front porch, light up a smoke, and keep pacing and wandering. Even go down to the bottom of the street to look out and flag down the squad car. Which gets here, Scott, four minutes after you place the call. And so, like you say, that probably explains why there's drops of her blood leading out and down to the road. 'Cause you had her on you when you just couldn't take being inside any longer.

"Gotcha. Fine.

"Too bad nobody saw you though, buddy. Ain't that strange? All these Neighbourhood Watch-conscious folks and not a single, solitary one hears anything, sees anything? Damn, what's the world coming to? Didn't even hear you pull up in the cab. Buddy, now that would have been good for us. That would've helped a whole heap of a fucking lot. But, no dice. They didn't hear or see anything all night.

"So you get my drift, Scotty, bud. We still got some problems here.

"Like the rest of the story. All the things you say happened earlier in the day. The shit you said should be here. Your clothes. That broken watch. Your keys. The broken mug. Where the hell is all of that stuff?

"Gone, Scott. Fine. You say she must've taken out the trash. Turfed it. Maybe. Yeah, all that stuff's probably at the dump right now. Garbage pickup around here happened between three and four. We checked. Good luck finding your shit now, though. We'll try. But it's a big fucking dump, Scott. And even if we find it, so what? But Jesus, buddy, I mean Christ, man, was she Martha fucking Stewart or what? I mean, bud, did she ever fucking clean this place up. There's like nothing here, Scott. It's as if she would've had to scrub every fucking inch of this place. There's just no other clear prints. A few smudges, here and there, and we'll check those Scott, but mostly, from what we can tell, it's just you, and her. Any dirt tracked in? Jesus, that could've come from you, right?

"And Scotty, I also got a problem with you saying she called your cell and left a message telling you to wait before coming home, that she said she'd call you again and tell you when to come. Too bad you didn't save that message, Scott. Too bad.

"Then, Scott, damn, we've got all this other disturbing information now. From her folks saying you two were having serious problems. That she'd told them you'd fought pretty bad before, Scott. Sometimes things got a wee bit out of hand, eh?

"Speaking of hands, Scott, sweet merciful crap. That thing looks like a goddamned football. You really should have it looked at, you know? Must've been quite a beating you laid on that phone, but, ha ha, that victim ain't corroborating your story either. It's possible though, right, buddy? I mean, you could've been that drunk.

"So, anyway, we know you've got a temper on you. And, oh, one of our guys talked to your neighbour earlier. Nice French lady. Wow, Scott. You threw a fucking newspaper at her fucking head yesterday. What were you thinking there? Jesus. This Colette woman – you see her fucking paintings, bud? Jesus, freaky fucking shit. Beautiful stuff, there's these absolutely mindblowing seagulls. Anyway, this Colette person, she says you were hurling obscenities at her like they were fastballs. Is that true? Says, and these are her words, she 'was afraid you were going to kill her.' Scotty? The neighbour?

"And then there's this other thing. See, we've checked with folks at your work, bud. Seems like there was something going on there, too. Something fucked up. But we'll figure all of it out. Don't worry. I'm talking to that Chisholm woman, Margaret, is it? Yeah, Margaret Chisholm, I'm talking to her later this afternoon. Nice lady. She said she'd be happy to talk about you, buddy. Pleased as fucking punch.

"But I'm a busy man, Scott. With a murderer to catch and all. So why don't you just tell me what she's gonna have to say? Is Margaret

Chisholm gonna tell me you ever threatened her?

"You like to get rough with the girls? Is that it, Scott?

"Oh, your buddy, whatshisname, Tony something.... I gotta tell ya, Scott, he's not being that helpful here. Not too co-operative. But he left the bar early, so he's actually not much good to you anyway. Said your hand was fine, though, when he left. Still, when we asked him about you and your job – and you can call this a vibe thing – if I was a betting man, and I am, I'd have to say he sounded a bit uncomfortable. More than a bit.

"Everybody we've been able to reach from Shooting Stars gave me that feeling. Oh, they weren't about to say anything. That's for damn sure. Nothing incriminating. But I've got half a mind to start digging, you know? Who knows, maybe they're covering their own big fat rich asses? Am I right, buddy?

"And then there's the small matter of evidence. I mean, help me out here, where the fuck is it? Where's the evidence of the fucking intruder? No forced entry, nothing missing but the shit you say you left here earlier, no sign of motive yet.

"Of course, you say maybe Amanda made an enemy. But other than that, genius, you don't have a fucking clue, do you? I mean, do you know anything about what the fuck your wife had been doing for the past few days? The last fucking month?

"Nope.

"Now, as bad as all this sounds – and any cop'll tell ya it sounds real, real, bad – I'm not saying you did this horrible thing. But, just so we're clear, I'm not saying you didn't, either.

"Ah, hell, most crimes like this? Most of these murders? It's the boyfriend or husband. And that's you, buddy.

"I know this must be hard. If you didn't do it. Hell, even if you did. But you're gonna have to give me more to go on, 'cause right now you're my number fucking one, grade A, prime fucking suspect.

"So, how about this? How about you tellin' me where I'm going off track here? Okay? Anyway, this is it: here's a little theory I got. Just one of the ways my mind's working on this thing. I'm thinking maybe you got yourself into a little jackpot up there at your fancypants work – Jesus, what I wouldn't give to have your job, free fucking tickets to everything, I figure – and somehow you weasel out of it. Good for you, buddy. Really, good for fucking you. Screw 'em if ya got 'em. I mean, they're all overpaid bums, right? And so you go out to celebrate, with your pal, Tony, whatshisname, and you go and have yourself a couple pops, check out the fucking rippers. Great way to spend a Friday, right? Anyway, you're drinking, enjoying yourself a bit too fucking much, getting loaded, and then this call comes in. From the deceased. And then you got your marital hell intruding on your good time, right? Maybe she's bitching at you – I dunno. Anyway, I'm thinking you get good and pissed, right? And you start to stew, and drink, and drink some more. Get yourself all loaded. And like I said, we know you got a temper on you, and maybe it gets the better of you. And you smoulder, slow, drinking yourself mean. And then, half out of your fucking mind, you leave the joint. Only you get here a bit fucking quicker than you're letting on. And you ain't tentative, and the door ain't open. No, you knock, 'cause you're locked out. And maybe you're pissed at having to do that, too. And then maybe you're pissed cause she's bitchin' at you, for knocking, for being drunk. And maybe you're pissed because she's thrown your shit out, Christ man, even your keys, on top of every little fucking thing else. Maybe, maybe not. Anyway, maybe you lose your freakin' mind. It happens, buddy, yeah it does. And then things get out of hand. Then, before you know it: bam! Dead fucking wife. Or maybe, just a dying one. You know? Like you just realized what the fuck you've done and Christ, you're freakin out, and you don't know what to do. And so you just sit around and wait, trying to figure things out. But while you wait and think, sonofabitch, she up and dies.

"I don't know, you know?

"But Scott, you didn't call us till just after four. And they're tellin me they're fixing her time of death somewhere between two an' four. So she could've died slow. Real slow.

"And yeah, buddy, yeah. Another thing. That fucking clock she was busted up with? Too bad the hands went flying everywhere, 'cause we don't even know what time she was hit at. The fucking thing just disintegrated. But there are prints there. Two sets. Hers. And yours.

"So, yeah, you could've been here, buddy. You could have done this and then watched your own fucking wife bleed to death.

"So Scott, c'mon, tell me where I'm wrong. Show me the error of my ways. I'm not as smart as you, maybe. What am I missing here?"

Sitting at his dining room table, Scott Venn could hear the budgie chirping madly as he ran his thumbnail under the rim of the stale large cup of Coffee Time coffee he'd been nursing for what seemed like hours.

The little guy must be starved.

"I've told you everything," Scott said. "I don't know anything else. I've gone over it a hundred times."

The detective was unmoved. He toyed with the bottle of Excedrin Migraine that sat in front of him.

Scott rolled his neck: "Look, can I at least feed my fucking bird?"

"Can't let you do that, buddy. We still gotta talk. You do. Where's the food? I'll get one of my guys to help the little fella in a bit."

Scott waved his arm out, a violent, crazy fling. "Kitchen, over the sink."

Buddy peeped: Finally, thank Christ.

"And what about the wedding?" Scott's voice was beginning to sound desperate. "Look, I don't mean to sound so callous, but I told you, me and Man, Amanda, we were supposed to go to a wedding today. Part of the wedding party."

The detective just nodded and smiled: "We called them, buddy. Told them you wouldn't be able to attend. Sent your sincerest regrets."

Scott Venn sized up the guy; he'd never hated anyone's face more, never felt more inadequate. "That supposed to be funny?"

"Not to me, buddy, not to me. None of this is fucking funny to me. I don't like to look at dead fucking women at five in the fucking morning with nothing but a spoonful of Raisin Bran in my fucking belly." He flipped open the Excedrin, popped out two tablets, cupped them into his mouth like beernuts, and took a harsh, dramatic sip from his own cold coffee.

Scott stared down at his rim again. One of the beat cops brought four large Coffee Time double doubles in on a moulded cardboard tray. Three for the detectives. One for the suspect. Despite the horrible sugar sweetness, it was the last nice thing anyone had done for Scott Venn.

Since then he'd answered the same questions over and over again, trying not to look into his living room.

The detective had opened the heavy archway curtain Man always kept drawn closed. It was a dare, a trap. A torture.

Try not to look. Try.

Try not to look at the chalk outline of where your wife's body once lay, dying.

At the blood that seeped and spread. The crust of it, drying.

Scott Venn looked up at the detective. The dishevelled man leaned confidently on one elbow, staring, impassive, his left eyebrow arched. "Tell me what you're thinking. I'm here to listen, buddy."

"I think," Scott said, his rage barely contained, "that while you're sitting here, questioning an innocent fucking man, the real killer's getting away."

The detective sneered. "Hey now, OJ, take it easy, will ya? I'm just doing my job here. And listen, seriously, if I had a dime for every time I heard that crap from some guilty motherfucker, I'd be a rich fucking man. Got it, buddy?"

Just as the detective hoped, Scott snapped.

"I'm not your fucking buddy!" Grinding his heel into the carpet below him, hard, with all his frustration, he pointed at the man who sat across from him and raved: "I did not kill my fucking wife! I did not hurt Amanda! I swear to fucking God I did not hurt her."

"For your sake, *buddy*," the detective said, "I hope so."

While Scott Venn slumped back down on his dining room chair, exhausted, nauseous, cored, his budgie called to him from the living room.

I'm your Buddy, buddy. I'm here, and I think you need to get a grip. Think, buddy. Think. They're out to screw you, buddy. Don't lose it. Don't be a dufus.

Composing himself, without the benefit of a sweet little bird's encouragement, Scott did it then, finally.

He unrolled the rim, thinking: Remember, Man?

You Can Win!

Big fucking joke.

He read the words the flap revealed and, thoroughly defeated, relaxed his grinding heel: *Sorry, Try Again!*

Between the sole of Scott's deck shoe and the willing fabric that covered his dining room floor, a happy little blue grey chip of Vicodin had been buried deeper, neatly and cunningly hidden, between the infinitely complex weave of the soft, plush fabric.

"So?" the detective asked, changing the subject, the tack, cracking his knuckles. A new role: a slightly better cop now.

"So what?"

"I won another free cup. Third one this week. An unbelievable hook, this promotion. Christ, it seems like I win all the time. You?"

"You're the detective, *buddy*. What do you think?"

Another peep from the living room, another sad aria: I think, buddy, that you win some and you lose some. But, buddy, these jokers? Forget about it. They don't have a clue. Listen to me, buddy. For once, just listen.

"I think my fucking head's gonna explode and I'd better feed that little guy in there, or he's never gonna shut up." The detective, tough guy, pushed back from the table, stretched, got up, then sauntered into the kitchen. Whistling through his pain, he picked up the sorrowed melody of Buddy's song.

Buddy seized the opportunity.

Okay, Scott, while he's distracted, listen to me. There was another guy. I'm sorry, but there was. Look into your heart. Think. Listen. Why else would she tell you to wait before coming home? Why didn't she ream you out then and there? And where the hell are the extra keys? Think, buddy. Listen! I'm sorry. I'm sorry, but it's true. So tell them she was seeing another guy. Tell them to check where she was two nights ago. Use your fucking head. Why wasn't she at home? Talk to them about that. They'll check and see she wasn't at her folks' place. Tell them. Listen to me. Tell them and it'll be over, like that. Listen to me, buddy. For once, listen. Are you listening, buddy?

Buddy?

Scott Venn was heating the back off the foil from his third pack of Dunhills in less than twenty-four hours, glad he'd thought to pick up more in the donut shop. He carefully wrapped the impossibly thin metal around the tiny ball he'd started earlier and rolled it compulsively between the thumb and forefinger of his right hand: old habits die hard. When it was a smooth, perfect bead, he placed it on the table in front of him and removed the first smoke from the deck. He tapped it three times, for luck, on the dining room table, before flipping it up into his mouth.

Scott flicked his Bic. Greener, burning, hovered and hissed in front of his face while he listened, carefully, his heart full of wonder, to the beautiful rising and falling tones of Amanda's pet.

I hear you, buddy. Yes, little fella, I hear you. . . . He worried about the little guy. Buddy'd miss her.

He lit his smoke, took a deep pull, held it, tilted back his head, and then pushed out a perfect O.

Oh man.

In the living room, the detective opened the bird cage. "Here ya' go, buddy," he said. "You must be starved, you handsome little guy. You know, I used to have a little fella, just like you, buddy. Just like you. Breaks my heart, this. See, my little Bud's been missing for a couple of days. The kid. Left the cage open. Messed up, too, buddy, he is. Yeah, we miss the sweet little guy. I bet he's fine, right? Right, pretty, pretty boy? I bet he's found himself a good home. Maybe a girlfriend, eh? Miss him like hell now. So damned sweet, buddy. Just like you."